Speaking in Tungs

Speaking in Tungs

Karla Jay

First Hedgehog & Fox Edition, May 2015

Library of Congress has catalogued the Hedgehog & Fox edition as follows:
Jay, Karla
Speaking in Tungs / Karla Jay. - 1st ed.
p. cm.
1. Humor — Fiction. 2. Thriller & Suspense — Fiction. 3. Romance — Fiction 4. Family Secrets — Fiction. 5. Language — Fiction.

Cover design by Julia Hardy. Special Font, Frost, by Fenotype.

More information can be learned about Hedgehog & Fox at warnerliterarygroup.com

Printed in the United States of America.

ISBN 978-0-996-19500-3 (original paperback)

ISBN 978-0-996-19501-3 (ebook)

In loving memory of Begonya Garcia. You left us too early but you will always be the president of my fan club.

"When I die, I want to go peacefully like my grandfather did - in his sleep. Not yelling and screaming like the passengers in his car."
– Bob Monkhouse

Ashes to Ashes

That hazy summer morning the humid breeze smelled of grass and something swampy. Cicadas buzzed in the nearby woods increasing the intensity of their drone, raising their pitch with each line the mercury climbed.

Already turning into a hell of a day, I pushed through the screen door of the Ash Country Store and Souvenirs looking for another human being. But the place looked empty. Then just as I turned to leave, the linoleum creaked behind me.

"You want a rattlesnake tail?" said a muscled storekeeper in overalls who approached the front counter.

"What did you say?" I asked, thinking I'd heard him wrong.

He wore a grease-smeared shirt and a scowl he'd probably been born with. Hulking over a gray-speckled countertop, he picked up a crossword puzzle and turned his attention to the page. Without looking up he repeated, "I said, do you want a rattlesnake tail?"

"I'll pass," I said. "Just directions to Tungston, please. Apparently it's around here."

Here's the thing. I was already irritated. I was tired and frazzled from driving cross country. In a moment of humility I reminded myself about my plans in coming here. I wanted to establish a place to live, albeit short-term, while I searched for my parents. *My biological parents.*

He ignored my question and asked me another: "Which high school you from?"

High school? "I just graduated college. Grad school to be exact." I tried hard not to sound bitchy. I didn't want to come across as unfriendly. I was here to find connections, not create barriers.

"Sorry," he said, and continued writing, head down. "Just saying. You look about 16."

"Really?" I raised my hands in a what-the-hell gesture. "Because I'm short?"

"Yup."

When I was 13, my grandfather on my mother's side got throat cancer and had his larynx removed. He spent five frustrating years trying to get people to understand his buzzing speech, those mechanical tones amplified through a hand-held throat vibrator. It wasn't until he lay in his coffin that he finally looked relieved.

I hit college and became obsessed with every aspect of retraining people to talk – from fixing broken language, unraveling mangled speech, to helping people with no speech - words frozen in the nerve bundles, unable to move toward a mouth, opening and closing, a dying mackerel with no word flow. I couldn't fix Grandpa, but I'd made a vow to his memory to repair everyone else.

If only I had spent as much time learning to follow directions.

My trip had gone well according to Google Maps until about an hour ago when my phone lost its signal. That's when the road signs disappeared altogether, and the trees pressed closer, their branches interweaving above the road, narrowing it down to a two-lane strip of spider-veined tarmac. Verdaphobia. If it wasn't a real word to describe the fear of tight, green spaces, then I'd just created it.

I studied the store's sagging interior. The aisles narrow, floorboards warped, shelves loaded with jars – jars filled with what I assumed must be stewed squirrel, pickled tadpoles or something equally inedible. "Nice place. Quaint and homey."

He squinted my way. "As an FYI. Rattlers are hard to catch."

I took a moment to search for words. "I can only imagine."

"Great souvenir for folks in California."

He'd read my license plate. I smiled. "You do look up once in a while."

His face firmed as if he'd come to some decision. He pushed off of the counter and narrowed his eyes. He looked to be maybe 35 years old, carrying about 290 pounds on a five-foot-ten frame. His dark hair, moussed back in long spikes, resembled a hedgehog's. "I've got a deadline before the mailman shows up." He tapped the sheet. "I'm multitasking by waiting on you."

I was ready to claim a headache or upset stomach just to get going. "Sorry for the interruption. I'm relocating to Tungston, staying at the Pfoltz Bed & Breakfast. I was heading in the right direction then my phone died. Now, I'm driving in circles. Or triangles. I don't know which." I pushed a smile onto my lips, although that wasn't what I was feeling inside.

I left San Francisco to seek life's answers locked away in rural America. Something thickened in my chest every time I remembered why I had come here.

"*I found information about your birthplace.*" Gary Karlinski, the genealogist I hired explained. "*Your parents' names are listed there, but not much else.*" The day he handed me the sheet of information, he also boob-grazed me too many times for it to be an accident. I had gotten all I needed from him.

My parents died three months earlier and I found myself completely alone at age 24. *Adoptive parents,* I reminded myself. I had a new life landscape to try to absorb. I'd been walking around in the pleasant scenery of my known world, oblivious to the false backdrop it was built against. I found out I had been adopted only one month ago. Now I wondered if the woman–and man–who had given me up for adoption at age two might still be out there?

A hollow draft of sadness swept through me. I shook the chill away.

The shopkeeper was back at the crossword puzzle.

"Tungston?" I asked. "How do I get there?"

"We just say Tungs."

"What?"

He said it louder, as if my hearing had suffered in those few seconds. "Not Tungston. Tungs."

"You're serious?"

"Why would I lie?" He looked directly at me for the first time and his deep-set, brown eyes flashed something I wasn't going to question.

"No, that's not what I mean." I shook my head. "It's the town's name. I'm a speech therapist." I drew in a lungful of air, so ripe with the scent of ancient wood I could taste it at the back of my throat. "Living in *Tungs.*" There were sure to be jokes about why I didn't choose the towns of Vocal Cord or Cleft Palette for my first job.

"You gotta love irony; I know I do." He pointed at me, his silver watch gleaming on his beefy wrist. "I've heard about you. You're gonna be working with my mother."

I sorted through the unsettling idea that someone at the ass-end of nowhere knew I would be arriving. I suddenly missed the anonymity of my private life in a very crowded city. "What have you heard?"

"Therapy on Wheels hired a new speech therapist. Not a local girl this time."

I offered my hand. "I'm Marleigh Benning."

He offered his. "Elyk Ash."

My hand disappeared into his giant paw, his handshake gentler than I anticipated. "Nice to meet you, Alec."

His forehead knotted. "Not Alec. Elyk, E-L-Y-K."

"Oh. Sorry."

"My mom liked the idea of words going backwards. 'Kyle' seemed boring to her." He reached for his pen and twirled it between his thumb and index finger. Nodding as if we'd exchanged all there was to exchange, he returned to writing words in the spaces on the paper.

"Well, what the 'lleh'," I said, looking for a connection.

He lifted his eyes as his lips compressed.

It occurred to me now – and I found this recognition troubling because it meant I was a snob – that I expected this man to be dimwitted because he lived in a rural area. If this is where my parent's were from, what did it say about me? My biological parents. I needed to keep practicing those words to make them more comfortable. "Kyle — Elyk. Got it."

"Short 'I'. E-lick."

"Elyk." I'd remember it as the sound of a cat hacking up a hairball. *Snob. I was a snob.* I hadn't always been this way, had I?

"Exactly," he said, and turned back to his puzzle.

Mr. Backward Name took a phone call; my directions to the Bed & Breakfast were on hold. I wandered the aisles until I found an office supply shelf. I grabbed a small notebook; positive I'd be writing detailed directions to my patient's houses now that I'd experienced the winding roads. Returning to the cash register, I noted it was old, the kind that dinged when the drawer opened, something able to kill a man if it landed on him. Next to it was the crossword puzzle. I leaned closer to read some of Elyk's answers. I was never one to pass up a word game.

Elyk finished his call and turned back to the counter. He stood across from me, drumming his fingers on the chipped Formica.

I pointed toward the paper. "Why's there a deadline?"

He scratched his ample rear end, the denim moving up and down under his thick fingers. "It's a national contest. Solve 60 puzzles in 60 days and get $60,000. It's been pretty hard so far."

"Want me to take a look?"

"Have at it." He snorted and stepped back, parking his hands in his pockets, a satisfied look, knowing he had thrown out an impossible challenge.

I read the hint for the first missing word. "To be ready or prepared. Nine letters, in—n—us." I thought for a few seconds, mentally scrolling through possible letter combinations. A word flashed in my head.

"Ingenious," I said, and reached for the pen to write the letters in.

"Don't!" he bellowed, lunging forward like he was pushing me out of the way of a bear. He grabbed the pen. "It has to be in my writing or I'll be disqualified."

"Sheesh! Calm down." *Maybe lay off the Red Bull a tad.* I stepped away from the counter. "I wouldn't have helped if I'd known you'd get in trouble." The puzzle had the number two written in the top right corner. Fifty-eight more to go. I felt sorry for the big guy.

He squared his shoulders. "I would have figured it out."

Under normal circumstances, I would have taken on a more agreeable tone especially since I needed the directions and he was the only human being around. But I was tired. Not just worn out from the last four days but from the last three months. Death has a way of slipping into your pores and feeding on any extra energy you manage to muster from minute to minute. "Hmm." I indicated the last blank in the puzzle. "What goes here?"

He fidgeted with the pen again. It was duct-taped to an old-fashioned, blue spiral phone cord, the end of which was nailed into the counter. Finally he said, "I have the word 'Asswipe' stuck in my head."

I grunted, and quickly tried to cover it up by clearing my throat. I read the clue aloud. "To relieve or soothe." I paused for emphasis. "And you're thinking it's, 'asswipe?'"

He scowled and snatched the sheet away. "It fits in the blanks."

"Not really. It's hyphenated; not one word." I shrugged. "Try 'Assuage.'"

He started to protest, then stopped and neatly printed block letters in the spaces.

He wouldn't have gotten the answer, but I held my tongue. "How much for this notebook?"

"Just take it. Been trying to unload it for months."

"Thanks. How about those directions and I'll leave you alone?"

"Follow me."

We walked outside and I pulled my sunglasses from my hair where they'd been acting as a headband. My blonde, blunt cut hit my shoulders again.

He pointed in the direction I'd come. "Go back to the first intersection and turn left at the log pile. About two miles up on your left there's a road that Ts. Turn left again. It winds around but you can't miss it."

"Thank you." I headed for the car then turned. "What's your mom's name?"

"Ivory."

"I look forward to meeting her."

"Hold those benevolent thoughts until you meet her." He smiled for the first time, and the gesture changed his face completely. I was instantly over my superior attitude. I'd been wrong about Elyk. Despite his hick exterior, and weird name, he wasn't illiterate. His face went from beady-eyed to civilized. He'd gotten the word "vociferous" in the puzzle. No slouch there. And I'd be shocked if I didn't find myself back at his store needing directions. Although I might get points for knowing a lot of words, I had no internal compass.

"Lost" was one word I was very familiar with, more so now that I had no one to call family.

The Pfoltzes

I parked in the driveway of the Pfoltz's Bed & Breakfast (that's pronounced *Folt-z*). The red brick Victorian rose as if out of a fairy tale in the blush of the mid-morning sun. A creek bubbled along the right side and I knew from the Internet photos about the Koi pond behind the main house. Farther back in the woods hid a crumbling private cemetery.

Richard and Rose Pfoltz had been very understanding when I'd called the night before, explaining I'd made it as far as Pittsburgh and I'd be arriving a day later than planned.

"You must be Marleigh," a man called from the side of the inn. He had a head of neatly-trimmed white hair and looked like he had just stepped off a yacht, not someone in possession of maintenance skills. A canvas tool belt lay at his feet, the pockets full of wrenches and pliers. His attention had been on a window-mounted air conditioner, its face-plate propped against the wall.

"Yes. Are you Richard?"

"Guilty." He brushed his hands on his pants, and walked toward me. "Rose and I were getting worried." He indicated the front of the house.

A tailored woman stood there, at the edge of the steps. Rose could model for drug companies pushing vitality meds to senior citizens, she looked that good.

I felt a stab of pain; they reminded me of my parents–*adoptive, adoptive, adoptive parents*–robust and healthy, in the moments before a Malaysian jumbo jet rolled over their Cessna 170 at the John Wayne airport. Only in their 60s, they seemed much younger to everyone who met them.

Over Rose's head, green tendrils from a flowering clematis crept across the gutters, softening the roofline, like lace at the edges of a starched gray dress.

"How was your trip?" she asked.

"I got lost this morning. The rest of the trip went smoothly, even with leering men in truck stops, dense fog in Indiana and a herd of cows blocking the road in Ohio."

Richard chuckled. "Well, you're here safely and that's what matters."

"I agree."

I touched the necklace at my throat, which held my adoptive parents' wedding rings. I wasn't sure they'd be happy I was here searching for answers. They kept this secret from me all these years and they must have had good reason to do so.

Rose squeezed my arm and said, "Come meet Richard's father." She pointed to the porch. "That's Milt. He's staying here until his nursing home gets remodeled. They had a tiny fire a few weeks back."

From a distance, Milt looked about a 150 years old, with shocks of white hair on each side of his head. His withered face was flaccid, like someone had unplugged him and forgot about it. Completely asleep in a rocking chair, his head was tipped back, his dentures askew in his mouth.

Rose tried to shake him awake then gave up. "You'll have to catch him between naps and introduce yourself."

"Good luck," Richard said. "Dad sleeps more than a narcoleptic cat."

I chuckled and Rose shrugged.

Richard carried my bags to the house through the beveled-glass door. There was a library on the left with pocket doors, the interior of the room lined with floor-to-ceiling, *filled* bookshelves. I knew where I'd be during all my free time. A sweeping staircase flowed upward on the right, the kitchen straight ahead.

San Francisco is known for its Victorians, one grouping aptly named The Painted Ladies. Had I chosen this Bed & Breakfast because of its similarity to home?

What I knew is that I'd picked the Hyacinth Room upstairs because it had a bigger closet. Some people go for long walks to think or they stare at a sunset. I was a closet retreater. Give me a medley of wool, leather, silk and cotton, and I could sit in the dark and nose breathe for hours. If the need for a refuge hit me, I'd be prepared.

But maybe things wouldn't be as topsy-turvy here as I'd anticipated. I unpacked. I liked the coziness of the small bedroom. My apartment on Golden Gate in San Francisco was 700 square feet. Everything in the apartment was within a few steps from the kitchenette. I sublet it to a guy in my department in grad school before leaving town.

Searching for the wall socket, I plugged my dead cellphone into the charger and headed downstairs to ask the innkeepers for directions into Wellsfield. Tomorrow I would start seeing patients, but today I'd meet my boss, Jake, sign my contract and pick up patient files. Tungston, or Tungs, was just what I'd envisioned; a quaint speck on a map, down home, but above all, somehow a part of my roots, in other words, me.

DARKNESS

Milt was missing from the front porch when I returned to the house an hour later. He also wasn't around when Rose served chicken breasts stuffed with Brie and currants with a green-bean salad on the side. Dessert was strawberry tarts. *What was I thinking?!* I originally debated about paying the extra cost for the dinner option.

Before bed, I hung up the rest of my clothes and stuffed my suitcase at the back of the walk-in closet. I lingered a moment amidst the interwoven scents of the different boarders. It made me lonely. I felt reduced to one point of energy facing the endless edges of the surrounding forest. I'd been obsessed with life and the temporariness of it. We strive for full days of accomplishment, pack in chores and friends and ways to stay healthy, yet, in the end, we leave only a bit of ourselves behind. I wasn't even sure that was the point, to leave something behind. However, despite my existential tail-chasing, I still needed to know.

I slipped under the lavender-colored sheets and listened to the crickets warming up in the darkness beyond the lacy curtains and screened window. I was grateful for their thrumming. The night's darkness encased the exterior of the house like a black cloak. Anything, or anyone could be moving around out there. I'm used to the cacophony of traffic, random sirens, and multi-ethnic midnight shout-outs; this stillness was freaking me out.

I moved deeper under the quilt and replayed my move to Tungston.

'*We just say Tungs.*'

"Perfect," I whispered.

From graduation to tonight – a mere three weeks – the only parents I had known dying two months before I received my diploma. Marc and Janette Benning. Made their money building storage units, strategically placed in the downtown area of twelve large cities. They had just landed from Houston, my father an amazingly safe pilot. And in a matter of seconds, with one wrong instruction from the tower, they were gone.

The weeks leading to graduation blurred, steeped in pain and loss and trying to reason why I should even graduate. But taken under the care of my parents' friends, I finished my finals and crossed the stage. The big shock arrived with the discovery of my adoption papers in their safe. This revelation confused me, and then made me angry. I could have handled knowing I was adopted. Why keep it a secret? These new documents eventually pushed me into action. I hired a genealogist to help find where my biological parents were from. Once he nailed down Northern Pennsylvania, it was only a matter of finding a job. I dreaded the four-day drive, but I'd need a car to get around. I was also very jumpy now about flying. I wasn't sure I'd be on a plane anytime soon. I questioned my intentions a hundred times as I crossed the country. Why I was leaving the Bay Area, especially since I could research my birthparents online, could easily access genealogy records from any number of websites?

I needed a change. My friends were concerned when I announced I was driving across the country, alone. Like a missile honing in on some yet-to-be-defined target, I'd quickly packed up, deciding to stockpile some healing time between my parents' deaths and the possible reincarnation of my birth parents. A temporary exchange of morning walks on the waterfront with the balmy marina aromas of fish, seaweed and engine oil for thick pine, grasses and corn.

And Tungs seemed like a stable place to start my career. Not to mention... it was *home.* It wasn't the coveted job in the shiny UCSF Medical Center, but a bigger facility could wait. Tomorrow I would roll up my sleeves and get to work, discovering what I was made of, literally *and* figuratively.

Beryl

I felt so much emotion standing on the porch of my first patient's home. Pride, satisfaction, a tinge of nervousness. The whole speech-therapy-healing-the-world idea. I pushed the doorbell and waited for Beryl Holmes to answer. The air smelled green, like I'd stuck my head in a freshly chopped salad. I breathed deeply, comparing the scent to San Francisco's salty-gray aroma and tried not to miss home.

Two minutes passed so I knocked loudly this time.

The chart said Beryl was 72 years old, ex-military, lived alone with his dog, and had trouble swallowing since he'd rolled his car a month earlier.

No one was more surprised than me in grad school that speech pathology covered not only speech and language problems, but swallowing issues as well. Drool, phlegm, copious amounts at times, words I hadn't initially thought I'd be writing in any chart became part of my daily notes on my externship at a local care center.

I studied Beryl's house and yard. The white, cottage-style home was neat, the windows edged with green shutters, his yard shorn so short a quarter could bounce off of it.

The telltale *thunk* and *squeak* of a walker sounded on the other side of the door. Once the door was wide, I held up my identification lanyard tag. "Hello, Mr. Holmes. I'm

Marleigh Benning, the speech therapist from Therapy on Wheels."

Beryl was tall and angular, with a gray brush cut and strong looking hands, the joints extra large and pointy. He squinted at my car and scowled.

I was required to attach huge magnets to the car's doors. The black plastic sheets showed a set of speeding tires with cartoon smoke spitting out from behind them. The words above the tires read, "Therapy on Wheels - Wheely Good Care in your Home."

Silliest motto on earth. Since I wasn't hired as their marketing director, I attached them as told.

"The hell does that say?" he asked. His voice was surprisingly strong and clear, even though a five-inch scar, still in its angry red stage, crossed his throat.

"The company's name. Vicky must have had them on her car."

Vicky Pascerella was the therapist I replaced. The local girl. She finished work three Friday's earlier as usual, then she quit by texting something about the job being too hard. Too hard? I was relishing a job that seemed so simple: working with only five patients.

"Negative," he said. "She never had those on." He rolled his shoulders and readjusted his hands on his walker before peering harder at my car. "That's not a Jap car, is it?"

He was insulting my aging silver Accord, my first big purchase when I started college. I lowered my voice, "I'm pretty sure it was made in America."

"So is Chrysler. Now they're putting out Kraut cars. Whole world's gone to shit." Balancing with one hand, he reached to unlock the door. "Come on in, young lady."

Glad the car debate was over.

After he backed away, I pulled open the door. In the next second, he cursed and the walker clattered off and he collapsed down like an accordion into a heap inside the stoop.

I yanked the door wide as I reached in to help. A blur of gray and white fur streaked past and brushed my face. The big dog's nails scratched the cement steps as it bolted from sight.

Beryl's gnarled hand clamped my arm, surprising me, and he yelled, "Go get the dog!"

"Are you okay?" I asked, my heart jack hammering. What if he'd broken a hip, or ruptured something in his neck? Would he even get into my Japanese piece-of-shit car to go to the hospital? And surely getting an ambulance out here would take a lifetime.

"Shit. My legs are like bad cardboard," he said. "Buckling all the time."

"I'm sorry," was all I could think to say. I retrieved the walker where it lay folded on the floor. Erecting it, I staggered against his weight to lift him to an upright position. We both wobbled drunkenly as I held him under his armpits. Bright spots flashed behind my eyes from the exertion, and my heart couldn't seem to control itself, banging out an erratic beat.

He growled, but this time not about his weak legs. "You have to get the dog," he said. He summoned superhero strength as he used the walker to push me backwards out onto the steps. "What are you waiting for?"

Vicky's note in the chart had read, "Hold the dog." I could have used something more helpful, like, "Watch out for the wooly mammoth - he's a runner." This was all wrong. Beryl expected me to drop everything and run after an animal? I doubted the dog could go far. The thick forest bordering the property looked impenetrable, with no more than a foot of space between the trees, and even those were chockfull of brush and briars.

I offered my professional assessment: "I'll get him right after our session." I waited to be let in again.

He closed the screen door between us and flipped the lock. Anger came off him in waves and I knew I now ranked just below the manufacturers of Honda and Mercedes.

"Okay, okay," I said, raising a hand in defeat. Although absurd, the sooner I brought the dog back, the sooner I could get his attention focused on rehabbing his swallowing problem.

I scanned the yard. Something moved beyond the garage. I jogged toward the back of the house, grateful I'd chosen the flat shoes over the wedges this morning. I spotted him – a large Malamute with beautiful markings. He sniffed a line of bushes while a breeze rippled his thick fur. The panic in Mr. Holmes's voice had been real but I didn't know why he was so distraught. I never had a dog but I suppose all dogs return to their owners in good time. Right?

Moving to within three feet of it, I reached for his collar. He bolted, lapping the house going about 50, and then he headed off toward the woods.

I called him for a few minutes before realizing how ridiculous the situation was. I didn't even know its name. Yelling "Hey dog" and "Come here" wasn't working. Beryl remained behind the screened front door. His scowl had notified the rest of his face, so now his mouth was set in a hard line."What's your dog's name?" I asked, panting harder than I liked.

"The dog," he said.

Was he demented or trying to irritate me? *No, not the dog. I need the name of the freaking cat you don't own.* "Yes. Your dog's name," I repeated, not liking the forced patience in my voice.

Just as I was nearly out of earshot, he said, launching into a coughing fit. "Lord Almighty."

Five months as a veterinarian's assistant had clarified one thing - never question what people named their pets. Cats can be named "Big Balls," a Mini Pinscher "Brutus," and I remembered a bright-blue parakeet called "Kitty Kitty."

I raced toward the forest and said authoritatively, "Lord Almighty, come!" The dog didn't even flinch, nor did it slow down. It dissipated like smoke into the emerald trees.

I stopped at the forest line and listened. In the distance a car engine turned over. A chainsaw buzzed. My breathing was echoing like my head was in a metal bucket. I held my breath and leaned toward the trees. I swear I heard the sweat run down my back as some of my hair fell out of its clip. I called the dog's name as I walked the edge of the woods avoiding what seemed to be the inevitable: actually going in there. There, that - the forest - was not my comfort zone. Mine was streets, buildings, a misty view of Alcatraz. The densely packed wall of green was disconcerting, and the weight of the humidity wasn't helping.

Rustling brush indicated he was on the move again. I took one step into the woods and thought I saw eyes watching, and a flash of gray fur.

The dog took off, crashing through the underbrush as he headed for the road. I'd easily catch him if I stayed along the tree line, while he'd be slowed navigating the woods. When we both reached the road, and if he didn't change direction, I'd grab him.

Fifty yards to the road and I was running at a sprint, amazed at how fast the dog moved.

Reaching the pavement first, I turned right, toward the spot where it seemed the animal would exit. Dry sticks snapped, growing louder, and then the branches flicked apart.

There he was, a blurry image of gray and white, still in the trees but charging straight toward me. I planted my feet, ready to throw myself on him if I had to, preparing myself for the impact.

In that same instant, a horn blared, and the scream of rubber sheared from four tires deafened me.

I covered my ears and spun.

The heated grille of a huge pickup truck had stopped no more than 18 inches away. I didn't know what a heart attack felt like, but I was pretty sure I'd just had one.

The cab door flew open and a man hopped out and ran to me. "Are you okay?" He took my arm, steadying me as I swayed, just as seaweed rocks under the wash of overhead waves.

I shook my head. "What just happe...happened?" My breath was ragged and I was sucking air in and out like I'd torn a lung. I looked toward the woods. No movement there. "Where did he go?"

"Who?"

The man looked to be a few years older than me, his thick brown hair swept back in soft waves. At five-foot-ten, he bent over to look me directly in the eyes. "Where did *who* go?"

"Lord Almighty," I answered. I hoped I didn't have to start the chase all over again.

The man's forehead bunched in confusion.

Returning to my senses, I realized what I must look like and I was suddenly self-conscious. "He escaped. Ran into the woods, so I chased him here. I almost had him when you scared the hell out of me."

"You were trying to catch the Lord Almighty?"

"Yes." My back straightened against his mockery. "He's huge and really moves fast."

"I think that's the general belief."

I wasn't sure we were talking about the same thing.

He cocked his head to the side and studied me like I'd found my way out of the mental hospital. "And what's your name? The Virgin Mary?"

"No." I held out my ID as if I were FBI. "Marleigh Benning. I just took a job here as a speech therapist." Why was I telling him all of that? I had a dog to catch.

"Well, Ms. Benning, let me explain what I saw. I came over the hill, and out of nowhere, a fairly good-sized gray wolf was within seconds of jumping on a young woman. My horn scared him off."

He let go of my arm.

I swept a lock of hair off my forehead and studied him. The temperature and humidity ratcheted higher the more I observed. He had caramel colored eyes and thick lashes, but it was his mouth that held me. My occupation had me watching a lot of mouths but this time it was different. The urge to press my mouth against his lips, to discover their softness, to test out his tongue, was overpowering.

I shook the image away.

He stepped back as if deciding what to do with me. He said, "I don't know if this is a speech therapy ritual, or if you're a religious…uh, person, but that is a *very* dangerous position to be in."

I knew I had a post-tornado-interviewee-look with my clothes askew and half my hair hanging loose. An awkward silence fell, the kind expected when two people realize they were strangers. I hoped he was just driving through the area and we'd never meet again.

"I was chasing a *dog,* not a wolf." Then I noticed the emblem on his truck. *Mapleton Fire Department.* Mapleton was ten miles away.

Crap. Local guy.

"Okaaaay." He stretched out the word.

"Do you know Mr. Holmes?" I pointed toward Beryl's, the driveway barely visible.

"Yup. Beryl and my Dad played a lot of poker."

Of course they did. "It's his dog. Lord Almighty. I let him out by accident."

"Uh oh," the fireman said. "That's not good."

"I *know.*" I shrugged to emphasize the defeat. "That's what I was doing running all over the place."

He smiled. I gave it a three-alarm ranking.

"I'll give you a ride," he said.

I didn't try to argue.

He led me to the passenger door, and after opening it, swept his hand toward the seat. "You look too shaky to walk. Besides, I haven't seen Beryl since his accident."

I climbed into the truck and we rode the short distance in silence. The interior was very clean. A Coke can sat in the cup holder and a popular hit from Chorus Line played quietly through the speakers.

Was he gay? Living in the Bay Area, I had good *gaydar* but here I couldn't be sure. The bigger question was did I feel relief or disappointment?

He'd said something, but I'd missed it, something about a lawyer.

My attention turned to him. "You don't think I'll need a lawyer, do you?" I didn't want to get into any legal issue, possibly putting my job in jeopardy. "Dogs get out all of the time, and really, is there a law–"

"My name is Lawyer. Lawyer Hunt."

"Oh," was all I managed before we parked in the driveway behind my car.

"Nice magnets," he said as we walked toward the house. "Wheely nice."

"Ha ha," I said flatly.

He was about to speak when Beryl opened the door.

We entered and stood in the kitchen, as Lawyer explained how we hadn't caught the dog but he would alert other county workers to watch for him.

I liked how he said "we." Maybe he wasn't gay.

Beryl's forehead scrunched up and my heart sank. This hadn't completely been my fault.

"I'm very sorry, Mr. Holmes. Vicky didn't tell me much about Lord Almighty."

Silence followed my statement. The kind of silence where the clock stops ticking to allow space for what's about to go wrong. Both men waited. Lawyer's eyebrows rose like croquet wickets and his mouth tugged to one side.

Finally the old man spoke. "What in the blazes are you talking about, young lady?"

Hazy thoughts spun through my head like cotton candy building around a paper cone. My therapy time with Beryl was nearly gone and it looked like neither of us was going to leave this encounter any better off. I spoke slowly, hoping to help him track the events. "Vicky didn't tell me the details – simple things like your dog's name."

An electronic squeal filled the kitchen. Beryl poked his gnarled finger in his ear, adjusting his hearing aid.

Lawyer leaned toward me. "His dog is deaf. Beryl just calls him 'The Dog.'"

"Deaf? That can't be true," I said, "He *told* me his dog's name was Lord Almighty."

Something shifted in his face. "I *think* he was just angry. Wouldn't take much to get him cussing when it involves his dog."

I held up my hand as I replayed the exchange in my head.

"What's his name?" I'd shouted.

"The dog," Beryl had yelled back.

Not a question but a statement.

Vicky's note had read, "Hold The Dog." Capitalized words. A name.

I tipped my head back, trying to relieve the stress in my cramped neck muscles. I expelled a long hiss and turned to Lawyer.

He was smiling.

"So this makes you happy?" I snapped.

"It kinda does." He grinned wider. "It sure beats car accidents and raging fires."

"Good to know." *Jerk.* "I'm leaving."

Lawyer straightened his face into a serious look. "Stay away from the woods. Hunters have been trying to trap that wolf for a month. So far, you've gotten closer to it than any of them."

"The wolf is back?" Beryl interrupted, his hearing aid working just fine now. "It'll kill my dog."

As Lawyer mollified Beryl, my mind went numb and my legs started to shake. A wolf really had tried to attack me? It had happened so fast, the animal nothing more than a blur. And if it was a wolf, where was The Dog?

Lawyer indicated the door. "I'll walk you out."

I tried to reschedule with Beryl for the next day but he dismissed me with a wave. "Only if you have my dog with you."

At the car, Lawyer waited while I packed my therapy bag in the trunk.

"Thanks," I said.

He shrugged. "I hope the rest of your week goes better." He sounded sincere.

"There's no way to go but up after this mess." I slid behind the steering wheel.

"You'll do great."

I nodded my appreciation; relieved I didn't have to check in every day with my boss. I could put this behind me and forget it.

I felt his eyes follow my car. He was an unexpected find.

I headed toward Tungs, a 20-minute drive. A large crow alighted on a telephone pole, flexed its wings once and turned its black gaze to the ground. In the rearview mirror, it dove to the earth and flew away clutching a small wriggling body. I shuddered. My quaint town, with roots to my parents didn't feel so innocent anymore.

When I reached the Bed & Breakfast, Richard was polishing the inn's van. He looked up when I approached. "You're back so soon. How did it go?"

"Well. I let a deaf dog loose, almost got chewed up by a wolf and a fireman nearly ran me over with his truck." I took a big breath. "Oh. And my client fired me."

He stopped. "Hmmm. Well, you're the one with the degree. So I guess you know what you're doing."

"Oh, yeah. I sure do." I headed for my room and unlocked my door. I flopped face-first onto the purple eyelet bedspread and fumed. What a day. I didn't even get a fair start with all of the miscommunication with Beryl. And while I didn't know everything about wild animals, I sure as hell knew gray wolves weren't indigenous to Pennsylvania. Just my luck to have flushed out a lone wolf.

Milt

The weather the next morning brought wavering, pearlescent banners of fog, obscuring everything outside, so that even the red maple shack behind the house lay hidden. I willed it to lift sooner than later since I had three patients to see.

I killed time by helping Rose clean up after a breakfast of smoked salmon, French toast stuffed with sweet Havarti and raisins, and chocolate cups filled with orange yogurt and raspberries. The woman could cook.

Richard entered the kitchen and hung a tan work jacket on a peg. "Pea soup out there. You'd better give it another few minutes before you leave. It's dissolving fast, but not as fast as trust fund money."

I laughed.

He winked. "Definitely not the kind of day to go hunting wolves."

"Ah, man," I muttered. Of course, not only had I mentioned the close call with the wolf, but the story had reached Elyk's store and Richard heard an embellished version while at the gas pumps.

Rose said, "He shouldn't tease you. Nobody knows where the wolf came from. And worse yet, it could be rabid. They don't usually come close to humans."

"I'm sorry," Richard said, much more serious. "I'd stay away from the woods altogether."

"Oh, I plan to. Car to house - house to car."

A couple from Arizona descended the curved stairs from the front sitting room. Another staircase led from the kitchen upward to the bedrooms at the back of the house where I slept. The huge Victorian, built in 1838, had been a busy mortuary for over 100 years. The historical plaque at the entrance stated sometimes funerals had taken place several times a week, depending on the season. Apparently cutting lumber was dangerous business but so was delivering a baby in a shack. Whooping cough, polio, influenza. The 15-room house was the custodian of many hushed stories of death.

The Pfoltzes shifted into their hosting roles and turned their attention to the couple. Milt sat in a green, velvet-covered chair in the tiny parlor off the living room. I waved and it seemed like he might have moved his head in reply. I would formally meet him later when I had more time.

I jogged up the stairs, the floral runner silencing my footfalls as I returned to my room. I swiped mascara on my pale lashes and brushed my hair, leaving it loose on my shoulders. I don't know why it mattered but I recalled how I'd looked in front of Lawyer yesterday. The more I thought about him, the less he seemed like a local yokel. I bet he didn't have "small-town" tattooed on his butt. With my current far-flung driving schedule, I'd probably never see him again.

I stalled in front of the mirror. Really? What was I thinking? I didn't need a new relationship, another way to feel attachment, then perhaps sudden loss. After my parents died, I'd been literally shut down, almost non-functioning, lying on the carpet of my closet, cocooning as much as possible, trying to forget what I could about the details of the accident. I filled time with sorting clothes according to fabric thickness, then by color, and finally sleeve length. I rearranged all my shoes from the highest heel to the flats, ordered the belts on hooks from the newest to the oldest, and prearranged the panties and bras in categories of "date night" and "not date night." Buoyed by days of organizing my life, I stepped out into the world again; ready to accomplish all the things my parents had hoped for me. Now, I was a mere two months into finding out they had died with the secret about my birthparents.

The floating mist separated itself into fingers outside the window, the fist of fog finally opening. I grabbed my therapy bag and headed for the car.

Luella and Margritte

Thirty minutes later, I arrived in the town of Swell, so small it didn't really qualify for its presence on the map. I found my patient's house by locating the quarry on the right and the swamp of dead trees on the left, exactly according to Vicky's instructions.

Luella Bledsoe lived with her sister, Margritte. Their mobile home sat dead center on several rolling acres, which was checker-boarded with rotting outbuildings and a crumbling white barn. Luella had suffered six rounds of aspiration pneumonia and she was lucky to be alive. I'd be teaching her how to thicken drinks so she wouldn't choke on faster moving fluids.

An auburn-brown hen pecked the dirt near the house. It'd be a wolf's lunch if we were closer to Milepost and Beryl's house, but 50 miles buffered the hen from death. Fear edged upward from the pit of my stomach – hopefully the wolf wouldn't kill The Dog. Weren't they from the same hood, genetically speaking? It was a connection I hoped would matter.

When I stepped from the car, a feathery tsunami of chickens flowed out from under the trailer skirt and I knew I was about to die. I've seen Alfred Hitchcock's *The Birds.* This would get ugly. The hens fought each other, taking random stabs at my therapy bag and jabbing at my shoes.

"Go on," I said, trying to shoo the birds away without actually touching them, but it couldn't be avoided. The *bawking* and *clucking* grew so loud I barely heard my own words. I stepped around the blotches of chicken crap to avoid tracking it into the house.

A short woman pulled open the door. She resembled a bowling ball on two sticks, her shape pushing the Spandex waistband in her violet stretch pants to their legal limit. Bright-red hair flamed out like dandelion fuzz and her face held a huge, toothy smile.

"Come in, come in," she chirped happily, stepping aside. "I'm Margritte and your client is the ornery woman inside." She hooked a thumb over her shoulder.

I searched for the right response as I held up my ID tag. I'd learned to handle difficult patients during my internship, so her sister didn't scare me. "Nice to meet you, Margritte."

Standing ten feet inside of the home, my eyes had to acclimate to the dimness before I spotted more hens roosting on the furniture. My entry inside brought about lots of head-bobbing and wing-flapping, which I could only assume was disapproval.

Luella, unlike her bulbous sister, was scrawny and looked like an old leather belt sitting at the crooked dining room table reading a newspaper. The loose skin on her neck and face suggested she might have once filled out her sagging flesh.

"Hi'ya, new teacher," she said over a pair of maroon-colored reading glasses. "Don't listen to my sister's trash-talking."

And ignore the chickens roosting on the couch.

She put the paper down. "Hey. Did you know one of Angelina's babies was fathered by an alien?"

I supposed she meant Angelina Jolie and her adopted children. "You mean the father is from another country?"

"No. An honest-to-God bug-eyed alien." She pointed to the paper. "Says right here."

I smiled when I recognized the tabloid. "I never heard that." I switched to mouth-breathing mode, trying to avoid smelling the toxic air. The humidity unhinged my taste buds, the tang of chicken crap settled at the back of my throat. I took a breath to say something but let it go.

You are not here to judge. You want to be here, and a trailer full of chickens is your new adventure.

"Grab a seat." Luella indicated an orange-and-brown-plaid couch.

If there was one positive thing to say, and there was really only one, it was that the orange material nicely complemented the color of the chickens nestled there.

"Just scoot the babies over," she added.

Once again, I wanted to throttle my predecessor, Vicky, a person I didn't even know. My main question to her would be, "Why not mention the filthy conditions inside this home? "*Chickens everywhere-wear rubber pants and boots.*" That would have worked.

I said, "I'll just stand. I'll be moving around, mixing up different types of drinks for you to try."

Luella pointed toward the living room where the chickens had settled down. "Just don't startle Bo Peep. She's the one on the hassock who's been giving us double-yolkers lately."

The words left my mouth before I could curb them. "I guess getting something like a parakeet didn't appeal to you?" It sounded more judgmental than I wanted it to.

The sisters didn't flinch.

"Oh, Golly no! Parakeets bite," Margritte said. "Those little peckers are kept in cages for damn good reasons."

I nodded, as if these were my very same thoughts.

We worked for a half an hour until I'd made certain both sisters knew how to thicken all thin liquids using a powder called Nice & Slow. Then Luella practiced a series of swallowing exercises to help strengthen the weakened muscles in her throat. I explained, "The reason you aspirate liquids is because the muscles are slow to act on the information when something fast is moving toward your trachea. A slow reaction doesn't leave time for the epiglottis to close off the windpipe and liquid trickles into your lungs."

"Nobody explained that before," Luella said. "They've just been bossy about me not drinking."

"Practice these ten times a day," I said, handing her a list of the exercises. "You'll be drinking your coffee skinny before you know it."

"Can I thicken anything?" she asked, running one delicate hand through her thinning red hair. "How about my old friend, Jim Beam?"

Alcohol might explain Luella's thinness.

I said, "If you're taking medication, I'd stay away from alcohol."

"Fine." The answer was snippy and something changed below the surface of her face. She pushed her glasses back on her narrow nose and flipped open her tell-all paper.

I was dismissed.

A short distance later, I pulled onto a roadside rest area to write in Luella's file. Therapy on Wheels needed daily notes turned in each Friday in order to bill Medicare or insurance.

I wrote: *Both sisters are motivated to follow a thickened liquid plan. Client is coherent and oriented to the reason for the adapted program. Luella did not tolerate thinner sips of water or nectar and she choked on 85% of the attempts today. Swallowing exercises initiated, 8 sets, 10 each. She cannot perform a dry swallow yet - other exercises completed with 70% accuracy. Good prognosis if she sticks to the program.*

I needed to talk to the home-health nurse about the chickens. Pets or not, I didn't believe for a second they were disease free.

I dug my cell phone out of my purse to let my next patient know I'd be arriving early. The phone had no signal and I realized how far away from my old life I had gotten. Remote enough my major phone company had yet to stick a phone tower on a ridge.

I would just have to arrive early and hope she was ready.

Ivory

I'd be seeing Ivory Ash, Elyk's mother, the woman who liked words going backwards. Despite previous rural driving upsets, this 25-mile drive to the tiny hamlet of Proxy was beautiful with bristly forests and meandering roads; it felt like I was shooting along a lush bobsled course. I passed a white-steepled church with a huge marquee reading:

"When you are DOWN to nothing—God is UP to something!"

A weathered sign announced, "Proxy, Pop. 171." A few scrappy houses hugged the sides of the road as I passed through town, following the directions, "Find two tall silos and the 35 MPH sign." A minute later, I turned into the driveway of a two-story log home with an attached garage. Acres and acres of grass surrounded the house, making it appear miniature. Apparently a lot of people here had time to mow a lawn the size of New Hampshire. In San Francisco, I was happy my balcony had room for a few flower pots.

The porch's floorboards were covered with colorful gnomes and whirligigs. I rapped on the door and waited. After a minute passed, I tried the doorbell. It chimed out two stanzas of the Disney tune, "Whistle while you work."

No response.

I checked the number on the wooden placard beside the frame to make sure I was at the right place. The numbers matched. Ivory had to be here; she was classified as "homebound," meaning she was unable to leave home without assistance. She'd be dropped from her home-health services if the clinical records stated she wasn't present for the session.

I went in search of a back door. I heard singing. Scanning the yard, I saw a large floral sheet hanging over something bulbous near the edge of a huge garden. Then the sheet stood and turned toward me, and her startled look probably matched my own. This was definitely Ivory; her son was a prickly haired version of the woman now staring at me.

"I tried the bell," I yelled across lawn.

Ivory was close to 300 pounds. She wore a sleeveless, pink top, a floral skirt, blue surgical gloves and lime green Crocs. She'd swept her dark hair up into a beehive cone, a popular style from four decades ago. Lumbering up a gentle slope toward me, she peeled off a latex glove and stuck out her hand.

"I'm Ivory," she croaked. Her vocal cords sounded like they were sutured together with rusty wires. "My son said he met you."

I took her hand and nodded, but my mind spun through the notes in her chart. I knew I was here for vocal therapy but nothing indicated her voice was *this* bad. Two other questions simultaneously popped into my head: Why did she have a thermometer sticking out of her hair and who'd been singing?

"Do you have company?" I asked, looking around. "I heard someone."

Ivory shrugged her shoulders and pointed to a small table beside the garden with a rectangular box sitting in the middle. "Just the radio."

Music drifted across the yard. I nodded. "That must have been it."

I hated making Ivory talk. Her voice sounded crackly and dry, like she had a 20-pack-a-day cigarette habit. Gazing at the perspiration trails running down her neck, I said, "Should we work inside?"

"Let's. Vicky and I liked the kitchen." Ivory waggled the blue gloves toward the house, indicating the screen door at the top of the steps. "A shame she quit."

Vicky's departure had worked out well for me, but I said, "Yes. But I'm here to pick up where she left off."

The kitchen was decorated in Modern Rooster. The bird motif was on everything from dishtowels, a copper cake pan hanging on a wall, to the curtains and rug in front of the sink. I sat in one of the spindle-back chairs at the table and pushed a Beautiful & Big catalogue to the side to make room for my paperwork.

Ivory dropped her girth in the chair across from me. She peeled paper towels off of the roll behind her and blotted her face and arms. Pulling the thermometer from her hair, she stuck it under her tongue, then held up a finger to signal she needed a moment.

I busied myself by slowly writing the date at the top of the notes.

I felt her eyes on me as she waited for the thermometer to beep. She removed the stick, squinted and pushed it back into her hair. "Good," she croaked.

"Are you sick?"

"No. But a full-bodied gal like me needs to be careful in this heat. If I go down in the garden, it would be the living death of me. I'd be yelling, and even if someone heard me, they'd think it was bullfrogs. I try to stay under 99 degrees when I'm working."

The fact she managed strenuous work at all was surprising. She was built like a twin bed. Incredulous, I asked, "*You* planted this huge garden?"

"A third acre of my specialty corn. I registered it under the name of White Knight. Like the guy in shiny armor."

People registered corn? Was it like a car, with inspections and all of the paperwork? I didn't have a lot of exposure to the art of farming but I knew there was something about rotation, which eluded me at the moment. "Good name," I said.

She cleared her throat, a sound akin to an ancient engine cranking over. "You know the old saying, "Corn has to be knee high by the 4th of July?"

"I'm not accustomed to farm terms."

She frowned so I admitted what the woman already knew. "I'm urban, born and raised. I'm lucky to keep a pot of petunias alive for a month."

She said, "Where you're from, you can get a pot of pot growing, I hear."

"True. If I were so inclined."

"Bet my White Knight's worth more than your Mary Jane." Pride rippled through her horrible voice. "By August people will pay big bucks for this corn for their muffins and breads."

"Very nice." Her voice sounded horrible, so I said, "Let's get back to why I'm here. How did you hurt your throat?

"A steak bone tore it to Christmas and back," she rasped. "Been a long recovery." She dropped her eyes to her hands. "People don't want to talk to you with a scary voice like this. They hang up on me thinking I'm pranking them."

"I'm sorry." Any voice sounding like a mix of broken glass and gravel would actually be a great voice for a prank. Especially at 2 AM. "*I'm in your kitchen and I've found your cleavers.*" I refocused. "What have you been practicing with Vicky?"

"I do this." Ivory tilted her head back and slowly eased out the sounds, "Aaahhhhhh. Eeeehhhhh. Oooohhhh." Her voice didn't crackle or break.

"Good. How often are you practicing those?"

"About ten times every hour."

With such a strong practice rate, the poor state of Ivory's voice was even more baffling. Starting with easy vocalization therapy, then increasing to more pressure on the vocal cords was the standard procedure for vocal trauma. "I'm surprised you haven't had more improvement. What does the doctor say?"

"Keep at it." Ivory wiped at a fat tear building in her eye. "I scare the bejesus out of my grandbaby." The tear raced down her round, flushed cheek.

Earlier when I asked, the Pfoltzes had said Elyk wasn't married. That didn't necessarily mean he hadn't fathered a little spiky-headed Elyk. "Is this your son's child?"

Ivory snorted. "Criminey, no. It's my daughter in Virginia. Elyk will never get married unless he pulls his nose out of a crossword book or away from NASCAR races." She shook her head, then perked up. "Do you follow the races?"

First I didn't know anything about raising crops, now car racing. All I knew about NASCAR was that getting really drunk was mandatory and the drivers were worshipped like God, but unlike God they had their own posters and clothing lines. I shrugged. "I know a little bit."

Ivory's face brightened. "I've got a mad crush on Jeff Gordon. Who's your favorite?"

Heat worked its way from my chest onto my neck. Searching around for a name, the only word coming to mind was something about Flintstone. *No, wait. Was it Firestone?* My eyes met hers. "Uhhh..." was all I managed.

"You don't know squat one about NASCAR, do you?"

"I don't," I confessed, tucking my hair behind my ears. "Nor squat two. But will it really matter?"

Ivory sighed, and rasped. "Just don't let on. Killing your kids is less frowned upon than not following the races." She pointed to her head. "Here's a tip. Just remember the names Tony Stewart and Jeff Gordon. You'll be all right."

Once again we were off track and Ivory's voice was moving from trashed to useless. The woman needed to quit talking. I tapped the sheet of exercises in front of me. "Here's how we're going to get your voice through the scary stage and back to normal."

We practiced for half an hour and she produced a quiet voice without its raspiness for about ten seconds. I reminded her I'd be back in two days, and I asked her to avoid talking. She stabbed the thermometer under her tongue and nodded.

Beryl

Outside of a town called Blackout, I passed a Get Petrol-fyed Plaza, with a dozen big rigs nuzzled up to the giant, plastic dinosaur in the parking lot, like metal suckling pigs. A wooden sign on top of the station advertised "loads of night crawlers, good eats and beer." I assumed these were for separate activities.

Richard Pfoltz said Blackout got its name from the miles and miles of old coal mines around the village. He warned me to stay on designated roads at all times near Blackout, unless I wanted to find myself nose-down at the bottom of a 2,000-foot shaft.

I made it through town alive and braced myself for my meeting with Beryl. I felt like I'd handled the chicken situation at Luella's really well and I think Ivory liked me. Two for two today.

I assured myself that when I got to Beryl's, I'd find The Dog safely inside his house and I'd end my day batting a 1,000. Lord Almighty I hoped I was right.

I edged up to Beryl's door, watching my back, leery of what might come from the woods. I rang the bell.

"The door's unlocked," he shouted. I opened it and hurried inside.

No big furry animal rushed by, and my heart dropped.

The living room was walnut-paneled and dim, like the inside of a coffin. Beryl sat on a wooden chair, facing his couch. Spread on the blue-tweed cushions was a mass of metal parts, bolts, wires, and something resembling a bicycle seat. The newspapers he'd placed on the sofa before putting the greasy parts on top were transparent from motor oil.

"You see my dog?" he asked. His gaze was on a sheaf of schematic drawings, lying across his lap.

"Regrettably," I said. "I haven't found him yet."

My words hung in the air like stale smoke, both of us recognizing its pungency but neither of us knowing how to blow it away.

We locked eyes for a fraction of a second, sharing the same thought - Was The Dog okay?

He dropped his gaze to his project.

I cut the distance between us. "What are you doing?"

"I was in the Army," he said. He shoved the drawings toward me. "Make yourself useful. Hold these."

Reflexively, I reached for the large pages of paper and waited there, clutching them. Although we needed to work on his swallowing problems, I decided to take a few minutes to get to know him. "You were in the Army," I said.

He picked up a wrench and started fitting parts together, mostly by trial and error.

"I was a mechanic. And a damned good one. I could build a jeep out of a garbage can and bubble gum if I had to." He nudged my leg with the wrench. "Hold that second page so I can see it better."

I complied, irritated at his bossy demeanor. Some people live alone for good reason. My gaze dropped to the papers. The heading above the diagram read, *Segway Personal Transporter.*

"You're building a Segway?" I didn't try to mask the disbelief in my voice.

"You can read." He fiddled with more parts and wires.

I studied the schematic and then looked back to the dirty parts lying on the couch. They'd come from a junkyard, not a Segway plant. Whatever he was building, and no matter how well he'd used a trash can and bubble gum in the past, this contraption wasn't going to look like the picture on the front of the plans.

He held a small metal box with droopy wires. "Go out to my garage and fetch the big brother to this one. It's on a work bench."

His intentions on how we'd spend our time together completely differed from mine. I wasn't going to devote one more minute on auto mechanics or running errands. We had therapy to do and it wasn't going to get done if I agreed to fetch oily parts from a shed.

"We need to stop this for awhile and work on your–"

He nudged me again with the wrench, this time hard enough to make me step back. "These are your choices," he said, turning a sharp gaze my way. "Either you go find The Dog or you help me make this set of wheels so *I* can go look for him."

My eyes narrowed but I tried to keep my face calm. "This isn't what I'm here for." Even though I felt responsible for his predicament, letting him dictate how our therapy time was used would be a bad precedent.

A tremble ran along his jaw line as he fought something internally. I softened my opinion of him. He was trapped in the house, barely able to get around with the walker, while his dog was deaf, lost, and hungry. And there was the added bad news about a wolf.

"Let's compromise," I offered.

Beryl laughed. It was a stubborn sound.

"I'll even take dog food to the back yard before I leave but first we have to do some therapy." I handed the sheaf of drawings to him and he accepted them without argument.

Apparently, I'd reasoned with him.

He spoke slowly, "Okey Dokey." He struggled to stand, swatting my arm away when I moved closer to help him with his walker. The wheels fishtailed and the whole contraption rattled as he pushed it toward the kitchen. "I'll let you take Kibbles to the back yard." He opened a closet door, reached in and brought out a rifle. "But you're not coming back inside to work with me. I don't like you so much."

My heart dropped into it my stomach. *What was he thinking? He didn't need a gun to persuade me.* I grabbed hold of the chair, fighting off the weakness in my legs. It was the proximity of the gun; I hadn't seen it coming.

I held up both hands and backed away. "I'll leave. You don't need to do anything like that."

Beryl looked from the gun to me, and chuckled. "Hadn't thought about shooting you, but hey, not a bad idea you got there." He laughed again and his eyes squinted into slits. "I'm going to be in the back bedroom, aiming from the window." He pointed the gun barrel toward an empty dog bowl and then at the bag of dog food under the counter. "I've got you covered since you smell like chickens and there's a wolf out there." He balanced the gun across the top of his walker and rattled away into the dimness of the house.

Something buzzed inside my head as the chunky brown food clattered into the metal bowl, loud like hailstones on a metal roof. *Should I just run while I had the chance? The man was a complete psycho. Backwoods scenarios like this were how people just disappeared without a trace. Another thought hit me. What if I was related to him?*

I studied my surroundings, looking for evidence pointing to him actually being dangerous, or for reasons to tell my boss why I couldn't come back. On top of the stack of mail lay pictures of a couple with two young children. Next to it, the local newspaper was open to the sports page. Photos taped to the fridge catalogued The Dog's life from puppyhood to current times.

Not a killer. Just a lonely guy who no longer had his pet for company. I related to lonely.

I carried the food bowl outside to the last place I'd seen the dog.

I felt Beryl's eyes on me and I didn't need to turn around to know he was at the window. I should have been flattered that he cared about my safety, but I had a hard time feeling comforted knowing a gun was pointed at my back.

I set the bowl near the edge of the woods and listened. Nothing but *burrumping* frogs and leaves flittering in the warm breeze.

I needed to talk to someone about how to lure a deaf dog out of hiding. I had no idea. And although I hated to say anything, I'd have to let my boss know I'd apparently been fired. Pretty embarrassing when I only had five patients to start with.

The sensation that something was off raised the hair at the back of my neck. I peered toward the tree line again. Even though it appeared just as it had seconds before, I swore I felt something, or someone, watching me.

I studied the house, spotting the sheer-white curtains fluttering around the shiny barrel of the rifle.

I lifted my hands for Beryl's benefit and shrugged, then let them drop. There would be no reason to try to talk to him again. If the finality in his voice wasn't enough, the rifle spoke volumes about how he felt. Somehow I needed to find his dog and win my way back into Beryl's house.

Lawyer

Over dinner dishes, I talked to the Pfoltzes about Beryl and my dilemma with his lost dog. Richard said he'd see the local dogcatcher at the evening town council meeting, and asked if I wanted to go along to meet him.

Half an hour later, Richard took me in his blue '72 Ford along Sawmill Road, a dirt strip, supposedly a shortcut to Route 6.

The sun held its last hour of daylight; its rays flickered through the trees as we bounced along the dirt road's washboard surface.

"So how do you think you're settling into the job?" Richard asked. We reached a stop sign and he took a left onto Route 6.

The paved road reduced the noise of rattling metal by half. I let a few seconds go by as I thought about my answer. "Okay, I guess. It's more rural here than I imagined, but I wanted a small place."

He nodded. "This part of the state is nicknamed 'The Pennsylvania Wilds' for a good reason. You'll get a taste for homegrown folks all right. But I understand you specifically chose to come here?"

"I did. Over a few other places. I like a challenge and rural was my goal. A place with limited distractions, so I could focus completely on being a therapist."

And finding out why, and by whom, I'd been given away at age two.

"Very mature of you." His thumbs tapped out a jazz beat on the steering wheel. "We'd like to show you around one of the local festivals held over in Happenstance in about two weeks."

"Oh?"

"The Rattlesnake Round-up."

I shook my head, laughing. "'Rattlesnake' and 'round-up' should never go together."

"I think you'd really enjoy it. And for ten bucks they'll let you hold a snake."

I shivered and noticed his smile. I shook my head, "Not even if they paid me 2,000 dollars."

He explained the purpose for tonight's meeting. The leaders of the towns of Tungston, Swell, Blackout, and Milepost were meeting at a Baptist church to help plan the annual Bark Peeler's Convention taking place over the 4th of July. I hadn't been paying attention to where we were going so when a sign along the road said, Mapleton 8, I felt my stomach jitter.

A pleasant image of Lawyer Hunt popped into my head. I couldn't formulate a whole picture of him since the incident on the road had taken place so fast. What I remembered were broad shoulders and the tiny smirk at the edges of his smile when he was amused, which seemed to be the whole time we'd talked.

Richard said, as if reading my mind, "The event is sponsored by the Maple Hose firemen, short for the Mapleton Fire Department."

Of course it was.

Richard signaled and turned into the parking lot.

The Baptist church filled a shady spot underneath two towering maples. It was white, two-stories, and topped with a 20-foot steeple. I scanned the lot for Lawyer's truck.

Not there.

Entering the side of the building through two wide dark-green doors, we turned down a set of creaky, linoleum covered stairs. The smell of musty old books and a 100 years of specialty dinners greeted us. The room in the basement was arranged with folding chairs facing a podium and another table with three additional chairs.

Richard introduced me to several of the people already seated, including the mayor of Mapleton, who had curly black hair and a Hollywood tan. "There's Troy, the dogcatcher. I'll introduce you later." He pointed to a man deep in a conversation by a wall plastered with kids' drawings. I'll introduce you later.

We sat in the center of the first row of chairs as the Mayor approached the podium. After the welcome, the secretary handed out the proposed program for the 35th Annual Bark Peeler's event.

A door opened and closed above, and quick footfalls thumped down the stairs. When Lawyer entered the room, his eyes immediately met mine.

And did he hesitate just a bit before walking to the table facing the audience and taking the empty chair? It looked like he had. A smile tugged at my mouth as I dropped my eyes to the sheet of paper in my hands. At least I looked better than the last time we met.

Lawyer offered a quick apology to the Mayor who nodded and handed him the agenda. The next half hour was awkward as I sat facing him, not more than ten feet away, trying not to look in his direction. When his turn came to speak about the fire department's role and the plans they were making, I tuned out the discussion and studied him.

He wore a light-brown checked dress shirt with the sleeves rolled to just above his wrists. Jeans and a casual pair of brown shoes. And he was better looking than I remembered. I pictured him in a calendar, probably Mr. August, wearing red suspenders, no shirt, of course, and his head would be cocked to the side under his helmet. His chest would have a sweaty sheen over ash smudges.

Richard nudged me. Everyone was chuckling and looking my way. My face flamed, having no idea what had just been said.

Lawyer raised his eyebrows and met my gaze. "I was just saying how the turkey-wrangling event should still be safe to hold since you've shown good promise in nabbing our stray wolf." He shot me a wide smile and I hated him. He'd purposely made fun of me.

With all eyes on me, I suddenly didn't know what to do with my hands, and my feet seemed to be crossed the wrong way.

Five agonizing minutes later, the meeting crawled to an adjournment. I headed straight for the steps but Richard pulled me toward Troy Twittler, the dogcatcher.

Troy's sandy-colored hair was thick and as straight as straw. He looked to be about 30 years old. He wore a wireless phone earpiece, inevitably indicating a self-proclaimed importance.

I explained what happened to Beryl's dog and asked if he could help me retrieve it.

"A speech therapist, huh?" Troy finally asked, studying me. "If you can say my name five times fast, I might be able to help you." Bits of tobacco chew stained his grin. "Go ahead."

What the hell? Even Richard seemed to be waiting for me to say the tongue twister. This would be my last community meeting since it seemed I'd been nothing but the new kid to pick on.

"The name's impossible to say," Troy said, predicting my defeat, crossing his arms and waiting.

I took a breath and said, "TroyTwittler-TroyTwittler-TroyTwittler-TroyTwittler-TroyTwittler."

Troy's eyes widened, then narrowed.

"So what should I do to get the dog back?"

"Probably a lost cause," Troy said. "It's deaf, you know."

I shook my head. "This is where you come in. You must have some ideas seeing this is your job?"

A rotten smile touched his lips. "We can ride around together and look for him. Could take weeks though."

He was hitting on me. I fought the shiver starting in the base of my spine.

"I don't think it would work with my job. Besides, I won your tongue twister test Troy Twittler."

"Barely." He turned and left the room.

"Uh-oh," I said, to Richard. "Is he mad?"

Richard whispered, "Well, he's kinda funny about losing. Troy loses to the game warden *every* election. Give him a few days to recover." He looked over my head and squeezed my shoulder. "I'll be right back. I need to grab the sheriff for a sec."

Left alone while five pockets of conversations filled the room, I glanced to where Lawyer had sat. The chair was empty. *Good. He'd left to go roll up some hoses or try on his shiny rubber boots. Maybe find someone new to berate.*

"I need to apologize."

I spun. Lawyer stood three feet away, his hands in his pockets, shirt untucked. "I'm sorry I teased you about the wolf episode. That was completely wrong."

I stood still, studying his face. He seemed sincere, and the smirk was gone.

"Really," he added. "I feel terrible,"

"Great," I said. "Now there's two of us."

We stared at each other for several beats. I held his gaze, refusing to look away.

He sagged a bit. "Not that it matters, but in my defense, you had a faraway look on your face when I was talking." He tilted his head to the side, raptor-like. "What were you thinking?"

You. As a calendar pin-up, walking out of a mist. Shiny and hot.

I shrugged and shook my head. "Probably work."

He nodded, and although I knew he didn't believe me, it looked like he'd play along.

I cleared my throat.

He pointed to the exit. "I heard you shut Troy down. Nice work. He deserved it." He paused, "Is fast talking a skill in your field?"

"Diadochokenesis," I said, hoping to be done with him.

"Bless you." There was his smirk again. "I hope you're not catching a cold."

Although I didn't want to, I smiled, rewarding his humor. "No. It means the rapid movement of the tongue. Diadochokinetic rate is measured to see if someone has a motor speech problem."

"Hooow aaam I doooiing?"

"I suggest you stop talking immediately."

"You know," he said. "I can start using big firemen words, too."

"Like?"

"Blaze. Heat. Smoky."

I leaned closer to him. A clean lemony scent floated from him. "Ooooouugh. Those *are* big words," I whispered.

"Incombustibility. Conflagration."

I nodded. "More impressive."

He crossed his arms and tilted his head. "Hard to impress a girl from San Francisco."

I inched back and said, "More than you know." I looked over his shoulder and spotted Richard heading our way.

Lawyer followed my gaze and turned to stick out his hand. "How are you, Mr. Pfoltz?"

"Dandy. How about you, Lawyer?"

"Doing great."

"Are you ready to go, Marleigh?" Richard motioned toward the exit.

"All set." I turned my back to Lawyer, but felt his gaze follow me to the exit.

Upstairs, Troy gave me a long, hard stare but didn't say anything as he stood with a group of men. I hoped he wasn't permanently angry. I wouldn't have done the tongue-twister challenge but he was so smug about my expected failure. And it was a word game, a contest. I couldn't resist.

Richard and I rode home in silence, both lost in our own thoughts. During the meeting, I had heard the sheriff whisper "Grady's dangerous" to Richard and Richard had frowned. I decided I would ask him about it at another time. For now I was content to sit quietly, replaying my interchange with Lawyer. I watched the moon hanging in the inky sky, seemingly closer tonight because of its brightness. I couldn't help but feel a genetic tug as I thought of my birthparents, decades ago growing up under the same view. Had they fallen in love under a moon like this?

Just before we pulled into the driveway, I realized I had never told Lawyer that I was from San Francisco. I hadn't said anything about where I was from — or where I was staying.

He must have been asking.

Richard interrupted my thoughts. "Are you worried about Troy?"

"I shouldn't have ticked him off." I shrugged. "I'm not much of a negotiator."

As he shut off the truck, the engine convulsed a few times, then died. "Don't worry. Troy isn't much of a dog catcher."

Smartphone

"I need a new cell phone plan," I said the next morning as the Pfoltzes worked in the flowerbeds in front of the B&B.

The sun had yet to break over the sea-green hills to the east but it sent out soft morning feelers of mauve and gold across the lawn.

Richard said, "We have an extra phone on our network you can take. It's just sitting on the counter most of the time."

"Are you sure it's not too much to ask?"

"You know. We could make a trade if you want." Richard rested on his hoe, his thick hair lifting in the breeze. "You help us around the place or shuttle people on the weekends, then you'd be justified in having the phone in order to keep in touch."

"You've got a deal."

I switched subjects.

"Does your father talk?" I'd been near the elderly man four times now and he was either asleep or staring at nothing in particular. One time I thought he was dead.

Richard shook his head. "No. And nobody knows why. He just stopped one day."

"That's so unusual," I said. "Maybe I can help."

Richard winked. "You get him talking and I'll throw in some unlimited texting on the phone."

I nodded. "I'll give it a shot." Grandpa Milt and I would have a little chat in the afternoon, right after I got home from work.

I stopped under a thick canopy of trees to try out the new loaner phone. First I dialed my boss and gave him my new number and told him about my troubles with Beryl.

"I heard about your run-in with him. He called to ask if Vicky was coming back."

"Aw, jeez," I said, sighing. "Jake, I'm sorry. I had no idea his dog was deaf. And I really tried to catch him. I ran all over the back yard."

"The chart must have said he was deaf." His voice held a challenge. "Vicky left fast but her notes seemed detailed."

I was determined not to swear, but he was defending her when she had left him hanging without a therapist just weeks ago. "The note read, Hold The Dog. Nothing about deafness."

"Understandable. You're new at this."

I blocked the word "fuck" from leaving my mouth by jamming my lips tight.

"Just stop by Beryl's this week and try to make friends with him. He'll cool down."

"And, Jake. Are there wolves in these woods?"

Jake was silent then said. "Not usually. Nothing for you to worry about since your job is inside."

I told Jake I'd see him Friday at the office. After I hung up, I leaned my head against the steering wheel for a moment. I was used to being at the top of my class, the straight 'A' student. Being labeled "new at this" felt as good as a sandpaper thong. I would have to show him I was quite the opposite.

Melvin and Sandy

I reached Ruttsford having only gotten lost twice. Progress, for sure. I found the home of my patient, Melvin Carlisle. The large, yellow home was all about being tall, with bay windows and wisteria vines as thick as an arm crawling the sides.

Melvin had had his second stroke in six months and developed word-finding problems. Vicky's note reported Melvin was the pastor's assistant at the Presbyterian Church. "A very devout man."

His wife, Sandy, a petite woman with close-cropped white hair, greeted me at the front door. "My husband is in his favorite chair, my dear. This way."

I followed the woman to a den with wall-to-wall bookshelves, surrounded by furnishings in rich maroon and gold-plaid colors.

Melvin was not overweight but he looked soft around his middle. He was nearly bald with a sprig of gray wisps combed across his shiny crown. He reclined in a chair, sipping a Coke. While he swallowed, he motioned for me to sit in the chair next to him.

"Hello," I said. "I'm Marleigh."

He set the red can on a wooden table between us. "Son of a bitch," he replied, staring right at me.

I froze. *What had I said wrong?* I looked down to see if my blouse had popped open.

His wife broke in. “This is why we desperately need your help. This stroke has left him nearly mute except for this ability to swear and use foul phrases. I’ve been trying to anticipate what he needs so he wouldn’t *have to* talk.” Her face sagged. “He’s cussed most of our church friends right out of the house. No one comes to visit. We’ve gone from popular to unholy outcasts.”

“Really?” It seemed liked church would embrace its members better.

“Like the Catholics,” she whispered.

Melvin watched quietly as his wife talked, then he pointed to the stack of large picture cards I had removed from my bag, and said, “God damn asshole.” He smiled and waggled his fingers in a “let’s get started” motion.

“Okay,” I said. “You and I are going to solve this problem. Let’s see what you can do.” I held up a picture of a car. “What’s this?”

“Shit bastard,” he said, tapping the photo, his face full of pride.

Amazing.

Next, I held a picture of a lawn mower.

“Bitches,” he said.

Then he called a hat, “a whore ass.”

He wasn’t upset by his choice of words, and in fact, he seemed happy. He couldn’t possibly be registering what he was saying or he’d be freaking out of his Godly head. I showed him the hat again. “Is this really a ‘whore ass?’”

He recoiled and his face overflowed with disgust. “Suck it!” he yelled, his voice matching his raised fist.

“Oh, Marleigh,” Sandy said, stepping closer. “He gets really upset when people swear.” Her hands fluttered in front of her chest, like sparrows tied to the ends of her arms. "And I know. You were just feeding back to him what he said. We've all made that mistake."

I quickly apologized and he calmed down. I felt a blush build under his scrutiny. His look said my soul was headed for a hot place, and it wasn't Death Valley in July.

Grabbing a tablet and a pen, I wrote the same words in large print, "CAR, LAWN MOWER, HAT." I slid it onto his lap and said, "Point to 'LAWN MOWER.'"

He did.

"Great! Where's 'HAT?'"

Bingo again. He could read, which was good. I touched the word 'HAT.' "Say 'hat.'"

"Dammit to hell," he announced proudly but his wife deflated behind me like a week-old balloon.

I turned to Sandy. "We'll take one victory at a time. His input system seems okay, but his output is broken."

For the next half hour I wrote out words and directed him to point to them, match them, or try to repeat them after me. Repetition of words was still unsuccessful.

"Haammoocckk," I drawled.

"Daammiitt," he slowly said, and smiled.

I patted his hand and promised to return two days later with a word board. Effective communication didn't always involve speaking. Maybe, if he learned to *not* talk, he could point his friends back into their house.

I drove to an overlook I had passed on the way to Melvin's. From this perch high above a valley, the view was spectacular. A bumpy, green topography, like a giant alligator's back stretched in every direction, cloven only by a blue lake rippling with silver-tipped swells.

Melvin's chart lay open on my lap. He must be so bewildered by what had happened. I wrote: *He's friendly and his wife is helpful.*

He has no ability to communicate his wants and needs. Speech is limited to foul language and he cannot repeat words. On the plus side, he reads. He needs to learn to point to words as his speech returns. I'll make a basic needs word board for the next visit.

I pulled away from the overlook and headed toward Tungs. This job didn't feel much like work. I was used to having ten sessions a day in the Bay Area. As the summer passed, I hoped I might find more patients. But in truth this was what I needed; I would have time to search out my parents, which was what brought me here to begin with. This was such a big deal sometimes it was easy to forget.

Maple Grady

An hour later, I was in the maple grove behind the Bed & Breakfast, holding a bucket while Richard and I walked from tree to tree removing the taps and spikes. My agreement to trade labor for the cell phone had begun. On the way to the grove, he said, "We'll cork up the maples. The sweet ladies are done for the year."

We weren't really putting corks in the trees, I learned. After we removed the taps, the trees would seal themselves.

"We had a late start this year," he said, kneeling beside a maple with a set of pliers in his hand. He pulled and dropped the last of the five-inch spikes into the bucket. "That should do it. We had a good season. Got 35 gallons of heavy grade and 26 of light."

I followed him to the maple shack. The building was ten feet wide by 20 feet deep and he built it out of red brick to match the house. The one and only door opened onto the main floor, which held the evaporation pans, a stove designed for boiling the syrup, and a large metal sink.

He took the bucket from me at the entrance, walked inside and set it on the lip of the sink.

"Can I ask you a question?," I asked from the doorway.

"Shoot."

I was reminded of my grandfather. He would point his finger and mimic pulling a trigger because saying "shoot" took too much effort. He'd have to turn the voice vibrator on, get it in the correct position on his throat, then speak. The regret of not being more help to him crawled through my chest close to my heart. Did helping others make up for not knowing what to do to help him talk? I hoped so. I missed my family. It was time.

"If I wanted to find some people who used to live in this area, do you know where I might start looking?"

He scratched his head. "Mmm. Well. Some people, eh? Do you know the town they are from?"

"Butterfield. I think it's next to Wellsfield. I have their names."

His eyebrows lifted. "Who is it? I know almost everyone in these parts."

"Kingston. Amber and Daryl."

He scratched his cheek. "Never heard of them. Your age?"

"No, they'd be about 45 or 50." I wasn't ready to say they were my parents. I wasn't so sure of what I would find.

"Butterfield is small. I'll put in a call to a poker buddy I have over there. Marvin Jewel."

"Thanks." I paused, then asked, "Also, and unrelated, I heard the name Grady last night at the meeting. Something about him being dangerous. Who is he?"

Richard stopped in the middle of dropping the taps into the sink, frozen for a second before answering. "We're not sure he's really in this area."

"Hmmm. Well there's clearly more to *this* story."

He nodded. "Okay. It's good that you brought him up because I was planning on talking to you about him." He ran hot water into the sink and added several pumps of soap from the dispenser above the tubs. "There isn't much to tell but you should know what we know."

"*Is* he dangerous?"

"Yes, in a way. Apparently he beat up a doctor in upstate New York about three months ago. And then two State Troopers near Elmira were nearly run over during a routine traffic check. The car dash camera didn't get any footage and the troopers didn't see it coming, so nothing about his description got called in. They think he steals cars. A few people in the Elmira area ended up with their houses broken into and money missing."

"Maybe it's different guys doing those things."

As Richard washed the metal pieces and put them in the rack to dry, I grabbed a towel and wiped.

"Good point except he leaves a calling card behind. That's the connection between them all."

"Like a business card?"

"No, he has these little notes, like a teacher might have, with apples or school buses on them. He writes a grade on the note. In the case of the doctor, he wrote a D-. The State Troopers got a B+ and a C- thrown from the car window. The burglaries all have the same type of notes."

I stopped drying. "Wait. Is this how he got his name?"

"Yup. Grady. Like I said, no one knows who he is. If it weren't for the notes, the police wouldn't have linked the cases in the first place."

"Why are you worried? It sounds like he's in New York State, not here."

"A farmer over in Cameron County, about a 100 miles west of here, had some turkeys stolen from his barn about a month ago. He got an A-."

Luella and Margritte's chicken patch popped into mind and I felt a finger of worry trace my spine. I described the sisters and their chickens.

He assured me the town of Swell was in a different direction than where the turkeys had been taken.

We walked back toward the house. He said, "Of course, our first goal is the safety of you, our guests. We're in constant contact with the sheriff's department. The good news is no one has been hit-n-run or had anything disappear for weeks. Law enforcement believes he's still heading south and has probably hit Maryland or Virginia by now."

He opened the screen door for me and smiled. "Now, let's see what this wonder woman has cooked us for lunch."

Milt

Later in the afternoon, I crossed the backyard and settled into a padded chaise lounge under a trellis heavy with ivy where I found Milt. The leaves shaded the large Koi pond. Several dozen torpedo-shaped orange and white fish moved slowly under the surface.

Milt stared at the fish, not even flinching when I took the chair next to him.

"Hello, Milt. You probably know by now that I'm staying here this summer. Like you."

A bee droned in the foliage above. Milt slowly lifted his eyes to meet mine.

They were sky blue, set in fleshy folds indicating a long life. Nothing registered in those blue chips, but his gaze held steady.

I could either wait an hour to see if he would speak or I could strike up the conversation. I chose the latter.

"I know you're from around here. Ever see a wolf in these parts?"

He swallowed slowly, his Adams Apple jumped and then eased back down.

"Right? Wolves aren't around here. But I almost got flattened by one a few days ago. Over by Milepost. You know Beryl Holmes? I'm learning everybody knows everyone here."

He hadn't moved a muscle but I sensed he was listening.

"He's all about his gun and protection, or so that was his story. I let his dog loose and he's really mad. I don't blame him. I'll go back to visit him because I don't believe he can hate me like this. It seems unfair, doesn't it?"

Milt dropped his eyes to his hands, and studied them like they'd just shown up at the ends of his arms.

An airliner flew overhead and left two fluffy streamers behind, they contorted and wavered, meshing into each other.

I waited for any sound or word from him.

The phone rang from inside the inn.

He focused on his right thumb.

A few seconds later Rose appeared holding the portable receiver.

"For you," she said.

My heart skipped a beat. I had no idea who'd be calling me on the B & B main line. My cell phone couldn't receive calls so no one in California would know how to reach me. I lifted the receiver to my ear. "Hello?"

A man's voice growled into the phone. "I need a seven-letter word. I'm really stumped."

Elyk. Why waste time with a silly "hello" when he needed a seven-letter word, stat?

"Hi, Elyk. How about manners? Manners has seven letters." I'll admit it, I sound crabby whenever I speak to him.

"What?"

"Hi, Marleigh," I coached.

"Oh, hell. Hello. You got anybody else calling and asking you for words?"

"Not really. But you could help me catch the attention of a deaf dog."

He paused. "Is that a metaphor for something?"

I let a few seconds tick by. "You know I let one out a couple days ago, since I heard you've had some fun retelling the story." I waited for him to argue but he didn't. I continued, "I also pissed off the dog catcher."

He laughed. "I heard he's pretty mad at you. Not like it matters. Troy couldn't find a dog if it latched onto his crotch."

I chuckled. "So everyone says. Which reminds me. How did *you* first hear about The Dog?"

"A fireman stopped in. We had a good laugh."

I knew one fireman. "Great." I paused. "Since you're a country boy, I need you to tell me how to find this animal." Elyk hunted rattlers so he must have some inkling on how to find a tame pet.

"Help me with this word first."

I hated making bargains for everything, but he seemed pretty stubborn. I sighed. "Give me the clues."

"Remember. Seven letters. The clues are, 'Facial, usually disagreeable.' Second and third letters are 'ug' and the last letter is 't.' I think it's 'bugshit,' but I'm not positive."

I was pretty sure it wasn't "bugshit" since I've never known a puzzle to use foul language. "Give me a second." I spun through letters that could come before the 'ug.'

"C'mon," he said. "I gotta go pump gas for some bluehair who's blowing the horn out front."

A man who loved the public. Then the word hit me. "It's 'mugshot.'"

I heard him clear his throat, then a pen scratched on paper. "I would have gotten it," he said, and hung up.

I said to the dial tone, "What about helping me with The Dog now?" I hit the disconnect button. If he'd been given a normal name, he'd be different.

Or maybe not.

I'd bug him later about how to catch The Dog.

Milt had slumped to the right and was fish-gazing again.

"Do you know there might be a criminal running loose not far from here?"

Nothing.

"I'm a speech therapist, Milt. Did you know that?"

He closed his eyes and straightened in his chair.

"Anytime you feel like talking, I'll listen."

His deep breathing signaled that sleep was not far off. His face relaxed, his jaw dropped open and the long, throaty intake of air announced I was now talking to myself. Again.

"I know." I stood. "I'm riveting."

CASEY

Vixonville was in a direction I hadn't traveled yet, sitting ten miles north of Mapleton. As I passed by the Mapleton firehouse I couldn't help but glance toward the building, wondering if the men would be outside. Maybe shirtless, sunning themselves, holding those metal-reflector sheets to even out their tans. No one was outside and the doors were all closed.

No reason to gawk.

Once in Vixonville, I turned onto Collard Street and after a few more miles I found Rutabaga Drive, a wannabe dirt road. I bumped along the rutted trail for a quarter of a mile before stopping at its end, in front of a two-story house with chipped gray paint and patches of shingles missing from the steep roof.

Casey Lester lived here. He was new to Therapy on Wheels, so at least at this house I wouldn't be compared to Vicky. Casey was five years old and had briefly gone to speech therapy in Wellsfield, but they quit after the first visit. The dad, Karl Lester, was a long-haul truck driver and the mom, Honey, would have the previous testing for me to peruse.

I grabbed my therapy bag and headed for the house. The steps creaked as I climbed them. The wooden porch hadn't seen paint since Vietnam and the doormat read, "The bell is hooked to explosives - you decide."

I pressed it anyway.

A woman's voice yelled, "Get the door," then footsteps quickly thumped down some stairs.

The door flew open and a boy stood there. Casey was stocky, with thick blonde hair and big blue eyes. He jumped up and down, wearing a dirty red-striped T-shirt with a frayed collar and "camo" shorts with bulging pockets on each side of his sturdy legs. The jam mustache above his lip looked fresh but the gum stuck in a tuft of his hair above his right ear had been with him awhile.

"Hi!" I said. I bent over and offered my hand. "My name is Marleigh. Are you Casey?"

He looked at me for a second, then grabbed my hand and licked it. Then he dropped onto the floor, running away on all fours like Gollum in Lord of the Rings.

Nice greeting.

I dried my fingers on my shirt and wished I had some wet wipes in my bag. Hopefully Casey was just nervous and this weirdness would soon go away.

A woman appeared at the door. She looked to be about 27, but deep lines on her face said she'd covered a lot more miles than that.

"I'm Honey. He's being a little shit today, so good luck." Her lanky copper hair was held on top of her head with a tortoise shell clip, and her ample, freckled cleavage pushed up from a tight yellow tube top.

"He's just nervous, don't you think?" I stepped into a high-ceiling foyer where a dusty chandelier hung in the center. To the sides of the entry sat a living room to the right and a dining room to the left.

"Naw, he didn't want to get his hair cut so I had to smack him a few times. Still didn't get the damn gum out."

My stomach lurched at the word 'smack.' Casey returned, still running on all fours, then he stopped next to Honey's leg and panted like a dog. Honey rubbed his head and said, "Good Boy. This is your new teacher."

Oh, no. She was reinforcing his ridiculous dog act.

I had to stop this behavior immediately or I'd be licked and pawed every time I visited. "Casey, stand up so we can get to work."

He scooted toward me and grabbed my leg like a Hero sandwich, and dragged his tongue along my shin.

"No, no, no! Stop, Casey!" I moved backward and put my hands on his shoulders to keep him away. I shot a desperate look toward Honey. "He shouldn't be doing this."

"Casey, stop all this shit. I told you it don't bring your daddy back any faster."

He rose up onto his knees, his hands curled in front of his chest, begging. "Ah ant a oo-ay," he said, his raspy voice an indication he did a lot of yelling.

Vocal nodules grew on the vocal cords with prolonged abuse from yelling, or in Kenny Roger's case, from singing badly. Casey wasn't born with this raspy voice - he'd earned it.

"Okay," Honey said.

His mom understood him? Casey talked like his tongue was tacked to the bottom of his mouth, kind of like Frankenstein's first words, just a bunch of vowels and grunts slung together.

"Go get a small one," Honey added, "but come right back. And stop being a jerk and try to walk."

He ran off on all fours.

"Brat," she said to his retreating back. Then she turned to me. "I thought you could work in here." She indicated the living room.

"Okay." I followed her into the room where a long, brown couch slumped against the back wall. A tweed area rug, curled up at its ends, exposed worn floorboards around the edges of the room. "I'm impressed you understood him."

"I spend enough time with him to catch what he means but I don't always understand him." Honey pointed toward a wobbly folding table she'd erected in front of the couch. "You can take the cushy seat and put him in the chair. And if you don't like his dog shenanigans, just let him have it."

I dropped my bag on the floor. The house had an old musty smell, but nothing looked dirty, just lived in. I wanted to know about "daddy coming back." Raising a child nearly alone was a major recipe for stress. "You mentioned his father being away. Is that why he does this dog thing?"

"His daddy drives truck. He's gone for ten days, back home for one or two, and out on the road again. It's hard on us but it pays good bank." She pointed to the ceiling. "He paid back his grandma for this house in about year. But Casey didn't act this way until we got Chipper a few months ago."

"Chipper?"

"A mutt my husband found along the road. I've let him pretend to be a dog because they've played together so well. You can see why Casey don't have many friends. Everyone thinks he's dumb as cabbage, but he's smart enough. I thought having a pet would be good, but maybe it wasn't."

I hadn't seen any sign of a dog and hadn't heard barking. "What breed is he?"

"Shepherd mix. Shaggy white-and-gray thing. You'll see him when Karl gets back next week."

I had an 'ah-hah' moment. "Oh. He rides along with your husband." Casey must think that if he acted like a dog, maybe his father would take him along, too.

Casey headed our way, carrying a very full glass of something red.

I started explaining my thoughts on the subject, "Sounds like he's trying to get his father…"

Casey tripped on one of his untied shoelaces and the red punch left the glass, a complete organism, rippling through the air like a sheer swathe of red satin before it splashed the front of my white Capris.

"Uuugghh!" I sputtered, first at the shocking coldness of it all, then at the red stain left on the crotch. *No! I looked like I'd miscarried an elephant.*

"Casey!" His mom snapped. She twisted his ear, but he squirmed loose and scooted out of her way.

"Ah ihhint een it," he whined and dropped to all fours again.

"You meant it," she snapped. "And dammit! Stand up!"

He continued to crawl around, ignoring her.

I jumped in to rescue him. "It was an accident. I can wipe this off in your bathroom."

She relented and led me through the dining room where a narrow path wound between stacks of newspapers covering the floor, the dining table, and every free space. The room had been rendered completely non-functional for eating.

"Newspaper drive?" I asked.

She handed me a wet peach-colored washcloth. I scrubbed my pants but the stain clearly wasn't going away without bleach.

"Oh, those dumb things," Honey said, looking embarrassed for the first time. "My husband picks newspapers up from all over."

"Impressive. I barely read the headlines on MSN." I wiped the sticky liquid off of my legs.

"He hasn't read *any* of them yet. He just has a thing for paper. Some guys drink or gamble or screw waitresses. He just finds the newspapers interesting."

Karl obviously had a major infatuation with wood pulp products.

Honey accepted the cloth when I gave up trying to get the stain out. She offered a weak smile. "Welcome to my damn world. Casey will mess you up faster than an afterthought."

I looked at my wet clothes. I *felt* like an afterthought. I couldn't go to the rest of my patients' houses this way. Could I get to Tungston, change my clothes and still stay on my schedule? Nope, it was too far and I'd be late.

"Let's reschedule so I'm not sitting in wet clothes on your furniture. How about tomorrow?"

There was resignation in her face and it was clear she knew I wasn't worried about her furniture.

Casey charged past us and hit the backdoor with both hands, before disappearing into the yard.

"Christ! That kid never listens. I told him to stay inside." She leaned out of the door and screamed his name several times.

He was swinging on an old tire tied to a tree branch, totally ignoring his mother, singing an unintelligible tune to the skies.

On the way to the front door I remembered something. "I heard you have a copy of his speech and language evaluation. Could I look it over tonight?"

She shook her head. "He didn't get tested. He'd just started this dog phase and all he would do was bark at the lady. We never went back."

I nodded. "Okay then. I'll test him tomorrow."

Downtown Vixonville covered two blocks. Several stores sat empty, with weathered doors and boarded-up windows.

I passed Sherrie's Furniture Nook, Ned's Hardware & Pet Complex, and an antique store called Old Fashioned. The last store on the end was the largest, with a sign announcing "Groceries & More!" I hoped once inside, the "& More!" meant shorts or Capris.

Wooden beams framed the interior of the warehouse-sized building, which was divided down the middle by a long wall.

"Howdy!" A man called from behind the counter. He looked to be about 40, completely bald with a chestnut-colored handlebar mustache. "What can I do ya for?"

"I need some pants." I pointed toward the non-grocery area. "Or a skort, sweats, anything like that."

"This way, city girl," he said, leading me into the other side. "My name's Bill and I carry several brand names but probably not the ones you're used to." He stopped and studied my sandals. "I think I know just the look for you."

I squinted at him, and said, "What makes you think I'm from a city?"

"Easy." A toothpick appeared out of nowhere between his lips. It magically moved from one side of his mustache to the other without his mouth opening. "You said skort." A toothy grin flashed below the thick cascade of lip hair. "Nobody here can even spell skort."

He was outfitted in work boots, faded jeans that bagged at the butt, and a dark-red cowboy shirt with pearl buttons. All that was missing was his horse. Apparently, though, this cowboy was a fashion-ista trapped in lowly Vixonville.

He dropped his hand on my back, nudging me toward the clothes. "Let's get you suited up." He pointed to four circular racks. He pulled a pair of blue bib overalls from the nearest rack. "This here's Round House, one of the finest names in overalls." He held them in front of me.

"Aren't these for construction workers?"

"Yup, and linesmen, painters." He hooked the hanger on the rack. "I thought we were trying to solve a problem here." He stared at my ruined pants.

I didn't have the time to find another town. "We are," I agreed. I lifted another pair from the same rack and studied them before putting them back.

He pointed to the last rack of overalls. "That's the Dickies brand."

I'd bought pants with a Dickies label before so we were moving in the right direction. I had my choice of one color, dark denim.

"Those are lightweight and preshrunk."

The man knew his overalls.

"Sold," I said, with mock enthusiasm. "Can I change into them before I pay?"

"Right there." Mark pointed toward a curtained-off alcove. "Meet you at the register."

I pulled the curtain shut and surveyed the area for a hanger. It obviously wasn't a changing room since it was stocked with fishing poles, bags of hooks, and an entire shelf of small bottles of bloated insects with catchy names like Trout Tantalizer and Catfish Connoisseur.

Did I come from people who fished? People who chewed toothpicks and said, "What can I do ya for'?"

I slid into the pants, and threw a strap over each shoulder and hooked the buckles in the front. The leg length was easily six inches too long, so I rolled each into a thick cuff at my ankles and slipped on my shoes.

At the cash register, I saw a grin twitching under Bill's mustache.

I didn't care. Dry clothes felt amazing.

I thanked him for the plastic sack for my wet Capris.

He nodded, studying my new look. "You put a spaghetti strap tank on under those bibs and wear a pair of high heels, you'll have a look that really talks."

"I'm taking your word for it, Bill. You are the kingpin of overalls."

Lawyer

I rolled to a stop at a light in Mapleton, across the street from the fire station. In my absence, the fire trucks had been brought out onto the cement in front of the building and three firemen were using long brushes and hoses to wash them down.

I stared, trying to see if I recognized any of the men.

A tap on my passenger window, made me flinch like I'd been electrocuted.

Lawyer stood there, a half grin on his lips. He made a tumbling motion with his index finger, so I buzzed the window lower.

I squirmed under his steady gaze as he took in my outfit. I forced my chin higher. "Hi," I said.

"More like Howdy. Did you get a new look?"

"Nope. Just trying to fit in." It was a mean thing to say, but I wanted to drive a stake through this conversation.

"Are you seeing patients out this way?"

The guys washing the trucks had turned toward us, staring.

"In Vixonville." I thought of the stacks of newspapers. "I just left a house you'd call a fireman's nightmare."

I saw interest in his light-brown eyes. "Why's that?"

"I'm seeing the son of a major hoarder; newspapers, thousands of them, stacked all over the house. You know. One lightning strike?"

He scowled. “Who is it?”

I wished I hadn’t brought this up. “I can’t give out their names.”

He stepped back from the window and pointed to the magnets. “I’ll call your boss and ask him.”

That wouldn’t be good. I really shouldn’t have gossiped about Casey’s house. “The last name is Lester. I’m not saying anything else.”

“Lester the Molester,” he said. “Easy enough to remember.”

“Don’t go out there, okay? I really need to keep seeing their son, and they’ll figure out it was me.” The light changed, and a car behind honked.

“Okay.” He tapped the roof and stepped back as I pulled away.

Ivory

I was annoyed all the way to Ivory's, so when I felt her analytical gaze fall on my overalls, I said, "Don't ask. I got splashed with a drink and these were the only clothes I could find in a hurry."

She studied me a bit longer then rasped, "You know. With a cute tank top and some high wedgies, that's a sharp look."

"So I've been told." I turned the session around to her issues rather than my failed wardrobe. "I've been thinking about your voice. And I know it will be hard, but you need to go on complete vocal rest for a week. Give your voice a chance to heal."

Ivory winced. "I don't think I can." She tugged down the hem of her bright pink and yellow blouse, causing her breasts to burst upward like two pale hams. "I get my hair done every Friday," she croaked, "and I do a lot of talking."

Her "get my hair done" comment stopped me for a second. Could a beautician really style Ivory's hair in this fashion? Wouldn't they be worried about their reputation?

I tried to strike an agreement. "How about you just nod and listen as the other ladies talk?"

"Can't. I retell stories from Elyk's store. It's the only laugh we get sometimes."

There really were no secrets here. It made me think if this Grady guy had been in the county, someone would have reported him by now.

I took a gamble, although it wasn't much of one. "Then you've heard about my crazy first day of work?"

Ivory tilted her head to the side, her beehive a missile pointing toward Russia. She pursed her lips. "No, he didn't mention much about you except that you were pretty fair at crossword puzzles and you were the size of an eighth grader."

Who designated a person's size by a school grade? And five-foot-three wasn't so short. I took a deep breath. I'd saved his big, canvas-clad ass by giving him the word "assuage" *and* "mugshot," so I deserved a ranking higher than "pretty fair."

I let the frustration dissipate. "He didn't tell you I'd let out a deaf dog?"

"Nope." Then it seemed like a light switch snapped on and a crimson flush rose on her cheeks. "Wait. What deaf dog?"

I waved my hand dismissively in the air. "A man in Milepost owns it. I can't tell you his name, but he has this–"

"On the Cross of Christ!" Ivory rasped. "Not Beryl's dog!"

Ivory heaved herself up from the chair, leaned on the counter and ripped a rooster motif paper towel from the spindle and mopped her forehead. She spat, "He was two weeks from shaving him. This is terrible!"

I was stunned into silence. Why wasn't I surprised that she knew Beryl? Once I shut my gaping jaw, I said, "Well, he'll come back soon. Besides, I'm out looking for him and I even talked to the dog catcher."

The information did nothing to calm her. Why did she care if the dog got shaved in two weeks? I saw why Elyk had decided not to tell his mom this piece of gossip. "Not to be rude, but what does cutting the dog's hair have to do with anything?"

She rasped, "I told you I have this prized corn."

"White Knight. Got it."

"When my corn sprouts, raccoons will eat it up like fat kids on a cone of Ben and Jerry's. I'll be ruined if he doesn't get his dog back soon." She lumbered into the next room, muttering under her breath. When she came back, she held a 50 dollar bill and a list.

"Here's some money to get my groceries and make sure you get some ground beef to leave out for The Dog."

I sat back in my chair and shook my head. "I'm sorry. I can't get your groceries."

"Well, Vicky used to make a quick run to the store on her way here."

Vicky again. I had to remind myself I wasn't in a competition with the last therapist. I met Ivory's gaze. "I can't shop for you; it's not allowed. I'm already on the outs with my boss for making Beryl upset. I'd hate to straight-up lose my job."

Ivory flapped the money and the list in my face again. "I make six-thousand dollars a year on my corn sales. That and my military pension is all I got. I'll lose my house."

"Military pension" and this hefty woman were like trying to force pieces from two very different puzzles together.

Ivory continued rasping out her story. "Beryl combs his dog all spring and saves up the hair. Then he shaves him come June and brings the bag to me. The Dog is skinny under his coat."

"As skinny as an eighth grader?"

Her eyes narrowed, her brows bunched up. "I spread it around the edges of the field so coons will take their ugly masked-faces to the next county."

Although this country folklore was interesting, the excessive talking was very bad. "I'll make a deal with you. I'll get your groceries, and some meat for The Dog, this *one* time, but you *have to* stop talking. If you agree to this, nod 'yes.'"

Ivory studied me with animosity. She slowly nodded.

"Good." I collected the money and grocery list, putting them in my massive overall pocket. "I'll be back tomorrow."

"Great–" she started to say.

"Uh-uh! Remember. You're a mime. Start thinking like one." I smiled. "You can do this, Ivory. And you're going to have to show me pictures of your grandchild next time."

Ivory's face lost its hard lines, softening to fleshy folds. She nodded, plucked the thermometer from her hair once again and popped it under her tongue.

As I crossed the yard, I studied the garden where tiny green sprouts poked up from the terraced ridges of dirt. There had to be a dog groomer within 20 miles that I could call.

I pulled away and drove to the church with the lighted marquee. Today, the message felt like it was meant for me. It read.

"If you're drowning, get the lifeguard who walks on water."

Maybe I wasn't drowning. It was more of a belly-flop day; the sting of rejection, one of making another patient unhappy, stayed with me like a hard slap onto flat water.

As I headed for Tungs, I planned out the word board I would design for Melvin. It would be simple to make and would give me something productive to do.

Yawning, I cruised along the roller-coaster roads, breathed in the woodsy smells, and watched the afternoon sun flickering through the leaves onto the windshield. Fifteen minutes later, I was lost. I crested the top of a long hill and the thick forest broke apart into fields on both sides of the road, with a squatty barn on the right by a tree-lined creek.

"Where the heck am I?" I muttered.

I'd learned a technique in the past three days. I'd drive until I reached a larger road, then I'd get its name and locate it on the map. Looks like that was my plan once again today.

My eyes stopped on something moving across the far end of the field to my right. Something furry.

I slammed on the brakes and the car skidded in the loose stone at the edges of the road before stopping. Lifting my sunglasses, I honed in on an animal.

A dog?

Could be.

I squinted harder. *Holy crap! It looked like The Dog!*

This had to be 30 miles from Beryl's. Had The Dog traveled this far?

I took the dirt road running down the middle of the field to get closer. The road was hard-packed and pot-holed, and as I bounced I tried to keep track of where I'd seen the dog seconds ago. There was no farmhouse on the property, just the barn, so I wasn't worried about being accused of trespassing.

At the center of the field, I parked the car. I was hoping to catch a deaf dog, and I had no food for bait.

I spotted movement again. It was definitely Beryl's dog. Zigzagging in and out of the tree edge it looked pretty darn healthy.

"Thank the Lord Almighty."

I could return Beryl's dog and he could stop building his ridiculous machine. I got out and walked toward the trees, then froze remembering Richard's warning about open mine shafts. And a wolf. Don't forget about that. The dog was apparently a long-distance runner and I was in no position to chase him through the trees. Hopefully for now, Beryl would be happy just to *hear* his dog was alive.

I let a few seconds pass, then I remembered Beryl's anger. He wouldn't be happy with a verbal report, he would need proof.

Retracing my steps to the car, I dug out my cell phone. It might have no coverage, but the camera worked. I might only have one chance to snap the shot. I couldn't use the Pfoltz's phone because it's a different kind and I don't really know how to do anything beside make calls.

I waited for the dog to reappear. Minutes ticked away. Just when I thought he wasn't coming back, he raced into view, oblivious of me. Snapping two quick photos, I checked the screen and saw I'd been successful, but by the time I lifted my eyes, The Dog was gone.

I slid behind the wheel and backtracked out of the field. When I reached the road, I turned left, retracing my journey here, from Ivory's town of Proxy. I might be lost at the moment but I had to be able to give directions to Troy Twittler so maybe the dogcatcher with the tongue twister of a name could actually do his job.

ELYK

When I returned to the inn, it was free of guests. Rose said we'd have a quiet dinner together before more visitors arrived the next morning for the Memorial Day weekend. When I told them about spotting The Dog, Richard made the call to Troy Twittler. After hanging up, he said Troy knew the area I was talking about and he'd head out the next day.

Before dinner I drove to *The Ash Country Store and Souvenirs* to try to find some heavier paper to use to make the word book for Melvin.

"Pathetic," Elyk said, restocking a shelf with maple syrup bottles shaped like leaves. "Helen Keller would get lost less than you."

I'd told him about my last three days. "Nobody here seems to care about road signs and I'm kind of used to those."

"Didn't take you long to start dressing like a hick though, did it?" His gaze slid to the denim overalls.

"It's a long story involving red punch."

"Uh-huh," he said, still studying me.

His fashion choice put him in a blue-flannel shirt with the sleeves cut off at the shoulders, a pair of faded-black jeans and black work boots.

He stood. "You know what would dress those up, don't you?"

"Yeah. I've already had that news flash: A tank top and some high heels."

"Hell, no. That would look stupid. I was going to say a rattlesnake tail hanging off your belt loop." He walked to the counter, and reaching under, produced a package with a four-inch-long rattlesnake tail hooked to a key fob. "Take it."

I accepted. Once I had it out of the plastic, I gave it a shake. The dry scratching sound inside the decreasingly smaller segments sent a shudder through me. I extended my arm, holding it toward Elyk. "I don't know."

"It's yours." He nudged my arm back toward me. "My girlfriend says I need to be nicer to you."

Another shiver went through me, about as strong as the first, but this one in reaction to the fact he had a girlfriend.

He said, "She wants you to come for dinner."

I imagined a meal of chipmunk and leeks. "Why? What did you say about me?"

"Nothin." He squirmed uncomfortably and dropped his eyes to the scarred counter, shooing away a fly.

I remembered his mother's comment about my size. "Are you telling everyone I'm the size of an eighth grader?"

His smile left and the color in his face followed. "God, no. I wouldn't tell Dottie that."

She must be a plus-size gal.

He took the packaging and threw it away under the counter. "Dottie thinks we should be nice to you since you've helped a little with this puzzle contest."

"A little?" I snorted. "I'll have to straighten the truth out when I come to dinner. Does Dottie like crosswords?"

"No, she just wants me to win so I'll buy her a diamond."

"I think I'm going to like her," I said and holding the tail up by the smallest end, I dropped it into one of my many coverall pockets. "Thanks."

"We could go to the Rattlesnake Round-up together," he offered. "I got a cousin we could hook you up with."

I raised my hands. "I'm not interested in getting hooked up in any way."

"Sorry." He looked hurt. "Just trying to help you meet a few new faces; get you familiarized with the local tradition of seeing some snakes up close."

"I'm almost positive snakes are nothing I want to see." I'd prefer having an appendectomy to seeing snakes in a box. Again he looked like I'd insulted him, and I was here to try to fit in. I said with a tiny whine, "Alright, I'll think about it."

I asked him for the poster board and he located a few dusty pieces in the backroom and said there was no charge.

"Need any help on today's puzzle?" I asked.

"Nope. "Perspicacious" had me for a second, but I got it."

"Nice. You are an enigma, my friend." I picked up the paper.

He offered his cross-toothed smile. "Be careful out there. You're about as safe as a sugar-coated boy scout in bear country. I have a lot to teach you. My friend." He nearly choked on those last two words.

Elyk sure was unconventional, but clearly, he was my ally. I smiled.

Milt

I helped Rose with dinner. She claimed we were eating light yet I set out a plate of yam and corn pancakes, baked white asparagus with toasted sesame seeds, and mixed berry shortcake.

Grandpa Milt shuffled to the table, without the assistance of his duck-headed cane I'd often seen him leaning on. He eased into his chair.

Rose said, "Dad eats with us when there are fewer guests. Don't you, Dad?"

The man raised his rheumy-blue eyes my way and stared as if I were a mirror.

"Hi again," I said, choosing the chair next to him. "How long before your apartment is remodeled?" He wore a polka-dotted bow tie and powder-blue sports coat.

He didn't seem inclined to answer. He lowered his gaze to his plate and never spoke. He seemed content enough, just a man with nothing to say.

"He should be able to move back in about a month," Richard said, squeezing his father's shoulders with a tender touch. "Right, Dad? Get back to the ladies and the card table."

Ladies and cards? I couldn't imagine him dealing with either. He slowly sank into his coat and looked to be a few breaths from a nap.

ʏ cards with you sometime," I said to his profile.
't respond.

Rose and Richard circulated bowls of food, dropping piles from each dish onto Milt's plate.

He slowly moved into action, picking up his utensils and, at a snail's-warp speed, carefully cut and ate the meal. He'd be here all night at this rate but, really, what else did he have to do?

I felt Rose's eyes on me.

She said, "He stopped talking about two years ago, although nothing happened, like a stroke or anything. We figured he just ran out of things to say. One of these days he'll surprise us, won't you, Milt?"

Milt chewed with his eyes closed, his knife and fork held in the air in front of him. He looked like an orchestra leader, enjoying an exceptionally beautiful composition.

I wasn't so sure he'd talk again. Milt looked pretty content as a mute. Mutism could start for the simplest of reasons and then advance to a permanent state. I'd have to get online and see what more I could find out about this.

I offered to do the dishes so the Pfoltzes could retire to the screened-in porch and focus on their own projects. Rose helped Milt into the library where he lay on a gold-velveteen settee, staring at the curlicue pattern in the high ceiling. I checked in on him and wondered what he could be thinking. The fact he hadn't talked for years piqued my curiosity. A speech therapist's dream: cure the mute.

I stopped by the porch to build Melvin's word board. "Mind if I work in here?"

"Come on in," Rose said.

"Thanks." Gathering my supplies, I sat down on the braided rug. I cut the poster paper into pages and smaller flashcards. There were lots of reason why this felt right. The

Pfoltzes had been welcoming, adding me into their daily activities like I was family. Coming here was hard, but it felt like forward movement, progress. My urge to break away from such loss was finally leading somewhere and I was succeeding outside of my comfort zone.

The sun was within an hour of setting and the elongated rays drained the tint from each object outside, like a colored photo reverting to black and white. The barn lost its red hue and morphed into a warm rose. The pines became light sage, the maple shack, mauve, until everything turned gray, ready for night's arrival.

Thirty minutes later, I finished gluing the cards onto the big pages and sat back to admire the book. This should help Melvin stop all of his bleeping swearing.

"I'm calling it a night," I said to the proprietors.

Richard snapped his fingers. "I called Marvin over in Butterfield. He's going to ask around but he can't recall any family named Kingston. Maybe they have another name?"

I remembered the information the genealogist had found. Something called an entrustment. *Maria Louise Kingston. Born August 26, 1990 to Amber and Daryl Kingston. Township of Butterfield, Tioga County, Pa. Closed adoption on October 12, 1992. This entrustment is made in the best interest and nurturing aspects of the child.*

I had been Maria Louise Kingston when I got to California, but I soon became Marleigh Lynn Benning.

"I'll look up the information again," I said. "Thanks for asking around."

"And thanks for spending an evening with us oldsters," Richard said, taking off his glasses and setting his book on the tiny table by his over-stuffed chair.

"It was my pleasure." I turned to go and nearly knocked over Milt who was right behind me in the doorway. He must have been inching his way toward us over the last hour from the library.

"Oh," I said. "Sorry."

He held up two dice and looked surprised as if noticing for the first time they were in his hand.

"Uh-oh, Pops," Richard said, quickly standing up. "I thought we hid those, but I guess we didn't do a very good job." His tone sounded like he was scolding a child.

Milt closed his hand around the cubes, staring at his son, his gaze flinty and much stronger than his physical appearance.

Rose and Richard looked at each other and a signal passed between them.

What would be wrong with having dice? Even if he had a hellacious gambling problem, it would take him a decade to walk to the nearest house to get a game going.

"Can I hold them tonight, Milt?" Rose said softly.

Milt clenched his fist tighter. His mouth twitched. He turned toward the library.

Richard sighed. "Well, no secrets between us so we will warn you. You may hear noises throughout the night but don't be alarmed. It's just Dad moving things around."

I nodded, then paused, processing his words. "May I ask what this has to do with the dice?"

Richard ran a hand through his hair and reached for his wife. "As far as we can figure, he looks at the numbers after each roll and goes from room to room moving as many objects. Like he'll roll an eight and take eight books from the library and move them to the kitchen. Roll again, get an eleven and he finds eleven forks and puts them in the umbrella stand."

"Lock your door," Rose said, with a weak smile. "No room is off limits."

Richard looked toward the library. "I'll see if I can distract him." He followed his father down the hall.

"He can keep this up all night?" I asked. The man could hardly lift a fork to feed himself. How was he packing around heavy objects and staying at it for hours?

"The house will be in complete disarray by morning. He'll get exhausted, fall asleep, drop the dice and we'll be good again."

"Why not throw them out?"

"We have board games requiring dice. I hide them until a guest wants to play, and then after, I do the same. I have no idea how he finds them. He's sharper than he looks."

I was struck by another fact; Milt purposefully created disorder in his world. It made me even more curious as to what was going on in his mind.

I assured Rose I would be able to sleep through anything. I climbed the steps and left them below.

Sometime during the dark night, I startled awake. A wolf's howl cut through the blackness. I slipped deeper into the comforter and bed, pushing away the unwanted feeling of dark eyes watching me, a ridiculous thought since my room was on the second floor, and gauzy curtains covered the window. It still took me another heart-thumping hour to return to sleep.

I made it to Friday morning. My first week of work was almost behind me and I hadn't gotten anyone, or myself, killed. I also hadn't slept well, between the wolf howl, and picturing Milt moving around all night, turtle-speed but purposeful. I rolled out of bed early to help put everything back where it belonged, a job taking the three of us 45 minutes to complete. My greatest find was five bars of unopened soap in the toaster oven. Richard found bread in his roll-top desk and Rose recovered a set of napkin rings in the medicine cabinet.

I dressed for work, grabbed my things, and thumped down the back steps to the kitchen. It was time to get out of there because a family of nine had arrived and they were yellers.

"Good morning!" shouted the man.

"Isn't this the loveliest breakfast nook!" screamed his wife. The kids tumbled inside and the noise level hit a painful decibel. They came from Wisconsin to raft the Piney Creek River, which ran through the bottom of the Little Grand Canyon, the number one draw to the Wellsfield area.

I whispered "good luck" to the bewildered Pfoltzes as I left. It would be a long, loud day at the inn.

Casey

A half an hour later I pulled into Casey's driveway. The day was warming up, as the sun peeked through the cottony fluffs overhead.

Honey and I needed to discuss why Casey acted like a dog. It could be argued this topic was better left to a counselor, but it didn't seem likely Honey would be calling one. Just as I stepped out of the car, Casey burst from the front door and charged, scrambling on all fours.

"I a oggie," he said, hopping into my front seat and doing his dog routine, jumping up and down, barking and licking the window.

I leaned in the car. "You're not a doggie, buddy."

Honey yelled from the porch, "Get out of there, you little scamp! Marleigh, just drag him out."

I reached toward him and smiled. "C'mon, Casey. I have some fun things for you to do."

He growled and then grabbed the steering wheel, yanking it back and forth, all the while barking.

I tried another tactic. "I can't give a *dog* a treat, but little boys can have one." I showed him a candy container. That got his attention and he sat up with his hands curled in front of him, panting.

"You need to work with me before you get one." I reached in, took his arm and tugged. He plunged from the car and ran, thankfully upright, toward the house, yelling something incoherent.

"He's excited to see you," Honey said. "The card table is up and waiting."

Casey was sitting on a putty-colored folding chair when I walked in. His chubby legs swung in the air below, his hands banging on the wobbly tabletop, with thankfully no drinks in sight.

"Ae-dee," he said loudly, his voice raspy.

"You're working for the candy." I set my bag by the couch and said to Honey, "Does he talk this loudly all of the time?"

"He's been screaming since he popped out. Good thing we live in the country." She left, saying she had work to do.

I began testing him. Because he was impossible to understand, I gave him a vocabulary test where he only had to point to pictures instead of naming them.

He watched me closely as I said the name of each photo he needed to find, and he took his time in choosing one of four pictures. I'd score it later but he seemed to perform at his age level, meaning he understood age-appropriate vocabulary. I checked his tongue movements by having him mimic sticking out his tongue in several directions and making a tongue click. He sounded tongue-tied, like his tongue was stuck to the floor of his mouth, but it was the opposite - he had great lingual movement. "Well, Casey. Why is your speech so gobble-dee-goo?"

"Ahbo-dee-oo," he repeated, and laughed.

"Right. Gobble-dee-goo. It's an official term."

Minutes later, the phonological test confirmed what I already knew; he had a severe articulation disorder, meaning that out of the 73 possible sounds he could make in English, he couldn't produce one-fourth of them correctly.

"Ae-dee ow?" he yelled, kicking the underside of the table. It bucked up and down and nearly knocked off my supplies.

I understood that one. "Candy now?"

"Almost," I answered, holding the table down. "One more thing to try and then, if you stop kicking the table, you can have a piece."

I'd start therapy with the earliest developing speech sounds of /b/, /p/, and /m/, the sounds an infant makes, and teach those first. I pulled out a therapy book with /b/ and /p/ pictures in their names and put them in front of him. I pointed to my lips and said, "B. Ball. You say it."

Casey said, "Aw."

"Pop your lips." I performed some "b-b-b"s and indicated he should try them.

"B-b-b-b," he said.

"Good. Now, b-all," I over enunciated. "You do it, b-all."

"Baw," he mimicked.

"Yay! You did it." We continued working through /b/ pictures and another set of /p/ pictures. He caught on quickly.

With all of my cheering, I thought Honey might come see what we were doing, but she didn't. When we finished, Casey chose his candy and ran out of the room, yelling, "Ee yoo ate-ah!" which sounded like, "See you later."

Wondering where she had gone to, I wove my way through the newspaper stacks, which grew even higher along the walls at the base of the stairs. I heard a TV coming from the second floor.

I hoped Lawyer would respect my request not to check out this house. I didn't know him well enough to think he could put his fireman role away when asked to. I wanted that to be the case.

I found Honey on a king-sized bed watching a soap opera. A stack of newspapers, serving as a night table, supported a bubbly clear drink with a lime bobbing among ice cubes. The smell of gin wafted in the air as a ceiling fan chopped the air.

"Want a drink?" Honey asked, pointing to a makeshift bar along one wall. She held up a glass beaded with moisture, "My 'momma's little helper.'"

So much for housework.

"No thanks," I begged off. "I can't find my way around this area even when I'm sober."

I explained Casey's success, the whole time competing with the drama on TV –over-dressed women and men in their mansions, their devastating lives. She nodded but her eyes never left the screen until I said, "Here." I handed her a list of /b/ and /p/ words to practice with her son.

Honey's forehead knotted. "How often do we have to do this?" she asked. "I'm busy enough without doing your job, too."

I bit back another "b" word. I studied her and recognized fatigue behind her pale-green eyes. Her lanky hair had fallen from its claw; her freckled legs were long but looked soft. She lived out in nowhere without much support. I mustered some empathy. "It's my job to guide his therapy program. But, if you could practice 15 minutes a day, his speech would improve much faster."

She released a long, slow, I've-had-it sigh, and pushed to her feet. "I'll think about it." She headed downstairs, tossing the homework on a stack of newsprint in the hallway.

Honey yelled through the backdoor, trying to get Casey to come inside. He ran around in circles, holding a hubcap on top of his head, making motor sounds.

Casey was scheduled with me for two times a week. I reminded Honey I'd see them the next Tuesday. I brought up his previous dog actions. "He was fine the whole time we worked. No licking or barking. Just a boy."

"I don't know why he does shit like this." Honey said, following me to the car. "Do you think he's autistic?"

I shook my head. "He's way too social. I think it's because he misses his dad. And the dog goes with his dad and Casey wants to be with him, too."

Honey glared at me. "Who asked you any of that bullshit?"

Her anger startled me and I stepped back. "You just did."

"No." Honey snapped. "I asked you if he was autistic. Unless you got a psychology degree while you were in my house, I don't need a lecture."

Her voice left no room for arguments. I'd just crossed a thin line of saying too little and saying too much. Some people take advice; others drink theirs with lime. Now I knew which category Honey fell into.

I said, "You're right. I have no basis for what I just said."

"Right." She burped. "For what it's worth, Karl comes home tonight, and he gets to be a dad for a few days."

Honey was burned out, and even though she seemed somewhat neglectful, she didn't appear to be abusive. I didn't think Casey was in danger, but I thought it would be nice if someone hugged him more.

Luella and Margritte

A bit later I reached the town of Swell and the Bledsoe sisters' home. This time I held my therapy bag up so the chickens couldn't reach it. Unfortunately, my shoes and ankles were fair game. I was developing an intense dislike of chickens.

Margritte answered the door wearing gray maternity slacks and a tangerine-orange shirt, about the same shade as her hair.

"Come in, come in," she sang.

I sat at the dining table since the chickens had beaten me to the other seats in the room.

Luella was in high spirits, having just won five games of Canasta against her sister.

"She cheats," Margritte whined.

"Don't cheat. Just got more upstairs than you." Luella pointed to her head.

"More what upstairs? You married that good-for-nothing brother of mine after I warned you away."

I'd thought they were biological sisters. "So, you're in-laws," I said, hoping to stop the argument.

"I guess we are. But he was a good man," Luella said, and together they both added, "God rest his soul."

"It's nice you live together," I said. I turned to Luella. "How long ago did your husband die?"

"Been about six years since he passed. But Margritte has always lived here. Family ties, you know."

Had the chickens lived inside before the husband died or had their migration into the living room begun after his death?

The smell inside was still ripe but it didn't seem as suffocating as two days earlier. I got to work, "So, Luella. Can you show me a dry swallow yet?"

This was a very hard exercise, even for someone with a strong swallowing mechanism. To perform a dry swallow, a person puts their tongue between their front teeth and gently bites down, holding it there, keeping the tongue from trying to help during the next step: the actual swallow. One repetition was hard enough, but I'd asked Luella to perform three in a row to increase her throat strength.

Luella's throat muscles were weak, which caused a slower swallow response. Thin liquids rushed down her throat and by the time she could send the message from her throat to her brain to close the epiglottis to block the airway, it was too late. The lungs are not designed to inhale Folgers, Coke or water. Within a short period of time, aspiration pneumonia strikes.

"We've been practicing our brains out," Margritte said. "I can do four in a row if she doesn't make me laugh."

"How about you, Luella? Any luck?"

"I almost get one, then it just stops. Yesterday, I was flustrated 'cuz it wouldn't work and I yelled pretty loud."

"I thought her legs had fallen off or something," her sister said. "But Bertha took off and left us a nice egg."

Bertha? Of course they'd named the hens.

I shrugged, "I guess the egg is a bonus." *Had I really just said that? Having a barnyard animal produce something in the house was a bonus?* "Let's practice."

Margritte excused herself while Luella and I worked through 20 different vocal exercises. Thirty minutes later, just as we were finishing, Margritte returned with a small wire cage. Inside stood two white chickens, looking like POW's pressed against a fence.

The indoor birds burst to life, squawking and flapping their wings as if a fox had shown up.

Margritte laughed, "Our inside babies understand the pecking order around here."

Pecking order. "Funny," I said.

The sisters stared at each other with arched eyebrows.

I let it drop. I reminded the ladies to use Nice & Slow to thicken Luella's drinks, and no Jack Daniels yet.

Margritte followed me to the car, still carrying the hens. She said, "We have a favor to ask. Could you run these to Burt at the Gas-N-Guzzle Hut?"

I wasn't putting any chickens in my car. I held up my hands. "I'm sorry. No."

Her chubby hand squeezed my arm. "Please. We make just a little money selling off a chicken or two."

"I signed a contract–"

"Vicky always helped. She'd buy groceries every Friday for some lady in Proxy at the Gas-N-Guzzle Hut. You're still seeing her, right?"

All of Vicky's helpfulness made me look uncaring, and diminished everything I tried to do as a therapist.

I drew in a long breath. "I still go to Proxy. I don't know what Vicky did but I don't want chickens in my car.'

"They're going to be dead in a day or so. It's not like the ASPCA is watching. Just crack your windows and they'll be fine."

"Wait." Then I realized what she was saying. And apparently I *was* taking them since I was negotiating which part of the vehicle they'd be sitting in. She interrupted my realization.

"You can't put them in the trunk! They'll get fumigated."

I shook my head. I liked the sisters-in-law and it was clear they struggled financially. My devil's advocate reminded me I already had to stop at the Gas-N-Guzzle Hut to buy Ivory's groceries. I'd get all of the home health sins out of the way in one day if I did the sisters this simple favor. The chickens were caged, so how hard could this be?

I opened the back door and made a sweeping motion with my hand. "You do the honors."

Margritte placed them on the backseat, baby-talking little good-byes to them. She smiled. "Thank you, Marleigh. We hoped you'd be a team player."

"Rah rah," I said, unable to keep the sarcasm from my voice. I even waved when I pulled away.

The clucking and squawking from the back seat filled the car as the chickens fought the wire cage trying to escape. If they arrived with feathers I'd be shocked since plumes already floated from the cage.

The chickens wouldn't shut up, even though I was the one who should be making the fuss. Not only did my car instantly smell like chicken shit, now I swatted away feathers as I tried to keep the car on the narrow, meandering road.

I turned on the air conditioning to super Arctic blast only managing to freeze myself. The birds remained frantic. With ten more miles to go, I fiddled with the radio, trying to find one clear airwave, hoping to drown out the squawking birds. I found a clear station, gospel, and the monochromatic strains of organ music filled my car. The chickens fell completely silent, like they'd been garroted.

"Really?" I tossed the questions to the caged hens on the backseat. "You're religious?"

A moment passed.

"Okay. Religious is good. You're headed to a small part of heaven you'll really love. It's called Cacciatore."

The second I said those words, I felt terrible. I didn't want them to die; I just didn't want them to be *my* responsibility.

This might be the last straw. I trusted my instincts as to why I needed to come to Northern Pennsylvania, to pine-scented air, profound greenery, and now, seemingly to a job that would soon unravel my last ounce of patience if things kept going this way. Really, I may have dramatically under-estimated the hazards of working in such a rural place. I needed to get going on the search for my birth parents so all of this frustration would be easier to take.

Ten minutes later when I reached the Ruttsford town limits, I really wanted to dump the chickens at the Gas-N-Guzzle Hut but that meant I'd have to go back later and buy Ivory's groceries.

I'd wait. The hens had fallen asleep anyway, their pea-sized brains lulled into a coma with The Old Rugged Cross.

Melvin and Sandy

The street in front of Melvin's house was torn up. Heavy equipment sat everywhere, and men were working in a freshly dug hole. There was no place to park, so two streets farther I turned onto a dirt trail leading off into green oblivion and parked in the shade. I cracked the windows, got out of the car, grabbed Melvin's word board and walked the short distance to his house.

Sandy let me in, apologizing for the mess in the road, saying a water main had broken earlier in the day. "You'll find Mel in his favorite chair," she said.

I set the word board in front of Melvin on the TV tray.

He studied it a few moments and started to speak. "Fu-"

I headed the rest of the word off. "Before you say anything, Mr. Carlisle, I want to explain this board. The book is divided into six pages. The first page has pronouns and basic verbs, and the next page has more specific words like specific drinks, clothes, and feelings. And there's space to write extra words in."

"Whore of a son," he said, studying the words, looking quite pleased. "Witches tit?" he asked, pointing to the bottom of the third page.

I laughed. "Well, I guess I know what you mean. These are your 'asking' words, so you have the WH-questions here. The next column you and Sandy will have to fill in with friends' names. But look. You can ask questions like this." I pointed to the words "How-Is-Pastor?"

He nodded.

"Or, you can tell Sandy where you'd like to go." I pointed to 'I-Want-Go-Movie.'

He smiled.

"Now you to try. Point to, 'Where is Sandy?'"

He studied the board for a few seconds and touched the correct words. Sandy leaned in and hugged him and he patted her hand.

"Damn gone it to hell," he said, happily.

Sandy shushed him by putting a finger to her lips. "Don't talk, Mel. Just point."

"Has anyone recorded his speech and let him hear himself?" I asked Sandy.

She whispered, "Oh, it went very badly. He threw the recorder across the room and he still won't speak to the friend who taped him."

I wouldn't be trying that then. I turned to Melvin. "Which leads me to the last page. You don't realize it, Melvin, but you're swearing and saying bad things."

Melvin scowled and studied my face. "Horses ass?" he asked quietly, which I understood to mean, "Really?"

I shrugged. "Yeah, you are. So, here are some appropriate words you could use instead. "Shoot, Shucks, Dang It, Cripes, and Heck."

"This is marvelous," Sandy cooed. "It'll help so much."

"Good. Now let's write in the names of friends and places he likes to go."

Sandy named people and places. I wrote them on the page.

Five minutes later we began practicing phrases and moved on to longer combinations, such as

"I-want-go-bed-after-news." The next 20 minutes flew by and my time was up.

I said to Sandy, "Use this all of the time. In creating sentences by pointing, he will eventually start verbalizing those same words and phrases."

I packed my things and stood. "Melvin, tell me 'Goodbye' with your board."

He did it.

End of Days

I left, pretty pleased with my experiment. I reached my car, hit the unlock button, popped the trunk and dropped my bag inside. Slipping behind the wheel, I turned the engine over before I noticed it was too quiet in the car. Not the-chickens-have-dozed-off-quiet, but rather the tomb-like silence of something worse.

I knew what I'd find even before I turned: dead chickens. Instead I was dead wrong. They were gone. Cage and all. "Dammit!" I said, banging my fist on the steering wheel. No word board would stop my swearing. I screamed a few more into the interior of my car. Who the hell had taken them? Then something else occurred to me. How had anyone gotten into my car?

I hopped out and looked at the back doors. No broken windows. I sagged against the car and contemplated what to do. I needed to make several phone calls; the police, the Bledsoe sisters and possibly my boss. I'd regret all of those calls, especially since the one to my boss might put my job in jeopardy and I really wanted to prove I could handle this job.

I dropped the F-bomb this time as I kicked a tire.

"Are you having car trouble, Miss? I spun around. A man had materialized from nowhere. Tall, built solidly, he was one of the construction workers from the street. I could see little of his face under the hardhat and sun glasses, but he looked very L.L.Bean-ish, with a tanned, chiseled jaw line.

"No. I've had some chii– uhhh, –something stolen from my car. I was just trying to decide what to do."

"Wasn't it locked?"

I held my hands up, resigned. "I thought so."

"Nobody else locks stuff. Maybe you just forgot." He looked at the magnets on my door. "Are you a nurse?"

"Speech therapist." I crossed my arms. "Should I call the police? I mean, is this something they'd even care about?"

"What was taken?"

I *really* didn't want to answer that. "Someone asked me to deliver some food to a store in town." *Sure, the food was religious and still moving, but he didn't need to know the details.*

"You should probably call them." He smiled. "I see you're not from here." He pointed to my license plates. "Do you have a phone?"

I pulled out Richard's loaner phone and saw that it had a strong signal. "Yeah. Is it 911?"

"No, you need to call the sheriff's department." He crooked a finger indicating I should hand over the phone. "Let me dial it."

I gave it to him, glad to let him take charge. I couldn't get my head around my car being broken into.

He turned the phone over in his hand, studying it.

"I know," I said. "It's pretty old."

He smiled, "These dinosaurs are hard to kill. Everything probably still works on it though, like the camera and the calculator, right?"

"Yeah, it works."

He held it in the air, "Wait right here and let me run back to ask my foreman *which* sheriff's department we are closest to. Don't touch or move anything - they'll want to look around first."

He jogged away in the direction he'd come from.

I was glad he'd spotted me, otherwise I would have had to bother Sandy and Melvin for help.

The less people who knew about the chickens, the better.

I suppose I might have left my car door unlocked. I was pretty excited about taking Melvin's new wordbook to him.

I imagined the conversation I would be having with Luella and Margritte. It wasn't going to be pretty, no matter how I tried to tell them I'd lost their chickens.

I opened the backdoors and let a breeze blow through the car, airing it out. When I realized the construction worker had been gone five minutes, I started getting a bad vibe. I locked the car and headed toward the construction site.

Several men worked in a ditch, another one on a back-hoe. Two men stood to one side talking, but the guy who helped me was nowhere in sight. I approached the two men and yelled above the noise. "One of your guys was helping me."

They both looked toward the worksite and back to me.

The taller man spoke. "I'm the foreman here. Which guy?"

"I don't see him right now. He borrowed my phone to call the sheriff."

The man's brow wrinkled. "Are you hurt?" He stepped over a ceramic sewer pipe and came closer so we no longer had to shout.

"No, not injured. But I had some things stolen from my car and he walked back here to make the call for me."

The foreman studied the workers again and put his hands on his hips. "You got a bigger problem than you might think, Miss, because none of my workers has left the site."

I called the sheriff's department with the foreman's phone. At the county jail, I filed a report with a young female clerk who acted like stolen chickens were not worth the effort of picking up a pen. She'd asked the mandatory questions, although my description of the fake construction guy was vague.

"Moles?" she asked.

"Who doesn't?"

"Scars?"

"Not on his face."

"Eye color?"

"Ray Ban gray," I said.

Her eyes met mine and she stopped snapping her gum. "You done being a smart ass?"

"I am." I was nearly done with being a therapist if this got back to my boss.

I pulled into the Gas-N-Guzzle Hut parking lot and turned off the car. I had no chickens and I'd just given away the Pfoltz's extra phone to a complete stranger. The construction guy had looked official in a hard hat, and he was so self-assured. *Who wouldn't have fallen for that?*

The Gas-N-Guzzle-Hut was a blue-shingled, squat building with tiered bins of fruit and vegetables out in front. I locked the car, twice, and taking a deep breath, entered the store with Ivory's list. I introduced myself to the owner, Burt Thomas, and explained the situation.

"I would have called to let you know about the chickens but I don't have a phone at the moment."

"Keyrist! Took 'em right out of your car, huh?" Burt barked. "No surprise there."

He wore an orange-and-green-plaid shirt tucked into faded jeans. His protruding nose hairs matched his head of thick black hair.

I asked the question I dreaded, "How much were the chickens worth? I need to reimburse Luella and Margritte."

"Aw. I can't let you pay. I usually just pay them with a sack of dried corn. Saves the IRS from taxing me and all."

I liked him. "Makes sense." I pulled out my wallet. "Let me buy the corn."

"You buy the groceries on your list and I'll get the sack. Just remember to stop in here when you go through town and I'll be happy."

I nodded. The squeaky cart fought me as I pushed it up and down the three narrow aisles. I found all of Ivory's food and added three pounds of ground beef for The Dog. I paid with Ivory's cash and added my own money for the meat.

While I carried the bagged food, Burt hefted a huge sack of corn on his shoulder and we loaded it all into the trunk. The rear of the car sagged under the weight.

He pulled a red handkerchief from his back pocket and dragged it across his sweaty forehead. "I'm not going to tell the sisters about your mishap. You didn't have nothing to do with some local nut-job taking advantage of you."

"Thank you."

"They're good gals. Just shouldn't have married that no-good brother."

"I heard that exact thing from them just a few hours ago."

His eyebrows shot up. "Then you've won their confidence. They don't tell everybody their business." He crossed his arms. "You might consider getting a cell phone."

I started the car, and before I closed the door said, "I definitely will."

I drove past the tiny church with the lighted marquee. Today it read:

"Running on Empty?—God has your fuel."

IVORY

After I parked in Ivory's drive, I juggled the two sacks of groceries out of the trunk. The dried corn would remain there over the long weekend until I returned to the sisters' house. I waddled toward Ivory's front door, where she let me in.

"Aren't you a dear," she croaked. "I hope it wasn't too much of a problem."

"No talking, please," I said.

Her eyebrows lifted at the irritation in my voice.

"I've had better mornings, but in the long run, it turned out I *had* to stop at your grocery store anyway. May I use your phone?"

Richard had taken the news of the lost cell really well. He assured me he'd call his provider right away and stop the service. He said he wanted to know more about what I'd just gone through, but I said I had to go since I was at an appointment. I almost mentioned losing the chickens until he teased, "At least you didn't lose any more deaf pets."

"At least," had been my reply before we hung up.

I unloaded the products onto the counter and Ivory put them away. We retired to the glider rockers in the living room and I asked about her ability to stay quiet for the last two days.

Ivory put her hand out flat in the air and swiveled it back and forth.

"So, so?" I asked.

She nodded.

"That's a good start."

Our 30 minutes were dedicated to the vocal exercises. Her voice sounded smoother and less strident.

"There is hope, Ivory. You need to not talk for three weeks."

Ivory shook her head and clutched her huge chest. Then she formed her index finger and thumb into a gun and placed it against her temple, pulling the imaginary trigger.

We both laughed.

"It won't require any drastic measures," I said. "Oh, I almost forgot. I have good news for you and your corn crop. I saw Beryl's dog yesterday and I'm heading out there in a while to feed him. You watch, I'll get him back."

She sat up straight and whispered, "Where is he?"

Well, there was a good question. Somewhere near a creek at the edge of a farm field and about 50 miles from either Blackout or Milepost, depending on how a drunken crow flies. "It's too hard to explain but he looked healthy."

Ivory nodded and smiled a full-toothed grin, showing off the same set of overlapping teeth Elyk owned. She gave me the thumbs up.

"Am I back in your good graces?"

She whispered, "You're on your way."

As I was leaving I thought of something. "Why don't you get groceries from your son's store?"

Ivory snorted, then whispered, "The Ash Country Store's there to rip off, I mean, to *cater* to the tourists. People on vacation will buy the dumbest things, and Elyk's the man to sell them."

"I've noticed," I said then paused before asking, "Just wondering. Do you like his girlfriend?"

She thought for a second before saying, "I like anybody who puts up with him and his odd habits."

"Like the crosswords?"

"Crosswords? Not just those. It's the ketchup issue."

"Ketchup?"

"He puts it on everything, and I mean everything. Course Dottie's got her own little quirks." She laughed and shook her head.

"Don't we all," I said. "I get a kick out of your son, though. He's really quite bright."

"Wait 'til you get to know him better. He's probably used up all of his smart lines on you already." She let out another 30-pack-a-day-gravel chortle. "I do love him though."

Beryl

I hit the road, looking forward to reaching Beryl's. If my own cell phone had had service, then it would have been the one I handed over to the *construction* guy. The picture of The Dog was on *my* phone, not Richard's, so I'd done one thing right today.

Beryl didn't know I was stopping by, so I didn't think much of the minutes that had passed after I knocked on his door. I tried his doorbell. After a few more minutes I grew worried. He couldn't have driven anywhere since he had no vehicle. And the Andy Warhol version of a Segway he was building wasn't going to be transporting him around any time soon. I supposed he could have been picked up by a friend and taken to an appointment.

Frustrated, I returned to the car and sat behind the wheel. The thought of surprising him had kept me going all day. I wanted his opinion of me to change; I *needed* it to change.

His animosity toward me had started so innocently and then increased quickly. I rushed to help him when he had fallen, his dog got out, and now days later he wouldn't see me.

I put the car into reverse and started to back out. Sometimes things feel out of place yet there's nothing to indicate why. I studied his neat house and perfectly mowed lawn. I pulled back in and parked.

I walked around to the back, taking a narrow path between the garage and the house. I remembered his willingness to lift a gun and point it toward a person's back, so my plan was to not startle him.

The backdoor to the garage stood open. It had been closed the last time I'd been in his yard. When I stepped into the dim interior, my eyes adjusted to the gloom. That's when I spotted him.

He lay sprawled on his back on the cement floor, unmoving. A toolbox had spilled, tools lay around his head and the image of a thorny crown came to mind.

"Beryl!" I rushed to him, dropping to kneel at his side.

No response.

I gently shook him and called his name again. Spinning through the steps I remembered from my CPR course, I checked his airway first. He was breathing. I reached for a pulse point on his neck but my heart hammered so hard I couldn't tell if I felt a beat under my fingertips or if it was just my blood banging through my vessels at a hundred and ten.

I moved my fingers and tried a second time. There it was: the weak but rhythmic beat. Unconscious, not dead. Reaching for my phone, I swore, remembering some jerk had the functioning one.

I dashed out of the garage and up the five cement steps into the house. The phone was in the kitchen; I lifted the receiver and dialed 911. I'm sure there was a sheriff's number I should have been calling but I had no time to figure it out. The dispatcher identified his address through his phone number and after my brief explanation, she said help was on its way.

I returned to Beryl's side and kept my hand on his arm in what I hoped was a reassuring touch. I fought the sour taste of fear climbing up my throat. These were the moments when I missed my closet, my sanctuary. It was where I headed as a child when my parents fought, and the habit prevailed ever since. Now, in this gloomy garage, I pictured clothes hanging straight, the warm smell of shoe leather and fabric softener. Clean silk, the thicker smell of cotton.

Beryl hadn't moved or made any sounds, but I kept talking hoping he could hear me. I told him help was coming. Said I had seen his dog, and I had a picture. I rambled on about my plans to feed The Dog and to catch him.

Sirens wailed in the distance and I slumped in relief. Moments later, two paramedics wearing white shirts, black slacks and bright-blue surgical gloves entered.

I stood to give them room as they swarmed around him.

"Has he said anything?" the one with reddish hair and a goatee asked.

"No, he was unconscious when I found him."

"Any idea how long he has been here?" He moved a stethoscope across Beryl's chest, listening.

"No. I just stopped by to show him something." I felt the presence of another person in the doorway and turned to see Lawyer Hunt and a blond emergency worker standing there. "When he didn't answer the door, I walked back here."

"Good thing you did," Lawyer said, entering the tiny garage now seeming to have shrunk by half. "Beryl doesn't get much company. With the long weekend starting, this would have been a disaster."

I hadn't thought of that. "I'm glad I checked in."

"More of your fast-talking, speech-therapizing stuff?" he asked, smiling.

His smile lit up parts of me that hadn't been ignited for a while. I knew without a doubt his mouth would be warm, eager, but soft, and his hands on my body could make me forget every part of my bad day. I smiled. "Yes, therapizing as much as I can." I felt some of the stress of the moment leave. "Mr. Holmes had asked me not to come back because he was angry about his dog." I saw the blond paramedic standing near us turn his head my way, and something registered in his eyes. I continued. "I stopped to let him know his pet is still alive."

The blond asked Lawyer, "Is this *that* speech therapist?" I didn't like the bemusement in his eyes.

Lawyer scowled, "Pete, they'll need the gurney."

Pete's grin evaporated. "Got it, Chief."

It felt like it was time for me to leave. The men were all business now but once they got Beryl into the ambulance, I bet the "chasing a wolf" jokes would start.

"I should go. It looks like you have it handled here." Lawyer nodded and stepped outside so I could pass through the narrow exit. "Beryl may have been mad at you before but I think his feelings will change."

I looked back at Beryl. The skin on his face looked tighter, his eye sockets sunken. "I hope he's okay."

"He's in good hands. They'll take him to Wellsfield Hospital." He pointed toward the front yard. "I'll walk you."

Turning toward my car, I felt the heat between us, something new, a connection feeling both familiar, like we'd known each other for a long while, and yet sexually exciting, with nerves flaring, all senses acutely on alert. I swear if he suggested a moment alone, I would make the first move. Was this attraction all from the nearness of death? The need to cling to a warm body to prove there was a future?

He must have felt something, too. A smile pulled the edges of his mouth and his eyes were bright. "It's good to see you again."

"Yes. It is." I smiled and then I couldn't make it go away.

After those highly creative lines, our eyes met. I felt the need to be as close as possible to him, to breath in his scent, to feel his weight on me. Pete pushed the gurney past us; the trance was broken.

I moved back a step and said, "I'll be in Wellsfield a little later so I'll stop by to see him."

"Do you know where the hospital is?"

"I don't, but I'm getting used to being lost then unlost this week."

"Just this week?" he cocked his head to the side, grinning.

"Hmmm," I said. "You must be a stand-up comic when you're not suffocating fires."

"Oh, yeah, and don't forget about rescuing cats from trees. I've had two of those within the last hour." Then he grew serious. "Thanks again, Marleigh. If you hadn't stopped by, the results would have been - well - terrible." He turned and followed Pete to the garage.

I pulled away, headed for the farm field where I'd last seen The Dog. I wondered if they would let me take a dog into the hospital. I'd soon find out.

The Dog

I reached the farm and pulled onto the dirt track in the field. If anyone asked me right then, irrational as it was, I'd have said in a very short period of time, I would be driving The Dog out of here. I popped my trunk, the hamburger was there, double-wrapped in plastic, still cool to the touch. Thinking ahead, I'd grabbed plastic bags from the grocery store to use as gloves.

Gripping the meat with one hand, I picked up the leash with the other and pushed the trunk closed with an elbow. I walked toward the edge of the woods, about a 100 yards away. Silence, eerie and heavy, filled the air. I stopped and studied the tree line, taking in the panoramic view. Nothing moved. Nothing rustled. Everything seemed to hold its breath and no dog ran out to greet me.

"You can't be gone," I muttered.

Now what the hell should I do? Leaving the meat was stupid if the dog was no longer there. And how did he get around so fast anyway? Then it struck me: maybe Troy *had* made a trip out here and picked up the dog after all.

I thought to call Richard, but I had no working phone. Blood pooled in the bag of meat. I couldn't keep it in the car because it would rot so I did what I had come for.

I picked my way around the thistle and tall daisies, and reached the trees. Green, unbroken latticework spread out before me, and the invisible antenna implanted in every human to signal danger started sending steady warning signs to my brain. What if the wolf was here? What if Grady was in Pennsylvania? Don't all serial killers come from small towns?

Hurrying, I used the bags to break off chunks of meat as I back-tracked to my car. I cleaned up with hand wipes and dropped it all into a litterbag.

Then I waited. I thought about the chickens. They were most likely in a soup by now and I felt bad. I'd make a terrible farmer. I waited some more.

Nothing came to eat. Or even look.

Twenty minutes later, I left, disappointed and tired. Why did I think I'd actually find the dog here again anyway? Being an optimist could be so disheartening at times.

Therapy on Wheels was easily 45 minutes away and I needed to be there before they closed. I backed away from my hamburger trail and turned the car toward Wellsfield.

If Troy Twittler had found Beryl's dog, then I should let him know Beryl was in the hospital. If Troy didn't have a place to keep him, maybe Richard and Rose wouldn't mind if I found a place for him in the barn. Just until Beryl recovered.

Jake

Parking in front of the Ace Hardware store that shared the building with Therapy on Wheels, I carried my files inside. Jake was on the phone when I entered, so I went into the charting room and began making copies of my daily logs and two-hole punching them for the main files.

"I see you're not turning in your magnets yet." Jake leaned against the doorframe, smiling. At six foot, he was on the chubby side of healthy, with tiny glasses reflecting golden orbs in the overhead lights, and an affable smile.

I touched the lanyard around my neck. "Haven't used the whistle either, which must count for something."

"Oh, yeah. No whistle-blowing is a good week." He turned a wooden chair around backward and straddled it, facing me. "And, I heard you probably saved Beryl's life."

True to form, news in the area moved faster than hummingbird sex.

"Yeah. I stopped by and almost left, but I got a funny feeling, so I checked again."

"Trust those feelings, funny or not. It can get a bit crazy out there. By the way. I answered the phone earlier because I saw your caller ID show up. I mean, I saw the Pfoltz's ID on the phone you're using. Were you trying to reach me?"

I was pissed. The guy who took my phone was already using it? And why call Jake? He should be wasting my minutes with his long distance friends and family.

I chewed my lip knowing the fake construction worker got my number off those stupid magnets. I was ditching them as soon as I got a chance.

"I lost my phone. I guess someone picked it up." The truth would not set me free so I didn't try it out.

"This was the same *new phone* you just got yesterday?"

His amusement did nothing for my mood. Had he ever done home visits or did he just dictate Medicare rules from this olive-green, 70s-stuck style office? Sure I'd fumbled the ball, or in my case, phone, but he had no right to laugh.

"Yup. That was the phone alright." Trying to divert him from this topic, I said, "Guess what I overheard? There's a bad guy running from the police and he might be in Pennsylvania. You know anything about him?"

Jake looked uncomfortable. He stood and switched the chair back in the right direction and pushed it under a table. "We didn't want to panic you with a 'what-if.' As it turns out, the sheriff's department believes the guy who is stealing things is halfway to moonshine country in the South by now."

He checked his watch. "I've got a few more calls to make before I button it up for the weekend."

I stood and closed the cabinet drawer. "Jake, is there a rule against visiting Beryl in the hospital?"

Jake brightened. "No rule. And stopping by would be very nice. Last I heard, he was still unconscious. Crazy old coot. They said he was trying to get something from the garage. Did he say anything to you?"

All I would have had to do on my last visit was to get the stupid part he'd asked for. What would have taken me three minutes, probably took him a half an hour just trying to navigate the five steps off the porch.

I tried for casual but I'm sure guilt still hung on my face. "He's a very determined man when he wants something."

Jake turned to go. "Have a nice long weekend. You're watching the big NASCAR race, aren't you?"

"Sure," I said smiling. "Right after I poke toothpicks in my eyes."

He tried to look aghast. "That's blasphemy."

"So I hear. But I could have a beer, so maybe it's only half blaspheme?"

"Nope," Jake said. "Let me know when you get a new phone."

"I will." Something still nagged at me. "One more thing. When the call came in earlier on my old phone, did you talk to the person? Or get a name of who had it?"

"No. I heard someone breathing on the other end so I thought you'd butt-dialed me."

"Alright."

"I said your name several times thinking the connection was bad, but nobody responded, then the phone disconnected."

I felt the hair on the back of my head get up and look around. *The guy now knew my name and that I was the speech therapist. I'd be easy to find again.*

I left the building, frustrated with Jake for telling this thief my name. He couldn't have known the call wasn't coming from me, but still.

I would just have to watch my car better. And maybe my back.

Who's Calling

By evening, the B&B was almost unbearable as the "yeller" family shared their adventures. Over the lamb kabob's and mint jelly, they screamed about the hike they'd taken in lieu of the river float.

Still in work mode, I tried answering their questions in a quiet voice, hinting at an indoor volume, but it didn't change anything.

After helping clean up the dishes, I begged off any further evening activities and shut myself in Richard's study to check email and Facebook.

The phone rang on Richard's desk. I ignored it knowing the innkeepers would grab it downstairs. A minute later Rose tapped on the study door before pushing it open. "The call is for you."

"Who is it?" I said before reaching for the phone.

"A guy." She waggled her eyebrows and pointed to the handset.

My heart rate spiked. She couldn't know what those words could do to someone who'd been duped so easily. And if the construction guy found me at the Bed & Breakfast, I was going to get on the freak-out train and plan my escape.

Then I reasoned he couldn't know where I was staying just because he knew where I worked. This had to be Elyk. It was his usual time of day to call and beg for a crossword solution. As he was inclined to do, I answered with no greeting. "What crazy word are you looking for?"

"I was going for 'hello.'"

Shit. It was Lawyer. "Oh, hi. Sorry, I thought you were someone else."

"And you talk that way to whom?"

"It's a long story. How are you?"

"Fine. I'll ask about the long story later. I wanted to let you know Beryl is conscious and talking. I just left the hospital."

"That's great news." I felt a rush of relief. Beryl might be a grumpy man who bossed me around and told me never to come back, but in a short time he had become *my* grumpy man and I cared about him. "Did they say when he'd go home?"

"They're keeping him a few days for tests." He laughed. "*If* they can hold him captive that long."

"He will bluster his way out sooner than later," I said. I tried to think of something to ask Lawyer but I knew so little about him. "Are you watching the race in Dover?" I'd gotten the name of the NASCAR race from Ivory. He paused for several beats, and asked, "Why? Are you?"

"Well, of course. Everybody's going to have it on."

"*You* follow NASCAR?" His voice held disbelief, which was beyond annoying.

He didn't know me. I could very easily be a racing buff or a fan or whatever the hell the loyal followers were called. "I quite like Jeff Gordon," I said.

"Yeah. And who else?" I could almost visualize the smirk on his lips.

I rummaged around my memory for the other name Ivory had told me. It had 'Stewart' in it. "Payne Stewart," I blurted out.

He snorted. "Wrong. He was the golfer who died in a plane crash." His chuckle was deep and throaty. "I have an idea. Why not skip this *one* race and come to the Memorial Day celebration in Wellsfield? They put on a nice event for such a small town."

Was he asking me out? "Sounds good," I said a little too quickly. "I can stop at the hospital and see Beryl while I'm there."

"Precisely my thought too." He gave me the parade information and I thanked him again for calling about Beryl.

He said he'd look for me Monday.

I went downstairs. Each evening Rose set out pastries, cereals, hot chocolate and milk in the dining room around 8:00 p.m. where it remained available until 9:30.

I filled a small plate and went looking for the Pfoltzes. They sat on a loveseat in an alcove off of the kitchen, where they were accessible to their guests but could watch TV in private.

Rose asked, "Who was calling?"

Both of them looked my way, waiting for the answer.

"Lawyer Hunt. He called to tell me Mr. Holmes is awake. He was the patient I had to call 911 for earlier. Beryl is a family friend of his."

"She met Lawyer at our community meeting a few nights ago," Richard said to Rose as if I'd left the room. "They seemed to get on quite well."

I cleared my throat. "Actually, I met him the day I let Beryl's dog loose. He almost ran me over with his truck."

"Is he Huck Hunt's boy?" Rose asked me.

"I don't know." I held up my hands. "He's a fireman for Mapleton and he has a white truck." I skipped the part where he made me tingle from the neck down.

Richard answered. "That's him. Huck was the state fire marshal for years. He died about a year and a half ago, right about the time Lawyer came back."

Ah, the reason he didn't seem to favor plaid shirts. But show tunes? "Came back from where?"

Rose answered. "I don't remember where Lawyer was before. Do you, Richard?"

"No, the Hunts have always kept to themselves."

What secret did the Hunts have that I suddenly wanted to know? "Just wondering. Is the festival in Wellsfield worth seeing?"

"Absolutely," Richard said. "It's got old timey traditions and you should be a part of it. We'll be fine."

Going For A Run

Another couple arrived at the B&B on Saturday morning from Louisiana. I drove the B&B van to the Little Grand Canyon trail twice to drop off and pick up bikers and rafters. On Sunday morning, Rose made something called Eggs on the March, in keeping with a Memorial Day weekend theme. Surprisingly, the food wasn't wearing little uniforms – Rose was all about details.

In the afternoon, I decided to start my East Coast running routine. I'd begun running in college to blow off steam, and once my parents passed away, I added distance to test my limits and to make something hurt worse than my heart. Now I was hooked. Lacing up my shoes and seeing where they'd take me became a habit and at some level I was defying death.

I found Richard hoeing the garden. "I'm going to run to the Ash Country Store."

He stood and studied my shorts and tank top. "Literally?"

"Yeah. What is it, about three miles round trip?"

"More like four. With some big hills in between."

"Perfect. I'm looking for a challenge. I should be back in about an hour."

He shook his head. "No shame in calling if you need a ride."

I smiled. "I think I have it."

The temperature was perfect, in the 70s with a slight breeze, but I hadn't counted on the humidity factor. Before I left the property and began jogging down the long road leading to the highway, my running shorts were stuck to my legs and I was clammy all over. I stayed in the center of the narrow asphalt since the sides were uneven with loose stones. With no traffic on this lonely back road, I felt like the only person on the planet. The thick tangle of trees and bushes lined each side of the road and an unvarying buzz and hum of insects in the dark recesses left a veil of white noise over everything.

Falling into a comfortable rhythm, I let my legs take me for a ride. I loved it when this happened. At the bottom of the hill I turned right, onto a slightly bigger road that would take me toward Elyk's store. I kept moving, but this time I stuck to the soft shoulder.

I thought about my parents and the fact that they had adopted me when I was two. They were in their forties when I arrived into their lives. I always thought their success kept them from having me earlier, but now I find this wasn't the case at all.

My birth parents were probably younger, possibly overwhelmed with bills and made the decision to find a home for me. Maybe they had to get married but then realized how hard it was raising a child. But who gives a child away so easily? Was there any grieving or guilt or remaining shame over their decision? What did their family and friends think?

I needed to get to the town hall in Butterfield and go through records. No one seemed to know my parents but the documents made it clear they were here at one point.

Minutes later, I crunched across the gravel parking lot and found Elyk on a bench in the front, head down, labeling carved wooden bears.

"Someone steal your car?" he asked, squinting at the tiny label on the bottom of the figurine.

"You must have radar." The thicker air had given me oxygen overload and I felt a bit woozy. "Just thought I'd drop by and see what you're doing."

"Working in the free enterprise system." He put the last bear in a wooden crate. "Dottie wants to know if you'd come to dinner on Tuesday night."

Nothing could keep me away. "Sure. I'd love to." I looked around for a hose. "Could I get a drink of water?"

"I got water. I also got stuck on a word this morning. I've been sitting out here trying to solve it. Serendipitous of you to come by because I was gonna call."

He picked up the boxed bears and headed for the door.

Inside I spied a plate of unfinished breakfast food on the counter. It looked like bacon and ketchup. "What's with the ketchup?" I asked, pointing.

"What's with the running?" he replied.

"Fair enough. You say Heinz and I say Nike." Crossword puzzle #8 lay next to the plate. One space remained at #42 down. "A danger," I read. "Starts with an MA, has nine letters and ends with M. One R in the third spot from the end."

Elyk unloaded the wooden bears onto a shelf with a sign reading, "Made by local craftsman."

"A danger," I repeated. "Not 'to be in danger.'" I started clicking through letters that might fit.

"I thought Martyrdom," Elyk said. He crushed a cardboard box underfoot and put it in a stack by the door.

"No. Then the "r" is in the wrong place. But it's close." I rubbed my arms, trying to brush away the chill from the air conditioner.

A car pulled in and an older woman with long, gray hair got out and entered the store.

"Hi, Elyk."

"How are you, Mrs. Shoemaker?" Elyk asked.

"Doing fine. I need pepper salami and headcheese for my ceramic group. I'm hosting today."

He motioned her to the rear of the store and they chatted as they walked away.

Just as I turned back to the puzzle, the word "maelstrom" popped into my head. I wrote it on a piece of paper and left it sticking out from under his plate.

I yelled, "I got it. Talk to you later," as I pushed open the screen door.

I hit the road, feeling pretty good after my short break.

I churned up the long rise and my legs started protesting. Sweat poured from my hairline and I leaned into the hill. Rustling from the bushes to my right made me stutter to a halt. Leaves swooped together like something had been there a moment earlier and then jumped backward.

Not good. I gulped in air and tried to decide why I should be waiting around. I bolted for the house.

Once I took a hot shower, I calmed down. The movement had probably been a deer, a squirrel, maybe even a wild boar. When Rose asked me how my run was, I said, "Refreshing." I'd feel stupid saying a branch moved and I had a heart attack.

Milt

In the late afternoon, I found Milt on the front porch, dressed in a peach-colored, short-sleeved shirt. "You're looking dapper," I said, dropping into the other wicker chair. His glass of lemonade dripped cold sweat onto the square table between us.

He slowly turned his milky-blue gaze my way.

No response.

"You have a secret," I said.

He continued looking in the vicinity of my face.

I smiled. "I do, too, but I want to hear yours."

He slowly looked away.

We sat through a long silence, broken only by the chirp of baby birds. The silver lace white flower growing along the roofline sent out ribbons of sweet air.

"Okay. Not today, I guess." I smiled. "No problem."

He leaned forward and reached around to his back pocket. Getting a handkerchief? It seemed like an old fart thing to do.

He drew out a deck of cards instead.

"Ah. Do you want to play something?" This was progress. The initiation of a joint activity.

He put the cards on the table and in excruciatingly slow motion he reached back into the other pocket. At this rate, it would be nighttime before we dealt a single hand.

He produced a ten-dollar bill and laid it on the table and then sat still.

"We're playing for money?" *The old guy wasn't completely gone.*

He reached for the cards and held them.

Obviously a nod or a headshake was too much to request. "What are we playing?"

He didn't move.

"Give me a sec." I went inside, jogged to my room and came back with my purse. "Here." I dropped a ten on the table next to him. "Let's do it."

He dealt three cards each and set the deck down.

"Twenty-one?" I asked.

No answer. He slowly lifted his cards, studying them.

I peeked at mine. Two fives and a six: sixteen points. *Kind of risky to take another card.* "I'll stay," I said. "What about you?" I was encouraged that he could sequence enough to play a game. Then I remembered his dice obsession – an activity that had sequencing down pat.

I picked up the deck, ready to deal to him.

He tapped the table.

I turned up a four. Minutes passed.

He knocked again.

I dealt a three. More seconds ticked by. Gnats were born and died. At one point, I thought he'd spaced out and we were done.

He knocked a third time.

I turned up a ten. *He had to be way over.* I'd dealt him seventeen and he already had three cards before that. It occurred to me he might not have a clue the game only went to twenty-one, not fifty one.

Bees buzzed. I slapped a mosquito on my leg and it left a tiny splash of blood. Cooking pots rattled around inside as Rose started dinner.

I didn't want to blurt out, "I won," but this was getting ridiculous.

He slowly laid down the cards and spread them out. I was still adding the points when he reached for the money. Darned if he hadn't had a two and two ace's to start. He had twenty-one.

He pocketed the bills with a motion that was the fastest thing I'd ever seen him do.

I laughed. "You were very lucky, Milt. Let's play again, but just for fun."

He held the deck for a moment, then he put them away.

"Hey! One hand isn't fair." I'd been hustled by a wrinkled prune in a bow tie.

Richard pushed open the door. "Dad. Let's wash up for dinner." He looked at me and asked, "What were you folks doing?"

I could mention being hustled, but I said, "Your dad's a good listener so I was going on and on about nothing in particular."

I squeezed Milt's arm. "Good talking to you. I hope it was a *lucrative* use of your time." I wasn't sure, but I think his lips quivered.

WELLSFIELD

On Monday morning, before heading into the Memorial Day festivities, I removed the beastly-big magnets from my car and put them in the garage. I could put them back on before work tomorrow.

Once in Wellsfield, I circled the town for half an hour, looking for a parking space several blocks away from the park.

The parade had ended so I followed the crowd toward the commons. The barbeque and military festivities would take place here according to a flyer someone handed me.

Folding chairs were set up inside a large white tent where performers would entertain from the raised wooden stage.

I walked around for a few minutes before I spotted Lawyer near the barbeque pits. I watched him talking and laughing as he moved along the lines. He wore his dressy "fireman blues" which made him go from good-looking to handsome. My hormones moved from hot to flaming. The man-in-a-uniform thing had always worked for me, and it kicked into overtime now.

Lawyer turned and walked toward me. I stepped away from the cake-walk area and moved in his direction.

He smiled.

I smiled back, but then realized he was looking just somewhere beyond my shoulder.

I ducked out of his line of sight and watched him approach a young woman about my age, with long, shiny hair. She owned a dancer's body and a hundred-watt smile. My failed aspirations as a dancer came rushing back and I felt my body deflate.

He kissed her on the cheek and they hugged. A long hug. The girl said something close to his ear and he laughed.

Jealousy struck hard and I had to look away.

I drew in a slow breath. He hadn't been asking me out today. It had just been a nice gesture, inviting me to see more of the local towns. Nothing more.

Disappointment hit, warm and fluid, but it was brief and I was able to push it away. I didn't need him with me to enjoy this day.

I studied the park and decided it was the perfect time to visit Beryl at the hospital.

Skirting the festivities, I walked against the crowd as everyone poured into the park. I crossed Main toward the street leading to my car.

The street was deserted when I dug around in my purse and found my key fob. I unlocked the driver's side.

In a flash, I was smashed flat against the door and my purse was ripped off my shoulder. Needles of pain shot through my head and arm.

Time slowed but it didn't help me process what was happening any easier. "Don't!" I choked out. Panic cut my airway off and black spots floated across my eyes. I struggled to get away but whoever had me pinned was strong, holding me with one hand pressed between my shoulder blades as if I were a bug pinned to a display.

Gulping air, I whipped my head around, trying to see who held me, but I couldn't turn far enough.

Then I caught a glimpse of him in the window. He wore a white military hat, like Marines on commercials when they invite young men to be all they can be.

"Let me go!" I rasped, then I stopped talking because bile threatened the back of my throat.

"Gladly," he hissed in my ear. He grabbed me by the hair and with a quick jerk, he slammed my forehead into the window frame.

My legs buckled and I slumped to the ground, my body turning so I landed on my back. Against the sky, I caught the outline of a man in full military uniform.

Right before I blacked out, I thought, why does a Marine need my purse?

I woke up with a view of the rust and oil stained undercarriage of my car. Irrelevant thoughts ran through my head as the fuzziness cleared, like how huge my car looked from this perspective, or how the insides of the wheel wells were caked in dirt. Then the hard ground under me registered as being completely wrong and the throbbing pain in my forehead brought my attention back to reality.

I was mugged.

Not in New York City nor even in the Tenderloin at home, but in a charming town advertised as one of the "crown jewels" of Pennsylvania. I had gotten a royal treatment all right.

How long had I lain here?

Fear set in and I scrambled to stand, clawing my way up the car using the door handle. My legs jittered and my heart slammed as I leaned against the car to catch my breath.

The guy was gone.

I still held my car keys, one thing that seemed to have worked in my favor. Slipping behind the wheel, I locked the doors, turned the engine over and tore out. I had no idea where I was going but I needed to tell someone what had happened before I started crying, which was seconds away.

I refused to return to the park. My legs were so weak I couldn't drive to Tungs at the moment.

The only place I had memorized on a map before coming here was the location of the hospital.

I drove there.

Egbert Memorial

I turned into the Egbert Memorial Hospital entrance. The main building complex consisted of a two-story, beige brick edifice housing the doctors' offices, the emergency room and the surgical areas. A three-story wing with a punch card of windows along the sides looked to be patients' rooms.

I parked close to the main entrance. As soon as I turned off the car, the tears I'd been fighting plunged from my eyes and gushed down my face.

I wanted to be tougher than this.

After a few minutes, I pulled myself together and examined my face in the mirror, where a blue-ish contusion rose from the left side of my forehead. A dried trickle of blood led into the hair above my ear.

I brushed the wetness from my face and blew my nose on a napkin I found in the glove box. Before closing the compartment, I grabbed my useless cell phone with the picture of Beryl's dog.

I think I know why Vicki quit without a notice. Fighting back new tears, I bit my lower lip hard to keep from crying again. I couldn't help but feel orphaned, by everyone.

I left the car, wobbling toward the building. The steadiness in my legs had not totally returned. I think I was still in shock. Once inside the doors I let out a long sigh.

I approached the nurse's station passing a supply closet full of towels. A warm, clean scent drifted from the dark room. I almost walked in there and stuffed my face in the pile of white comfort. It would just be for an hour or two – that's all. Safe, cocoony, protected.

A woman with extra-big, brown hair leaned over the desk and glanced at me, and then she did a double-take.

I willed myself farther down the hall to her counter, where I could see her name badge. I leaned on the counter and spoke first since her jaw needed to close before she would be able to say anything. "Rhonda. Hi. I need to call the police and wondered if I could use your phone." I wavered a bit and nearly slid off the counter.

The woman dropped the clipboard she'd been holding. "Starfish on fire! What happened to you?" She scurried toward me and grabbed my arm, leading me to a row of orange plastic chairs.

I let her take charge as I sagged into the seat. I mumbled, "A guy in uniform, a Marine, he hit me, and took my purse."

Rhonda swore loudly then left to call the police. Shortly after, she returned with an ice pack. "Someone will be here in a jiffy. They're just at the park."

I know.

She held the ice to my forehead and I was glad for the company. She chatted on and on about her kids and how they had decorated their bikes for the parade I'd missed.

Parker York

A few minutes passed and the glass doors slid open. Two policemen entered and introduced themselves.

Harvey was older and had gray sidewalls, while Kent was younger with a trimmed, black mustache. Dressed for business, they wore wide belts loaded with crime-stopping gear.

Rhonda led us to a break room. We pulled out chairs around the rectangular table. She excused herself, leaving the door open.

"Does this happen all the time here?" I asked.

Kent raised his eyebrows. "Oh yes. Rhonda is very good at what she does."

It took me a second to figure out what the hell he was talking about. "No. I mean people getting beat up. Does that happen?"

Kent quickly shook his head. "Nope. It's pretty rare."

Harvey leaned forward and placed a tape recorder on the table. "I'm going to ask some questions about how you got hurt."

I nodded and swallowed hard. Still queasy, I willed myself to focus on Harvey's Adam's apple as he talked.

Up and down.

Halfway up, up some more, and then down.

Watching the pure mechanics of speaking calmed me.

Kent produced a notepad and cleared his throat. "Is your husband active duty?"

"I'm not married."

"Well, that's usually the case around here. What I mean is, did he just get discharged?"

Why did I have to get the stupid cop? He thought this was a domestic abuse case. I turned my head toward Harvey, hoping for an IQ above a Pekinese.

I said slowly, "A stranger in a uniform attacked me at my car. He smashed me into my door, took my purse, and threw me to the ground."

The two deputies looked at each other and then back to me.

Harvey spoke. "A serviceman attacked you, for no reason?"

I snapped, "Do servicemen get to hurt people if they *have* a reason?"

Kent put down the notebook. Disbelief preceded his words. "It's just hard to believe one of the men at the festival would do this."

I shot back, "I can believe anything. I had my cell phone and some chickens stolen yesterday by a construction worker."

After a light tap on the doorframe, Lawyer walked in and looked my way. "I just heard what happened." The skin was drawn tight across his cheeks.

"Hey Cap," Harvey said. "You know this young lady?"

Lawyer was still in his dress blues, but at the moment, I was way over the whole you're-so-handsome-in-navy-cloth-and-gold-buttons bit. If I never saw a man in a uniform again, I'd be fine.

Lawyer said, "This is Marleigh Benning. She's staying at the Pfoltz Bed & Breakfast in Tungston and works for Therapy on Wheels."

He took the chair next to me and draped an arm across the back of mine. "Are you okay?"

The only thing to come into my head and out of my mouth in the blur of the moment was something my Grandfather used to say before he got his voice cut away. "I'm finer than frog's hair and that's pretty fine."

The three men studied me for a few seconds before Kent spoke. "She was talking about chickens right before this. Now it's frogs. She really must have whacked her head."

I grunted and touched my damaged head. "It's just a saying. And I did have chickens taken from my car."

"You had chickens in your *car*?" Kent asked.

"Yes." I held the "S" to show my impatience. I turned to Lawyer for help.

He tilted his head. "I have to say I'm curious. You were carrying hens and someone took them?"

"Outside of Ruttsford. I filed a police report." I shrugged an annoyed 'whatever.' "The chicken story isn't important. I'm ready to go home."

"First, I'm going to get a doctor in here," Lawyer said. He stood to leave. "Have you called the Pfoltzes yet?"

I shook my head. "They have a houseful of new guests. I didn't want to disturb them. I can drive home. Give me a few minutes to regroup."

"I'll make arrangements to get you there." Turning to the officers, he said, "Go easy on her. She hasn't had the best of weeks."

With his statement, I thought maybe he still looked a tiny bit handsome. He left the room.

The interview proceeded and it seemed to go logically now. They established the Who, What, Where, When, with the Why still the unknown.

No, I hadn't flashed money around and I hadn't talked to anyone on the street.

The officers concluded I'd been in the wrong place at the right time. They'd send my limited description of the "perp" to local sheriff departments in case anything similar surfaced.

As far as being robbed of chickens and now of money, they saw no connection. Harvey said, "It was probably some out-of-work guy trying to feed his dogs and kids; in that order, mind you."

I explained how the construction worker had taken the time to call my work.

"Just someone checking you out," Kent responded. Your company makes you drive around with its advertising, right? It's no biggie calling up the pretty girl behind the wheel."

I said, "But he called from my stolen phone."

Lawyer walked in, followed by a 30-ish doctor wearing fashionable eyeglasses and green scrubs. The doctor introduced himself as Parker York.

"Everybody please leave us," he ordered, moving toward me.

The deputies began discussing the big car race before they turned the corner.

Lawyer said, "I'll be in the lobby."

The examination took place with me sitting on the lunch table. He determined the contusion on my forehead would resolve with ice and Tylenol. The cut didn't need stitches, and except for minor scrapes, I'd been lucky.

He washed my forehead and applied antibiotic and a bandage. I liked his touch and his clean, soapy scent.

We started talking. He had an easy unassuming style. I explained how I'd gotten here, my job, the crazy week I'd had. Then I washed my hands at the sink, and caught my reflection in the window. There was no hope for my dress, especially since road-grease stained the back.

He must have noticed my disappointment. "You still look pretty."

I knew I blushed and my mouth opened and closed once. I said, "Thanks."

"It's been really nice meeting you." He leaned against the table, one leg crossed over the other.

"Likewise," I said. "You've been the one singular moment of calm in my crazy week."

Lawyer tapped the doorframe where he had been standing. Something crossed his face as he looked from the doctor back to me. "What's the verdict here?" His casual tone didn't match the hard line in his jaw.

Parker touched my back and said, "She's going to live to be 25."

Lawyer nodded. "Not at the rate she's going." When Dr. York left the room, Lawyer reached for me, gently taking my arm. "C'mon. I'll give you a ride home."

"Are you sure?" I held the keys in my hand. "I've taken you away from your … from your day, long enough, and really, I'm good as new."

He bent toward me. "Do you have a current driver's license, young lady?"

He had a point. I had no identification, but I argued anyway. "I do. It's just not on me at the moment."

"Exactly. How about your insurance card? Money? A library card?"

I snorted a half-laugh. "I'm going to need a library card to drive to Tungs?"

"Most people wouldn't, but you might. The point is, I'm driving you home and one of my guys will follow in your car." He led me to the doors.

I suddenly remembered. "I wanted to visit Beryl while I was here."

He studied me before speaking. "Don't take this the wrong way. You're quite pretty."

It was nice hearing this twice. "Uh. No offense taken."

"I wasn't finished." He took a step back from me. "You look like you spent an hour in a dryer with a couple of good-sized rocks. I don't think you want Beryl to see you right now."

Truth was, I didn't want *anyone* to see me like this, but here I was.

"I have a picture of his dog to show him." I held up my phone and noticed my hand still shook. I clicked through the pictures until I reached it. "See?" I handed it to him.

He squinted and moved it closer and then farther away.

"My suggestion would be this," he handed it back to me. "Get it blown up first. Beryl will appreciate knowing the gray speck in the center is really his dog."

I looked again and knew he was right. "Good point."

We left the hospital and turned toward the parking lot.

Lawyer said, "Did you tell Twittler where you saw the dog?"

"Richard called him. Troy may have found the dog already, because when I stopped out there again to leave some food–"

He halted me with a hand on my arm. "You did what?"

"I left hamburger for him." I stumbled over my words, taken aback by his reaction.

He scowled at me.

"What?" I said, anger rising inside.

"Where did you put the meat?"

"In the field, making a trail back to my car."

"How Hansel and Gretel of you." He let out a long sigh. "You can't do that anymore."

I'd never done well with "can't." When I heard "can't," it always sounded like "I dare you." I'd done my first road race with a "You *can't* possibly be in shape to finish this race." Completed high school early with, "You *can't* take all of those credits and still do well." I'd broken up with boyfriends, hiked through Peru, and eaten oysters because of the word "can't."

I would be buying more meat in the morning.

I said, "Noted." Suddenly irritated with everything, I marched ahead of him to my car. A younger fireman stood there and I stuck out my hand. "Hi, I'm Marleigh."

He shook my hand, confused at my fast approach. "I'm Jim Brough."

Lawyer reached my side and started giving Jim directions. "We're going west on Rt.6–"

I broke in. "That's not necessary." I handed my keys to Jim. Then I walked to the passenger side of my car. "I'll tell him where we're going." I opened the door and after dropping into the seat, flipped down the visor, blocking out Lawyer.

I saw Lawyer pause, then he turned and crossed to his vehicle.

As Jim drove, I sank into my seat, feeling about as deflated as Milt often looked, a weighty exhaustion pushing me down.

My chauffeur seemed content to let me rest.

Clearly I *wasn't going to make it here.* I'd wanted rural, a place allowing me to commit fully to the patients in my caseload, a place with no distractions. I should have chosen the Native American Indian reservation in Yuma. At least if there was danger, I'd have seen it coming across the wide-open desert.

It wasn't too late to switch. Therapists were needed in other places. I'd call Jake in the morning and give him my notice. He'd be mad but he wasn't the one getting his butt kicked. And where were my birth parents? I could keep searching for Amber and Daryl Kingston online. Tears filled my eyes. I hated losing.

And I didn't like firemen who said, "can't," especially if they already had a girlfriend. I pushed away the earlier, hotter thoughts I'd had of jumping Lawyer and focused on the gentle touch of the doctor. He had no wedding band and from Lawyer's reaction, Dr. York had been flirting. Maybe I could get to know him and see the more normal side of Tungston.

Lawyer

My anger dissipated by the time we arrived at the inn. I thanked Lawyer and Jim for getting me home.

Lawyer leaned toward me and said, "I'm sorry I made you mad. And I feel even worse this happened to you since I was the one who invited you to the festival."

I realized I'd been a bitch. "I was rude. I apologize. And what happened wasn't your fault. I'm just not built for this, it seems." I shrugged. "I'm going to resign tomorrow."

He slowly nodded, his eyebrows pushed together in concern. "I hope you'll change your mind. This isn't typical at all."

I protested, "But you know about my week. Really. Nothing has gone right."

He stood with his arms crossed, his head cocked to the side. "If you go, who will work with your patients?"

I shrugged, and every part of my body screamed that I should stop moving. "Here's what I bet. At this rate, if I stay, they will still be without a therapist because I'll be in the hospital."

"I don't think so." He stepped forward. Uncertainty made him hesitate and then he said, "Come here." He carefully folded me in his arms.

I let him hold me, knowing I could stay this way for weeks. Maybe I would make it until August.

Tears threatened again. He smelled wonderful, like wool and sweat and some great cologne all rolled into one heady aroma.

He spoke into my hair. "Remember this. Call me anytime you are in trouble. I'll be there."

"Thanks," I mumbled to his chest. "You'll drive to California?"

He chuckled.

I liked the throaty sounds next to my ear, at which point Parker York and his tableside manner became a gossamer memory.

"You're helping people here. They need you. Your part in their lives counts for a lot."

"Let's review your idea. I've lost a man's pet, put a lady's corn crop in jeopardy, and had chickens stolen." I sniffed. "Yup. I'm working miracles."

He stepped back and smiled. "I'll give you advice my dad gave me: "You have to lay down the fine print before you can tell your whole story. You, Ms. Benning, are stuck on punctuating the fine print. Keep moving."

I nodded. "I'll think about it."

He said again. "Call me any time."

Jim tipped his hat as they headed for their vehicles.

The B&B was quiet. The Pfoltzes had taken Milt with them as they shuttled their guests to their rafting and biking activities. I'd explain the attack later when they returned. For now it was nice to have time alone. I climbed the steps to my bedroom and sank into the padded rocker, staring out across the wide expanse of the property.

From here, the whole mugging seemed surreal, yet when I closed my eyes I saw myself falling and the outline of the attacker against the morning sun. I felt the hard ground under me.

I hadn't had my radar up because I hadn't expected danger. The tears came again. They were from pure frustration. I was a competent speech-language pathologist, but who would know by watching me?

I reviewed what I'd done with my patients so far and even the tiny breakthrough I'd made with Melvin wasn't much to celebrate. Someone else could pick up and run with it from here.

I crossed the room and stalled in my tracks when I caught my reflection in the mirror. My forehead rose under the bandage and it pushed down my left eyelid. I looked like a bee sting victim. "Nice," I said. I'd even had my picture taken at the hospital for evidence.

I closed my eyes and planned my future, or at least what I needed to do tomorrow. Besides making the calls to get a new driver's license and Social Security card, I'd have to call the bank to report my stolen credit cards and checks.

All four of my patients were scheduled for therapy tomorrow because of the holiday today. I knew I couldn't just up and walk away like Vicky had, so I'd give a two-week notice, but nothing longer.

I showered and dressed in soft clothing that didn't hurt. Richard had left a new phone on my bedside table. I must be such a nuisance to them. They were busy enough taking care of his father and the guests at the B&B, and now they had an accident-prone adult in the house as well.

I familiarized myself with the cell phone. Lawyer was right to caution me about heading out into the wilderness again. Not that I *couldn't* do it, because I sure could, but I didn't even know where the animal was.

I'd have to decide later what I'd do about The Dog. Maybe Troy already had him.

Elyk

By the time the Pfoltzes arrived home they'd already heard the news. They were apologetic and appalled at the same time, saying, "This never happens around here."

"So I've heard."

Elyk called, but not because he was stuck on a word. He asked if I was still coming to dinner the next night.

"I was planning on it." Even if I didn't stay in Tungs, I wanted to say goodbye to the only friend I'd made. And of course, I *had* to meet Dottie.

"Good. I couldn't deal with Dottie if you backed out."

"I'm not backing out. What can I bring?" I realized I was looking forward to something normal. A nice dinner with friends. A two-way conversation, lots of word play.

"Nothing. We got it covered." I could almost hear the gears in his head clicking, trying to decide what to say next as he hung on the line. He spit it out. "Want me to go after the guy who did this to you?"

I snorted. "By doing what?" I tried to imagine him in a cop uniform but I couldn't picture that much blue material.

"I'd ask some people – you know, at the bars, truck stops, then wait for some dumb-ass to brag."

I was forming a picture of Elyk's "people" - silent woodsmen, axes in hand, fresh from the hills, secreted in bars, waiting for his word to spring into action with the payback, which I translated as "to kill the bastard."

"You'd get into trouble, Elyk. I don't need one more thing on my conscience."

"I wouldn't either, but let me know. Come by the store for directions to our house." He abruptly hung up.

I'd miss his weirdness.

Milt

Within an hour, the story of what happened to me made its way around the county. I suspected the Pfoltzes kept most of the phone calls from me, which I was grateful for, but Jake got through and said he was incredibly sorry. When he stopped for a breath, I gave him my two-week notice, stunning him into silence.

"Will you rethink this?" he finally asked.

"I did. A dozen times. It's how I got to this decision."

After he hung up it was obvious he immediately called my patients. Each one in turn rang to say how much they needed me, how much I'd helped them. Melvin got on the other line while Sandy talked and said, "Whore's of a shit." Sandy said it meant, "Don't leave me now."

I had to smile.

Ivory rasped through the line that she liked me. Luella begged me not to leave until she could toast her progress with a "snort of something smooth." Beryl was still in the hospital and Honey probably hadn't heard the phone through the blur of gin.

After the flurry of calls, I sat on the porch and tried to decide what to do. Milt slept in a chair next to me while the guests did a historical tour of the property.

"I don't know," I said to his sleeping form after I'd presented the pros and cons to him. "Do you think I should stay?"

He snored. His false teeth sat on his leg, smiling my way.

You have to lay down the fine print before you can tell your whole story, Lawyer had said.

I studied the woods beyond the house and kept up my monologue with Milt. "The tiny things I've done so far seemed nothing more than fine print, but if I put *enough* small events together, I guess I'll eventually form a success story, right? The main problem I have is I can't take the unexpected events." My parents' sudden death made me so vulnerable to anything slightly shocking. I'd lost a tougher side of me the day the police came to the door, hats in hand, stating the facts they were taught to say. *Your parents were killed in a tragic accident.* No use of the ambiguous words like 'passed away' or 'gone.' They made it very clear. 'Killed instantly.'

I pushed ahead with Milt. "Oh, I'm good with speech therapy and walking into the most shocking of rehab circumstances, but this? Nope. This is not working for me."

A glance showed he was still asleep.

"Did I tell you I worked with a guy who shot his lower face off? I was very cool from the time he walked into the room, and throughout all of the months I worked with him. I just can't take this unexpected *environmental* stuff that's been happening. Do you know why I'm here? Well, one reason. I was given up for adoption 22 years ago and I just found out about it a month ago."

Cold fingers touched my arm and I flinched. It was Milt, awake and staring my way. My lungs hitched with emotion. He'd been listening. Whether it was meant this way or not, I interpreted his gesture as one of affirmation.

I put my hand on top of his. "Thanks. I'll do what I've come here for. I'm going to work and I'm going to find my parents. I'll stay." I patted his hand and stood. "I have to call back my boss."

Casey

The next morning arrived outwardly bright and sunny, the perfect opposite of my inner gloom.

I hadn't slept well. A wild storm had rocked the rafters for over an hour before the rain began to splatter the eaves. It fell in buckets and the thunder rumbled long and loudly. Eventually, I closed my eyes, but details of the attack returned, like flipping through snapshots, each one presenting itself with perfect clarity.

My reflection in the car window. The terror in my eyes.

The hand on my back. And the voice, whispering, "Gladly."

I'd awakened each time, reminding myself I was safe.

I pulled my aching body from the soft bed, crossed to the antique dresser and pulled the bandage from my face. The person in the mirror looked like the battered wife the police suggested.

Dabbing on extra makeup, I covered the contusion on my forehead. It was the size of a plum and turning a beautiful shade of one, which nicely matched my bedroom. The good news was the swelling had gone down so I'd lost the unicorn look. Splashing a few drops of Visine in each eye, I hoped the redness there might fade to pink by the time I reached Casey's house.

I said good-bye to Richard right after I put the magnets back on the car. I got paid 23 cents a mile with the advertising on the doors, although I didn't need the money. A trust fund from my parents deaths had set me up for life once I reached age 30. Then I would inherit their wealth. But I'd trade all of the money for more time with them. They'd been amazing parents, fun, smart and always on my side. I wanted them back. I also wanted time to ask about my first two years of life as Maria. I snapped the magnets in place now because it was my job to have them on.

I lugged my therapy bag to the car. It was so heavy it felt like it held a dead body. Even places on my body with no bruises protested in pain. Like my armpit muscles. Earlier I'd had to stifle a scream while rolling on deodorant.

I thought about this job on the long drive to Vixonville. I'd learned one thing. Speech therapy wasn't as much about technique as it was about being there for the family. I knew tons of technical terms and medical words, but when I was with a patient, most of that didn't matter. A person who slurred his speech didn't want to know about his hypoglossal muscle damage, he wanted to be understood.

And it's why getting fired by Beryl really bugged me. He didn't like me at all, and I'd had no chance to make up to him. Maybe once he was home from the hospital, I could improve my standing with him to "tolerated."

I didn't know Honey well, but she could use a parenting class, or a trip up the twelve steps of AA.

As I bumped down the long lane toward Casey's, I saw a black tractor-trailer rig with blue and orange flames fanning the sides parked there.

Karl was home.

Today no boy ran to greet me even after I knocked on the door. I waited. It was eerily quiet. Doves cooed in the eaves. Bushes scratched against the porch rail. Something tiny buzzed my head.

I tapped louder. A sick feeling grew in my stomach and terrible scenarios of death wheeled through my mind just as the lock snapped open. Clearly I was still traumatized from being mugged.

A man cracked the door and growled, "Who're you?"

From what little I saw, he needed a shave and he wore a white wife-beater that was a few inches too short, leaving a clear view of his hairy paunch, hanging over black sweat pants.

Karl was a real looker.

Pointing to the magnets on my car, I held up my ID tag. "Casey's speech therapist."

His face scrunched and he studied my nametag. "You're at the wrong house." He started to close the door but I blocked it with my foot. I had to make sure Casey was fine.

I quickly said, "I've been here twice already."

"Wait here," he said, pushing my foot away and closing the door.

After a few moments of silence, Honey and Karl's arguing carried from the upstairs window. The gist of the conversation was she *had* told him Casey had a therapist, and then Karl reminded her that *no one* was allowed in the house. Honey saved her skin with the lie, "They work on the porch."

Maybe she had more guts than I thought.

Five minutes later, the beige card table and two chairs were erected on the porch. I thanked Honey for always setting them up. "I'll gladly help you next visit."

She nodded for show, but whispered, "Who hit you?"

"Some guy grabbed my purse and I fell." I shrugged as if to imply "these things happen."

Karl remained outside, his look a permanent glare. He struck a match on the porch railing to light a cigarette.

Casey was a changed boy; no jumping around, no dog antics, no yelling. A flash of anger blazed through me. I missed the loud, clumsy, leg-licker. Chipper raced around a tree, barking toward the branches.

Casey and I worked through the /b/, /p/ and /m/ pictures again and practiced more words. He hung in there and repeated the words over and over again, no matter how many times I asked.

"You're such a good worker," I praised. If Honey had warned me Karl was here, I'd have come another day. Instead, I had an over-weight guy in a mini-shirt observing my every move.

"Is he retarded?" Karl asked, flicking his cigarette butt into the dirt.

"He's completely normal. He just has a really bad speech impediment."

He huffed. "Is it because Honey lets him watch TV all day? I think that's what's got his mind all twisted."

What an idiot. Maybe overexposure to newspaper print made someone crazy, too?

I said, "There's no correlation between TV watching and underdeveloped speech."

"So when's his speech going to straighten out?" He scratched his stomach, and it sounded like nails on sandpaper.

He actually seemed to be concerned. It wouldn't hurt to show at least *one* of Casey's parents my goals. I reached into my bag and found a spiral notebook. Opening it to the middle, I tore out a page and got my pen ready.

"What the hell are you doing?" He flew to our table, his face red, his eyes bulging.

Casey jumped up and ran for the backyard.

The hair on my arms jumped up, too. I sputtered, "I…I was going to show you how sounds develop—"

He grabbed the notebook and held it away from me. "Never, ever ruin paper in front of my kid again!" he thundered. "I've raised him to respect paper."

"What?"

"People are too careless with this product." Spit flew from his mouth. "Our country was founded on a piece of paper. It's a national treasure and yet, you don't get it."

I wanted to argue that the constitution was more than one piece of paper but was afraid Daddy Whack Job would take it out on Honey and Casey. And it was clear why Honey drank her lunch.

He said, "I'm saving paper from thoughtless acts, like wastefulness."

Under his anger was something else. What had he lost, making him hold on so tightly to one thing?

With no rebuttal, I held up my hand in an act of surrender. "I understand now." I packed and left the porch. There was nothing to say to calm him. I'd call Honey before my next visit to make sure he was gone. The man needed serious therapy. He must fall completely into seizures around the art of origami, and bags of confetti must slay him.

Luella and Margritte

My drive to Proxy was a blur.

I arrived at the Bledsoe sisters' trailer and walked to the trunk through the cluster of pecking hens to retrieve the bag of crushed corn.

Dragging the huge corn sack to the lip of the trunk, I tried to heft it in both arms. It was like picking up an uncooperative pig sliding around in its skin; just as I got my arms around the center, the corn shifted and the weight dropped to another part of the sack, and fell from my grasp.

I finally managed to get one shoulder under it like I had seen Burt do at the store, and my hands grabbed onto the burlap. I regretted this as the muscles in my arms screamed and my lower back spiked with pain. I staggered up the steps and balanced the bag as I rapped on the metal door.

Was I really glad to be back to work? Not at the moment.

"Oh, hi'ya there," Margritte cooed through the screen after opening the inner door.

"Hi," I gasped, realizing I was holding my breath. "If you don't mind getting the–"

"Oh, God no, we don't want the feed in the house. Just take it around back and I'll show you where we put it."

She closed the door in my face.

Forty pounds wasn't too much weight, but I wasn't sure I'd make it. I cussed, shifted the bag, and lurched toward the backyard.

Once there I saw a jumble of rusting cars, a silver water tank listing to the left, and an enormous bare board chicken coup, raised three feet off the ground with a platform serving as a door at night and a gangplank for the chickens by day.

Margritte poked her head out of a window. "Just put it in the bin next to the building, please." She pointed a meaty hand toward the four-foot long metal container resembling a miniature city dumpster.

I hate myself.

Build a story from the fine print. What made Lawyer's dad a philosopher anyway? The fine print right now was, "This sucks." I staggered to the bin and gently rested the sack on the ground. Catching my breath, I turned to walk away.

"No! You have to pour it inside," Margritte protested, then called over her shoulder, "She just dropped it next to the bin." She turned to me again. "You *know* we can't lift the bag."

I sucked in a slow breath. *Obviously.* I could hardly do it. Turning to the bin, I pushed the lid open and studied the sack. I located the burlap string holding it closed. I lifted the bag, pressed my back against the metal storage tub and reached the top of the sack and pulled the white, nylon string on the burlap bag. The contents hissed downward into the container.

Chickens danced and fought each other around my feet vying for kernels dropping there.

"That's good," Margritte called. "You got it."

I raised my hand. "Yeah." I mumbled. "And I got jittery legs and a headache." I left the empty sack on the ground and retrieved my therapy bag from the car. I scraped bird crap from the soles of my shoes onto the edge of the side-walk. When the door opened, I kicked the canvas shoes off and carried them over the threshold.

"Sorry," I said, standing barefooted. "Could I rinse the bottoms of these off before we start?"

Margritte grabbed them. "I'll do it while you visit with Luella." She shooed me across the room with the back of her hand. "Sure glad you didn't quit on us."

"How did Vicky ever carry that sack?"

"Oh, lands no. She couldn't ever carry it. We had a neighbor drive over and get it out of the trunk. We could of asked him but he's out in Happenstance today, trying to catch a monster rattler."

Luella jumped in, "For the big round-up this weekend. Are you going?"

"I don't think so. I'm a bit overloaded in the excitement department." I crossed the carpet and tried not to be too concerned about what was on the floor. I wished I'd worn socks.

Luella spoke, "And thanks a million for selling our chickens."

I swallowed hard and debated whether to tell them the truth about the birds or just let it go.

She continued. "Burt said he had a real nice chat with you."

Solved. Letting go.

Burt had been true to his word of keeping the incident between the two of us. "He's a nice man," I said. "Helpful. Very helpful." I opened her file. "Now let's talk about you."

We worked through the exercises. Her swallowing strength had improved to the point that she could perform one dry swallow. At this rate, I would be discharging Luella within the next few weeks.

Margritte carried my shoes back into the room and sat them by the front door. "Squeaky clean," she sang.

I really wished she had brought them to me since the crunchy things in the carpet had been more than a little disturbing on my first crossing and now I had to do it again.

After the session wrapped up, I tip-toed to my flats.

They were so wet my feet squished in the lining. Apparently Margritte had submerged them instead of simply washing off the rubber soles. They were ruined, but worse, I'd have to wear them the rest of the day.

"I'll see you two on Thursday," I said, somewhat uptightly. I kept my face smooth, calm, not wanting my frustration to bleed through.

I drove toward Proxy, chewing a thumbnail, scrolling through the things I had to do. I needed to get new shoes and burn these, but more immediately, I needed to pick up a bottle of wine for dinner. I should have asked Elyk what Dottie was serving, but I hadn't. I'd get a red and a white.

Ivory

Ivory was in her garden when I walked around the house. The large woman wore a pink tank top. Her tanned arms were surprisingly strong and firm for such a robust woman.

The sprouting garden looked like a dark-brown quilt, tied at perfect intervals with spring-green yarn.

"I couldn't find you," I announced. I set the therapy bag at my feet and tried to stretch out my upper back where two nerves had been pinching each other back and forth like squabbling siblings for a half an hour. I blamed the sack of corn.

Ivory made a slicing motion across her throat with a finger and then shrugged with both hands turned up in front of her.

"Good," I said. "You aren't talking."

She indicated we could work at a picnic table under a maple tree. I kicked off my shoes in the sunshine to continue with the drying process. The skin on the bottom of my feet had wrinkled and the bright red polish I had recently applied to my nails was sloughing off.

When we were seated across from each other, I said, "Your garden looks great."

Ivory leaned across the table and whispered, "Thanks. It's loads of work. Is Beryl talking to you yet? He wouldn't answer my phone call this weekend."

Ivory wouldn't have known Beryl was in the hospital. And since the *only* work rule I hadn't broken was the one concerning patient confidentiality, I said the most truthful thing I could think of. "I didn't get his dog back yet."

"Why not?" she croaked, her face a knotted scowl. "You said you were going there last time."

"Keep whispering." I took a big breath. "I *thought* I could catch him but he didn't show up. I left food, and the dog catcher is still looking, too."

Ivory spoke louder, defying me with her eyes and exorcist voice. "I need a bag of fur within a few weeks or I'm finished." Her face blossomed with red splotches as she crossed her arms onto the natural shelf of her bosom. An over-sized pouty five-year-old.

"How about a dog groomer?" I asked, forcing a smile. "They have loads of hair."

She banged her hand on the table and the slats vibrated. "You think folks here spend money prettying up their dogs?" Her voice was cracking and breaking all over the place. "Most folks can't afford to eat."

"Okay." I held up my hand. "I'm still hunting for The Dog." Continuing this conversation would set her back weeks if she sustained this volume. "Please whisper, Ivory. This is hurting your voice."

Ivory continued ranting, a bit louder now. "Here's the deal." She removed the thermometer from her beehive hair and waved it in front of me. "I will start following your rules when you bring me a bag of hair. And not from a beauty parlor. It doesn't work." She stuck the thermometer in her mouth, signaling the conversation was over.

I stared off into the distance, reigning in my feeling of desperation. How had it come to this? Another patient wouldn't work with me.

Had I made the right decision? I would have been done with this. Getting in the car and driving west seemed like the easiest thing to do. But if it were just about an easy solution, I'd have left the first day.

"I'm too heated up to work anymore," Ivory rasped around the thermometer between her lips. "I'll see you on Thursday."

"I'm sorry I upset you. I really am trying to get Beryl's dog back. I don't want you to lose your corn."

"Okay."

"Okay." I slipped on my damp shoes. "Would you compromise and stop talking while I'm gone?"

Ivory narrowed her eyes. She pulled the mercury stick from her mouth. "Do I look like the compromising type?"

I forced a smile onto my lips. "See you in a few days."

I hoped Elyk had insight into getting along with his mom. I'd see him soon enough.

The day was beautiful and warm on my return to Tungs. Twenty shades of green wove together in the long stretches of verdant tunnels over the road. I relaxed, no longer feeling the oppressiveness of the thick greenery. Somehow, it had dissipated. I forgot my aching back, my wet shoes, and my angry blue-ribbon winner.

Elyk

Twenty minutes later I parked in front of the country store. It had only been eight days since I'd first met Elyk. So much had happened it seemed much longer. It wasn't until I was locking my car I noticed the magnets were gone.

"Dammit," I said, looking around. I tried to remember when I'd last seen them on the car. They were there at Ivory's, I was pretty sure of that. Why would anyone want them?

Elyk wasn't in his usual spot by the register when I pushed the door open. Again that buzzer that sounded like a basketball scoreboard announced my arrival.

He called from the recesses of the room, "I'm back here."

Pickles and cheese scents filled the air as I neared the deli case. He worked the stainless steel meat slicer. "You didn't quit, I hear."

"Still working, if you can call it that," I said.

Instead of gray coveralls, he wore a faded-green, button-down shirt the color of dried mold. I wondered if he would be changing it before dinner.

"I'm picking up the Pfoltz's groceries." Since Elyk knew everything about everyone, I asked the question that had been bugging me. "What do you know about Milt? I can't get anything out of him."

His muscular arm moved the automated handle back and forth. A pile of ham slices grew on the plastic bag below. "I heard he made his nursing home unlivable. Something about mixing up chemicals from the garage with something from the cleaning closet. He was moving shit around at night and it created some chemical reaction and started a fire in one wing."

Obviously, the dice fascination wasn't new. "He has this thing about redecorating rooms."

"You should know something," he said. "My mother is not a flexible woman."

This thought, clearly out of left field, took me a minute to process. I let him continue, unsure where the ball would land.

He switched off the machine, and put the pile of sliced meat under the glass shield of the deli case next to a tub labeled pig's knuckles. The knuckles were exactly what they claimed to be; a jumble of tiny cloven feet with fleshy pink leg warmers around each ankle.

"She doesn't like you much." He squinted over the glass case. "Even if you are sort of helping me with the contest. She's about to miss out on an entire year of income because you lost her friend's dog."

I made a scoffing sound. "This has been so blown out of proportion. No one is paying attention to what I'm doing to get him back."

"Uh-huh." The slicer dropped creamy white layers of cheese below. "What are you doing?"

"I left food for him after I spotted him in the woods. And the dog catcher knows where I saw him."

"Uh, huh."

"I'll even go to a groomer to get hair for her."

"Exactly what she said. My mom doesn't like change."

Obvious from the woman's hairstyle. "You've talked to her today?"

"Yup, she called all upset, yelling and things."

Ivory had said she wasn't going to follow my directions to be quiet and it appeared she was going forward with her vow.

"You know, she is supposed to be on complete vocal rest."

"What for?" He turned the cutter off and leaned on the stained wooden counter. "So she'll stop telling people about you?"

"No. Her voice. It's so bad."

"Well, I don't know how you're judging that. Anyway, we'll talk about this at dinner because I can't have my mother calling and harassing me."

He lifted two brown paper bags stuffed with groceries. "These are yours." He carried them to the front and I held the spring-loaded door, letting it bounce on my hip as the buzzer sounded. He squeezed past and I followed him to my vehicle.

His face softened and he almost smiled. "See you at seven?" he said, waiting by my trunk as I closed it. He handed me a sheet of paper from his back pocket. "It's easy to find."

I guess his tantrum was over. "Thanks. I'll need these." I put the directions in my back pocket just as my phone rang. "See you soon."

Elyk walked away with an over-the-head wave while I spoke into the cell. "Hello?"

"Marleigh? This is Harvey."

He was the older policeman from my interview at the hospital.

"We found your purse."

"What? Wait. I'm just about to start driving. Can you possibly meet me at the Pfoltz's Bed & Breakfast in ten minutes?" I asked.

The Purse

I was back at the Bed & Breakfast in five minutes and helped unload the sacks of groceries.

When Harvey arrived, I asked, "Who took it?"

"We don't know. We found the purse in town, thrown into a hedge, only a few streets from where you'd been attacked. Here you go."

Except for a few scrapes and a dirty spot on the bottom, the leather satchel looked the same as when it had been ripped from my arm. I undid the clasp. Rummaging around inside I found the thing I was most worried about losing: my black wallet. The thirty-five dollars was missing. Expected. The cards were all accounted for, including my Visa, driver's license, and insurance information. And yes, my library card.

It looked like nothing else had been taken although everything was jumbled around like someone had pulled things out and thrown them back in. Too bad I hadn't had a mouse trap inside.

"Thank you," I told the officer before he left.

Elyk and Dottie

I was so excited about my purse, I forgot to get wine! Wellsfield was in the wrong direction from Burdock where Elyk lived. Rose fixed up a to-go tray of crab, artichoke, and cucumber appetizers to appease me. I loaded the tray in the car and headed to Elyk's.

The driving instructions got me there without a problem, the "there" being a smattering of three mobile homes and two small cabins along an open stretch of cleared forest.

I turned down a rutted path toward a rambler-style cabin at the edge of a pond. A roadrunner weather vane by the pond slowly chopped the breeze floating off the water. The outside of the log home was neat with a few plastic animals arranged in the flowerbeds by the steps.

I carried the food tray up a wooden ramp serving as the front steps. They must have bought the house from someone in a wheelchair.

I shrugged off the dull pain thumping in every part of my body except for my hair. My hair was doing fine.

I knocked and waited.

Seconds later, Elyk opened the door. He wore a clean blue T-shirt and the same black jeans as earlier.

"You found us. I made a bet you'd be an hour late."

"Well, you lost," I said, smiling. "Here," I held out the tray. "Mrs. Pfoltz sent these over. She said they go with everything."

"Thanks. Dottie's in the kitchen." He turned and I followed.

The living room was woodsmen-casual with a strange mix of children's furniture and a long brown leather sectional. The house was more modern than I'd imagined with a wall of electronics and a computer to the side. Everything was also very pink from the throw pillows and decorations to plaid pink-and-brown curtains.

I pointed to the animal heads mounted on the walls. "You shoot all of those, Elyk?"

"Those are the keepers. I've shot hundreds."

I was still processing his last statement when we turned the corner into a rectangular kitchen, opening into a mudroom beyond.

A dozen old conversations raced through my head the second I saw Dottie. The main one being Elyk's panicked voice saying, "*God, no. I wouldn't tell Dottie that*" when I asked if he'd said I was the size of an eighth grader. And his mom had said Dottie had a bunch of "tiny quirks," and then she'd laughed.

From those bits of insight, I had concluded Dottie was a plus size gal with tiny quirks.

I was way off.

"Hi there!" Dottie piped in a voice right out of Munchkin Land. "Welcome to our home."

The miniature woman stood on a chair stirring a pot on the stove. If she was even four-foot-five then I was Wonder Woman. Her long, curly black hair was pinned up on the sides with pink clips and cascaded down her back. She wore a pair of girl's shorts and had tiny running shoes.

"He didn't tell you I was a shorty, did he?" She laughed and climbed down from the chair. "This happens all the time."

I resisted the urge to pick her up; she was so childlike.

"I'm really glad to meet you." I'm pretty sure I stammered right before I blushed.

She and Elyk went together about as well as mustard and strawberry ice cream.

Slapping Elyk's butt, she said, "Just describe me as petite or use one of your big words, like 'diminutive,' you big lunk."

He said, "I don't need to explain anything, Hon. You're my gal, no matter what size."

"You have a romantic streak, Elyk," I said, forcing away the thoughts about how these two have sex.

Dottie hopped up onto the chair again. "You'll get used to the idea. Want to help by setting the table?"

"Sure." I'd chop wood or milk a buffalo just to have something to do besides think about them.

She pointed to the cupboards below the counter top. "The dishes and silverware are down there."

Elyk walked to the outer room and said, "I'll drop the meat on the barbeque."

I unloaded the dishes from the lower shelves and realized why there was a house ramp. Conventional steps would be too tall.

As I set the table, Elyk asked, "Do you like elk? It's fresh."

I laughed. "Only with creamy mint-sauce over the top."

He stared at me and then asked Dottie. "Do we have any of that stuff?"

Dotty paused and shook her head.

Their faces informed me we were having elk.

"I'm just teasing. I like it however you're preparing it." Then I asked, "Is this one of the 'hundreds' you've shot?"

He inflated, which put him at Paul Bunyan status next to his girlfriend. "Sure is. But it's our little secret, okay?"

"Okay." Then I paused. "Why?"

"The game warden doesn't need to know stuff like this."

I love it. Elyk was a criminal and Dottie was in on it. Not Bonnie and Clyde, but Minnie and Clydesdale.

"Well, of course he doesn't," I said, laughing. "I'd be stupid to give up my connection to fresh elk."

He waved me toward the room off the kitchen.

I followed. The elk was extremely fresh since its head stared my way from the blood-stained wooden table - the same table with a cleaver stuck in the top.

Elyk loosened the small ax by rocking it up and down, the muscles in his forearm bulging below the surface. He adjusted a chunk of shiny, maroon meat under his hand and hacked off a piece.

I flinched as the *thunk* vibrated to my backbone.

The smell of the blood made me woozy and I grabbed the speckled tabletop. I tried to breathe through my mouth but then I tasted pennies and gagged. The last thing I needed was to throw up or pass out. The thought of waking up on *this* floor with the pooled blood and chunks of hair sobered me up fast.

"I'll go help Dottie," I mumbled.

Elyk continued whacking more chunks from the huge mother ship of meat but I put distance between the butchering and myself. *How could Dottie let this go on in the house?*

"You're really pale," Dottie said, alarm in her voice.

"I've had a few scares lately and I think it was all the blood." *And the dead eyes staring at me.* "Sorry."

"Oh, your mugging was so terrible!" She was off of the chair and sliding bowls of food onto the table. "And the bruise on your head looks terrible." Dottie brightened. "I'm a Mary Kaye representative if you ever need any makeup. You could even host a party in your house."

I looked at the pink room. *I should have known.* "Thanks. I'll keep it in mind."

Had to be tough qualifying for a pink Cadillac out here.

"You could use a better foundation to cover that bruise." Dottie pointed to her own head in the same spot as my injury. "We have one good enough to hide a tattoo."

I quickly raised my hand, trying to move my bangs around, and I changed the subject. "Did you hear? I got my purse back today."

She let out a tiny giggle. "Oh, great. Did they catch the guy who took it?"

"Not yet."

"Well, forget all that and let's eat."

The meat had been slow-cooked, crockpot-style, so it was tender, and with barbeque sauce it went down easier than I expected. The appetizers Rose had made were a hit and Dottie's cole slaw and corn bread were perfect compliments. Ivory had been right-on about Elyk's ketchup fetish. He added it to everything, even the appetizers.

We briefly talked about Ivory. It became clear Ivory was a handful for the couple and they didn't have any more advice on how to make her happy.

Then I thought about The Dog. "Elyk. You were going to give me tips on finding The Dog. I'm getting desperate."

"Easy. Can't let him see you coming," Elyk said, wiping his mouth with a napkin. "You've got to become one with the forest."

I pictured Elyk in the woods, buried under a cover of leaves and dirt, only his eyes showing. *Like I'd ever do what he does.*

"I'll take you out someday." He laughed. "Teach you survival."

"I've never shot a gun," I said. "Might be a dangerous offer."

He snorted. "Who said I'd give you a gun? I don't have a death wish. You'll learn other stuff."

"Hey, I'm not completely incompetent." I looked to Dottie for support.

She smiled sheepishly and shrugged. "I hear you're really good with words."

After dinner a Scrabble game appeared. Naturally I was delighted. Dottie begged off and watched from her cushiony throne as Elyk and I slugged it out, word by word. I finally won with "Adz" on a triple-word square.

When we started yawning, I thanked them and said goodnight.

I followed the dirt road to the highway, still smiling. I'd had a fun time, and who knew elk was edible? Although I took some frozen slices with me, I promised Elyk I wouldn't divulge my source. Besides, I had other plans: If Lawyer asked me if I'd *bought* more meat to leave out for the dog, I could honestly say "no."

It was all semantics, but it wouldn't be a lie.

Healing

I reached the Bed & Breakfast during the evening social hour. The guests had gathered in the dining room while Milt was in the library, asleep. He'd had a big outing, riding along into town with Rose.

Rose handed me a piece of pie. "Grab a shower and go relax." When I reached my bedroom, I closed the door to the laughter and voices floating up the stairs. I hooked my purse over the closet doorknob and sank into the rocking chair. Balancing the plate with one hand, I forked the pie in with the other.

Maybe tomorrow I'd go shopping since I had the afternoon free. Not in any obsessive, fill-my-closet kind of way but I needed new shoes after Margritte drowned my comfortable pair.

Loneliness swirled in on the cool breeze. I wished I had a sister or a brother to call to unload on. I could call Bethany or Morgan, my good friends through college. Their numbers were in my California cell and it needed a charge before I could find them. Who kept numbers memorized anymore; they were just in a contact list. Scroll, locate, push. Bethany's family let me spend nights at their house when my parents died. They were generous people, aloof in their lush lives selling Bentleys to the next level of income above them. Bethany and I had roomed together freshman year, but it didn't work out. My purpose in college was to be able to support myself in six years, while Bethany was there to appease her parents, making her time in college like high school, but with more unsupervised party options. She barely earned a bachelor's in psychology and for the last two years has run a children's clothing boutique in Beverley Hills. We stayed in touch although the disparity in what we were doing made our calls less frequent. My stories of finals, thesis completion and getting her a ticket to my graduation ceremony weren't relatable any longer. She'd already hauled in more money than I would make at any top speech pathology job on commission selling Gucci, Dolce & Gabbana, and Fendi dresses and skirts for toddlers with price tags of $500 and up.

Morgan came from San Bernardino, the high dessert city known as a lame neighbor to high-kicking LA. Her parents were psychiatrists at Patton State Hospital. After one dinner with them, I understood why she chose the field of communication. Her parents required no response or feedback on their one-sided monologues concerning current thoughts on psychiatry, the newest antipsychotic meds, or the latest horror story out of their prison facility. Morgan accepted a newsroom job in Salt Lake City hoping to work up to reporter or anchor. At the moment, she was in Bali then off to Vietnam and India before retuning. I tried not to get my hopes up, but maybe the Kingston family came with half sisters or brothers.

I'd email both of my friends later. I took the empty plate and went looking for Milt.

He was stretched out on the gold settee, a calm look on his face. I slid the library door shut so I wouldn't look like a complete idiot talking to a sleeping man.

"I'm waffling again. Quit, don't quit. These patients. I'm carrying huge sacks of corn around, getting yelled at."

He moved his head to the side, still fast asleep.

"Someone took those magnets off my car." I paused. "I know. Thank God, right? Did you know Elyk's girlfriend is a third his size? Teeny-weeny. I was shocked, and I thought I'd be immune to shock by now. And I'm still jumping at every little noise. I guess that's to be expected."

I sat a few more minutes with him and then said, "Thanks for listening."

I closed the door and saw streaks of green lights flying across the backyard. The guests were playing horseshoe toss with glowing circles out back. The metal stakes were 15 feet apart, and with the help of a full moon, it made it easier to get a ringer. It sounded like a teenage boy was winning.

The phone rang just then and since no one was inside, I dashed down the hall and grabbed it on the fourth ring.

"Pfoltz Bed & Breakfast," I chimed, trying to sound upbeat like Rose. "May I help you?"

"I think you can," Lawyer said, his rich tenor voice igniting something smoldering inside of me. "But first, I need to hear how you're feeling."

After how I'd treated him yesterday, I was surprised he bothered calling. "You know those crash test dummies? I feel just a little bit better than them."

"Feeling better than a dummy; always good." He laughed. "Did you quit your job?"

"I quit and unquit ten times today, but I'm going to stick it out."

"I'm glad. And impressed. You actually went to work today?"

"I did. It got my mind off of my aches and pains. Oh, and the police found my purse with only the cash missing. Getting it back compensates for a few bruises, I think."

"At least two." He remained quiet for a moment. "I called to see if you have any free time tomorrow."

Let me think – shoe-shopping or time with the hot fireman? "I'm free in the afternoon. What's up?"

"Well, a report came in that some parts of the county have been chaos-free in the last week, so I thought I should take you around–"

"Hey!" I said, and laughed despite myself. "Not fair. This area is a magnet for criminals and wild things."

"*You* are the only magnet I see. But, in your defense, and someone needs to defend you, with all of the talk—"

"What are people saying?"

"Not important. It's just idle gossip. I'd like to show you the softer side of our towns and," he paused, "maybe have dinner together."

Had Lawyer caught the flirtatious tone Parker York had used with me? He was trying to beat Parker to the punch – admittedly a bad metaphor at the moment. I would accept, even as I wondered what Lawyer's girlfriend would be doing during this time. "I *have* missed the finer qualities of the area."

We agreed on 2:00 o'clock.

"See you tomorrow, Marleigh."

I liked how he said my name. I realized a silly grin was on my face as I headed to my bedroom.

Melvin and Sandy

The next morning, Melvin met me at his front door with the word board. He pointed to, "Come in" and then, "I want to sit."

Sandy was all grins. "Oh good Lord. Your word board is working great. He still swears his head off, but he's been content to point if I remind him."

"Exactly what's supposed to happen." I was pleased this device was working so well. For 30 minutes, we practiced sentences for feelings, needs, and thoughts. He was about 50 percent accurate but still mixed up some things when he touched, "I want knife for bed" for "I want knife for bread."

Then we shifted to trying out the hard stuff - actually saying words. Foul-language still predominated anything he repeated but now he produced a few real words. For homework, I asked them to work on reading a word, then writing it and then repeating it again. He walked me to the door and as I headed down the driveway, he yelled happily, "Take a piss!"

I laughed and shook my head. *One step, or in his case, one word at a time.*

BERYL

I drove toward Beryl's, excited to see him, hoping he'd let me in. I *had* saved his life, although it would be unprofessional to work that angle.

I'd gotten used to the narrow two-lane roads and could finally enjoy the scenery while driving. The first week I had a death grip on the wheel, hugging the right side of the road at all times, afraid of a head-on collision.

A movement caught my eye and I backed off the gas. My eyes darted across the tree trunks, waiting for something to appear. Deer-crossing signs everywhere already had me alert: I did not need to hit a deer. I craned my neck as I rolled slowly along the road. Nothing moved.

I returned my gaze to the pavement when a huge gray wolf burst from the evergreens, nearly jet propelled. I stomped the brakes. And it disappeared into the trees to my left. From what I saw, the wolf looked just like the one from last week.

I could see how big it was this time. The forest changed in an instant, it turned dark, and the beautiful flora I noticed earlier now felt like a tight, green coffin.

I punched the gas. It wasn't like the animal could get in my car, but I'd learned weird things happen.

Five minutes later I passed the field where I had last seen The Dog and where I left the burger trail.

"Aw geez," I whispered. It was probably the wolf who enjoyed the hamburger, not The Dog.

I dug the new phone out of my purse, dialing the inn.

"Marleigh," Richard said after he heard my voice. "How's your day cooking up?"

"I just saw the wolf again."

I was out of breath and my voice sounded piping-high like Dottie's, but I couldn't calm down. "I'm near the farm where I saw Beryl's dog last week. The wolf was in the thicker forested area just before the farm."

"Don't get out of the car!"

The alarm in his voice shook me. He was always the calm, cool guy.

Did he really believe I'd go near it? "I won't. I almost hit it though."

"You're driving, right?"

"Yes, I got out of there fast."

"Keep going. I'll call the Sheriff. The hunters around there will want to take a crack at that bad boy. Are you done for the day?"

"No. I have one more patient in Milepost." I couldn't hang up without asking another question. "Do you think a wolf would eat a dog?"

He hesitated just long enough, knowing he'd contrived his answer for my sake. "Naw. It would be like eating its brother. No worries there."

"Right. See you in a few hours."

Hanging up, I realized I had forgotten the elk meat in my trunk! There was no way I was going to drive through the field again and leave it for The Dog. Quickly stopping my car, I got out and popped the trunk. Strangely, I felt a hundred eyes watching. If a guy in a Marine uniform stepped from these woods, that would be it, my heart would simply stop beating.

I put the bag of now-defrosted meat – not too keen on the smell – on the passenger-side floor and drove back the way I came. I wouldn't stop, but I'd perform a safe, drive-by discarding.

Reaching the same dip in the road, I slowed, and coasted as I untied the bread bag. Leaning out the window, I dropped the sloppy mess onto the side of the road. If the wolf scented the meat, then someone driving along the road would have a better chance of shooting the animal while it ate. Or if the wolf was full, he might hesitate before killing The Dog, if he hadn't already.

I arrived at Beryl's anticipating something bad to happen since bad had been my history there, and history seemed to repeat itself.

My legs were wobbly. What were the odds I'd seen this wolf twice when no one else had?

When Beryl opened the door, he was relying heavily on his walker as he let me into the kitchen. "Hello," he said, and either he smiled or had a gas pain, because his mouth did something different from his previous greetings.

"How're you feeling?" I set my bag inside the door. "I stopped to see you at the hospital on Monday but it - well I -, let's say it didn't work out."

He pointed to the chairs around the tiny breakfast table. The tabletop was covered with a blue-and-white plastic table-cloth. In the center was a brown circle where the plastic had melted, probably when a potholder had been forgotten.

We sat across from each other before he said awkwardly, "You got hurt, I heard."

I sagged into the chair and my hand went to the circus of colors on my forehead. Of course he would know. He was nearly dead in his adjustable bed at the hospital but obviously the news still reached ICU.

"Oh. Yeah. Someone wanted my purse. Or apparently just the money in the purse, since I got everything else back yesterday."

"I was so sorry to hear about that."

I fought back tears. What was with the crying? I hadn't cried in two months.

"Thank you," I said, touched by his sincerity. "I was lucky. Just a few bumps and a bit of embarrassment."

"I want to thank you for calling 911 when you found me."

I raised my eyebrows and before I could utter a word, he said, "And I'll thank you by teaching you to defend yourself. The only thing that pisses me off more than foreign cars is men who beat up innocent things."

I was now a thing? "Well, that's not necessary–"

"As a woman, you're born handicapped. Nobody bothers telling you how to take care of yourself and then, *Blammo!* some sucker decides to hit you."

Handicapped? Not even the slightest hesitation when he said those words. "Well, I wouldn't use a word as strong," I began. "This guy was military and tough. Even if I knew –"

Like a snake striking, he reached across the table and jabbed his index finger into the soft spot below my Adam's Apple, gently hitting my windpipe.

I choked and raised my hand to my throat for protection. Shocked by his speed and the fact he'd actually shoved his crooked finger into my neck, I jumped up, trying to get air.

When I could breathe again, I sputtered, "What was that for?"

"To show you how you can drop Goliath," he said. "I could have just told you how to do it, but now you won't forget it, will you?"

"Uh..." I still held my throat.

"Damn right, you won't. When the army wanted me to learn to shoot, they didn't *tell* me about it, they put a gun in my hands and gave me a god-damn moving target." His face was red with exertion. "I got a few more things you should know."

I panicked. *Would he kick my feet out from under me next? Show me how easily an elbow snaps? I had to put a stop to this.*

"Really. I think I'm good." I decided to deflect any more Jujitsu moves with a change in subject. I dug my phone out of my purse while I searched for the photo. "I saw your dog last Thursday. That was one reason I came by to see you on Friday." I smiled, "I also knew you missed me."

He squinted my way. "Huhn."

Afraid of another fast move, I said, "I have a picture of him in here." I scrolled some more. "Anyway, I bought some hamburger and left it for him. He looked fine. Here it is." I handed the phone to him, remembering how tiny the photo was and Lawyer's suggestion to enlarge it, which I hadn't done yet.

He held it like a policeman holds a car microphone, kind of claw-like, squinting at it and moving it closer and farther away from his face. "Bunch of damn trees," he snarled.

I leaned over the table and tapped the gray spot at the tree line. "Right here. I'll get this enlarged since it's not easy to see."

"Mosquito dandruff is not easy to see - this here's impossible."

"Aren't you happy he's alive?"

"Maybe." He handed the phone back. "You can show me firsthand where you saw him when you take me to get my glasses adjusted. They got twisted when I fell."

"I didn't know you wore glasses."

"Like I said, they're twisted."

I frowned. He hadn't needed glasses to read the Segway instructions.

"Only need them for distance," he said, as if reading my thoughts.

The day I carried food to the backyard - while he trained the rifle on my back – he hadn't worn glasses.

The man was a lunatic.

He snapped his fingers and I flinched. I didn't trust any hand movements anymore.

"There's a copy shop in Wellsfield right next to my optometrist. We can kill two birds there: while you enlarge the picture, I'll get my specs fixed."

"I can't drive you in. It's against the home health rules."

"You'd leave me here with limited sight? What if someone with a muddied conscience comes along?"

I checked my watch, estimating the 30 miles to town, the wait, the return time. If we left immediately, I'd make it home before Lawyer arrived.

"If someone 'muddied' shows up, just poke him in the neck."

When his mouth made that strange movement again, I decided it *was* a smile. We might never be great friends, but we'd get along well enough to work together.

"Let me help you to the car."

He took his glasses case and a small backpack from the kitchen counter. When we were outside, I folded his walker in the backseat, made sure Beryl was secure in the front, then we started on our way.

His demeanor softened and he talked non-stop, like an excited kid headed for Disneyland, telling stories as the land blurred by.

"The bog right there is where I shot my first turkey. They aren't as dumb as they look. Oh, and this next farm coming up on the right is owned by a Kraut named Franz Heikel. Locals torched his barn during World War II because he didn't sign up to fight. He lost about 200 head of cattle and a year's supply of silage and hay. Come to find out he had a clubfoot and had gotten turned down at the enlistment center right before the fire. No one knew much about them except they bought a lot of cabbage and vinegar. Turns out they're good people."

The sprawling farm had a well-manicured yard, fresh paint on all of the buildings, and neat fences surrounding the corrals; a perfect puzzle picture.

"Liking sauerkraut makes a person a Nazi?" I asked.

He unzipped his backpack and brought out a silver flask. "It did during the 40s." He unscrewed the cap and took three gulps from the container.

The scent of whiskey hit my nose. "Uh…we have an open container law in California prohibiting that."

"Thanks. I'll remember not to visit you when you go home."

He screwed the cap back on and returned it to the pack. "In my day, a Kraut was a Kraut and a Spade was a Spade. We called it as we saw it and nobody got all squeamish about labels."

He looked so satisfied I couldn't resist, "You know Kraut means 'herb' in German, right?" I'd taken German in high school and this was one thing I remembered. "Sauerkraut means 'sour herb.' Not much of a slur, when you think about it?"

His eyes narrowed as he stared my way.

I'm sure he had a non-squeamish name for me. I shouldn't have challenged him but I had a hard time with this rant.

"You aren't married for a good reason," he snapped.

I bristled. "Yeah. I'm only 24." Marriage was the last thing I needed.

"That ain't it." He drew in a breath and pointed to a crumbling stone building at the intersection ahead. "Right there is the only school house in the area when I was a kid."

I let him talk - my own personal, bigoted tour guide. As long as he wasn't challenged, his stories were interesting and I learned more about my home. My parents may have had relatives who went to school there.

After arriving in Wellsfield, I helped Beryl into the waiting room at the eye doctor's before I walked to *Copy That* next door. A woman about my age, with hoop earrings the size of baseballs and dark bangs over her eyes, showed me the computer to print the uploaded photos from my phone.

Moments later she dropped a 5x7 photo into an envelope. "Done." While she rang it up, I slid the picture out far enough to see The Dog. He was a bit fuzzy because of pixilation in the enlargement process but it was clearly Beryl's dog. I'd caught him mid-bound. His fur rippled in the wind, his mouth open in a dog smile.

At the optometrist's, I waited 15 minutes before the scrape of Beryl's walker headed my way.

Once in the waiting area, he stopped and patted his shirt pocket holding his black glasses case. "We're good to go. Did you get your picture?"

"You're going to be dazzled."

On the drive to Milepost, I handed him the envelope. "There's your boy, as you call him."

He slid the photo from the sheath and studied it. I returned my attention to the road, where vehicles sped toward me, the only thing separating us was a mere five inches of white paint.

Beryl held the picture closer to his face.

Didn't need glasses? Any closer and he'd be in the photo. "He looks good, don't you think? We just need to catch him. The dog catcher–"

He interrupted, "Which one are you talking about?"

"Troy Twittler. I thought you knew him."

He shook the picture back and forth. It made a *fwaka fwaka* noise. "No, in the picture. Which 'he' looks good?"

What the hell was he talking about? I slowed down and cut my eyes from the road to the picture and back.

He moved his finger from the dog to the far right of the picture. Standing just inside of the woods was another blur.

I hadn't seen it. With the grays and the greens in the picture it could have just been a tree. "Maybe a deer?" I asked, as a huge logging truck blew by us, rocking the car in the suction of its aftermath.

"No," he said, moving the photo into a stream of sunlight. "Sure as shootin', it's not a deer."

And then a bad thought hit me and I silently asked for one huge favor from wherever favors sprout from: Please not a wolf.

Lawyer

Lawyer's dark brown hair lifted in the afternoon breeze and shy patches of sunlight touched his cheek. I had never been one to study jaw lines or cheekbones before, but I found myself admiring both.

As promised, he arrived at two and we visited two towns. In Roseburg, our third and last stop before dinner, Lawyer parked the truck at the town cemetery, where we climbed a hill and retreated to a bench under an ornate iron trellis, a break from the sun. The structure was laced with fragrant Wisteria vines thick with leaves. The bench overlooked the cemetery, and to our back stood a hushed forest.

We sat a few feet apart, both studying the sky. It was full of racing cumulous clouds the size of buffalos. The sun appeared, then disappeared again. The cemetery was quiet, quilted with the noises of chirping birds, chattering squirrels, and a distant lawn mower.

"This is nice," I said. We'd been speaking in hushed tones, just because it seemed wrong to do otherwise.

"Which 'this'? The company or the scenery?"

"Both."

"Good. It's one of my favorite places to think. I spent a lot of time here when I was younger. My first job," he said, nodding.

I studied him from behind my sunglasses. His legs were stretched out in front, crossed at the ankles. Today he wore running shoes, jeans and a white golf shirt.

"*This* was your first job?" I paused. "Let me guess — grave digger? Body snatcher?"

"No." He chuckled. "Those were my second and third jobs. I mowed; I was in charge of grass maintenance."

"Grass maintenance? You mowed this whole thing?" The cemetery was hilly and went on forever. My guess was, using a sitting mower was beneath him. Now I knew how he'd gotten those amazing shoulders.

I suddenly felt self-conscious, as if he could tell my thoughts were lingering on his body.

"What was your first job?" he asked.

I stalled, not wanting to answer.

When I met his eyes, he raised his eyebrows. "You don't have to tell me."

"Pet sitter. When I was eight."

When he laughed, I shut him down with a scowl. "I didn't laugh at your job."

He held up his hands. "And now you're a speech therapist."

I nodded. "A bit like going from a grass mower to a fireman?"

"I was a teacher in between," he said.

"Really? Where did you teach?"

His demeanor changed slightly and his body language became defensive. "Taught history for four years in a private high school. Near Philadelphia. I moved back last year."

I remembered this from the Pfoltz's discussion, but they couldn't remember where he'd been.

"Was that hard? I mean leaving a few million people and coming back to the rural life?"

"Sometimes you just need to come home," he said too quickly. He reached for my hand and gently urged me up from the bench. "Come. I want to show you something few people know about."

We wound through the plots and stopped in front of a large willow tree draping its pale-green skirt onto the ground.

I looked around and saw nothing unusual – just a big lacy tree. "And this is a secret?"

"Wait." Lawyer parted the hanging tendrils. "In here."

I followed. Weak sunlight filtered through the stringy bows and I saw this was also a gravesite. As my eyes adjusted, I read "Wilson" on the main monument beside the gnarled tree trunk.

Twelve headstones, spaced about three feet apart, circled the base of the tree like preschoolers sitting for a game of Duck Duck Goose, their leader the willow tree in the middle.

Lawyer walked to the nearest headstone, knelt down and brushed some leaves away from the inscription. "They start here. January 19, 1919. Emily, aged 4 years, 3 months." He moved to the next granite marker. "David, January 21, 1919, aged 8 years, eight months, and then, on the same day, this one," he pointed to the next marker, "Joshua, aged fifteen months."

Every family member except the father, Harold Wilson, had died within a week of the first child. The father lived 40 more years. "What happened to them?"

"Influenza," Lawyer said. "The big cities in Pennsylvania were hit hard the year before and that's when most of the pandemic precautions were taken. The rural populations got slammed in 1919."

I pictured young Lawyer mowing around all of these concrete stories. "Is this why you became interested in history?"

He took me by the hand again, which I was starting to like, and led me out into the open toward his truck. "You might be right. Let's head to dinner."

We had a 20-minute drive to Marshall, where he had said we'd try a restaurant and bar famous for its drinks. Its slogan was, "Fifty Ways to Please your Liver."

We fell into a comfortable silence as we walked around the graves, then he finally asked, "So, have you heard from Dr. Parker?"

I'd wondered if his name would come up. "Not yet," I said, and smiled. "I'm sure we will be in touch over the next couple of days."

He hesitated. "Yeah. He seems interested in your – health." A moment passed. "No boyfriend back in Frisco to make jealous?"

I loved the fishing expedition and I knew I was smiling too widely. "Nope. Not anymore."

"Hmmm," was all he said.

I switched subjects. "I saw the wolf again."

"Where?" His voice held disbelief.

We were almost to the truck when I started to answer but then I noticed the name. "Kingston" was carved near the top of the simple headstone. I stalled and then stopped altogether. I leaned closer to see the names carved on the sides of the stone. Amber and Daryl. My breath caught in my throat and I stumbled backward.

Lawyer grabbed my arm to steady me.

I hadn't thought about this possibility. "They're dead?"

Unaware of what I was seeing, Lawyer said, "Yup, all of them." His hand swept the hillside.

I knelt in front of the stone and touched my parent's names as if tracing them would make them go away. Not really be here. My father had been born two years before my mother, in 1965 versus her 1967. They were 25 and 23 when I was born. The death date read October 6th, 1992. Four days after I was given up for adoption.

Lawyer must have recognized where I was looking. He knelt beside me and studied the names. "You know them?"

Tears began to fall from my eyes, down my cheeks, off my face and into the ground. After several minutes, I said, "These are my parents. My birthparents." I wiped my face with the back of my hand, "I just found out I was adopted only a month ago."

He wrapped his arm around me and pulled me closer. "I'm sorry."

"I had no reason to think they'd be dead. All I have is the documentation for my adoption so I thought I could look for them while I was here. It never occurred to me they could have died."

He leaned closer. "And on the same day."

I felt hollowed out, and I immediately started erasing all of the homecomings I had built in my mind. If I let them go it wouldn't be as painful. But sadness overwhelmed me. I had counted on having a family in Pennsylvania, on reuniting and knowing I belonged.

Lawyer gently raised me to my feet and held me for a few moments as my shell-shocked mind reeled. I kept saying, "This can't be right."

I pulled away from Lawyer and studied the gravestone again. "I wanted to meet them. It's all over now. I'm officially an orphan." Tears spilled from my eyes and I let them blur the image of the headstone.

Lawyer touched my back. "I'll take you home."

"Thanks."

Once we were in the truck, his phone rang.

"Excuse me," he said, and took the call. He launched into a long string of "uh-huh's," and then said, "Can we talk about it later?" He listened again before saying, "Alright." Getting off his phone, he flexed and relaxed his jaws several times. "Something has come up anyway."

"A fire?" I asked, even though I'd heard a woman's voice on the other end, crying.

The image of Lawyer hugging the girl on Memorial Day popped into my head. I didn't want to get in the middle of anything involving crying, more sadness, or more loss.

"No fire, but let's take this as a rain check." His smile sat uneasy on his lips.

He shouldn't have spent the day with me if he was this attached to another woman. I probably shouldn't have accepted either, but I liked his hug. It felt like a once-in-a-lifetime hold.

Fat raindrops exploded onto the windshield. I pointed. "Looks like you get the rain part."

He cut his eyes toward me. "And what about the second part?"

I didn't want to say no. I liked how he didn't have a hero complex and he was so comfortable to be with. And the instantaneous sexual attraction – something worth exploring. "Give me a call in a few days. I'll see if I have any reason to stay here now that I've found this out about the Kingston's."

He nodded. "This is why you are really here, isn't it?"

I paused, and then smiled with, what was at this point, a weak heart.

I had nothing more to say and between the discomfort of our words and the water banging on the roof, he fell silent, too. Once we arrived at the inn, I didn't wait for him to open my door. "Thank you for the tour." I stepped out and hurried to the house. I think he said something, but it was lost in the noise of the storm.

Milt

My mind was still spinning as I sat through another dinner of wild game. This time it was crab-stuffed pheasant and had little in common with barbequed elk. The guests remained for rhubarb strudel, but I excused myself and went looking for Milt. Not sure if I'd be here much longer, I spent an hour online researching mutism and discovered a person suffering from this social anxiety was hardly ever completely silent. I wanted to see if he would initiate a game of cards again, or better yet, talk to me. He was in one of his usual places, on the front porch with a cup of tea on the side table. Dressed country-casual today, in jeans and a short-sleeved white shirt sans bowtie. He stared across the road into the woods and didn't budge when I took the seat next to him.

"Anything exciting out there?"

He turned toward me, his neck as wrinkled as a turtle's, his eyes slowly reaching my face.

"I saw a wolf today while driving. You never know what can come out of those trees."

His eyes didn't even flicker.

"A big wolf."

Nothing.

"And my parents are dead. All four of them." I didn't go on. As soon as the words crossed my lips a bleak darkness moved into my chest, a muffled loneliness acknowledging I would never have family again. I needed to stop or I'd be bawling like a baby. "I'm wondering something. When you stopped talking, was it all at once or did you keep talking to certain people for a while?" I'd also read selectively mute people at times had someone they would talk to - just not the world at large. It was rare a person became completely silent.

He tipped his head to the side and watched me. He was tough; most people couldn't ignore a direct question. I was just planting a seed in his head so if he decided to talk, he would then know I would be there to listen.

"If you want to write something down, just let me know. Or we could go for a walk and have a chat. I'll be here." Since a walk could take a half a day, I'd have to plan accordingly.

"Do you have your cards?" I pointed to his pocket.

He slowly returned his gaze to the woods and kept his hands in his lap.

I waited. Just when I thought he wasn't going to respond, he slowly reached for his front pocket. Even before I saw what he pulled out, I heard the telltale clinking. He had a set of dice.

This wasn't good. The family had just recovered from his last rotation through the house.

He held them out with the same glint a naughty four-year-old gets right before he throws spaghetti at the cat.

"How do you keep finding these?" I asked. He watched me as he slowly closed his hand around them. *What was going on in his mind?*

One of the therapies for mutism was called "shaping." The patient wasn't asked to speak but to just follow a non-verbal movement. After success there, they were asked to make sounds, eventually moving into the act of whispering simple words. Maybe I could use the dice to try a shaping technique.

"Milt? Roll one of the die and let me show you something."

He waited a lifetime then opened his hand and let one drop onto the glass table between us. It was a four.

I touched each dot and hummed an "M" each time. "M-M-M-M. Your turn."

He picked up the die and rolled it again. A two. A minute later, he touched the dots and seemed to get excited. He panted a few times and then tried to stand up.

"Stay. We don't need to move anything around. Let's just play while we're sitting here," I said. "Just make a sound or hum."

He took the game piece back and closed his hand again.

"Roll for me," I said.

A die hit the table and stopped on a five. I did the same thing as before, touching the dots and made five "M" sounds.

His number was a six. Again he was excited. His breath came in short bursts. Suddenly I realized he was snorting air as a way of counting the dots. He'd pushed air six times.

"Oh my, gosh! You're saying something." I touched his arm. "Do you do this when you are rearranging things in the house? Is it your way of trying to talk?"

He stared at the die and then at me.

Is this how he coped with not being able to get words out? Did he use the numbers to plan these pushes of air, like stutterers learn to tap their foot or swing their leg to get unstuck when they're blocked?

"If you add some sounds to what you're doing, Milt, maybe you'd be able to say words." I really wanted to believe this.

The dice disappeared into his front pocket and he turned his head toward the trees and retreated back into his own world.

Maybe he didn't want to talk again. I hadn't thought of that. Maybe in his eight or nine decades, he'd said enough. He'd used up his word allowance and he was broke.

Rose appeared with a handful of herbs from the garden. "What are you two chatting about out here?"

Should I rat Milt out? Maybe he always had dice but only messed up the house once in a while. "I was just humming. What a peaceful view from here."

Rose turned to her father-in-law. "Do you need anything else to drink?" She waited a half-second while he stared beyond her. "Just let me know if you change your mind." She turned and left.

Here was a problem: they didn't *expect* him to answer. It had been so many years since he'd spoken, Milt was just someone to talk "at," not "with."

Like a pet. He was their shriveled Shar Pei.

The sun sank below the horizon and dusk dropped a soft cloak of mauve and gray over everything. Milt and I sat for another half hour without speaking until Richard convinced him to get ready for bed. Would Milt be sleeping tonight or rearranging the house? I'd wait to see.

In my room, I sat propped up in bed, ready to write in the charts, but unable to do anything but think about the Kingston's. *They had died right after I was adopted.* Did they know my parents? Or was it anonymous. The papers had called it a closed adoption. I wasn't sure what that meant.

Elyk

The house phone rang. After a few minutes, my cell phone rang.

When I answered, Elyk barked, "Dottie wants you to have a makeup party."

"Hi, Elyk. Good to hear from you, too." I was going to model manners for him until he got it. "I would love to host something, but she is the only female under 50 I know here. I'm not going to be very helpful. And, I'm not sure I'm staying much longer."

He yelled something away from the receiver. "She said she doesn't want to, Hon."

"Elyk! I did not say that." Dottie would be hurt to think I was dismissing her. "Let me talk to her."

"Okay, then, Marleigh. You think about it some more." He was obviously saying these things for Dottie's benefit.

"Elyk! Put her on."

He said, "Well, before you hang up at least help us out with a word."

I was going to kill him. He was pretty good at one-sided conversations. "Do you really need a word?" I huffed. "Or are you going to keep showing off?"

"Thanks. Here's the clue – 'Mine.' Starts with C-O-N-C and has nine letters."

I scribbled the letters out on the back of a page in Casey's file and tried to imagine letters in the blanks. "That's the only clue?"

"Yup. One word: 'mine.' I think its 'Concubine' but I'm not positive."

"You would think that." Maybe the clue had a different meaning. Was it "Mine" as in "I own it," or "Mine," like the hole in the ground? Then the answer hit me.

"It's concavity," I said, smiling.

"Well, okay Marleigh." I heard him scribbling the answer down. Then a dial tone buzzed in my ear.

I wanted to drive to his house and give him a *real* concavity right where it counts. I would tell Dottie of course why he deserved it!

Amber and Daryl

I crawled under the covers and closed my eyes. The house phone rang again. Moments later there was soft knock on my door and Rose said, "Marleigh? You still awake?"

"Yeah." I switched on the bedside lamp. "What is it?"

Rose opened the door and crossed the room, holding a slip of paper. "Sorry to bother you but Lawyer Hunt said to call him right away. Use the cell."

I glanced at his number. Fire Chief Hunt wanted me to call him.

"Thanks, Rose."

As she shut the door, I debated dialing or just ignoring his request.

I dialed.

"Marleigh. I need to know you're okay."

"The cemetery. It's all I've been able to think about."

"I'm sure." He paused as if debating his next words. "I have more news about your parents," he paused again, "if you want it."

"What?"

"Unfortunately, it's not great news."

My heart seized. How could it get any worse. They're dead. I swallowed a breath I didn't know I was holding. "Because?"

"The names on the headstone were given to a young couple from Pittsburgh who died in a car accident while they happened to be here, in this county."

A steady pulse beat in the bruise on my forehead. That didn't seem so unusual. They moved here, and had me, then gave me up, and then died. "I'm not clear. Why is a car accident such unfortunate news?"

The phone was silent for a beat too long. "They were given those names when they went into the Witness Protection Program. You may never know who your real parents were."

"Witness Protection Program!?" I wasn't sure I could handle many more surprises today.

"I hope you don't think I was prying. I thought you needed more answers than a headstone."

"No. I really appreciate this, Lawyer. Thank you for looking that up." I suddenly couldn't talk any longer. "I have to go," I said and hung up.

I headed into the closet and closed the door. Breathing deeply I sorted through the facts. My birthparents were young but not so young. I mean they got to a point where they needed to change their lives completely. Butterfield was hours from Pittsburgh and seemingly a long way from danger. No matter, at the end of the day, this day, I was without family. Any family.

But then I wondered if this really changed much. Maybe I needed this. I stuffed my face into my shirts and drew in long breaths. Finally calm, I left the closet and crawled under the sheets, but sleep was elusive. In the dark, with the new emptiness in my mind, the mugger's voice returned, all whispery, a deep rumbling sound, playing over and over. I didn't know how it would happen, but I wanted him out of my life. Everyone else was gone, why couldn't that apply to him as well?

I needed to know more about Amber and Daryl and Lawyer might be able to help me do that. Plus it still seemed that staying in the area made more sense than heading back to San Francisco. Something good and successful needed to come from my time here. And I still had clients to help.

Richard

I startled awake before daylight, a voice whispering "gladly" ripping me from my sleep. Milt must have slept through the night since there had been no early morning hustle to put things back in place.

I found Richard on the back patio, studying the yard.

He said, "I'm thinking about getting a life-size chess set. Found one in a recreation magazine. Sure would be unique."

"Would it really top a private cemetery, a maple syrup sugar shack and glow-stick horseshoes?"

"This is neater. The pawns are four-foot tall and the king and queen are five."

The word "cemetery" made me think of Lawyer, us holding hands, walking, laughing, then the shocking news. Our speedy goodbye. If we went out again, I'd get the subject of his girlfriend cleared up first.

Richard wrapped the garden hose around the storage wheel, and then surveyed the clean patio. "Troy put together a bunch of hunters and they went looking for your *canis lupus.*"

It was good to hear the dogcatcher was finally taking this seriously.

I asked, only half joking, "Did he make them all say crazy tongue twisters first?"

"No. But let's give the poor guy a break. He still lives with his mother and has an up-to-date marble collection. He's got a lot *not* going for him."

"You're right. As long as he keeps looking for The Dog and the wolf, he can be the oddest guy on earth."

We headed to the house. "Troy said he hasn't seen either of the animals, but he's pretty fired-up because he thinks he's discovered a poacher."

My stomach dropped. "Why's that?" I asked, knowing the answer.

"He found a pile of meat along the road and when they tested it, it turned out to be elk."

"Oh." I played innocent. "You can't hunt elk here?" I quickly replayed how I'd gotten the meat from Elyk, driven it around while I forgot and it defrosted, and then dropped it by the roadside. It couldn't be traced to either of us.

"Pennsylvania only has about 700 elk in the whole state, not like some states out west with hundreds of thousands. We have a very limited hunting season, only in the fall, involving a lottery. This meat was a fresh kill. Killing elk is a no-no in June."

"Oh, wow," was all I said. They wouldn't trace ten pounds of elk to a guy living in the back woods, a guy I didn't want to make angry. I had one friend, well, one-and-a-half when I counted Dottie, and I didn't want to lose them. "That should keep Troy busy."

Casey

I'd be seeing Casey today so I called to make sure Karl was on the road. Honey apologized and thanked me for pretending we always worked on the porch. "You don't want to see Karl when he's mad," she added.

I thought I already had.

Luella and Margritte

At Luella's, I began what had become routine: nudging away hens, slowly sweeping one foot forward, then the next, on my way to the front door. Chickens seemed about as intelligent as insects hovering outside of a bug zapper; the bugs never learned the light was not their friend, even after thousands before them turned into sizzling sparks. Each and every visit, the chickens investigated me like I was made of food although I'd never once fed them.

A note with my name on it was taped to the front door.

It read: "Luella had a bad night. Might have new monia again. We are at the docters. Sorry, Margritte." She'd drawn a happy face after her name.

I wrote I was sorry and added my phone number, asking them to call when Luella got home. I re-taped it to the door, did the chicken-step dance back to my car, and slipped inside.

"New monia," or pneumonia, no matter how it was spelled, was very bad news and I worried. If Luella had been following my diet restrictions and avoiding thin liquids, it shouldn't have happened. She had gotten pretty good at the dry swallow and other exercises, so a recurrence like this was baffling.

I sat in the car and dialed Therapy on Wheels and left a message for Jake, updating him on Luella's status.

Casey

I drove to Mapleton and turned toward Vixonville. Again, there were no firemen out in front of the station but this time I was relieved.

At Casey's, I found his mom on the front swing, crying, her head on her arms, her short shorts revealing way more than I wanted to see of her butt. Casey was nowhere in sight. No loud singing came from the back yard. No licking boy scrambling around on all fours.

About the same quiet as the visit before.

She's killed him. I pinched my arm to clear the bad thought away; statistically most people didn't kill their kids.

"He knocked over a couple stacks of newspapers," Honey whined when I asked what happened.

"I'll help you pick them up." I dropped my hand onto her back. "This is easy to fix." She was over-reacting for a few newspapers on the floor, but after meeting Karl, I think I'd be crying, too, if I were in her shoes. "Where's Casey?"

"He's in his bedroom watching TV." She wiped her eyes with the hem of her green haltertop. "I needed some time to get my shit together."

Karl had accused Honey of putting Casey in front of the TV too much. "You know," I said. "TV can be a good baby sitter. Why don't you take a few minutes for yourself and I'll go sit with him? We can clean up together."

"You're nicer than I thought you'd be," she said. "Coming from the city I thought you'd be a bitch."

And I thought you'd be wearing a bra. "Oh, I keep that side locked away."

Honey came along with me to Casey's bedroom. It was upstairs, just past the master bedroom. She pushed the door open and said, "Your teacher is here, Casey."

I followed her in but stuttered to a stop just inside the doorway. It wasn't the chaos of toys or the mattress on the floor with the disheveled Buzz Light Year comforter that panicked me; it was that Honey had literally tied Casey to the chair in front of the TV.

He looked toward me with his big brown eyes as she untied the blue bandana from his mouth.

Now *I* wanted to cry.

She cooed to him as if he'd just awakened. "Did you like Winnie the Pooh?"

He nodded and said something unintelligible as she freed his arms and legs from the bathrobe tie.

"What did he say?" I asked, trying to stifle the uproar in my stomach. I wanted to grab the braless woman and shake her to pieces. This was child abuse. Karl might not be the only bad influence in Casey's life.

"He asked if you brought more candy," she translated.

I stared at Casey.

He bounded free of the chair and ran over to me, smiling, happy, not traumatized. He shoved his hand into my therapy bag and started rooting around.

"I have candy for you, but let's work first."

When he ran for the stairs, I turned to Honey, trying to put words together, but my mouth just opened and closed. Nothing came out.

"What?" she snapped, while chewing a cuticle.

"Because he knocked over some papers, you felt compelled to tie him up? It's dangerous."

She snorted. "It wasn't just the papers. Karl stressed me out this weekend. He's got to take some longer hauls or lose his job. I'm pissed off because he's never here as it is and now he'll be gone more. Makes me wonder if he's doing cab scabs."

"Is that overtime?"

"No. Truck-stop hookers." She rolled her eyes as if to say I was dense.

I'd seen plenty refueling stations on my cross-country drive but none with those.

I visualized Karl's unshaven face, his protruding belly and confrontational attitude. "I'm pretty sure he's not *doing* anything but driving."

She shrugged, suddenly looking smaller.

"I'm sure it's overwhelming having to raise Casey alone, but it's also really dangerous to tie him to a chair."

"Why?"

A shiver ran up my neck and tucked itself under my scalp. "What if there was a fire? Or he choked? We need to come up with something to do when you get frustrated. Maybe get a babysitter for a few hours."

She rolled her eyes again. "Who's gonna take care of him? He talks Martian mumble, doesn't listen to anyone, and he's clumsy."

"Not really. He's a cute kid. Has a mind of his own but I don't think he'd be difficult to watch for a few hours. I bet he'd like TV even if he wasn't tied up."

Her face reddened. "Good, it's settled. My backup plan is to call you." She huffed down the stairs.

I might have just volunteered to watch Casey at some time in the future, which I would deal with if it happened.

Casey sat at the card table waiting for me, his legs swinging back and forth, the tips of his dirty sneakers barely scraping the worn-out carpet.

I brought out all of the picture cards he and I had practiced with the last time. I knew Honey hadn't done any work with him, yet he remembered how to make the /b/ and /p/ sounds clearly. So we moved on to harder things. We used the words in phrases, like "bounce a ball." This was more difficult, but he was so attentive watching me say them first, he did quite well. Of course, every few minutes, he'd asked, "Heh ahdee?" which I knew meant, "Get candy?"

I assured him he would.

He needed to learn as many sounds as he could, as fast as possible. He was heading into kindergarten in three months; he needed to be understood. I introduced the /f/ sound as what the "mad kitty" says, and we practiced f-f-f-ing each other like two cats fighting. He got the giggles and rolled off his chair. I helped him back up.

Returning to the cards we tried to say, "fall" but he could only say "all." This obviously would take longer but at least he could now produce the /f/ sound correctly in isolation. On each visit I would try to add another new sound to his repertoire. We'd keep practicing the old ones and hopefully by the end of the summer, he'd be more understandable.

I gave Casey a choice of candy and he took one, squeezed me around the thighs and scampered off. On two legs. Another improvement.

As I gathered my things, a wave of sadness washed over me. I couldn't fathom tying a bandana in his mouth. Who could do that to anyone, let alone someone they loved? I would do anything to have my parents back, to tell them all the things I just assumed they had heard enough. The "I love yous," the "thank yous." Do we ever say those phrases enough? And what I would give to meet the people who made me. Just to get to talk to them, see them, look for characteristics we shared. I shook my head.

I found Honey in the middle of the mess, holding up a newspaper and studying it. I wasn't going to lecture her about restraining him, but I'd keep reminding her there were other alternatives when he got on her nerves.

I dropped to my knees beside the scattered newspapers and helped restack them.

"They have to be in order from the oldest to the newest," she said. "He'll know if they were moved."

Her voice had an edge that I didn't like. "Okay." *This might take longer than I thought.*

We worked through the mess, putting them in ascending order. The pile grew against the walls.

Honey worked slowly, staring hard at each paper before deciding where it would go. When we finished, I said what was bugging me. "I know I'm not a mom. But tying up and gagging your son is child abuse. I'm supposed to report abusers." I waited for her reaction.

She sagged against a stack of paper, looking hollow and empty. "You know. I can't read past a fifth-grade."

Her announcement shut me up. No wonder she overreacted when the papers got knocked over. The effort to re-order them must have been overwhelming.

"I quit school to work in my parents' diner and when they lost the restaurant for bad taxes I never made it back to school."

Back taxes or "bad taxes" was about the same. But I knew state education rules. "They let you quit school at eleven?"

She shook her head. "Oh, I was 16 when I quit but I only read at a fifth-grade level. I get by, but stuff like reading these dates is more work for me than skinning a squirrel."

She needed a boost. "You can be proud of everything you've done then." I had to force cheeriness into my voice. "You're married to a man who has a good job, you own a house and you have a healthy boy." None of those statements seemed to help. "And you're pretty."

She smiled for the first time and flipped her lanky blonde hair off her shoulder. "Yeah. For now anyway." She grew serious and folded her arms. "Are you turning me in to the cops?"

I chewed my lower lip. Calling Child Protective Services was an anonymous call so people felt safe making a complaint. There would be no secret here about who had called. "What do you think I should do, Honey?"

"I get it now. I didn't treat Casey right. And, you said I could call you if I needed a break. Right?"

"Sure, call and we'll talk about what's going on." I didn't want her to think I was a babysitting service, but I had no problem talking to her.

She walked me out and dug at the ground with her big toe. Something else was on her mind.

I raised my eyebrows, "You okay?"

"Don't tell anyone I can't read, alright?"

"It's nobody's business," I assured her. I was taken aback. Her shame didn't come from being harsh with her son; it came from the fact that she couldn't read.

Grady

On the way to Ivory's house, on the outskirts of Proxy, I passed the church and the new sign read:

A Get Out Of Hell Free Card Can Be Yours.

My phone rang, startling me. I fumbled for it as I watched the road, found it and punched the green button. "Hello?" I said without looking at the caller ID.

"Hi, Mareigh."

It was Rose.

"Where are you right now?" Her voice was different, twined with nervousness.

Something had happened. "I'm near Proxy. "Why? What's wrong?"

"Well, we don't want to worry you, but Richard just got a call from the sheriff's department. The guy they call Grady is apparently in Pennsylvania after all, and he's struck again. This time a bit closer."

"Where?" Selfishly I hoped it was a town I had never heard of.

But that wasn't the case.

"Outside of Blackout," she said.

A town I drove through every day.

Ivory

I promised Rose I would call after my next patient's house, that I wouldn't talk to strangers, and I wouldn't stop for anyone along the road. She had started treating me like a daughter, which I liked. My parents were smart, witty, and adventurous. They we also hands-off, not physically warm or nurturing. They raised me with the idea that I needed to be independent, seeming to start this idea at birth. Or in my case, at age two.

Parking in front of Ivory's home, I searched the enormous yard before exiting the car, even though I was at least 15 miles from Blackout. I rang the bell and hoped Ivory had changed her mind about further ruining her vocal cords.

Voices came from inside. The TV was on, which meant she was home. I knocked louder on the door and the voices stopped.

Ivory opened the door, smiling, and whispered, "Thought I'd scared you away."

"I don't scare easily." We walked to the dining area. "What were you watching?"

"Nothing. Why?" Ivory wore plum-colored slacks and a pink and purple swirly patterned blouse.

"I heard someone talking."

"Oh, you know." She squinted at me. "Just a dumb soap opera. Background noise for the lonely."

Ivory didn't fight me when I asked her to go through the smooth vocal exercises again. We practiced for 20 minutes as if our confrontation during the last visit never happened. Not wanting to ruin our rapport, I avoided all conversations with the words, "dog, corn, prize winning, hair, or fur" in them. Next I had her answer questions using a quiet voice, just at the point where it didn't sound raspy. She had no problem with this, although it should have been hard.

Out of nowhere she asked, "What did you think of Dottie?"

I pondered my answer, then said, "A little shorter than I imagined."

She laughed. "I should have warned you."

"Yeah, thanks." I paused. "I found Dottie to be incredibly nice. I'm going to see them again this weekend."

"They could use normal friends like you."

"I'm glad you see me as normal," I said, chuckling. "Will you give your voice a rest?"

"Depends. I'm a big, stubborn woman."

"So your son says."

"He said that about me?" Ivory's face went bright red. "He's an ungrateful twerp."

Uh oh. I didn't need Elyk pissed off at me. "He just said you *could* be stubborn — he hadn't mentioned the 'big' part."

"Hells Bells! I *am* big. Anyone that isn't blind can see that. It's the 'stubborn' part I don't like." She put her hands on her hairdo and straightened it although the inverted tornado hadn't moved an inch. Shellacked so thick with hairspray, I could see my reflection in it.

Ivory sighed. "What's your compromise?"

"Cut the talking by 50 percent. And try to whisper just to the point before your voice engages, like we practiced today." I demonstrated in a dramatic whisper, "Hi Elyk, it's your mother. I'm cutting you out of the will."

She laughed and slapped the table. She whispered, "Good idea. That's exactly what I'll tell him."

I groaned inside as I prepared to leave. I had to stay out of this bickering or I was going to be in the middle of a messy family feud.

At the door, Ivory handed me an envelope. Inside was a $100 bill and a grocery list.

Not this again. "I can't keep getting your groceries."

"Yes, you can," she whispered as instructed, offering a toothy smile. "But you only need to do this until you find The Dog. The inconvenience of shopping will help you remember you're making my life a *living hell* without my dog fur."

I suddenly understood why there was no Mr. Ash.

"Living hell?" I couldn't cut the irritation from my voice. "Well you're in luck. The church up the street is offering Get-out-of-Hell-Free cards."

"What are you talking about?"

"Nothing." I sucked in a long breath. "I'll have your groceries tomorrow. And I'll be doubling my efforts to find Beryl's dog."

"That's all I'm asking," she rasped. "I'm not impossible."

"You're a little bit impossible," I said. "But I like you."

Grady

I checked in with Rose before heading back toward Tungs, through Blackout. The only recent news on Grady was that he had taken some rabbits and left behind his usual grade card–this time with a pun: "A clutch." They weren't a herd, a pride, or a pod, I learned. The bunnies were missing and probably weren't coming back, but no one had been hurt, and once again, no one actually saw Grady.

Sheriff cars patrolled the back roads leading to Blackout. Once I reached the edge of town, I was halted at a road stop.

Two Pennsylvania State Police cars sat across the road, noses facing each other, reducing the thoroughfare to one lane. Several State Troopers guarded the opening, their hands on their holsters, their legs splayed wide. Some fellow officers in New York State had been outwitted by Grady once before and it appeared they wanted to avoid having it happen again.

One policeman approached my car, and I buzzed my window lower.

He asked for identification, which thankfully I had back in my possession.

"Long way from California," he said, squinting from under the brim of his dark felt hat. He was built as solid as a bronze statue and had a belt full of gadgets and weapons. His nametag said Reardon.

"I'm about two weeks into a summer job as an itinerant speech therapist. I'm staying at the Pfoltz Bed & Breakfast."

He nodded, checked my car registration and asked to look in my therapy bag. Another officer, older and less clean-shaven, looked through the trunk.

The first deputy returned my ID and asked, "Where are you heading?"

"To Tungston."

He wrote something on the paper on his clipboard. "What's the nature of your visit?"

"I live there." I paused, then said, "And I lost a dog about 15 miles from here. If you see a big Malamute, could you call it in to the local sheriff? He's deaf, by the way."

The state trooper inspecting the trunk walked forward and joined the policeman at my window.

"What do we have here?" the new guy asked.

"A chatty speech therapist," Officer Reardon answered. "She says the local sheriff is deaf."

Idiot. "No, the *dog* is deaf. The sheriff is fine."

Officer Reardon nodded. "You can go. Call us if you see anything out of place." He touched the brim of his hat. "Miss."

"Sir." I made it through the car barricade but not without two sets of eyes on me.

In the center of town, policemen walked the streets while others covered the hillsides. It was an honest-to-God manhunt. Surely this guy, with the evaporation skills of a ghost and the made-up-name would be caught today.

Sex

Rose peeled vegetables in the kitchen while Richard was outside poking at the coals in a charcoal pit convincing them to light. Tonight they were having a barbeque and a square dance. They encouraged me to come wearing my bib overalls.

First I needed to get some fresh air and run off about five pounds of Rose's home-cooking and I needed to blow off the heavy sadness that was getting heavier by the hour. They are dead. All of my parents are dead.

I asked Richard if he thought it was safe to go for a run since Grady was assumed to be 30 miles away.

"How far are you going?" He asked, his forehead creasing.

"Two or three miles."

"Just stay on the road leading up here from the turn-off. It's about a mile."

In my room I changed into a black halter bra, threw a gray tank top over it and pulled on black running shorts and tied my shoes. I stretched in front of the inn, realizing Milt watched from the front swing. I waved to him before jogging onto the road, then I dropped down the long hill once again, reaching a comfortable stride pretty quickly. My muscles ached less and most of my bruises were in their final stages of "yellowing," so the leftover pains from the mugging were about gone.

The temperature was near 80 and a soft breeze pulsated from the forest to my right. A quick rain the night before had left the air humid and heavy, intertwined with smells of moss, brackish water in the lowlands, and wood pulp from freshly cut logs. I liked the soft thump of my feet on the road as I fell into a steady rhythm, realizing I never ran without my iPod in the city.

I pushed away thoughts of being alone. I'd see Beryl tomorrow. I knew people were close to finding The Dog. I wanted to be the one to find him but I wouldn't be heading into the forest to look for him, especially since it was near where I'd recently seen a wolf.

I reached the log pile at the bottom of the hill and stopped to stretch again. The paved road at the intersection was still wet in the shaded areas. A car zipped by, its tires on the surface sounding like masking tape being pulled off of glass.

On my return up the hill, I thought about my time with Lawyer. In actuality, I couldn't stop thinking about him. I wanted to be pressed up against him again, wanted to try out his mouth against mine. I wanted to squeeze his butt, knowing it would be rock hard.

I valued his help in solving the mystery of my birth parents, and since he had gotten information already he must have connections. I decided I would ask him for more.

I pushed myself harder, trying to get the words "rock-hard" out of my head as new images of what they could mean came to mind.

Eleven weeks without sex was having a greater affect on me than I would have thought. Was it pathetic that I knew the exact amount of time that had passed since I had last had it? No need to answer that question.

Of course there was Dr. Parker York. Kind, decisive. Available. I liked available. No need for a rain check from him, from what I could tell.

A Square Dance in Overalls

The square dance music pulsed out over the dusky backyard as 30 people stood in box formations waiting for the caller's next Grand Right and Left.

I had planned on participating in only one set, but 30 minutes later I was still weaving through the line like a "shuttle on a loom," something Rose kept saying. I wore my overalls, classing them up with a white tank top with sparkly beads at the bodice and high heels. However, once the dancing started, I kicked off the shoes and danced barefoot. I should have saved today's run for another time because my legs were beat.

Neighbors and friends had arrived to make it a real gig.

The food consisted of ribs, slick with a red tangy sauce, cabbages stuffed with coleslaw, and baked beans served in Anaheim pepper skins. Rolling Rock beer and Hard Lemonade helped the adults wash it all down and loosen everyone up before the fiddler raked his bow across the strings.

Troy Twittler, the so-far worthless dogcatcher, arrived late with his mother. The woman was solid and looked strong enough to be the lead dog on an Iditarod team, if she could be harnessed in place. She hadn't touched the alcohol so I supposed her repeated introductions to me were a heroic effort to become my mother-in-law.

The music stopped and everyone reached for a chair or a drink. Troy sat at a picnic table watching, the place he'd been since arriving.

"I have to take a break." I grabbed a Hard Lemonade and plopped down on the bench across from him.

"It's harder when you don't know what you're doing," he said. He didn't crack a smile so I assumed he was just being an ass.

"So, you square dance?"

"Oh, I used to. It's one of those things that's only fun if you didn't grow up with it." He stretched both arms over his head and tried to look bored.

"Tell it to the American Square Dancers League," I said.

"I don't think they're called a league."

"I didn't think rabbits were called a clutch, either." He was irritating the crap out of me.

He squinted, rusty gears grinding in his head as he thought about my statement.

I still needed his help so I tried for nice. "Okay. What *do* the dancers call themselves?"

"The United Square Dancers of America is one group."

"Really? The USDA? Must get confused with the agriculture department." The challenge rolled off my lips.

Darkness crossed his face.

The music started up again, but only half the dancers took to the floor.

I spoke louder, leaning forward. "Any news on finding Beryl's dog."

"He's bear food by now." He made a show of taking a long slug from his beer, then he choked and tried to cover it by putting his fist in front of his mouth.

I hid my smile. "C'mon. I just saw him a week ago. Let's just pretend he hasn't been eaten by anything. He would still be alive, wouldn't he? Just skinnier."

"When I'm driving my route, I'm always looking for him."

He sounded like a garbage collector.

"What can I do to help? Mr. Holmes is pretty angry and the dog will die if we don't find him soon."

"Stay out of the way. Stay out of the woods. Anyway, I think we have a bigger problem."

I sighed. "The guy who is running from the police?"

He pursed his lips. "No, he's not my problem." Troy leaned his elbows on the table. "I'm putting all of my efforts into finding a poacher."

As the English say, he was on the wrong bloody trail, and because of me. "Isn't poaching something a game warden deals with?"

Then I remembered too late that Troy had run for Game Warden but lost time after time.

He snapped up, a puppet yanked from above. "I happen to be helping him out, Fannie Farmer." He pointed to my overalls. "Note to yourself, that's not a good look." He left, and a moment later I heard a truck door slam and tires peel away.

It seemed up to me to find The Dog.

After the dance, we cleaned for 45 minutes. The phone rang just before I headed up to my room. Richard's face hardened as he listened.

"Thanks, Jim. I will," he said before hanging up. He turned to Rose and me. "Sheriff's office. They didn't catch Grady."

An electrical shock zipped through me. "There were a 100 police officers in Blackout this afternoon. How did he get past all of them?"

Richard shoved his hands in his back pockets. "Well if that's true, then there are 99 officers now. One of the state troopers is missing."

Milt

I sought out Milt, thinking he could recreate the air chuffing thing and we'd try talking again. He'd been propped on a chaise lounge during the dancing but then Rose moved him inside just after dark. He sat in the library, in the same old settee, leaned back so he had only a view of the crown molding around the ceiling.

"You're up late." I pulled an over-sized chair toward him. "Been playing any poker lately?"

His gaze dropped to my face and I thought something twitched at the edge of his mouth.

"If you have the cards, I've got the time."

When he reached for the deck in his pocket, I wondered whether I had the time. The man moved at a blistering snail's pace.

He set the deck on the table, and brought out a $20 bill.

"Whoa! That's too rich for my blood." I hadn't gotten paid yet and I'd already been robbed of what little cash I carried.

He waited. Finally he put the $20 away and brought out two $1 bills.

"You're on." I reached into my pocket and matched his two dollars from the eight dollars I had found in my jeans, left there from my cross-country drive. It was all I had until payday tomorrow. "Deal the cards."

He dealt one card apiece, face down and then put the deck in his lap. He turned over a nine.

I didn't know what game we were playing but I flipped my card. A seven.

He raked my money toward him with his gnarled hand and left his two dollars on the table.

"War? We're playing War for two bucks a draw?"

He looked from my hand to my purse.

"One more time," I said. I was more intrigued by this gambling elf than I was intent on winning. He sat around all day looking so helpless but then there was this shyster side having no problem taking my money.

He dealt two cards. Mine was a Jack of diamonds. "Uh oh," I said. "You're in trouble."

He stalled in midair, as if considering what defeat might be like, then reached to flip his card. A king of spades.

"Amazing." I shook my head and waved away his offer of losing another two dollars. "I'm taking you to Vegas someday."

Over the next five minutes, he packed away the money, then the cards.

No more than half a minute later, Richard popped his head around the leaded opaque door. "What are you two up to?"

"Talking about poker," I said, and winked at Milt.

He didn't move.

"You don't want to play poker with my dad. He's legendary for taking home more Friday paychecks than anyone else. Right, Dad?"

Milt stared at the crown molding. It stared back.

I knew when to say goodnight.

Dr. York

The next morning arrived overcast and gray. The fog hung a few feet above the ground and the world lay veiled behind cheesecloth thick air, every object in the yard nothing more than a gauzy outline.

Richard handed me the home phone, saying Doctor York had called to check up on me. His office number was on a slip of paper.

I waited through three rings and got his voice mail. I told him I was better and left my cell number.

Richard took me aside and said the story of the missing state trooper wouldn't make the news until evening, so I wasn't to say anything. He handed me a small canister of Mace. "I wanted to practice before you left today but in this fog, we'd only end up hurting ourselves."

Thanking him, I dropped it into my purse. I rummaged through my therapy bag, checking my materials, making sure I had the right picture book for Casey.

I curled onto Milt's settee in the library and stared out the tall windows, willing the floating mist away. What did Milt think of during his long days parked here? At some level he trusted me. Or I was just a sucker.

Melvin and Sandy

Although I'd called all of my patients to let them know I would be late, I felt bad arriving at Melvin's behind schedule. Standing on his steps, I cringed, hearing a tapestry of curses through the open kitchen window. My word board had failed.

I let myself in; the doorbell was as effective as a bird peep in a tree full of starlings.

Melvin paced the kitchen holding a pair of scissors, stringing together words whose paths were not meant to cross.

"That two-balled bitch!" he yelled.

My point exactly.

Sandy leaned against the dishwasher. The word board lay on the tile counter looking tattered and used up. She quickly walked my way.

"I don't know if you want to hear this," she said, her face flushed. "It's a slippery slope into hell for everyone's ears when he gets like this."

"What happened?" I asked.

Melvin stopped talking when he saw me. He seemed to be waiting for an answer to the question, too.

Sandy said, "We were watching a game show and the news broke in about a manhunt for a guy who's running from the law. Mel lost it right then. I tried to have him use the board but he can't seem to find what he wants to say."

I sighed. "It *is* very limited. I tried to think of common phrases, but it's not a dictionary."

"It's great, Marleigh. This is a different thing. He's acting like something bad is going to happen. He seems afraid."

Melvin approached me as he handed the scissors to his wife.

That was a relief.

He looked me in the eyes and slapped both hands on either side of his face, in an Edvard Munch scream and leaned toward me expectantly.

"You are surprised?" I asked.

"Mother hell!" He stormed.

I squeezed his arm. "Melvin, calm down so we can help you. Can you show me what you want?"

He grabbed my hand and walked me to the TV. He tapped the screen, then took his glasses off of his face and then slid them right back on. He waited for me to guess what he meant. From the look on his face, he thought he was making himself perfectly clear.

I had no idea what he was trying to say. Panicking, I looked to Sandy for a clue.

"Just so you know," Sandy said. "His pantomiming isn't very accurate. Last week he kept patting his back pockets and pointing to "little candy" on the board."

"What did he want?"

Sandy sighed. "For me to find out how our son's foot surgery went."

I shook my head. "Okay. I'll keep it in mind." I turned to Melvin and took a stab. "You were watching your game show..."

"Shit," he nodded, agreeably.

"The news flash came on about the guy they're looking for..." I watched his face for the reaction and so far I was still on the right track. His eyes were big and his head bobbed up and down... "And you got upset because he's dangerous."

He slammed his hand on a shelf by the TV. "Rectum bastard!" He shook his head and headed for the back door.

"Melvin, don't leave," I said. The loud cursing trailing behind him like foul cigar smoke.

"He won't go anywhere," Sandy said. "Let him cool down."

"I don't know what to say. He must think we're really dense." As the trained professional in the room, I wasn't very helpful.

Sandy sighed. "You should have known him before all these strokes. He was such a patient man who could sit for hours and help people with their troubles." Her face set itself in a resigned mask.

A movement outside the kitchen window startled me and it was my turn to let out a little scream. A man stood there, looking in with his hands cupped to the glass. It was Melvin.

He left the window and headed back inside.

I dropped my hand from where it clutched my chest. "Oh, my gosh," I said, fanning my face. "I think I know what upset him."

Melvin entered the kitchen and stopped in front of us. "Gooodd daaaammit," he pleaded, his hands in front of him, his palms turned up.

"You saw a man at your window and you're worried it's the guy they're looking for?" I held my breath, waiting for the barrage of anger to follow.

He sagged in relief, nodding vigorously. "Dumb ass," he said, patting my back in a congratulatory manner. "Dumb ass."

I laughed. "I'll take that as a compliment. Are you sure it wasn't a policeman? They have been going house to house near here for two days. They might have widened their circle."

He shrugged his shoulders and squinted, thinking.

I turned to Sandy. "What time did he become upset?"

"About a half hour ago."

"It wouldn't hurt to call the police, you know. You'll feel better knowing it's just an officer checking things out."

Sandy said, "I'll ring my cousin, Inez. She's a county dispatcher. She knows the who's-its and what's-its about everything happening." She squeezed my arm. "And, thanks for solving this."

While she placed the call, Melvin and I returned to the den to practice using the word board. I had him build sentences like, Call the Police, I Saw A Man, and Afraid Man Outside.

This relaxed him.

Sandy lingered on the phone, chatting away, catching up on family gossip. I waved to her when the session was done.

"Can you hold a minute, Inez?" Sandy put the receiver to her chest. "Inez is looking into it 'cause right off she doesn't know about anybody searching Ruttsford."

Weird. Who had Melvin seen? "Okay. Melvin's pretty relaxed now. Have a good weekend and I'll see you Monday."

I stayed on the little porch just off the kitchen and wrote my notes about Melvin. I'd usually drive to my favorite overlook but until Grady was caught, it seemed best not head to some lonely stretch of highway.

Melvin was making pretty good progress. He *had* slapped his face and removed his glasses which could mean, "I saw a face in the window," didn't it? Much better than when he'd patted his back pockets to say he wanted to call their son.

The second I stepped out into the sunlight I knew something was wrong. My car was where I'd left it but its sides were no longer naked: the *Wheely Good* magnets were back, slapped on all askew.

My head turned in all directions, while my heart banged out the beat to Camp Town Races.

Nothing moved. No one was near the car or the bushes edging the property.

When the magnets had disappeared, I'd imagined bored high school students had taken them on a dare. Take some street signs and move them around. Put toilets in the road. Boots flung over telephone lines. All hilarious activities.

But I wasn't laughing. This was getting creepier by the second. Besides, I really didn't want the stupid things back.

"Hey, Speechy!" The man's voice came from the street.

A silver pick-up truck idled there. Troy Twittler hung out of the driver's-side window. "I might have a lead on this."

Maybe I had underestimated him. Naw, he still wore his Blue Tooth earpiece and no one called me "Speechy."

"What did you find?" I asked, walking toward the road, stopping at the end of the driveway.

He pushed his sunglasses up on his forehead. "Found a hideaway out by Blackout. Little shack in the woods. Recovered those," he said, pointing to my car.

"My magnets were there?" That was really scary news.

"Yup." This time he hooked his thumb toward the truck bed. "And these."

I walked over and peeked in the back. A wire cage full of multi-colored rabbits sat in the center of the bed, the rabbits staring bug-eyed through the wire enclosure.

The famed missing clutch.

I was still stuck on the idea that Grady, whoever he was, had taken my car magnets. Maybe he used them to camouflage a car.

Troy said. "You can thank me now."

I approached his door. His shirt had a county seal patch on the sleeve.

"Thanks." I paused. "Just wondering, was there a state trooper tied up out there?"

"Don't be ridiculous," he said and rolled his eyes. "Why would there be a Statey out in the woods?"

I forgot that the news of the missing trooper hadn't been reported yet, but since it soon would be, I saw no harm in telling Troy. "A state policeman has been missing since last night and they believe this guy grabbed him."

The color left his face, like someone had pulled a plug on his toe. He rubbed the back of his neck and fidgeted like something was crawling there. He must not have known when he found Grady's camp, Grady might be more dangerous than expected.

I said, "You should call the police."

"I gotta go," he muttered and shifted the truck and sped away. Did he believe there was a reward? He was a strange man but he might just have figured out where Grady was hiding. Maybe now he could concentrate on finding Beryl's dog.

I pulled away and was 15 minutes on the road when I realized my magnets had *not* been taken while I was at Melvin's the week before, but they were gone after I'd been working with Ivory in Swell. I skidded to a stop on the side of the road. I didn't buy the idea Grady had been in Swell and Milepost and Blackout, and he was wasting time stealing car magnets while he was on the run. Troy was the guy with the grudge. He was messing with me.

Ivory

The day had turned hot and humid and my mood wilted. I pulled into the Gas-N-Guzzle Hut to get Ivory's groceries. I found Ivory's list, filled my cart within five minutes and paid Burt's daughter, Celia. I asked the girl to say 'hi' to her dad.

"Oh, you lost those chickens!" Celia squealed. "We laughed our heads off at that."

"All right then." I forced a smile onto my lips as I left. It seemed like the whole county thought I was a joke for about four different things. I packed the two brown sacks in my trunk.

Ten minutes down the road I passed the church sign I always looked forward to seeing. It didn't disappoint:

Exposure to this Son is good for you

I found a radio station with some contemporary music and I hummed along, thinking about my week, from getting attacked on Monday, to seeing the wolf again, getting my purse back, my day with Lawyer, right up until finding out my parents needed to be in the Witness Protection Program. What exactly had they witnessed?

My thoughts were cut short by my ringing phone.

"Hey, Marleigh. Jake here."

"Hi Jake. How are you?"

"Good. You done for the day?"

"I have two more people to see. Ivory, and I'm almost to her house, then Beryl. Then I'll be heading into the office."

He cleared his throat. "I need to pull the plug on you."

Was I being fired? What? My mind went to Honey. Giving her feedback about handling Casey got me fired?

I could smooth this over. "Did Casey's mom call you?"

"Nooo," he said cautiously. "Should she have?"

"Uh, no. I was there earlier and wondered if I'd left something at her house."

"We're asking everyone to finish up because this bad guy is still in the area. Just bring your paperwork by and you can make up the visits next week."

"Do you think I'll have time to work with Ivory if I'm there in five minutes?" Which meant, can I at least unload the groceries at her house?

"Stop in and explain why you can't stay. Really, I want you back right away."

I agreed.

"Thanks, Marleigh," he said. Then he laughed, "I guess this isn't the quiet country getaway you wanted after all."

When he interviewed me by phone, he asked why on earth, with my resume, I wanted this job. The "quiet get-away" had been part of my answer.

"I'm managing." I hadn't told him my magnets had been gone so there was no reason to mention they were back. I said I'd see him shortly and hung up.

At Ivory's house, I climbed the steps with my arms full of sacks, feeling that at any moment a camouflaged woods-man might pop out and grab me. I knew this worry was unfounded, but having been freshly mugged, I couldn't convince myself lightning wouldn't strike twice.

Since Ivory lived alone, I worried about her. She didn't lock her doors when she was out in her garden worshipping her corn sprouts. Anyone could slip inside her home.

"I can't stay," I explained as I unpacked the groceries. I told her about the manhunt, my boss's request, and how I was concerned for her. "Could you stay with Elyk and Dottie for a few days? Just until they capture this guy?"

"Not a chance," she croaked. She put the eggs away. "I'm fine right here. Got double locks on everything and I don't need to get out in the garden for a while."

Every time the subject of her garden arose, The Dog conversation followed, so I beat her to it. "And, no, I still have not gotten The Dog back. I just had a conversation with the dog catcher a half an hour ago and he talked about looking in the woods."

"Tick, tick, tick," Ivory rasped. "My corn doesn't have much time."

I assured her I was trying to help and that I'd be back on Monday. When I left, I waited to hear the door lock behind me before I descended the steps.

Beryl

I drove down the road to the church and parked. I made the call to Beryl to tell him why I had to cancel today and I'd see him Monday.

His only reply was, "Remember. Poke 'em in the throat if you get in trouble."

I laughed and said I would.

"And find my damn dog while you're at it."

Always a downer subject. By leaving the elk meat along the road, I had put Troy on the wrong path. He might have found The Dog by now if I'd just dropped the meat in the woods. And on top of that, thanks to my hint about a missing policeman, he was probably out in the woods, trying to be the hero by finding him.

Beryl's dog had been gone eleven days. He may have looked happy and healthy in the picture from eight days earlier, but it had been too long; he may not be alive. Maybe he approached someone, and they were caring for him.

I had to stay positive. The Dog would come home.

Elyk

I called Elyk next. "Need any help on your daily puzzle?"

"Nope. Got it and mailed it off. Day 13 and still in the contest. Where are you?"

"I'm parked at this cute church just past your mother's house. The one with the sign out front with a new daily message."

"Oh, yeah. Some new guy came in and took it over a while back. He let's people wear jeans and cut-offs to the service."

"Well, he's got a lifeguard that walks on water."

"Huh?"

I laughed. "Just one of the signs. Cute, I thought."

"You would." Papers rustled and the cash register *chinged* through the phone. "Hey, we're still picking you up around 6:30, right? You haven't chickened out?"

The highly touted Rattlesnake Round-Up started tonight. It was held in a town called Happenstance, which I thought was more than fitting. I now regretted agreeing to go with them, but they'd seemed so excited to show me some local flavor, I couldn't refuse.

"Is your cousin normal?" I asked.

"Why wouldn't he be? And I made it very clear you are not his date. We're just all riding together."

"Thanks for setting it straight. See you tonight."

I wasn't holding my breath that Elyk's cousin, Donny, was normal by the rest of the world's standards. I hadn't heard back from Dr. York or Lawyer, either one of which could have been a good excuse to not go hang out in a pit of snakes.

During the drive to Therapy on Wheels, my nerves were on alert.

Jake

I spent 40 minutes at the office, first talking to Jake, who congratulated me on getting through the week without needing a new phone number and for sticking with the job after I'd been attacked on Memorial Day.

"Yup," I said. "Still alive." That was more than could be said for the rest of my family.

Jake said, "The sheriff's office will keep me informed on the manhunt. In any event, I hope Monday's a different story and we can all get back to work."

I nodded. I sat at a worktable and finished my notes, made copies for the main files and turned in my time sheet.

Jake handed me my first paycheck for the previous week. It wasn't huge but it felt good. In my car, I tried to decide what to do with the extra time I had before Elyk and Dottie met me at the Bed & Breakfast. I needed a bank account to cash the check so I headed to Main Street to a bank I'd seen there. I set up a local account, deposited the check and left the building feeling a tiny bit wealthy.

Rattlesnake Round-Up

I skipped dinner at the B&B because Elyk said we'd eat at the Round-Up. I hoped it was something most of America recognized as edible and not possum-on-a-stick or rattler-touille. I changed into jeans and a sleeveless top and slipped into tan wedge sandals.

A horn beeped from the driveway.

The Pfoltzes were driving to the festival later with a van full of guests, and they said they would look for me.

A tall burly guy hopped out of the back door as I approached.

"Hey, Dude," he said. "You looking for a ride?"

"I am," I said, already annoyed. I hated people who stated the obvious like, "Sandwich, huh?" when you clearly held a sandwich. "But not 'Dude.' It's Marleigh."

"Yeah, I know. Elyk said you had a weird name. I'm Donny."

He stood back, making it clear I was getting in this side of the truck, behind Dottie.

"Hi Marleigh." Her tiny voice made me smile. I settled in and hooked my seat belt. "You look cute, Dottie." She wore lots of makeup; she almost looked like a doll.

"So do you," she said.

Donny nudged me. "Tonight's going to be bitchin'. You ever hear of Myrtle and the Dirt Turds?"

"No, and I'm afraid to ask." I squirmed away from Donny. He was sitting closer than necessary.

"They're the band playing tonight, Marls," Donny said.

"It's Marleigh."

"Yeah, I know." He touched his head. "I got a good memory. Anyway, they're a rockabilly group. Pretty famous." He reached under his feet and brought out a pint of Jack Daniels, unscrewed the cap and handed it to me. "Get you loose and ready."

"No thanks. I'm ready."

Donny tipped the bottle and drank several swallows. He held it between the front seats. "Cousin?"

"Nope." Elyk waved the bottle away. "I'm going to get us there in one piece. It's all yours."

Dottie said, "Donny, we don't need you falling out of the car again."

Again? "That explains a lot," I said.

He laughed and drank another swallow before putting on the cap. I sent a frosty stare back when he winked. He wore a silky blue shirt a size too small so the buttons couldn't close from mid-chest up. His cologne smelled like Mr. Clean.

I said, "Tell you what. If you stop drinking, I'll buy you a beer at the festival." It wasn't like I had money to throw around but beer was cheap.

"Now you're talking, Sweet Cheeks." He leaned into me, bumping me with his shoulder, his breath almost igniting my hair.

"It's 'Marleigh.'"

"Yeah, I know," he said, before digging a packet of Skoal chewing tobacco from his pocket and pinching some between his lower lip and teeth.

The drive felt longer than it had to and I was the first one out of the car. The Rattlesnake Round-Up took place in the center of Happenstance, in the huge circular ball field. A few homes were scattered around the edges but the focus was in the middle of the field where a large white tent was pitched.

We parked in a muddy lot with a few thousand other trucks, jeeps, and motor homes. The highlight of the night, outside of Myrtle and the Dirt Turds, was the ox roast. A humongous animal sizzled and rotated on a bowed spit at the center of the grassy area, its horns still attached.

I looked away.

The Happenstance Fire Company had their two trucks and one ambulance parked along the edges of the ball diamond. A wooden stage stood near home plate for the bands and announcers.

Elyk pointed to the white tent. "That's the big show in there: the live snakes."

I was in no hurry to see reptiles, so I bought Donny and Elyk each a foamy beer. Dottie and I wandered past the booths, looking at the trinkets and handmade decorations. Everyone stopped us to talk to Dottie. When I asked her how she knew all of these people, she said, "I was the skeet shooting champion in this area for five years."

"You're kidding!" I tried to picture her holding her little gun, yelling "pull" in the voice of a kindergartener, blasting away at clay disks.

"I was really good until a gun recoiled and knocked me off my step stool and I ruptured a disk in my back. I turned to cosmetics."

"Smart move."

In the meantime, Donny bought a segmented wooden snake so realistic it undulated when held just right. He spent the next ten minutes trying to scare girls, but only the ones wearing halter-tops and barely-there shorts.

Dottie and I used those ten minutes pretending we didn't know him and he eventually wandered away.

"Sorry," Dottie said. "Bringing him was a mistake."

"Don't worry about it. I'm happy to be with you and Elyk.

The Pfoltz B&B van pulled into the lot.

"I'll be right back, Dottie," I said, and jogged across the field to meet Rose and Richard before the crowd absorbed them.

"Rose. I was wondering if I can ride back with you whenever you leave?"

Rose tilted her head. "Of course. Anything the matter?"

"My ride here was a tad too crowded."

She smiled, understanding what I meant.

Richard dropped a hand on my shoulder. "You haven't held any snakes yet have you?"

"No. Not yet." I shivered. "I'm going to miss that event, I think."

We walked through some of the same concessions again and made our way to the corner of the ball field.

The B&B guests decided on a rendezvous time and place and moved off in different directions.

As if staged, Lawyer and his girlfriend walked toward us. She had her arm linked through his and I felt a stab of jealousy. I knew what his arm felt like. I turned my back and waited for them to reach us.

"Oh, hi, Lawyer," Rose said. "How are you?"

"I'm great. Mrs. Pfoltz." He introduced the young woman next to him. "This is Veronica."

I had no choice but to turn and face them.

He raised his eyebrows and smiled my way.

I sent my winning-est smile back.

"Veronica, this is Marleigh. And this is Rose's husband Richard Pfoltz. They own the old Victorian B&B in Tungston."

Veronica shook our hands. All I saw was flawless skin and straight hair lifting from the side of her face in the breeze.

"Oh, running the B&B must be so much fun," she said, directing the comment to me.

"I'm just here for the summer." *Now why did I said that?* "I mean, I'm working here for the summer."

"Doing what?" She had the carefree smile of the well-liked.

"I'm a speech pathologist for a home health company."

"She's really good," Lawyer said, the customary smirk on his lips. "She saved a guy's life last week."

"I did," I said, nodding.

"It must be so rewarding," Veronica added. "How fortunate for you."

"Yes, I'm fortunate." I pushed a question her way. "What do you do?"

She looked to Lawyer and he answered, "She's taking a break from Broadway. Just hanging out here."

I wanted to throw up. A beautiful stage performer, who didn't need to work. Perfect. Which explained why Lawyer listened to show tunes. It hit me fast. I wanted to be anywhere else but here. "Enjoy yourselves." I turned to Richard. "You promised to show me the snakes."

He looked startled. "I thought you said…"

"…I wanted a peek at the Cow Pie BINGO game." I grabbed Richard's arm and tugged. "They're done now."

A winner had been declared in the cow pie contest and the players all stood around laughing with cow crap half way up their arms, with more splattered on their clothes and faces.

When I walked away, headed for the snake tent, I felt Lawyer's eyes follow me.

It's better to be prepared than to just wing things. Five minutes later I found myself in line preparing to hold a rattlesnake and suddenly I didn't know why I thought this was better than talking to Lawyer. The snakes were in a large penned-in area, pushing straw around, guarded by the Environmental Protection Agency officers. One of the handlers would gently slide a noose over the head of the rattler chosen and lift him out to be held.

My knees shook the closer I got, but Rose was in line with me making this a team effort. Donny had drifted in but because he'd been drinking, he couldn't touch the snakes due to the strict rules of no drunkenness around the reptiles. I spotted Elyk and Dottie watching people heft five-foot rattlers. I waved and tried to smile but I felt like I was moving someone else's face.

"Which one should we pick?" Rose asked when it was our turn. We stood in front of a large pen with 60 snakes; other pens held more.

The gyrating snakes slithered around, the whispery sound made me dizzy. The hollow sound of the rattles made my heart skip. "You choose," I barely said.

Within a minute, we were holding a writhing serpent in our hands, the head held steady by the handler. My first thought was how heavy and dry it felt.

Not slimy at all.

A photographer got us to smile and then snapped our picture, which could be ours for $10 dollars.

We returned the snake to the handler. I moved along, still in an adrenaline haze when I heard the next person in line say they'd hold the same snake.

There was a fast movement behind me and something heavy, cold, and wiggly dropped down the back of my shirt. An electrical charge ran through me as the snake moved down my spine to my waist.

I screamed. Probably twice.

Then blacked out.

Someone called my name from far away but I fought against leaving the nice, dark place. The comfort factor was right up there with a closet full of warm clothes.

Someone said my name again. I ignored them. *No thank-you, I thought. I'll just stay right here if you don't mind.* Then someone touched my arm and I was shaken awake.

Three faces stared down at me: Rose, Lawyer, and a man I didn't recognize. I had no idea where I was but I was looking at a white metal ceiling.

"Marleigh?" the unknown man asked.

In tiny flashes, I registered the paramedic insignia and white shirt, surgical gloves, and the small space we were all crowded into. An ambulance.

We weren't moving.

"How did I get here?" I whispered. I felt clammy.

"I carried you," Lawyer said, kneeling at my side.

Had he thrown me over his shoulder in a fireman's carry?

"Donny put the wooden snake down your back," Rose said, her voice an apology. "I guess you thought it was real."

I hated that guy.

Lawyer's lips struggled; he was fighting a smile. He cleared his throat, then said, "Your date is in the back of a cop car right now while they decide what to do with him."

"He wasn't my date!"

I tried to sit up but the paramedic gently held me down. "Give yourself a few more minutes."

"I wasn't with Donny. He's Elyk's cousin and we all rode together."

"Uh-huh," Lawyer said. "Not quite his story."

I sighed and sagged into the pillow under my head. "Yeah. I'll bet it wasn't."

Rose asked, "What do you want to do? We could stay away from the snakes and watch the band for a while."

I said, "Myrtle and the Tirt Durds."

"Dirt Turds," Lawyer corrected. "If you want, I'll give you a ride home if you've seen enough hicks having fun."

"What about Veronica?"

"My mother is here with the Woman's Auxiliary League. Veronica can ride back with them."

By now I was sure everyone knew I'd passed out over a toy snake. "I'm ready to leave."

Rose hopped out of the back of the ambulance and waited for me to sit up.

When the smell of roasting ox hit my nose, I knew I had had enough for one night. I waited for my wavering eyesight to steady. I slowly got off the gurney, and tested my leg strength getting out of the ambulance.

Rose dug through her purse and handed me a set of keys to the inn. "Get some rest. Milt is at a neighbor's so don't worry about him."

Lawyer

Lawyer held my arm as we crossed the field. I liked the feel of his strong touch and I would have walked to Tungs with him. When he helped me into his truck, his hand on my ass was probably more for his benefit than it was for mine.

"Strong hands," I said.

"Nice glute." He jumped behind the wheel and when the engine turned over, the music kicked in, a song from the musical, Chicago. A female voice sang the Roxie Hart lyrics, "The name on everybody's lips, is gonna be Roxie..."

He pointed to the speakers. "That's Veronica. Last year on tour. Have you seen Chicago?"

"Yes. One good thing about San Francisco. Lots of theatre." I listened to more. "She has an amazing voice."

He nodded but said nothing.

This was as good a time as any. "How long has she been here, on her..., uh, I think you said her break?"

"Off and on for three months. She's thinking she might stay."

His voice said he cared a great deal about her.

He smiled. "I have a question for you. How do you feel working here of all places? I mean, come on. 'Tungs?' Speech therapist. Would be like me looking for a job in Fire Valley."

"The only parents I knew, Marc and Janette Benning, died in March in a plane accident. My plan was to stay in California and get a job there. Then I was going though the papers in their wall safe and I found my adoption papers. When the complete shock of the adoption news wore off, I knew I needed to look for them."

"And now you've had another shock. I feel responsible."

"Actually, you sped things up for me. From what I understand, if you are in the Witness Protection Program, no data can be found out about your previous life."

"Right."

"So, I could have searched all summer and never found out they were gone. The next step is to figure out why they were hiding out here to begin with."

"If I can prove I'm a good detective would you have room in your schedule for me?"

"You've already proven it."

We wound over a hill and down the other side, the high beams cutting through the dusk.

"Besides Beryl, who else are you working with here? Not their names, of course."

This was a comfortable subject. I told him about Melvin's problem with swearing, Ivory's torn-up voice, and Casey, Honey's lack of interest in her son, the house cluttered with newspapers, the obsessive truck-driving husband.

"Oh yeah. You talked about him."

He slipped his hand onto my shoulder and I liked the feel of it. "I still want to check the fire danger there."

I shook my head. "They aren't going to change. Besides, the mom's already mad at me for counseling her on why her son acts like a dog."

"Really? Like, he barks?

"And licks my legs."

"Smart dog."

I shot him a sharp look. "He's five."

"Kinda young, I guess. But still smart."

As we drove up the long hill toward the Bed & Breakfast, we both fell silent. He parked in front.

"Thanks for the ride."

"My pleasure." He turned to me. "I hope you're not embarrassed about what happened with the snake. I've seen men faint over less."

"Good to know."

"And don't think I have forgotten about our rain check." His hand dropped to mine and squeezed. "I haven't."

Why was he keeping this up? "You don't have to. I mean you're with Veronica. We'll just bump into each other, okay?"

"It seems I 'bump' into you in places like the middle of the road, or at the hospital after you've been attacked, or on the ground covered in sawdust near a snake pit." He smiled again. "Fun for me, but it's got to be wreaking havoc on you."

I laughed. "It *is* starting to add up."

Being so close to him, I couldn't think straight. "Okay, okay," I said, holding my hands up in surrender. "You've made your point. I've had a hard two weeks. Call me sometime." I reached for the door handle.

When he shot me a winning grin, I got all sweaty again.

"I'll get your door," he said, and walked around the front of the truck.

The headlights illuminated him and I studied his body. Hard, compact, and inviting.

He grabbed the door handle and pulled.

Snakes, wolves, Lawyer. All made me hot.

He walked me to the house. I fumbled the key into the lock under the porch light.

"One more question," I said after I had the door ajar. "Did you throw me over your shoulder to carry me to the ambulance?"

He shrugged, and a sparkle flashed in his toffee-colored eyes. "Is there any other way?"

He reached for my arm and pulled me toward him.

I fought his pull for a moment, then I met his eyes. They seemed full of need. I fell into his embrace, leaving the keys jangling behind. I'd been thinking about this moment for a while and it was better than I'd remembered. We pressed ourselves into each other, molded together like clay. I breathed in his scent, and as I lifted my face to pull away, he kissed me. His lips were soft and warm, his tongue quickly finding mine. I think I moaned.

We parted but not before I felt the hard press in his jeans. He kissed the top of my head and turned to leave. "If you want to experience the fireman's carry while you are conscious, just let me know." He was laughing as he walked away.

I stepped inside, relocked the front door and leaned against the wall to gather myself. My legs were weak and I couldn't think of another time when a kiss had affected me so much. Once in my room, I threw my clothes in the hamper, showered and changed into PJs. Even though the doors were all locked, the big house had a litany of sounds I'd never heard before. I was still jumpy from the snake incident, but the creaking and cracking noises and something scraping on the roof was unsettling.

I lay in bed, wide-eyed, willing my lids to close. After 20 minutes, I grabbed my pillow and a quilt and headed into the closet, closing the door behind. There was just enough room to stretch out on the carpet. I rolled up in the quilt and breathed in the soothing scents around me.

Moments later, I settled on thoughts of being in Lawyer's arms. My heart still pounded. He really turned me on, which I wasn't sure was good. He had a relationship with Veronica, yet he felt free to flirt and kiss me? I should have pressed him more about her when we were still driving, before he pressed himself against me. Now it would be the elephant in the room I'd have to poke a stick at to get an answer.

ANTIQUES

On Saturday morning, one of the guests asked who had put the forks in the bathroom sink and the towels in the library, and I knew Milt had gotten the dice out last night after he'd come home.

I walked to the old cemetery on the hill before the B&B came to life. Wandering among the 200-year-old headstones, I was content until noises in the bushes drove me back down the hill to the inn. I volunteered to drive a 60-year old couple from West Texas to several of the local art barns as they looked for antiques. Darius and Hannah Bergen, both retired educators, hadn't masked their disappointment when I explained I wasn't from the area. They wanted someone with local roots to answer all of their silly-ass questions like, "What's that weed growing along the road?" or "How much lumbering is done here each year?" or "Do the Amish buy their land in hectares or acres?" I deferred their questions, telling them Richard Pfoltz was the guy with the knowledge.

Our first stop was at Betty's Craft Barn on the outskirts of Rosefield. The barn was two stories high with a hayloft above. With its graying wooden exterior and double-sized roll-away barn door, it showed its age. Ancient tractors, a rusty windmill and a horse plow decorated the yard in front, exoskeletons of an era gone by.

Once inside the store, Hannah and Darius were drawn to the large fabric and homespun goods section. They had hopes of making handmade dolls in their second career selling "Yankee Doodle Darlings."

I left them "oooing" and "aaahing" by the pile of plaids, running their hands through the swaths as if it were a sensual experience. Maybe we had something in common after all.

I crossed through a kitchen display and went on to the next aisle. There were racks of long white nightgowns with ties at the throat in both women and men's styles. I held one up, and shook my head, wondering if men actually slept in these.

"It's not you," a voice said from behind me.

It was Lawyer, his eyebrows raised, a crooked smile pulling his mouth to the left.

His mouth! I wanted to get to it with my own. My heart instantly ramped up, as I thought about dropping him onto a rack of clothes and stripping him naked. What the hell was he doing here? And why did he look so fantastic in a pink golf shirt?

I said, "I'm buying some bells for you so you can't sneak up on people."

He smiled. "I only sneak up on you."

I nodded and circled my finger around the interior of the store. "One of your favorite places?"

"Not exactly," he said and then he looked over my head and past me. "Come meet my mother." He took my elbow and turned me around.

We approached an attractive woman, in her 60s, with dark brown hair held in a large silver clip. She was about five-foot five, and in great shape. I remembered the Pfoltzes had said Lawyer's father had died last year.

His mom stood in the birdhouse section, studying a tiny Victorian house with so many perches sticking out of the tiny doorways it looked like a hanging porcupine.

"Mom."

"Hi, honey." She didn't turn toward him, but she asked, "Is the blue on this roof a cornflower blue or more turquoise or teal?"

He glanced at the birdhouse. "It's the same blue as the chair cushions on your porch." He shrugged. "That's the best I've got." He touched her arm. "Mom, I want you to meet someone."

She turned and offered the same crooked smile I'd often seen on Lawyer's face. Her eyes, although the same toffee brown as her son's, were faded. Her vision was impaired.

"Mom, this is Marleigh Benning. Marleigh, this is my mother, Geneva Hunt."

I shook her hand, which she held out in front of her and waited for me to grasp. "It's nice to meet you, Mrs. Hunt."

"Genny. Just call me Genny." She clasped my hand with both of hers. "What a beautiful name."

"Thank you," I said. "I like yours, too."

"Marleigh is the new speech therapist working for Therapy on Wheels this summer."

He failed to mention he'd kissed the hell out of me 12 hours earlier.

Geneva seemed to ponder that for a second. "Oh, you work with Beryl Holmes. Lawyer's dad played poker with him for years, didn't he, son?"

"Yep, and they hunted a lot, too. Marleigh is the one who found Beryl unconscious last week, and called us."

"Well, thank goodness. Tell him we said 'hello.'" Her eyes were focused toward my face but her gaze floated just above my eyes.

"I will. He's home from the hospital and seems to be doing well."

"Great," Geneva said, plucking the birdhouse from the hook and handing it to her son. "I'm ready to go if you are, son."

"All ready." He accepted the wooden structure and took his mom's arm with his other hand. He turned to me, his eyes smoldering. "I'll give you a call."

I swallowed and nodded.

Genny said, "Please come by the house sometime."

"Thank you. I will."

He guided his mother through the aisles, and they laughed at something right before they disappeared from view.

Dammit. I had to give him points for being cute with her.

Darius and Hannah came through the checkout line, their arms full of prized "fat quarter" swaths of fabric. Hannah gushed about the colors: wheat, cream, mustard and green plaid, which looked like either a spring farm field or vomit.

We loaded our purchases in the trunk and headed home.

Darius tapped my shoulder. "I overheard something disquieting. A cashier she said there was a cop killer in the area. Is there?"

I defended my newly adopted home. "He's not a cop killer, just a thief, and he's been good at staying ahead of the law. There's a manhunt going on right now about 30 miles from here."

"So there's nothing to worry about?" Darius acted like I was in cahoots with Grady, playing Bonnie to his Clyde.

"In my job I drive all over this area and I'm not worried. Really, he's as good as caught by now." I felt better just saying the words because come Monday I wanted to get back to work.

"Uh huh," was all the man said, yet the tiny phrase conveyed complete distrust. Probably from my lack of knowledge about the damn weed along the road.

I said, "Oh. I remember the name of the weed you asked about. It's called Bosom Weed, or as the locals say, Tit Weed."

His eyebrows knit together. "Strange name."

I furthered the lie. "The explanation I heard was it only grows on hills, or mounds, so you know, 'bosom' came about."

They seemed really happy when I dropped them at the Bed & Breakfast, and they told the Pfoltzes I had been very knowledgeable.

I returned to the main highway to gas up the van. Tomorrow I would be dropping some river rafters and hikers off near Ansonia where they would spend the day in the Little Grand Canyon. Then in Wellsfield, I'd get the enlarged photo of The Dog.

Elyk

When I reached The Ash Country Store and Souvenirs, Elyk was helping an elderly woman load groceries into her giant yellow Cadillac. Her thinning lavender hair complemented the car nicely.

I parked by one of the two gas pumps, got out and waved to him. While the van filled, I studied Elyk. He wore dirty gray coveralls, but he'd tried to improve the outfit by tying a darker gray bandana around his neck, rendering a cross between a Texas chainsaw murderer and a train engineer.

He needs a personal shopper.

We finished our separate tasks and met inside the store. "How's the puzzle contest going? Day 14, right?"

"Yup. Dottie's stoked I'm still hanging in there."

"With a little help," I said.

He shrugged. "Very little." He started cutting open boxes and loading cans on a shelf behind him. The cans had a duck on the label.

"Liver pate?" Pate was one of those foods where one bite was one too many.

"Hell, no," he said. "This is a genuine French delicacy. Duck gizzards."

"Gross. Ducks live on insects. Essentially this delicacy is bug guts and grit, hardened inside a tiny stomach?"

"Sounds good, huh?" He smiled.

I changed the subject. "Would you let me take you clothes shopping? For Dottie's sake."

"Only if you let me take you snake hunting. For your sake."

"C'mon, those two activities are not at all alike." He was so frustrating.

"I know. Clothes shopping is hard work and torturous, while snake hunting is relaxing."

I laughed. "No, really. You need a new look if you want Dottie to stay around."

"She's not going anywhere." He looked down at his outfit. "I guess I could use a shirt or something. We can go after work one day and then you and I can head into the woods. Only way it's gonna happen."

I shrugged. "And Donny? What was he all about?"

Elyk moved on to canned spinach. "I heard he had changed for the better after getting the ankle monitor off." He rolled his shoulders.

"Monitoring? Like on parole?"

"Yeah. He had a few acres of weed growing in another county. Had a real green thumb, I heard."

"I could really have done without the embarrassment of passing out last night." I followed him along the aisle.

"You caught the attention of that cute fire chief, so stop your complaining. I hear all the local ladies been trying to get inside his suspenders."

"I caught *medical* attention."

He pointed to the shelf under the counter. "Help me with the puzzle and I'll tell you more about him."

Everything with him was a trade-off. I walked to the front of the store and found the crossword sheet with a ketchup stain.

Vixen was the clue for an eight-letter word, the first letters being "h-a-r." I saw Elyk had another sheet of lined paper underneath, this one with several dozen attempts at words, all crossed off. The word "hardness" was circled.

A vixen was a female fox. "Explain 'hardness,'" I said. I wanted to hear how these two words went together inside his porcupine head.

He shoved his hands in his pockets. "A vixen is like a female siren or a dick-tease. So you know, hardness would be something that happened from being around a vixen." I hesitated. "I see your reasoning." I turned back to the page and spun through letter combinations, but nothing jumped out. Elyk walked to the counter and leaned on the other side across from me. "I'm going to stick with 'hardness' if you can't think of anything."

I ignored him. I made phantom letters move in and out of the empty spaces, creating possibilities and failures. Then I had it. "It's 'harridan.'"

He scratched his butt with his thick fingers, the denim hiking up and down. "Oh, yeah," he said, writing in the letters.

"I guess you would have solved that one?" My smile was quickly evolving into a smirk.

"I'd have figured it out. I didn't have much time to think about it, you know." He folded the puzzle and slipped it into a mailing envelope.

I pointed to the lined paper with the word attempts. "Writing those would have taken an hour."

"I write fast." His tone said he had already dismissed the topic. Then he brightened. "I close early tomorrow. Let's clothes shop first, then I'll teach you to catch a snake. You could even make a little extra cash selling tails and skins this summer."

I shivered. "I'm pretty sure I'll survive without the extra money."

"Suit yourself."

A man got out of his truck in the parking lot so I used the moment to leave. "See you tomorrow, then." I'd probably cancel the hunting trip. I couldn't imagine going into the woods with him. Judgment wasn't one of his best qualities and I was afraid he'd teach me survival skills the hard way, like leaving me out in the middle of nowhere with a Q Tip and a match.

Closets

Returning to the Bed & Breakfast, I helped Rose make something called Pandora Fish on Farro Salad, a boiled whole grain, like couscous, with a mix of olives, garlic, tomatoes and basil.

It was Italian night according to the little menu she posted in the dining room.

The dinner was first rate, and accompanied by music from Il Divo, four hot tenors. The guests gathered on the patio as dusk settled in, to a serving of Italian ice cream and Tiramisu.

I found Milt in the tiny parlor off the entryway. A huge grandfather clock behind him ticked away, measuring our lives in seconds. Milt wore a light-blue plaid shirt, powder blue pants, and a black bowtie.

"You look handsome." I took the chair angled next to his. An end table between us held an expensive looking glass egg balanced on an ornate silver pedestal.

He turned to me but said nothing.

I expected nothing.

"You know," I said as I leaned in all conspiratorial. "I'm going to tell you a secret."

He stared, but there was no facial movement or flicker of interest.

"I knew you'd be intrigued. You see, I spent two weeks off-and-on in my closet back in March, trying to sort out some things in my life. Have you ever felt like hiding away?"

I waited. Something surely had happened in Milt's life making him as mute as a marshmallow.

"I rearranged my life in there. Literally. And here's what I learned. Sometimes you just have to face the bright ugliness of your life at the moment and move on."

I waited. "I'm still working through the pain, the loss, probably like you did when your wife died."

"Okay, change of subject. I have another problem. I've got a chance to go out with a fireman and a doctor. Now the doctor has a very kind bedside manner and adept hands, but the fireman kisses like he means it. What do you think? Go out with one, see where it goes? Date both, see where that goes?"

He didn't move. But he didn't look away either.

We sat quietly for a while, me smiling at him, his withered face staring back, his eyes sapphires in folds of skin.

I patted his hand and stood. "Back to the closet – and by the way, the one upstairs is quite comfortable – but, can you help me figure out this one clothing mystery? Why is the word bra singular and the word panties plural?" I patted his hand. "Think about it and get back to me."

I hoped he was laughing inside.

Lawyer

The phone chirped in the kitchen and I snagged it as I walked by since Rose was carrying a tray of dessert dishes. "Pfoltz Bed & Breakfast," I said.

"Did I catch you at a bad time?" It was Lawyer.

I recalled our kiss. "No, I'm fine."

"Good to hear it," he said.

A rustling sound came through the line as he shifted the phone to his other hand. "I called to say it's safe to go into the woods again. Not that I think *you* should ever go anywhere near the woods. But in general, it's safe."

"Hey," I replied. "I'm trying here. Why is it safe?"

"They caught the guy they call Grady in Maryland about an hour ago."

"Well, thank God." A shiver of relief ran up my back. "How do they know it was him? He seemed so evasive."

"He tried to steal from a rancher but the farm dogs cornered him. He was carrying newspaper stories about himself. They're still trying to determine his real identity."

"The missing policeman. Did they find him?"

"Oh, yeah. I thought you'd heard. He wandered into an auto repair shop about five miles from where he was last seen. Only wearing boxers, but he was fine."

"So, Mr. Boxer Shorts will confirm that the guy in Maryland is Grady?"

"No. The cop never saw what hit him. But obviously this is how Grady got away, dressed as a state policeman and all."

I thought of Melvin, and the person who had peered in their window. Could it have been Grady? And why would he be looking in windows instead of trying to get out of town?

I sighed. "I guess Troy's tip put people onto Grady fast. I just talked to him yesterday."

Lawyer paused, "Twittler had a tip?"

"Yeah. He found the rabbits at a campsite in the woods. And the magnets from my car. I'm not so sure he didn't take the magnets as revenge, but that's a different thing."

Lawyer was quiet.

"You still there?"

"Where did Troy say he found a camp?"

"In the forest near Blackout. He was pretty proud of himself."

More time ticked by.

"You okay?" I asked, not sure why he had gotten so quiet.

"Just thinking about what you said. I'm going to follow up with the police since Troy might have messed with a crime scene." He cleared his throat. "Hey, if you're free tonight, and would like to join me, I can show you something pretty cool."

Pretty cool, like him slowly undressing? "Okay. I'm intrigued. As long as we aren't going into the woods."

"Ah, hell no. I don't have a death wish." He laughed.

That hurt. Did he think of me as a bumbling fool? Then I recalled our times together and realized he'd only seen me after stupid incidents, which had been out of my control. "No death wish here either."

Lawyer and Marleigh

"These have been called the darkest skies in the nation," Lawyer said, looking up at the moonless night.

We'd driven to a quarry not far from Tungs and sat side-by-side on plastic chaise lounges in the bed of his truck. I was glad for the bottle of Russian River beer he handed me because it gave me something to hold. I was nervous but I couldn't pinpoint why. I blamed it on the darkness. He turned the flashlight off once we got settled into our chairs, a blanket draped across us. Night dropped in fast, the inky curtain coming down around us. "Kinda spooky," I whispered.

I felt him shift next to me. "You okay?"

"Well, I thought there were about 12 constellations, so, overwhelmed might be a better word." I was actually thinking about crawling on top of him but wasn't sure if the chairs would hold.

He draped his arm across the back of my chair. "Remember, the bad guy is behind bars."

"Good enough." I rested my head on his arm.

We were silent for awhile, each staring at the crystal sparks hanging overhead. I felt so small. Was anything I did important? Would it really matter in a 100 years if a few people spoke more clearly? Or swallowed faster? I knew one patient who could have done without my first visit; he'd still have a pet at home. Then I pictured little grubby Casey, his mom at her wits end, his dad a paper freak.

He needed me.

"What's going through your pretty little head?" Lawyer tipped his beer back.

"Just pondering the big picture and feeling insignificant."

"You'd never be insignificant." He squeezed my shoulder and pointed to the sky with his other hand. "I do like this perspective though. It's humbling."

"I can see where the 'humble' thing would take some doing on your part."

"That hurts," he said, and then chuckled. "I'll have you know, I cry during animal-rescue commercials."

"Uh-huh."

"I missed this when I lived near Philly." He squirmed a bit. "Hey, let me move my arm for a second." He pulled his arm away and adjusted the blanket over me.

"I can see why."

Then, he had the flashlight in his hand, flicked it on and swept it toward the tree line. Suddenly he drew in a sharp breath.

I jerked upright, my chair legs scraping the metal floor, and I squeaked. I dropped my beer in the bed of the truck and threw myself on top of him. "What is it?" I whispered, my eyes straining to see what was at the end of the anemic beam. All I discerned were dark brown tree trunks and deeper blackness behind them.

"Nothing. Just messing with you." He laughed and set the light down, then wrapped his arms tightly around me. "Oh. And trying to get you over here."

I grabbed my chest with one hand and collapsed on him. "I almost had a heart attack. You like doing that."

"I don't know why, but I really do." He laughed again. "I like doing this, too." He pulled me completely on top of him and raised his face to kiss me, long and soft at first, then more urgently.

I kissed the side of his neck, tasted his skin and then his mouth. Within seconds I'd forgotten about the darkness, about my bad week, about insignificance. My entire focus turned to the body under me: hot, hard and eager. We were both breathing fast and locked in a warm, long kiss.

He pushed his hand up under my shirt and cupped my breast. I drew in a sharp breath, never disengaging from what our mouths were doing.

When we pulled apart, our eyes met in the dim light from the flashlight on the floor. If my eyes were saying the same as his, then we were both surprised and ready for more of the same. I snuggled into his side with my head on his shoulder, breathing him in, as I tried to calm down.

"Next time," I said. "Skip the scare tactics and let's go straight to this instead."

"Deal." His hands still explored under my shirt. "Your amazing lingual skills cover kissing as well. I can see, or I should say, I can *feel* why you have a Master's degree."

I laughed. "Those are my undergraduate skills. You aren't ready for my advanced degrees."

He nodded comically. "Oh, I'm ready. I was a Boy Scout, an Eagle Scout, and now I'm a grown-up fireman. I can take anything."

I crawled on top of him again and he slid both of his hands into my jeans and squeezed my bottom. I responded by slowly grinding into him and dropping my mouth over his. The message was immediate and clear – we wanted each other.

I felt a vibration between my legs and for a second thought it was anatomical. When the vibration stopped and then started again, I rolled over and said, "You have a call." As he pulled his cell phone from his pocket, I added, "I like the feel of your ring tone."

He laughed as he touched the phone. He squinted at the text message. Then he closed the phone and let out a long sigh. "I have to go."

"Right now?"

His shoulders sagged. "I'm sorry."

"Sorry? You take me to the edge and then drive me home?" I rolled back to my chair and chucked the blanket at him. "Why not push me off a cliff?"

"I cannot tell you how difficult this is." He shook off the blanket. "Remember, I was there, on the same edge."

He straddled his lawn chair, then stood. He offered me his hand but I struggled up from the chair without his help. Was I being too harsh? He is the fire chief. Needed in emergencies. "Is it a fire?"

He wanted to lie; I heard it in his pause. "No. But something happened at home."

"Well, great. Let's get you home to your girlfriend and your little drama."

"Don't," he said, reaching for my hand.

I brushed him away and started packing. Disappointment marred my thoughts and I moved in a haze. I didn't want to feel this way. Jealous, all worked up, willing to tell him to go to hell, but already wanting to feel his body against mine again.

He drove out of the quarry and turned toward the Bed & Breakfast. His jaw clenched and unclenched as he pushed the truck along the dirt road.

I stared out the passenger window, sitting as close to the door as possible. My mood had soured and I should be relieved that we hadn't gone any further. But how to ignore our chemistry? It's not something you create – it either is there or it isn't. Couples either fit together or got frustrated trying.

"What are you doing with me when you are with Veronica?" I folded my arms. "Is this a game? See if you can get me all worked up and then, nothing happens? If it is, I'm not going to play."

He drew in a breath and turned toward me.

The dash lights highlighted his cheekbones, jaw and the hard set of his mouth. "Veronica and I used to date. The romantic stuff is in the past but we still have a strong connection."

"Undoubtedly."

"She's working through some things right now." We'd reached the long hill before the B&B. "I'll explain it when we have more time. And we've cooled off."

I snorted. "I don't need this. And the bucket of ice water you just threw on me – I'm cooled off enough."

He parked the truck and turned to me, "I want to see you again."

"I don't know. I'm pretty busy so I'm not promising anything." I jumped down from the cab, "I hope you and Veronica work things out." I slammed the door and jogged to the porch.

He revved the engine and left.

I stood looking at the sparkling night sky through two tall pine trees and thought about the evening. Voices floated on the crisp pine-scented air from the rear of the house where the company must be gathered. I settled into the porch swing and pushed it back and forth, my mind emptying itself of the images of us together, those blazingly good moments before his phone rang.

Closets

The front door opened and footsteps crossed the wooden porch.

"Marleigh?" Richard asked.

"Over here."

"Thought I saw a vehicle. You're back kind of soon." He approached my side of the porch and sat on the railing. "Didn't have a fight, did you?"

"He got a call."

"Happens when you're dating a fireman."

"We aren't dating. Just talking."

"Talking's good. Keeps the tongue strong."

I didn't need him mentioning tongues. I pushed away the feeling of Lawyer's mouth on mine.

"Rose has the victims, I mean the *guests*, playing games in Italian on the back porch. Want to join in?"

"I've got some writing I need to do, if it's okay." I stood and patted his arm. "I'll join them another time."

"Not a problem. And let me know if you see Milt. He's been wandering around and I can't find him."

Milt would come in second in a race with a glacier so I didn't know how it was possible to lose him.

I stopped in Richard's office, got on the Internet to look for stores in Wellsfield for my outing with Elyk the next day. I'd have one shot at getting him into a shop so I had to make it the right one. I wrote down the name and address of Bill Blythe's Big and Stout Shop. The name said it all.

Upstairs, I slipped inside my room and turned on the tiny light by my bedside. I shed my clothes and tossed them on the bed. They smelled like Lawyer. *I'd have to burn them.*

After slipping into my PJs, I sat in the rocking chair and stared out at the backyard. A soft halo of light from the back porch pushed out across the lawn and into the black velvet blanket of night. The crickets performed their nightly concert and a bullfrog randomly joined in with base vocals.

I didn't know much about Lawyer outside of the physical stuff. Now I wished I didn't know that.

A creak came from behind me and my head snapped around. The closet doorknob turned and the blood drained from my head. Grady, killers, dead bodies, all images of horror filled my head. I tried to call out but my voice wouldn't leave the safety of my throat. I sat frozen in place as the closet door opened.

Milt slowly stepped out.

"Oh, my gosh!" I said, as the wave of adrenaline broke.

He shuffled toward the bedroom door.

"Milt." I walked to him, peeking in the closet on my way. Nothing seemed out of place. "What were you doing?"

He reached the door, opened it and headed for the stairs.

I shook my head and locked the door. "What the hell," I muttered. I looked in the closet again and felt its pull. Now it smelled like old-man aftershave. I threw the Lawyer-fumed clothes from my bed into the hamper and closed the door.

This was a tiny success for Milt and me. He had processed my story about spending time in the closet and he'd been intrigued. He had become my main sounding board and had heard some of my fears, hopes. But was this really therapeutic for him, like I'd intended? I tell him a secret, but he tells me nothing in return?

I wasn't so sure. Maybe I was telling him my innermost thoughts because he was safe – a mute. I had to rethink my motivations.

Milt

Milt stared at me across the breakfast table and I smiled back. We'd bonded at some level. Both now out of the closet, so to speak. I cleared the dishes and loaded the washer while he was led to the front porch to do whatever it was he did all day. I'd agreed to help Rose and Richard so I dove into their list of chores. I would have done anything to distract me from thinking about broad shoulders and toffee-colored eyes and don't get me started on Lawyer's other warm, hard parts.

Parker called my cell phone at 10. He established I was feeling better before asking, "This is very last minute. But would you be free for dinner tonight?"

I had to take Elyk shopping mid-afternoon and he had to take me snake hunting after. "As long as it's around 8, I should be free."

He agreed to pick me up at the B&B. This felt like a revenge move on my part until I focused on the facts: Both handsome and appealing options, but the doctor was single and the fireman was not.

Errands

By noon, Richard waved the Texan couple away and sighed heavily after their car disappeared. "They were very strange. Kept talking about something called a tit weed. I had no idea what in Sam Hill they were yakking about. Any idea?"

I stifled a smile. "Nope."

Richard took the van, headed to Williamsport to load up on supplies and food. Rose was out in the backfields picking strawberries with the guests.

Lawyer called my cell, but I ignored it and regretted having given him the number. I couldn't think of anything to say to him except he needed to put his efforts into his "strong connection" with Veronica, and to stop calling me.

I phoned Elyk and confirmed I'd pick him up at 3:00 when he closed the store.

The phone rang, and since Milt and I were the only ones there, I answered it. It was Harvey, the policeman who had interviewed me at the hospital. After we exchanged pleasantries, he said, "We'd like to check those magnets on your car for fingerprints since it seems they might help us with finding whoever is messing with you."

I asked them if Troy's tip was correct and they said they were still investigating it but Lawyer Hunt had called and told them about the magnets coming and going.

"Will you be in Wellsfield anytime soon?" he asked. "We need to fingerprint you, too, to rule you out."

I told him I would meet him at the police station in a few hours. I initially felt angry at Lawyer for making the call, but knew he was doing what I should have done the second the magnets returned. This was probably why he had called me earlier.

I planned on a game of cards with Milt, but when I found him snoring on the front porch, I had to find something else to do.

I decided to drive to town and run a few of the errands then come back later for Elyk. I let Rose know I was leaving.

In Wellsfield, I walked to the copy store. "Your 8x10 print's there," the same pierced girl said, pointing to a large envelope.

"Thanks." I waved it in the air and left. Once I reached my car, I pulled the photo from the sleeve and there was Beryl's dog, big and happy in the center. Off to one side stood a man peering through binoculars.

Not at all what I had expected.

Originally I hoped someone would pick up The Dog and feed him. This man could be the farmer who owned the field. Beryl might be able to identify him; he knew a lot of the farmers.

Since I was so close to the police station, I followed Harvey's directions. I found the building at the edge of town surrounded by acres of close-cropped lawn. An American flag flapped in front of the white brick barracks.

The receptionist called Harvey's office and the policeman met me in the foyer a few minutes later. "You couldn't wait to see me, huh?" he flirted. "You're here earlier than you said."

I laughed. "I know. I'm stoked to get fingerprinted."

He carried a pair of blue latex gloves. "Pretty exciting when you're not a criminal, huh?" he said. Then continuing a conversation from earlier on the phone he asked, "Are you sure you won't get in trouble letting me have the magnets?"

"Keep them as long as you want. My patients know who I am now." *Hopefully I would never see these magnets again.* "If you have to, file them away as evidence."

He pointed toward the door. "Let's go round those rascals up."

When we reached the car, he gloved up and pulled them off, carrying one in each hand so they wouldn't stick together. We headed back inside. "Hold your breath. It's time to ink those fingers."

The fingerprinting was over in five minutes and I still had more time before I needed to pick up Elyk. I glanced at the envelope on the seat and knew what I would do with my free time.

Beryl

Beryl eyed me as I entered his kitchen. "You got a corn cob stuck sideways in your mouth? I don't think you could smile any bigger."

"Open it." I said and waved my hand toward the envelope. "C'mon. I went out of my way."

"Unless my dog's in here, you haven't gone out of your way *enough.*" We sat at his Formica kitchen table as he slid out the photo and studied it. He nodded and almost smiled.

Beryl hadn't seemed too surprised when I called to say I was on my way to his house on a Sunday, and he put out two iced teas and a plate of mint cookies by the time I arrived.

"Do you know this guy?" I pointed to the edge of the photo. The man was dressed in jeans and what looked like one of those greenish-tan hunter's shirts with a blend-into-the-forest pattern.

He leaned closer and adjusted his glasses. "I don't recognize him." Beryl squinted harder. "Course his face is almost covered by the binoculars and he's in the shade."

"Your dog looks good," I said. "I'm thinking this guy found him and is feeding him."

He pondered my words. "Then he stole him from *my* woods. The Dog was never adventurous and I can't imagine him covering 30 miles or so to this farm."

I hadn't thought of that. "The guy might have found him wandering around here after I chased him into the woods. He might be a good guy."

"Should have turned him over to the pound then," he snarled then studied me. "You're coming back tomorrow, right?"

He wanted to start working with me? Finally I'd won his confidence. I smiled. "Yes, does our usual time work?"

"Yup, it does." He tapped the photo. "Thanks for this. I'm going to call around and see who owns the farm. Then we can figure out where this bozo lives, and we'll go get my damn dog."

I smiled. I liked how he'd said "we."

Elyk

As I pulled into Elyk's store, I felt happy with what I accomplished today. Elyk and I agreed to meet at his workplace because he wanted to surprise Dottie later with his new clothes.

I drove to Wellsfield while Elyk told me how he'd met Dottie. "There was an article in the newspaper about her and how she'd won the State skeet-shooting contest. About three years ago."

The fact Dottie had persevered with this relationship despite Elyk's rough edges spoke volumes about her patience.

"So you just called her up?" I asked.

"Of course not. I started taking skeet lessons from her trainer."

"Aw. So romantic." I flicked his arm with the back of my hand. "You went through a lot of work to meet her."

"I did. The article said she'd had a tough childhood being a small person. You know the teasing and stuff. I related to that."

"You were *never* a small person," I said. "Who dared to tease you?"

He was quiet for a moment. "My mother. Ivory. But, you *cannot* tell her I said that. I can't have her screaming at me."

I felt sorry for him. Ivory was difficult but I thought her temper was mostly directed at non-family. "I won't say anything. Besides, she shouldn't be screaming at *anyone* with her torn-up voice."

He shook his head, puzzled. "You've said that before." He turned his hands up in front of him. "Her voice is perfectly fine. She's a singer, for God's sake. Why do you even go see her?"

I started to argue, then recalled my first visit to her house. The beautiful singing I had heard coming from the "radio." And the day she said she had the soap opera on or how easy it had been for her to do some of the exercises yet not be able to use a smoother voice. Now I was pissed. She'd been milking the Medicare system for months since Vicky had seen her, too.

Heat rushed to my neck at her dishonesty. All the tears about how she had scared her grandchild with her voice. I'd be talking to her on Tuesday for sure. "I can't discuss her. Patient confidentiality. But thanks for the tip."

I was saved from any further discussion when we pulled into Bill Blythe's Big & Stout Men's Shop.

At the entrance, Elyk grumbled about how much he hated this idea, but I pushed him through the door anyway. He let me pick out several casual polo shirts and two dress shirts, one a dark green and the other a blue-and-gray checked. He agreed to one pair of dark jeans with white over-stitching but there was no way he was buying dress slacks.

"I'll cut my legs off first."

I took that as a "no." He paid for the clothes and we returned to the car.

"You're welcome," I said.

"For what?" he grumbled.

"For your new look. When are you going to start wearing them?" I pulled away.

"I'm taking Dottie out Wednesday night. You want to come?"

"You don't need a third person. Where are you going?"

"There's this place in Marshall called Fifty Ways To Love your Liver."

The place Lawyer had almost taken me to. Now I really didn't want to go. "It's a bar, right?"

"No, it's the best food in a three-county area and very romantic. The building sits over a stream and the whole interior is like an English garden. You could ask Lawyer to come."

"We aren't speaking."

His eyebrows shot upward. "Since when?"

"Since about an hour ago when I refused to answer his call," I said. "I'm going out with Dr. York tonight. Do you know him?"

"Works the emergency room, faggot glasses?"

"Emergency room, yes. *Modern* glasses–not faggot glasses, seriously?! That's mean. Anyway, if we hit it off, I'll let you know about Wednesday."

As we neared Elyk's store, I tried to figure out how to get out of snake hunting. My insides quivered and I was getting a headache. I was dressed as he suggested and the jeans and tennis shoes felt hot.

"You don't want anything nipping at your ankles," he'd said.

I parked the car by his truck and said, "How about you just tell me how to set a snake trap and we'll call it good?"

"Hell no," he bellowed. "I put myself through torture in that store. Now it's your turn. And we're not setting traps, Daniel Boone. We're luring them out of hiding."

We entered his store and he set his shopping bags down. He grabbed a pair of knee-high rubber boots from a rack of hunting supplies. He held them out. "Size 8 is the smallest I have."

I could have argued that they were way too big, but I put them on and decided to go along with whatever he had planned. I learned about snakes at the Round-Up. They were shy and wouldn't strike unless they were cornered or attacked. I decided to make as much noise as possible once we started the hunt. Just because we went looking for snakes didn't mean we had to come back with any.

After ten minutes in the truck, he turned from the main road onto a dirt trail disappearing into the woods. The trees created a solid canopy over the narrow path as we bumped our way deeper into the green tunnel. My claustrophobia was coming back and a vein pulsed in my neck. Then the trail suddenly ended in a space large enough to turn a vehicle around.

"Perfect time of day," he said, pulling two long poles with snares at the end from the truck bed. He handed those to me as he reached back for a large tackle box and a tan canvas bag. "Snakes can't take the midday heat so they come out early morning and again in the early evening."

We pushed through the brush, with Elyk in the lead. I held my hands in front of me to keep the branches from slapping me in the face and because I carried the unruly poles. The wires at the ends snagged every stray limb if I didn't hold them just right. "How much farther do we have to go?" I shouted. The snakes needed to flee long before we ever reached them. "What's wrong with right here?"

"Not deep enough in the trees. They hate the sun so they'll be in a den or a log, someplace dark."

"Like your mind?" I said, only half-teasing. *He cuts up elk in their house.*

He stopped and turned, a wide grin on his face. "I could leave you here and then what would you do?"

I gulped. "Become one with the forest."

"Just remember good old Elyk gave you that advice."

I grabbed his muscled arm and squeezed. "I'm sorry. Onward to the snake holes is what I say."

"They're called dens," he snorted.

"'Den' let's get going."

He shook his head. "You can do better, Miss Fancy Words."

"I really can't," I said. "All the words have been scared out of my head." As we moved on, I hardly blinked, watching for anything slithering.

We followed a ridge and slowed down. My feet ached from trying to keep the boots on my feet while climbing over logs and smashing down bushes.

We reached a deer path and followed it for another few minutes. Elyk raised his hand and set the tackle box on the ground.

"What is it?" I asked, my voice inappropriately loud in the hushed cover of trees. The buzzing had disappeared.

He squinted at me, "I know what you're trying to do by shouting everything."

"I don't really want to see a snake. I passed out over a wooden one and I'm not sure I could handle a real one now." He had to understand where I was coming from. "We can even take your clothes back if you want."

"I like them, so, no, we aren't leaving until we have a couple of rattlers in the sack. And snakes are deaf, so yell all you want." He grinned.

I could have sworn snakes had ears.

He put on gloves and motioned for me to hand him a pole. Then he flipped open the lid of the tackle box and reached in and pulled out a squirming white mouse.

"Oh God," I said. "We have to chum it in?"

"Not 'we.' You stand still. Snakes don't need hearing because they pick up on vibrations and even though you're small, you move like a buffalo."

He walked toward a tangle of vines. In the center was a rotted tree whose trunk had broken in half. Elyk tied the mouse to the snare and held its wiggling body two feet in front of the hollow log laying horizontal in the vines.

"Get the bag ready," he said.

I picked up the canvas sack and walked a little closer to him. I held it open and felt a surge of panic. "Why don't *I* have gloves?"

"Poor planning on your part?" he asked. He moved the mouse closer to the dark opening and pulled it away. I felt sorry for the dangling rodent and was about to say so when the broad, triangular head of a rattlesnake shot from the opening and grabbed the mouse.

I screamed and jumped backward.

The snake devoured the mouse, but before it could retreat, Elyk grabbed the rattler behind its head and dragged its entire body from the tree. It writhed around his arm and thrashed back and forth in the air trying to get free. "I'd say it's a five-footer," he said. "Not too shabby."

I almost couldn't hear him over all the blood pulsing in my ears. Up until now I'd been pretty annoying; maybe it was time to cooperate. I held the bag open and walked toward him just to prove I was tough. "Okay. In it goes."

He stared at me and squinted. "You want to carry a live rattler out of here?"

"I thought that was the plan."

He pulled a knife from his leg sheath and slashed downward, severing the snake's head just in front of where he held it. The head dropped onto the ground, its mouth still opening and closing, the tongue flicking around before it finally stopped. The creepiest thing was the tail fought on much longer, even after Elyk dropped it into the sack.

I hyperventilated and made strange keening noises as I held the heavy bag, telling myself it couldn't hurt me. But that it continued to move after its decapitation was bothersome.

Elyk loaded up another mouse.

"Aren't we done?" I asked.

"I get $25 bucks a rattle and in case you didn't notice, the last one's noise maker was busted."

I hadn't noticed. A deaf snake with no rattle – the clan had probably pushed him out of the log as a sacrifice. "So how does that happen?"

"Smashed while crawling in a little space or something dropped on it." He dangled the bait in the exact same place as before. "The good news is he hasn't warned the others hiding in here."

"Others?"

"Oh, yeah. Could be a dozen or more."

The bag in my hands had stopped writhing and I studied the ground, wondering if some of the others weren't sneaking toward me to reclaim their headless relative.

Within ten minutes, Elyk had repeated the capture three more times until I could no longer lift the bag. The newest snakes were smaller than the first but their rattles were in great working condition. I had three separate bouts of chills.

He carried the bag and I grabbed the poles as we retraced our path to the truck. My legs wobbled as I removed the boots and put my sneakers back on, but I was pretty proud I hadn't fainted. One positive thing had come from today's adventure: The woods weren't as scary; there was a beauty I hadn't anticipated.

We reached the store and unloaded all of the hunting supplies. I let Elyk deal with the canvas sack.

"You want one of these tails as a souvenir?" Elyk asked, holding the bloody bag in front of me.

I shook my head. "I still have the one you gave me last week. One's enough, thanks." I had the rattle in my glove box with the mace from Richard. I was armed and probably dangerous, but most likely only to myself.

I crossed to my car and slipped behind the wheel. "Call me with any crossword puzzle issues, but I'm done hunting. Oh, and let me know what Dottie thinks about your new look." I had to start preparing for my date with the doctor!

DR. PARKER YORK

"Do you want dessert?" Parker asked. He wore a crisp white shirt and pressed khakis. He was on his third beer.

I was on my second martini, feeling the buzz, smiling too widely.

The restaurant had a lot of glass, chrome, and plants to break up the tables into quiet sections. The food was small portioned, rich, and presented as a work of art on the plates. I missed California.

"I can't." I patted my stomach. "Stuffed. It was very good."

I'd only thought of Lawyer a few times during the last two hours, and only to compare him to Parker. Parker was taller, but less broad-shouldered. His eyes were sky-blue, not toffee-brown. He had the kind of laugh making everyone want to join in, and he hadn't teased me about anything.

We moved through the mandatory review of our education; and how we each found ourselves in the Wellsfield area. We both had broken off a relationship before the move to Pennsylvania.

The night was ending with who had the most shocking story to tell.

"I removed a pitchfork from a guy's ass last week," he said. "The horse chucked him just as a grandkid was pitching hay."

He loved working the emergency room calls over having an established practice with hospital rounds.

My turn. "Well, I learned to hunt rattlesnakes today."

"You did not."

I nodded, laughing. "I did." I retold the details, embellishing them, of course.

When he smiled, his eyes crinkled perfectly at the edges. "I think you have me beat. I'm not much of a man in that category. I don't hunt things and I don't go in the woods."

I chuckled but something nagged at me. Something about earlier today. I pressed my lips together trying to force it to the surface, but the vodka veiled it.

"Let's walk," he said, as he paid the bill. Behind the restaurant ran a wide, placid river. We walked to the large deck, strung overhead with tiny white lights. We leaned on the wooden railing, watching the blue-black water move.

The stars lit the sky but I kept my eyes on Parker. After a few moments, he pulled me toward him and kissed me.

It was a terrible alignment. He bumped my lip with his teeth and I jerked backward. We both laughed and came together again. His mouth was open wide, and his lips were stretched thin, leaving me nothing soft to put my lips against. All I could visualize was Milt's mouth open wide, while he was sleeping, his head thrown back.

I pulled away, pretending I wanted a hug. He pulled me close. I pressed myself against him, trying to whip up feelings of lust and passion. He moved his hands up and down my back, but nothing was happening.

Then it hit me. This wasn't working because he felt like a brother or a colleague; definitely not someone I could get sexual with.

"I need to go," I said, the words tumbling out too quickly.

He pushed me to arms length and studied me. He wore his caring doctor's face. "Are you okay?"

What could I say? *I just got grossed out?* "My day has caught up with me." I faked a yawn. "And I've got to get ready for tomorrow."

On the drive back he talked about some of the fun things we could go see in the area. I agreed to nothing but nodded and smiled.

My buzz had worn off by the time he stood next to me under the porch light. A long hug and a quick kiss told me all I needed to know: we failed chemistry together. And he didn't seem to get it.

MILT

"Can I ask you about your father-in-law," I asked while Rose handed me dishes to dry. I arrived back at the B&B early enough to help with the evening's clean up.

"Milt's a complicated guy, isn't he?" she said. "What do you want to know?"

"When he stopped talking, was his wife still alive?" It would be easy to understand if he had quit talking the day she died.

"She died in a car crash coming back from Elmira. They still lived in their house at that point but he moved to the residential center soon after. He was very social for a few months, then he just stopped talking one day."

"Nothing else coincided with his refusal to speak?"

"No, we just thought he'd gotten tired of talking about losing Miriam. And about everything else, I guess. Do you think there's a bigger reason?"

I smiled. "The speech therapist in me thinks everyone should talk or there's something seriously wrong. But some people become mute because they have had a stroke in the motor-speech area and they can't form words. It's called total Apraxia."

She looked alarmed. "Should we take him to the doctor?"

"I don't think so. My feeling is he doesn't have anything like Apraxia, but I think he's on the verge of communicating again." I quickly told her about how he was puffing air that matched the number of dots on each die. I said, "Let me work with him some more."

The next day I found Milt in the parlor. He wore a red bow tie. It seemed significant.

"How was your day?" I asked, sitting in the other chair. I waited. And waited so long I felt my hair grow. I tried again. "I went rattlesnake hunting yesterday."

He turned his head to look at me.

"Right? Shocking, huh?"

He kept staring.

"It was really frightening and sometimes those things make me want to stop talking. Has that ever happened to you?"

Nothing.

"I also went out with Dr. York. It didn't go too well. He's a terrible kisser."

He stared.

"Do you want to play cards? I got paid a few days ago so I have money to lose." I crossed my legs and sat back in the chair and waited. He'd lost his wife so suddenly after six decades of being together.

"I'll bet you miss your wife." I wasn't sure if I should even bring this subject up but it just followed with the thoughts I'd been having. "I know you loved her lots and you probably told her often. You would have made sure of that, Milton Pfoltz."

I needed to get ready for work tomorrow. I stretched my arms over my head and started to say goodnight.

I looked over and tears bumped down Milt's craggy face and his lips quivered.

I was a horrible person! I leaned closer and grabbed his hand. "I am so sorry I brought your wife up."

He cried on, yet no sound came out. His eyes never left my face although he blinked the tears loose every few seconds.

I squeezed his hand. Had it been the part about missing his wife or when I said he had always told her he loved her? Maybe he needed to say it again. I had no idea where she was buried but driving him there would be worth trying to make him feel better.

"I'll be right back," I said, patting his hand. I found Rose in the pantry. "Where is your mother-in-law buried?"

She stopped stacking the plates and her eyebrows lifted. "She's in the old cemetery behind this place. Why?"

Should I tell her Milt had responded to something? "I have a hunch about Milt. I'm thinking he might talk to Miriam if we go visit."

She considered it. "We stopped taking him because it didn't seem like he wanted to go, but if you think it might help, then I guess it's okay. Can you get him into the car by yourself?"

"I can do it." I'd picked up a huge sack of grain recently; Milt couldn't weigh much more. I had already been to the cemetery so she explained how to find Miriam's plot.

When I came back, Milt had stopped crying but his face was still damp. He held a white handkerchief in his hand and stared at nothing in particular. I hoped I hadn't lost him.

"Milt. Why don't we take a drive to visit your wife?"

I expected him to remain seated as always but he surprised me. He raised his hand, and when I took it, he pulled himself out of the chair. I let him lean on me as I guided him toward the door. We trundled along and a few minutes later reached the front steps. I never saw him descend the steps but I knew he left the house, so he must be able to.

Ten minutes later he was belted in the front seat of my car and we passed through an iron gate at the entrance to the cemetery. The arch over the top of the gate had an intricate arabesque-like design welded into it. The cemetery was small, with no more than 50 headstones dotting the grassy areas. Tall trees sheltered the tombstones and a narrow gravel drive divided it down the middle.

I parked where Rose had said. "This is very pretty, Milt." I pushed my door open and walked around and opened his. He was a bony rag doll that I hefted to his feet.

We shuffled toward a large headstone with soft, green ivy up the sides, the fingers of the runners nearly reaching the angel on top. The dates of Miriam's birth and death were etched in the polished marble face, and Milt's name was next to hers.

We stood in front of the grave and I waited for any reaction from him. I hoped, but held no expectation that he would speak. If just being here brought him a bit of peace, it was enough.

A gentle breeze floated around us and the early evening shadows grew longer as the trees blocked the sun, darkening the area.

Tears formed in Milt's eyes and his lips twitched again. He whispered a word, shaking with the effort.

I wanted to whoop with joy. The man was talking for the first time in years and I thought he just said, "I."

I leaned closer. "Keep going. Pretend Miriam is standing right here. Speak to her. I anticipated what he might say next - *love you.* I steadied his trembling body with one hand under his elbow.

He turned to look at me and I smiled and nodded. "You can do it."

He took another step closer to the headstone and pointed a crooked finger toward his wife's name.

Tears pricked my eyes.

In a rusty voice trapped inside for far too long, Milt said, "I…hate…you."

"What?" I couldn't have been more surprised than if Miriam had stuck her arm up through the dirt and given him the finger. "Milt!"

He turned and shuffled toward the car. I heard him say the same three words again under his breath. "I hate you."

What the hell had I done?

Later in the evening, after all of the new guests had gone to bed, I prepared my books and therapy supplies for the next day. Exhaustion played with my focus. I was tired for a lot of reasons, the main one was I think I ruined Rose and Richard's entire vision of Milt and Miriam's 66-year marriage.

It wasn't bad enough that he had muttered, "I hate you" all the way back to the B&B, but then he wandered from room to room moving things around in front of the bewildered guests, saying those same three words to them. He dropped two containers of unopened Comet onto one person's lap and took *People* magazine out of her hand and traded it for a small banker's lamp. Richard cornered him and made him drink a shot of something to get him into bed and asleep.

The bright spot in all of this was he hadn't needed dice this time to speak. By the shocked look on my hosts' faces, it wasn't going to matter much if "I hate you" was all he said until summer's end.

I ignored another call from Lawyer. But to be fair, I didn't take the one from Parker either.

Luella and Margritte

I called Luella's house. Margritte answered and confirmed that her sister was home from the hospital. "And Marleigh," Margritte said loudly, so Luella would overhear, "You're gonna have to yell at Luella. She admitted she was cheating and drinking stuff with no thickener in it."

Luella responded in the background and within a few seconds they were fighting, sounding like their indoor pets going at each other.

"Hey, hey," I interjected. "I'll just wait to get the story when I see you."

They stopped squabbling, then Luella shouted, "Tell her we have more chickens to sell."

I was not taking any more chickens to market.

I had an hour before I needed to leave so I went looking for Milt. Rose said he was still sleeping.

"I'm sorry about what happened last night," I said. "I hope you and Richard can forgive me for prying into Milt's life. I truly thought I was being helpful."

Rose nodded and smiled. "Whatever comes of this, it's better than him not being able to say what he wants."

I sagged in relief, "Thank you."

Richard entered the kitchen, catching the end of our conversation. He dropped a hand on my shoulder. "At least you tried. We gave up on him. We should be offering the apologies." He sighed, "Anyway, different thought, the Wellsfield police called. And guess what?"

"They matched the prints to Grady?" I asked. That would have been the fastest turn-around ever on fingerprints. Then, the thought that I was forgetting something came back to pester me again.

"No. They caught Troy Twittler." Richard had a huge grin on his face. "His prints were all over your magnets."

"Oh, geez. I should have told the police. Of course, Troy's fingerprints would be there because he brought them back to me."

Richard shook his head, "His were the *only* prints there except for yours. And when they grilled him about the cabin he'd discovered, he cracked and admitted he took the magnets, the rabbits and hadn't found any hideaway."

What an idiot. No wonder he paled the day I told him a state trooper was missing. "Will he go to jail?"

Richard scratched his head. "He'll lose his job as dog catcher for sure but I guess they'll have to decide if he broke any laws outside of stealing magnets and rabbits. He did bring them back."

I thought for a moment. "So this whole scare and manhunt for Grady was kicked into gear when Troy took the rabbits?"

"Apparently. And the cost of the two-day search could go against Troy, which will not be pretty for him."

The solution didn't feel right. I asked, "Let me get this straight. Grady was a few counties over but went to Maryland where he was captured a few days ago. Troy made it look like Grady was actually closer to Blackout than he really was."

"Yup," Richard said.

My eyebrows bunched together. "But a state trooper was kidnapped? Was it really Troy?"

Richard answered, "Don't know yet. Troy's not talking and neither is the guy in Maryland."

"Why would Troy take my magnets?" I could see his reasoning with the rabbits; he'd be the hero once he *found* them, but taking stupid pieces of plastic?

"He was messing with you. He hasn't recovered from the tongue-twister episode."

"Could he have beaten me up for my purse? I mean, he could have gotten a military uniform. I never saw the mugger's face except for his reflection in the car window."

Richard said, "You know. I wouldn't put it past him. Did the guy who hurt you seem to be about Troy's height?"

"Actually, he did. And he whispered, so I couldn't tell you if it was Troy." I shivered. The voice saying "gladly" still had not gone from my mind.

Then the thing which had been bugging me bubbled to the surface. I snapped my fingers. "Would Beryl Holmes know Troy?"

"Probably not," Rose said. "Two towns away. Huge difference in age. Why?"

"Remember the picture I took of Beryl's dog on the farm? I had it blown up and there's a guy standing in the woods with binoculars. We couldn't see his face. I mean, what if Troy found The Dog right away and then was using him to mess with me? To make me look bad?"

Richard said, "I'd recognize Troy. Let me see the photo."

"I dropped it off at Beryl's. But I can get another from the copy store in town."

Richard nodded. "I'll have the sheriff's department request it. You might just be onto something. Troy might have been into all kinds of things."

I told him to let the police know they could call me with questions. I packed my therapy things and headed out, still shocked at how far Troy had disintegrated.

Melvin and Sandy

Sandy let me in. The blotches on her face showed she'd been crying.

"What's happened?" I asked. I didn't see Melvin in either the kitchen or the living room.

Sandy sighed, "It's just me. I didn't sleep well. He wandered the house, talking all night."

There was no money in the Medicare system for respite care, but it was exactly what Sandy needed. "Why don't you lie down for a few minutes?" I said.

She nodded and left as Melvin came up behind me.

"Christ Almightly," he said quietly, and then he put his finger to his lips, indicating we should be quiet. "Asinine cesspool bastard," he added, motioning me through the living room.

I nodded, mainly because I wanted him to stop swearing.

We reached the den and he grabbed the word board and started pointing. Need-Sleep-Tired-and-Sick.

"Very nice, Melvin. And your gesture telling me to tiptoe through the room was the right one." I grinned. "I'm impressed."

He touched the words, Thank-You.

"Today we're going to work on repeating phrases. It was really hard the first time I was here but now I think you're ready. I'm going to point to a word then I'll say it a few times slowly. I want you to say it with me, at the same time. Okay?"

"Dammit to hell," he said, nodding.

I chose the words Thank you since they were almost always automatic in a person's vocabulary. I said the words slowly stretching them out, "Thaaank-yooou, thaaank-yooou." I motioned for him to join in. "Thaaank-yooou."

"Thaaank-yooou," he said along with me and I grinned.

"You did it, Melvin. Say it again. I'll start. Thaaa..." I dropped out to see if he could finish it without my cuing.

"Thank-yooou," he said, and we both smiled. Progress. He was now getting feedback on his own speech, whereas two weeks ago, he had no idea what he was saying.

"Let's try Happy Birthday." I dragged the words out, "Haaappy-biiirthdaaay, haaappy-biiirthdaaay."

"Happy-birthday," he said. Then he stopped a second, scrunched up his forehead. Without saying anything he began humming the melody to Happy Birthday.

I added the words and sang along with his tune.

He joined in, singing along with me, "Happy birthday, Dear Sandy, happy birthday to you."

I wanted to shake Sandy awake so she could be a part of this. His first steps back to acceptable language for society. I felt like a proud parent watching my stumbling toddler run for the first time.

Melvin must have realized the extent of this breakthrough because he slapped his leg and exclaimed, "Hot whores alive!"

"Exactly!" I agreed.

We spent the rest of our time quietly singing popular tunes together. Most times he followed along and had the words correct but on a few other songs, like "When you wish upon a Star," I realized he probably had not known the words in the first place as he sang, "Makes no distance beer or bar."

I laughed and shook my head. "Okay, not that song." I caught a movement in the doorway where Sandy leaned against the frame, wiping tears from her cheeks. "I haven't heard him sing for months."

"I know," I said. "We stumbled on the singing idea purely by accident. And I think, just maybe, he can say a few words." I turned to Melvin. "I'll start. Let's say Thank you again. Thaaaank–"

"Thaaaank-yoooou aaagain," Melvin said.

Sandy and I broke into laughter and Melvin, not completely aware of what he'd said, offered a confused smile.

Sandy rubbed Melvin's shoulders. "We're gonna have to put you in the church choir, my dear."

I collected my things to leave. "Just don't let him offer any prayers."

"Goodness, no," Sandy said.

"Keep him singing until I get back in a few days. It will be the best practice he can get." I started to leave and remembered. "Did you know they caught the fugitive in Maryland?" I didn't want to add anything about Troy's escapades since it wasn't public knowledge.

"We heard it on TV." She patted Melvin's head. "He was upset the whole night and checked the locks a thousand times before we went to bed."

"Shit on a shingle," Melvin said, agreeably.

"Thanks for telling us," Sandy said, while walking me to the door. "It's a relief to everyone in town."

"Probably everyone in the state," I said then excused myself.

I quickly wrote out the notes on Melvin's session, realizing how far he had come in these weeks. Maybe he would be able to give the opening prayer at church before summer's end.

I munched on a granola bar as I headed the 15 miles to Luella's house. I was thinking about her new round of pneumonia. Maybe this stint in the hospital had scared her enough so she would start following the no-thin-liquids rules.

Luella and Margritte

"Whiskey!" I said to Luella, whose face held a sheepish grin. The woman was perched in a rocking chair with a black chicken sleeping beside her feet. "You've been drinking Jack Daniels?"

"*Sipping*. You all make me sound like a lush by saying the word 'drinking.'" She was on the defense.

"You must have been belting back whiskey every day," Margritte chided. "Which makes you a drinker just like our no-good brother. And you knew what you were getting into," she added. "All you had to do was look at daddy and see what Reggie was gonna turn out like."

"Our daddy didn't drink," Luella said.

I intervened. "Ladies, ladies. I'm thinking the past should just remain there, okay?"

They probably had been arguing all weekend about this since they both seemed pretty fed up with the other. Something about their argument set off a tiny alarm in my head but since I was still processing everything I had learned about Troy, I blamed it on that.

I said, "Enough, ladies. Let's get some swallowing practice in and see how you're doing. Luella, give me two dry swallows in a row."

Luella managed one clean, strong swallow. Her mouth quivered and went through several contortions as she tried to initiate another one, but the second swallow didn't go. "I can't get it," she said, exasperated. "The FBI should use this when they torture people."

"I'm not sure they are into torture," I said and then I regretted saying it. "And as far as a second swallow, Luella, the strength will come back quickly if you practice every hour for five minutes. Like you were doing before you went into the hospital."

Margritte jumped in. "She wasn't practicing much around all that drinking."

"Hush your mouth," Luella snapped. "I was managing both, thank you very much."

Margritte marched out the front door, which was fine with me. The chickens were enough to deal with and this bickering was more than I could take.

Luella and I continued running through the other swallowing exercises, especially those facilitating a strong cough. In case something ever got stuck in her trachea, she'd have a good chance of clearing it. She did better on these.

"This isn't forever, you know," I said. "You only need to practice for a few weeks, then you'll be able to drink anything you want."

"I get it this time," she said and tapped her chest. "No more pneumonia."

"Good." I packed my things and said goodbye, confident this stay in the hospital had scared her straight.

When I reached my vehicle, Margritte was standing by the rear door, her vibrant-green stretch pants reflecting onto the side of my car.

I didn't see the anticipated cage of chickens. "Thanks for helping your sister," I said, cautiously opening the back door of my car to put my therapy bag in. *No chickens there.*

"It's what family's for," she said.

At that moment something from their earlier conversation hit me. The thing seemingly wrong. I replayed the conversation.

"*You're belting back that whiskey every day, girl,*" *Margritte had said.* "*Which makes you a drinker just like our no-good brother. All you had to do was look at daddy and see what Reggie was gonna turn out like.*"

"*Our daddy didn't drink–*"

That was it. "Our." On my second visit Margritte had said, "*You married that good for nothing brother of mine after I warned you away.*"

Oh, my God. Luella had married her brother; *their* brother. Burt at the Gas-N-Guzzle had alluded to the sisters trusting me with their secret, but I hadn't caught on to what he meant.

"You having a stroke or something?" Margritte added.

"What?" I focused on her mouth, unable to meet her gaze.

"Your face was saying you were somewheres else."

"Oh, I was somewhere else, alright." *On the road paved with years of inbreeding.* Richard had said incest was rampant in some parts of these counties, but I hadn't given it a second thought. A weird tingle ran up my spine. I'm pretty sure it was revulsion. "Gotta go. I'll see you soon."

"We were going to give you more chickens but I realized we were taking advantage of you. I put a dozen eggs in your trunk as a thank you for understanding two old, crazy gals like us."

Even though she got the crazy part right, I was touched. "Thank you, Margritte. You're so nice." I popped the trunk and there was a clear-plastic carton with large brown eggs resting inside their half-oval seats.

"I'll put them up front where I don't need to worry about them falling over. Plus the air conditioning will keep them cool." I placed them on the passenger side floor.

"Don't worry about eggs in the heat. They sit in nests for days and don't go bad."

"Good point," I said.

"One of those old wives tales," she said and smiled.

Like the one about marrying your brother is genetically a bad idea?

It would take me awhile to recover from this new detail, but at least they hadn't had children.

I paused. Margritte had said the chickens were their only source of income. "Are you sure I can't pay you for the eggs?"

"Well, if you've got $2.50, it would cover the cost of the carton."

"I'll just bring the carton back," I said.

She waved her hand through the air dismissing the idea. "Naw, we don't recycle them. We'll just take the money." She stuck her hand out and waited.

What a con artist. Put her on a corner in San Francisco with a puppy on a leash, she'd be hauling in $400 bucks a day. I dug three dollars from my wallet and handed them to her. "I don't need change."

"Thank you, Marleigh." She folded the bills and tucked them down her shirt into the left cup of her DDs. "Like I said, we sure do appreciate you." She turned and left.

I shook my head and slid behind the wheel. Next stop: Beryl's. If he learned who owned the farm and it helped us find The Dog, that would make my day. I wanted to see the picture again. I drove toward Milepost, thinking of Troy. What was he thinking, imitating the criminal everyone in the world was searching for? I replayed the mugging, and the more I thought about it, the more I knew it was Troy. He almost got me to quit my job. Almost.

I called Richard and asked if Troy had confessed to anything yet.

He laughed, "Last I heard, they put his mother in the cell to get him to talk. Shouldn't take long now. She's a scary woman."

I agreed and said I'd be home by dinner.

Beryl

At Beryl's, I sagged with disappointment as I read the note he had taped to his door:

"Found out who owns the place. I'm off to leave a message at the barn with both of our phone numbers. Be back soon. If you write a note for Medicare suggesting I'm not homebound, I will fire you. Again."

I chuckled.

I waited in the car and ran the A/C intermittently since I didn't believe in Margritte's theory that heat was okay for eggs.

I didn't know how Beryl was traveling to the field and back. He had no car. Maybe a friend had driven him. Then I remembered the heap of parts he was trying to build into a Segway! On my last visit, it was still strewn across his newspaper-covered couch. Curious, I decided to see how far he had gotten in building the machine.

From the front step I could lean across to the window and peek through the cracks in the blinds. I stretched and grabbed hold of the green shutter nailed to the side of the window, balancing precariously while I leaned my face to the glass. The reflection of the sun forced me to lift a hand to shade my view.

I was able to pick out the carpet and then the coffee table. The couch was just a bit higher. I stretched a few more inches and suddenly lost my balance, scraping down the side of the house and crashing into Euonymus bushes.

But not before I saw that the Segway was gone.

I panicked. Beryl had traveled, or tried to travel, 25 miles to the field where I'd seen the dog. The roads were full of dangerous curves, blind hilltops and huge trucks going far too fast for a guy putting along on an under-powered Segway. I had no cell phone number for him. His note said he'd be back, but a half an hour had passed and I had to do something.

He'd kill me if I sent the police looking for him, so I drove the route he would have taken. I covered a lot of ground in a few minutes, and at each hilltop, I hoped to find him buzzing his way back.

My phone rang. I checked the ID to see who it was. I didn't recognize the number but it was a local area code. I brightened. It could be the guy who found Beryl's note.

"Hello?" I said, trying to keep the car on the road.

"Is this a good time?" a man asked, although the static on the line made it hard to hear him.

"Oh, yes," I answered quickly, telling myself to calm down. This had to be the farmer. "Thanks for calling." I didn't want to scare him away so I continued talking in an upbeat tone. "I'm glad you got the note."

"Uh, okay," he said. The phone crackled again.

"And I hope you understand about The Dog and why I want to get him back."

"I do."

Then the voice kind of sounded familiar.

I said, "So. Can we meet in the field or should I come to your house? Let's make this convenient for you."

"Okaaay."

I felt such relief! I was so close to recovering The Dog.

Then laughter burst through the phone. "What the hell are you proposing, Marleigh?"

Shit! It was Lawyer. "What? Lawyer? Is that you? I thought you were someone else."

"Of course you did because you're not answering my calls," to which he then quickly continued, "Interesting proposition: the convenience of a field or a house? Earthy, but sexy," he said and laughed again.

"Long story about The Dog."

"Did you find him?" he asked, surprised.

I gloated. "Well, not yet, but Beryl contacted the owner of the field where I saw The Dog. He left my phone number so I thought this was him calling."

"What makes you think the property owner knows Beryl's dog was even there?"

"I showed you the picture."

"The Dog was a tiny dot in a photo."

"I had it enlarged." My irritation grew. "There was a man standing at the edge of the trees, watching…um…" I didn't tell him the guy had binoculars on me. Lawyer was so paranoid, and not that I hadn't given him good reason to be so.

"Watching what?" he asked, his voice edgy.

"Watching the dog," I said. "Jumping and playing."

"Uh-huh."

I wasn't in the mood to talk to him and I wouldn't have even answered if I'd recognized the number. "Whose phone are you calling from?"

"The fire station. Can we talk about why you're not answering my calls?"

I let a few moments tick by. I didn't see how talking would change our situation.

"Marleigh? I want to explain why Veronica is here. And I have a lead on your birth parents."

And just like that he hooked me again.

"I'm a bit preoccupied right now. I'm working with Beryl so let me get back to you." I steered around a dead raccoon, keeping my eyes on the long stretch of road ahead of me, hoping to see an upright wheelie contraption.

Nothing.

"Okay," he said, in an overly patient voice. "Promise me you won't go into any stranger's home to get the dog. Make him meet you in a public place."

"I'll definitely keep it in mind," I said. *Another damn good idea from this guy.* "Oh, maybe we should double date sometime. Parker and I, and you two."

"You went out with Parker?"

"I did. Bye, Lawyer," I said and hung up.

He rang back but I ignored it. The phone *binked,* indicating he'd left a message. I'd get it later. I had a patient and his dog on the run.

The Purse

Twenty minutes later I headed back to Tungs, exasperated and driving too fast. I had not found Beryl and he hadn't returned home. A second later, a rock came cascading down a hillside nearly hitting my car. But I whipped the car around it and my purse cart-wheeled to the floor, spilling its contents.

"Great! Just Great!" I screamed and pulled off the road. I reached for the pile on the carpet and raked the items toward the mouth of the purse. One end of my special plastic tampon holder popped open. I waited for my two emergency tampons to fall out but instead a colorful square of paper poked out.

Strange. I tried to remember when I had emptied the case.

The slip of paper was a cute sticky note, like a teacher would put on a child's paper, with a large, red, handwritten A+ in the center of a green apple.

My heart pounded and my vision warped. *Grady had taken my purse?*

A Run

Thirty minutes later I was back at the B&B. I wanted to show Richard the grade card but he'd just left with guests, headed to the Lumber Museum. Milt napped on the front porch swing. Rose said he'd stopped talking altogether, which was kind of good and bad.

A brief rain shower had moved through and I breathed in the scent of wet dirt and grass. I decided to go for a run. I was pretty tense.

I was still a mess worrying about Beryl. I would try his home phone later, and if he didn't answer by dark, I would get help. Probably not the police, but Lawyer could check on him as an old family friend and it wouldn't seem strange.

The road was still wet so I avoided the puddles. The smell of skunk floated on the breeze and birds squabbled somewhere in the trees overhead. I'd have to thank Elyk for making the woods less ominous. I would never go in there again because it was crawling with snakes, but now I didn't have a heart attack every time a tree branch moved.

Elyk was slicing deli meat at the back counter when I arrived at the store. "Give me a minute."

I stood off to the side until the family left.

"Look," Elyk said. He showed me the rattler tails he had on display from "our" snakes.

"Nice," I said. I pointed to his shirt. "I thought you were waiting until your date this week for your new clothes."

"Dottie found them when I was unloading the snakes."

"And?"

I think he blushed. "She said they were okay."

I laughed. "You mean she loved them?"

"Maybe." He busied himself with washing the front window with spray cleaner and a rag.

It was all the thank you I was going to get. "Need any help with today's puzzle?"

He pulled the sheet of paper out from below the counter, along with another scratch pad covered with crossed-out words. "It's hard," he said. "I'm having trouble solving this one."

I read the clues. He needed an eight-letter word meaning, "A south of the border musical instrument."

"_ e r _ _ _a u?" I said aloud.

"Yup," he said. "I had to put it away. It was pissing me off."

"Give me a second." I spun through letter patterns that might make sense with an ending of "au" - but got nothing. Then I started at the beginning of the word and ran through the alphabet, putting letters in and taking them out. Still nothing.

"This *is* hard. When is it due?"

"Tomorrow, five PM. But I can't cut it that close."

I tried a few more letters and gave up. "I'll work on it tonight and call you if I get something."

He frowned. "You mean 'when' you get something?"

A car pulled up to the gas pump so I walked outside with him. "Right. *When.*" I said goodbye and headed back to the B&B.

I pushed myself on the return run, trying to hold a full sprint all the way to the top of the hill. I was still puffing when I walked through the front door. I wandered around the B&B looking for Milt, wanting to see if I could get him to talk. I worried again I'd done something destructive by taking him to his wife's grave. It had felt right at the time. Apparently no one knew his true feelings about Miriam until my actions ripped open his wound.

He wasn't in his usual haunts. Rose or Richard must have been keeping a close eye on him. I'd find him later but for now I needed to shower and change before dinner.

Once in my room I pulled clean clothes from the dresser drawers and started for the closet when I stopped short. The door had been closed this morning but now it was open a crack. I had the key to my bedroom so no guests could have entered. Milt?

I yanked the door open but no one was inside. Nothing was out of place. The clothes still hung from their hangers, with my shoes lined up below the hems. I turned to go but I heard something, a humming. As I looked more closely, I noticed a pair of old geezer shoes next to my black leather sandals. From there I followed the powder-blue pant legs upward, as they disappeared into the clothes.

Milt was standing with his back against the wall, mumbling something.

I walked in and separated the hangers so I faced him. He stared back at me, squinting against the outside light. His face showed no surprise.

There was so much I could have said. I could have made a joke about him just "hanging out," could have chastised him for invading my room. Instead I stepped inside and closed the closet door, rendering the small area almost completely black. I felt my way into the line of clothes until I was leaning against the wall, next to him, our shoulders touching.

Minutes passed. Since closets always calmed me, I didn't mind. Some things in life were a huge waste of time, but these moments were not among them.

"So, Milt," I said quietly. "This whole hating your wife thing? Quite a shocker."

He murmured something.

"Say it again?" I asked. I leaned toward him as the hangers scraped along the metal bar.

He whispered, "I hate you."

I needed to move him beyond this phrase. I was no psychologist but it seemed like if he could list the reasons for such a strong feeling, he could move on.

"Why, Milt? Finish the sentence."

"I hate you," he said.

Starting the thought for him, I said, "I hate you because..."

He whispered, "I hate you for..."

"Good. Keep going. Hate you for..." I had no idea what to expect. *Had she had an affair at 80? Hidden his money? Tried to poison him?* All highly unlikely since Milt and Miriam were still lovey-dovey before she died. I reached for his hand and gently squeezed. "Go on."

When the sentence came out, it did so in one long burp. "I hate you for leaving."

Tears rushed to my eyes. He was just desperately lonely, not filled with anger.

He said it again.

I tightened my grasp on his hand. "Keep talking, Milt. Get it out."

We stood in the darkness for five minutes longer while he repeated the phrase 30 more times, each time getting easier.

I fumbled the two steps to the door and eased it open. I parted the shirts and looked at him. "You ready to come downstairs and tell your kids?"

Milt shuffled out and we slowly made our way to the kitchen where Rose was chopping cabbage.

I had a huge grin on my face. "Is Richard here?"

"Just outside," she said, her eyebrows rising.

I walked to the back porch where Richard was unpacking a giant chess set. "Could you come into the kitchen for just a minute?"

He looked concerned. "Sure. What's up?"

"You'll see."

Once I had the two of them standing side by side, I looked at Milt. "Okay. Tell these kids what's on your mind."

He stared back at me but said nothing.

Don't do this, I silently begged.

We waited.

I finally said, "I hate you for–"

Rose groaned.

I held my hand up, *give us a moment.* I grabbed his other hand and squeezed, as if he was a stuffed animal you had to pinch to make a noise. This time it worked.

He said, "I hate you for leaving."

Three seconds of stunned silence turned to tears and hugs. I left the three of them huddled together as I headed back to my room. I smiled, contemplating the possibility of starting a closet-therapy program. It had worked once, so it only stood to reason there might be a market for it. It was nonsense, but I lingered on the idea anyway.

Dinner was a happy affair although Milt stopped talking again. He stared at me through the entire meal. I smiled at him and hoped this meant we would have more talks soon, in or out of the closet. After I helped clear the dishes, I retreated to the office to call Beryl. It was dusk and I prayed he was home.

He picked up on the ninth ring, just as I was about to hang up.

"Oh, my God!" I snapped. "Where have you been?"

"Nowhere," he said abruptly, with more gruffness than usual.

"Did you get The Dog?"

"I did." Now he sounded like he was holding the phone away from his mouth, distracted, as if this call wasn't important.

"Are you going to tell me what happened?" I couldn't believe I had to coax this out of him. He knew I'd been going crazy looking for his dog.

There was a pause, and then he said, "I don't want you to come by anymore."

"What? I haven't even started therapy with you yet." I was going to be in big trouble for this, but more importantly, I liked him. "We can start fresh now that you have your dog, can't we?" I was pleading but I couldn't help it.

"Don't make me shoot you," he said, then abruptly hung up.

I sat back in the office chair, stunned. *What made him change his mind? We were working toward the same solution and then, just like that, he fires me?*

My earlier elation over Milt was gone. Gloomy and mad, I might need to retreat to the closet for a little emotional repair of my own. One thing I knew for sure, I was *not* going to stop seeing Beryl. Even though his house was out of the way from my other patients tomorrow, I would drop in to talk to him.

Dottie called as I was getting into bed. She thanked me for taking Elyk shopping. I told her I was glad to do it.

She asked, "Do you want to come to the drive-in with us this weekend?"

I had no date, and a drive-in seemed very much a couple thing to do. "Let's talk about it as we get closer to the weekend, okay?"

"Okay. And I have some nice new lipstick colors if you want to come try them out."

I wasn't exactly a lipstick gal but I couldn't keep shunning her offers. I said, "I'll do that," before we hung up.

I was too keyed-up about Beryl to be tired, so I listened to the message Lawyer left.

It was long. "This is *not* how I wanted to have this conversation," he started. "Veronica gets panic attacks. For some reason, I'm the one person who can talk her down. I knew her when I was teaching in Philadelphia. When my dad died, I moved back to take care of my mom and I invited her to come as well."

I didn't know she currently lived with Lawyer. Another minus. "She's here to help watch mom and she sees a counselor in Elmira. It's as simple as that. I'd really like to…"

The message time ran out.

Did I wish the sentence had ended with "spend more time with you?" *I did.*

But the sentence could also have ended with "help her get better which is why I can't see you."

I needed to call him, but one more day wouldn't matter. My parents would still be dead. I needed to know what he found out but it could wait. He had it all: looks, kindness, humor, and an amazing kiss. I'd been pushing him away because I thought he was a player... moving in on me while he had a girlfriend. One call and I could sort out if he was available or not.

He was a constant distraction while I was trying to focus on my job and find my parents. My time here hadn't turned out as I hoped. Muddling along, running errands for patients, chasing dogs, hauling chickens... And sadly I got the answer to my question about my birthparents, my main reason for leaving California.

Damn! I'm so ambivalent! Was I really done here or not?

I thought of Beryl, imagined his dog curled at the foot of his bed, for the first time in weeks, both of them snoring in synch. Eventually those thoughts pulled me toward sleep.

Milt

It rained hard through the night. The drumming on the roof was a comforting sound; hollow, yet protective. I dragged myself from bed just as a few weak rays of sunlight announced the morning's arrival and the end of the storm.

I dressed in a pair of tightly fitting tan chinos, a soft pink stretchy shirt and my lopsided flats.

Rose was in the library straightening the books and DVDs the guests could borrow for their rooms. It was still too early for breakfast, although something in the oven smelled great.

"Crab quiche," Rose answered when I asked her what it was. "You look extra pretty today."

An exaggeration, I'm sure. "Thank you, Rose. How's Milt?"

She said, "He finally looks like he's not trapped behind those eyes. I think he's been trying to say that one sentence for all these years, and thanks to you, the man can die in peace now."

"I'm glad."

"How did you get him to talk?"

I wasn't going to tell on Milt. He *had* broken a house rule by unlocking a guest's room. "An old relaxation technique. It's been pretty effective in the past, so I thought, why not?"

"We can't thank you enough. Richard and I slept better last night than we have for months."

"I'm glad." I looked around. "Where is Milt?"

She pointed toward the porch.

I headed there, dropped into a chair next to him and smiled. "Anything new to tell me?"

He turned his head to look my way.

"I've got news. Did you hear about Troy acting like the fugitive guy? Pretty dumb, huh?"

Milt made a puffing noise and it looked like he would talk. An urgency built behind his eyes and he sat up straighter.

"What is it?" I leaned closer.

His face gained a scarlet tint and his lips quivered. He said, "Wolf and man."

"New words!" My face broke into a broad grin. "You said new words."

His eyes had never been more drilled into mine. He acted like he had said the three most important words in history.

"You heard us talking about the picture of The Dog and Troy. Wolf and man. Good, Milt."

He sagged in his chair, like his spine had melted. I patted his leg. "I'm off to work but we'll talk later."

I found Richard outside, setting up his new toy. He was drawing out the future black-and-white chessboard design on the cement pad by the maple sugar shack. Nearby, the tailgate of his truck was open and a jumble of large chess pieces was stacked beside it, like a pile of bodies.

"How's the chess set?"

"We'll be playing our first match by tonight." He grinned, like a kid with his long-awaited toy.

I nodded. "You're pretty happy about this."

"Oh, yeah."

I smiled. I reached into my back pocket and brought out the A+ card. "I wanted you to see this."

He reached for it.

"Troy must have done his homework when he decided to imitate Grady," I said.

His eyebrows knit together as he turned the paper over and back again. "Where did you find this?"

"It was in my purse. After Memorial Day when I got it back."

Richard was silent, which wasn't the response I expected. I thought we would laugh about Troy's dim-wittedness.

"Can I keep this?" he asked.

"Sure. But what are you thinking?"

"I want to show it to some sheriff buddies." He shrugged. "It might not matter, but we never told anyone about this part of Grady's technique. Definitely not Troy. And unless *you* let someone know, it's a little unlikely he would have found this out."

"I never said a thing."

He clapped a hand on my shoulder. "Gossip is viral here. Probably some young deputy in a bar, bragging about his insider knowledge. I'll check it out."

I loaded up my therapy supplies and left, headed for Proxy and my confrontation with Ivory. Like Troy, she put on such a good act! She really should go into theater. And why would she want to wreck her voice just to qualify for home-health services?

My phone rang but I was on a narrow road so I didn't bother with the caller ID before I answered.

"Come get him now!" Honey yelled into the phone.

I'd be to their house in an hour. "Honey, calm down. I just have to make one visit first then I'll be there."

"Nope. You said you would come get him if I felt like killing him, so that's right now." She sounded furious.

What had he done? My heart pounded and I had to swing the car off of the side the road because I wasn't thinking clearly. Although I didn't think Honey would harm Casey, I couldn't chance it. She'd already proven she would tie him to a chair and gag him. "Okay, I'll come right now but please calm down. Let him play in the backyard until I get there." I glanced at the dashboard clock, "Give me 20 minutes."

"Fine," she snapped and then hung up.

I'd be late to Ivory's, but I would call her. I pointed my car toward Vixonville and drove like hell.

Casey

I barely stepped out of the car when Casey ran to greet me, wearing just a graying pair of Fruit-of-the-Looms.

He threw his arms around my legs. "Ah ih uhoh," he said, looking over his shoulder.

I understood this to mean, "I'm in trouble."

Honey stood on the porch holding clothes in her hands. "Get back here you little shit."

Casey laughed and ran behind me.

I laid my hand on his curly hair and felt the sweat there. "Hey, Casey. Do you want to go to work with me?" I guided him toward the back seat of my car and he hopped in without further coaxing. I gave him a piece of candy and told him to wait.

When I reached Honey, I took his clothes from her. "What did he do?"

"He busted the card table you were using." She had both arms crossed over her chest.

It was a wonder the rickety piece of junk had stood this long without breaking. "I think we have an extra one at the place I'm staying. I'll bring it next time."

I didn't think the Pfoltzes would mind and I would pay for it if they wanted.

"Now you're talking," Honey said, snapping her fingers on both hands and pointing them at me like an outlaw with pistols. "Take your time today. Keep him away as long as you want." She turned away, snagged the can of Pabst on the railing, and headed inside.

"Bye," I said to the closed door. "And you are welcome."

Her behavior made me sad. Casey was a happy little kid who would know soon enough his mom wasn't going to be joining any PTA groups.

My phone rang as I reached the car. It was Elyk.

"Hey," I said. "Can I call you right back?"

"No, I need the crossword answer now." He sounded pissed off because I hadn't solved it yet. "South American musical instrument. Eight letters."

"I know, I know," I said, tucking the phone between my neck and chin while I unraveled the wad of clothes. I had to get something on Casey besides his underwear. "I have to do one thing first then I'll get back to you."

He hung up. I tossed my phone on the front seat. As I dressed Casey, he stared off into space, singing loudly. I turned him to face me, as I slid his tan cargo shorts onto each leg and pulled him to a standing position before tugging them up. He held onto my arms for balance, acting like it was no big deal having a person he hardly knew dress him. Next, a striped t-shirt went over his head and then socks and scuffed sneakers onto his feet. I buckled him in, then jumped in the driver's seat and pulled away.

Casey asked something but I had no idea what this slew of vowels and seesawing intonations meant. He said it again, but louder.

"Okay," I said, looking over my shoulder. "How about some ice cream?" I had no idea if he was lactose intolerant or not.

Casey chanted, "I eem, I eem," as I punched in Honey's home number.

She answered on the fifth ring. "What?" she barked.

Bitch. "Can he have ice cream?"

"He can have ice cream, cigarettes, or his first beer if you want. Just stop bugging me." The phone clicked in my ear.

I looked over my shoulder where he sat expectantly. "Good news, Casey. Your nice mommy said we can have ice cream."

We entered the Gas-N-Guzzle Hut walking hand in hand.

Burt greeted us and I explained I had a little friend with me for a few hours. We ordered the strawberry ice cream Casey pointed to and Burt began filling two cones.

He asked, "You still seeing the lady out in Proxy?"

I'm sure I had never given Ivory's name to Burt. "Yes. We are headed there right now."

"Don't play poker with her. She's good." He handed the first cone to me and I passed it down to Casey. Casey devoured it like a starving animal. Honey might not have fed him breakfast; it didn't look like it.

"We must be talking about a different woman. My patient is homebound," I said.

He stopped scooping and frowned. "Ivory Ash, right?"

I shook my finger. "I can't share confidential information."

"You bought her groceries last week, so no secret there."

"Obviously not." I thought over what he said about Ivory playing poker. "These poker games were before her vocal trauma, I guess." Her fake vocal trauma, that is.

He returned to his job. "I was just in a game with her this past weekend. She took me for over a $100 bucks." He shook his head. "She's crafty."

I should have known she was lying to me the first day I heard someone singing in her backyard. "Oh, she sure is."

Not only was her horrible voice just an act but she also was getting out of the house regularly.

Burt handed me my cone and I slid the money across the counter. He pushed buttons on the cash register and it *dinged* open. He gave me change and said, "I'll win it back this next Saturday. I figured out when she's bluffing."

Me, too. Even with all the fake tears.

I needed proof though. I needed to catch her using her normal voice, but the trouble was she had caller ID. If I used my cell, she'd shift into damaged-voice mode. "Could I use your phone to call Ivory and let her know I'm bringing this little guy?" I patted Casey's head. "My cell is acting funny."

Casey leaned into my thigh and licked his ice cream. I took a few napkins from the counter when I saw the mess already forming on his cheeks.

Burt picked the receiver off its charger, punched in a set of numbers and handed it to me. "It's local so don't worry about it." His daughter called him into the back room. He waved and left.

Ivory

Ivory's phone rang five times. I imagined her girth swinging through the house, getting to the phone and squinting at the caller ID.

On the sixth ring, Ivory said, "You still mad about losing your money, Burt?" She laughed loudly.

Her voice was clear and not the least bit traumatized.

"No, but I'm mad…you lied to me, Ivory." I waited. The silence stretched on and on, like an abandoned railroad track running across Kansas. "Just wanted you to know I'm on my way, but I have a little boy with me today."

She said in her horror-film voice, "My voice seems to be coming and going now, thanks to your help."

"Nice try." I hung up.

I settled Casey in the car again. My backseat would have strawberry handprints all over it in no time but it couldn't be any worse than chicken dander.

I turned toward Proxy. A few minutes later we passed the tiny church. The marquee read:

How do you spell relief? G-O-D. Now in a three pack.

I smiled.Ten minutes later I faced off against Ivory, each of us in a kitchen chair, our hands on the table, like two people prepared to arm wrestle. Casey was on the living room floor within sight, digging through a toy box Ivory kept for her grandchild.

"But you are *not* homebound," I said for the third time.

"Nobody would come visit me," she whined again. "Like you. You wouldn't come here and I quite like you." She was using her perfectly good voice. "Better than Vicky."

"Which reminds me," I said. "Did Vicky know about this?"

"No. She was beside herself trying to figure out what to do with my voice. You, on the other hand, jumped right in and put me to work." She chuckled.

Ivory acted like this had been a game. I already told her that lying about her condition was considered Medicare fraud. She didn't seem to care.

"I'm going to discharge you, Ivory, but to save you a lot of trouble, I'm not going to mention the fraud part."

Ivory fanned her face with a plastic plate. "Please don't discharge me." Tears built up in her dark eyes. "I won't have any identity."

"No identity?" I asked. "You *want* to seem disabled?"

Her face flushed pink. "I've defined myself by who I can make do stuff for me. Ever since I was a drill sergeant in the Waves, I found out I kind of liked it. If you go, I'm not going to know who to boss around." Tears slipped from the edges of her eyes and trickled down her plump cheeks.

They were real, and I was taken aback. She truly looked sad. "This is all about wanting someone to boss around?"

Ivory nodded.

"You have so many good traits, you don't need to *make* people do things."

"Name one."

I sputtered for a second. "You have a beautiful singing voice. And, you put in a winning crop of corn."

Ivory studied me, obviously needing more.

"And I hear you play a mean hand of poker."

She was silent while Casey made loud *vrooming* noises, pushing a blue car around on the carpet.

"I hate grocery shopping." Her eyes blazed. "Do you know how people stare when you're a full-figured person like me?"

"I'm sorry. People are jerks sometimes." Now we were getting to the truth. Ivory was embarrassed. "But you know everyone who lives here and you've got friends, right?"

She nodded. "I do have lots of friends. Could you just finish out the summer?" Ivory patted her beehive hairdo. "No one will know and maybe I can figure out something to do with myself by then."

I actually felt her loneliness. "I don't understand why my three visits a week make much difference to you."

"The daytimes are the worst. It's just me and the stupid TV shows."

"What about babysitting? You like children." They're easy to boss around, I wanted to add.

"There aren't many kids in these parts." She sighed deeply.

"You could volunteer at the hospital, or at a community center."

"Too many viral issues there," she said wrinkling her nose.

And then Sandy and Melvin popped into my head. Maybe Sandy's respite care worker was sitting right in front of me. "I just had the best idea. I'll have to make a phone call, but if it works out, you will be making a difference *and* someone would do your grocery shopping for you."

I hoped Sandy would agree to a trade.

Ivory chuffed and said, "That would be a perfect world."

We sat back and talked about non-therapy issues and I found out she'd had a pretty interesting life. She joined the military before it was "cool" and had been on a troop transport during Vietnam. She smoothed the sides of her blouse with her hands and smiled, "Of course I was more slender back then."

She sung in musicals and performed in small-town theatres before Elyk was born. She broke into the chorus from *Wouldn't it be Loverly*.

Her voice was absolutely beautiful.

When she finished I scolded, "You almost ruined your voice, Ivory, by pretending all this time. You were abusing it, you crazy woman."

Although I'd wanted to be the therapist who helped her using my stellar therapy ideas, I guess I had done it by simply enforcing the rules. I switched topics. "You'll be happy to know Beryl has his dog back."

"He does?" She nearly jumped out of her chair. "I've been trying to call him today but he hasn't answered."

"He's not much of a phone guy. I had a hard time getting him to answer all yesterday."

"Who found the beast anyway?" she asked.

Not wanting to tell her about Beryl's Segway, I said, "I'm not sure. But good news, huh?"

"The best. I thought for sure he was a goner."

"It's a huge relief for me." I tapped her arm. "And I'll let you know soon about my caretaker idea. I'll be in touch."

"You'd better be," she said, and then sighed.

I stood and turned toward Casey. "Hey Casey, we have to clean up now. It's time to go home." He ignored me and kept driving a car all over the floor instead. I tapped him on the shoulder and he looked up at me and smiled. "We need to go."

He dropped the car into the toy box and started picking up. And that's when it hit me. How could I have missed the signs? The loud singing? Him not following Honey's demands?

Casey couldn't hear!

He wasn't actually deaf because he responded when he was watching my face, but he no doubt had a severe bilateral-hearing loss.

I tried out my theory. His back was turned toward me as he scrambled around and collected toys. I said in a fairly loud voice, "Casey, do you want some more ice cream?"

He didn't respond.

I moved closer. "How about a new puppy?"

Nothing. He grabbed toys and put them away. This was such an easy solution. Once he got hearing aids, his speech would take off.

Ivory said, "The boy can't hear a damn thing."

"Apparently not," I said and shrugged. "This explains so much." His delayed speech development, his mom's frustration with him not listening. "Poor kid."

I felt like an idiot because I hadn't spotted his hearing loss the first time I met him, but in my defense, that was the day he acted like a dog and spilled a drink all over me. I'd had very little time with him without a crisis. In our one good session, he'd stayed focused on my mouth while we worked, and he was able to learn the new sounds. This meant he was good at reading lips.

Ivory said, "You're solving things right and left aren't you? Beryl's dog, this boy's hearing, and you got rid of me."

I gave her a half hug. "I'll miss you, Ivory."

We said goodbye. I couldn't wait to tell Honey about my discovery. Her stress level would immediately drop once Casey started listening to her. His loud voice would quiet down. He'd start talking and be able to tell her what he needed. It would make a huge difference, especially to this little boy who seemed to always be in trouble.

I smiled at him in the rearview mirror. I debated whether to call Honey right away and tell her the great news or surprise her when we got there. She made it pretty clear she didn't want to hear from me.

I had another choice, too. I could drive directly to Vixonville and take Casey home, or drive to Milepost and see Beryl and ask why he was done with therapy. Something seemed very out of place during our last phone conversation. He said, "I'll shoot you." Who said that to someone who was trying to help?

I could take Casey along to Beryl's house and use him as a buffer. Beryl couldn't yell too much with a little kid there and even if he did, the screaming wouldn't bother Casey, especially if he was playing with a huge dog.

I drove slowly, debating. Vixonville or Milepost?

My phone rang and I saw it was Elyk. I let it go to voicemail, feeling bad I hadn't solved his puzzle yet. He must be a mess after having come this far in the contest and was down to the wire on this word. I'd call him back in a few minutes when I got a chance to think about the clues again. I had to decide where I was going. I stopped at the intersection. Casey's or Beryl's? Casey was happily kicking the seat. I could let him decide. I made sure he was looking at me before I asked, "Do you want to go see a big dog or your mommy?"

"Ommy," he said. I wasn't surprised. A mom was a mom, even if she tied you up or died when you least expected it.

Ten minutes from Casey's, I dialed Honey's number. She picked up right away.

"I know you said to not call..."

"Oh, hi Marleigh," she interrupted.

There was something new in her voice. *It sounded like a fifth of gin.*

Her voice held the forced cheeriness of a waitress at a diner. "Are you on your way back?"

"We are. I have some exciting news about Casey."

"Okay. How far away are you?"

She hadn't even asked what the news was. It would have been my first question.

"We'll be there in about ten minutes."

She paused, "Okay. See you soon." She hung up.

A few minutes later we drove through Vixonville, then along another two-mile stretch outside of town before I turned onto the dirt road leading to Casey's house. I hadn't noticed until now how secluded Rutabaga Drive felt. I bumped along the quarter-mile drive and parked just short of the house.

A silver truck with a camper shell was parked near the front porch. I caught the backside of a man and a dog disappearing around the right side of the house.

I groaned. Karl was home.

No wonder Honey was all cheery; she'd put on her good mother act. I wasn't in the mood for his paper-fetish issues. I hoped my news about Casey's hearing impairment trumped Karl's strangeness.

We would see.

I unbuckled Casey figuring he'd take off after the dog. But he stayed next to me and slipped his hand into mine. If Karl were watching, he'd be furious.

I squeezed his hand in reassurance. There'd be no therapy today but I would explain how they should get Casey's hearing checked and how to get fitted for hearing aids. The progress he'd make once he could hear would be huge.

No one rushed out to meet us when we climbed the steps to the porch. I hesitated. Karl hadn't allowed me in the house the last time he was here and I was sure today would be no different.

Casey pushed against the interior door and it opened. He dropped my hand and went charging in yelling, "Ommy!"

I followed to make sure someone was actually in the house and I wasn't just ditching the kid at the door.

"Hello?" I looked around. I heard Casey running through the house calling his mom, and then he suddenly stopped. I crossed through the dining room and turned into the kitchen.

Shock does different things to different people. For me, my hearing stops and a high shrill noise fills my ears, like when I was told my parents had died in their plane. Now, when I turned the corner into the room, both happened.

I had no idea if I made a noise when I saw Honey tied to a chair, and a man–not Karl–next to her with one hand clamped over Casey's mouth and the other holding a gun to Honey's head.

All I heard was the high whine in my head.

And within nano-seconds, the truth found its way through the shrill hum.

Here was Grady.

His face was covered with a clear-plastic mask. He smiled through the cutout in the mouth, red and freakish, his lips distorted.

The fear in Honey's eyes told me this guy, Grady or whatever his real name was, had been here when I called. Probably why Honey had asked how far away we were. She had no way to warn me.

"Nice of you to come by, Marleigh," he said.

A chill raced down my back when he said my name. I tried to hide the shiver but he saw it and smiled wider.

He looked familiar but how was that possible?

He had brown hair, was young, and looked strong. Through the eyeholes of the mask I saw deep gray irises.

Tears slipped from Casey's eyes and spilled over the guy's hand. It got me moving. I stepped forward. "If you let them go, you can take anything. I have money, lots of it, in the car. You can even take the car. Just don't hurt them."

The man shoved Casey toward his mother. Casey threw himself onto her lap and wrapped his arms tightly around her, burying his face in her chest. Her arms were tied behind her but she dropped her head down to touch his.

The man crossed to me, impossibly fast. He grabbed my arm and stuck the gun into my side. He hissed "Gladly" into my ear.

My legs weakened and I nearly crumbled, but he held me up. This guy had attacked me beside my car, not Troy. He wore the state police uniform he'd taken when he left its owner naked last week. He'd obviously *not* been caught in Maryland.

The faint smell of wood smoke rose from him and another truth hit me; he was the construction worker who had taken the chickens and my phone near Melvin's house. But why?

"You've been a pain in the ass," he growled, and dug the gun deeper into my side.

I tried to get away from the metal prod, but I only managed to scoot a few inches and the gun followed.

I forced my voice to stay steady. "Why are you messing with me?" I was pissed now that I thought about everything he had done. I pushed back at him with the arm he held, but he didn't budge. "I moved here and a week later you are following me around, taking my phone, and beating me up."

Casey looked at me and rattled off a long string of vowels and fleeting consonants. I realized I would be dead before I ever get to tell Honey her son couldn't hear.

"What did the kid say?" Grady growled.

I was thankful for Casey's unintelligible speech. "He said his daddy is out back and he'll beat you up."

Grady laughed and scoffed, "Nice try. But there's no one here but us little mice."

I flashed to the four mice Elyk and I had used to lure the snakes. Now *I* was the one wiggling at the end of a snare.

It wasn't Karl rounding the house. My hopes the angry truck driver would barge in and save us withered.

Grady added, "Oh, and there's the old geezer and dog in my truck, so make that six mice."

Beryl and The Dog. Grady had gotten them, too. No wonder Beryl had been so strange on the phone last night. I'll shoot you if you come back. He'd been warning me away. And now he was in just as much trouble as us.

My stomach dropped as bile rose in my throat. "Did you hurt them?" I hated that my body shook.

"Define 'hurt,'" he said, chuckling. Then he added, "I *think* they're still alive."

I solved another mystery in that moment. "You've had The Dog all this time. And you were by the woods when I took the picture."

"You're a genius."

"Why not just give the dog back and leave the area?"

"I've worked too hard to stay ahead of the law. I was surviving here, hiding out in the most remote part of the state, and you snapped the only known photo of me. Dumb luck or just dumb, you tell me."

I was going with dumb.

And with his last statement, it all fell into place. He'd been able to find me through the magnets on my car, had gotten my name from Jake after he took my phone and called the office. He'd followed me to my patients' houses. Melvin had been so upset. "You were at the window of one of my patients."

"I was at most of your patients' homes. Seemed like the best way to catch you. And I almost had you that day. Then the dumb dogcatcher brought your magnets and the rabbits by to show you."

"So he *had* found your hiding place."

"He helped me out by trying to be the local hero. It sent the Stateys in a completely different direction. I took your magnets but I used gloves. He wasn't as smart, so it all pointed to him. I like dumb people."

There was his twisted smile again.

All of my clients had been in danger. By kidnapping the State Trooper, Grady had accumulated more serious charges, making him more dangerous than when he was just stealing food or running road blocks.

Done with the banter, he spit out the words. "Here's what we are going to do. You are going to give me the phone that has my picture. Then you are going to tell me how many more pict..."

The phone in my back pocket rang. We all stared at each other like an alarm had gone off. It rang again, the sound impossibly loud.

"See who it is," he growled.

I pulled it out. *It was Elyk.* I had one chance to get help and he was going to have to be it.

"It's my boss," I said. "He checks in every hour lately because of all the crazy stuff I've gone through. If I don't answer, they'll come here, following my schedule."

He took two steps away and put the gun to Honey's head again. "And I'll get nervous if you say anything you shouldn't."

I swallowed hard and took a big breath. I forced cheeriness into my voice and answered. "Hi. I was waiting for you to check in."

Elyk snarled. "The hell. *You* were supposed to call *me.*"

"Yup. Everything is fine." I looked toward Grady. His eyes were slits and his mouth was set in a straight line. I didn't doubt for a minute he would shoot Honey.

I was rolling phrases around in my head that wouldn't sound like "Call the police" or "I'm about to die."

"Are you on drugs or something?" Elyk asked.

"Oh, yeah. And I have the information you asked for earlier. Get a pencil and paper to write it down."

Grady looked impatient. He shifted his weight from foot to foot.

I raised a finger to stall gesture, but I knew I was down to seconds.

I knew what to say to Elyk. If only my denim-clad friend figured it out. I needed Elyk to call Lawyer since Lawyer knew Honey's last name and could get the address. We'd joked about it when I was explaining Karl and his newspaper hording problem. Karl Lester. *Lester the Molester.*

"I almost lost this contest," Elyk said. "This was close."

I'd forgotten about his contest. He was going to be furious when this wasn't the answer he needed.

Then a weird thing happened. The answer to his crossword popped into my head. It was "Berimbau"- A South American musical instrument. If I told him it right now, he'd hang up immediately.

"Ready," he said.

I said, "The problem is there's a *maelstrom* that needs to be fixed. It's in *Harridan*-ville."

Would he remember harridan meant vixen? God, I hoped so.

"What the hell, Marleigh. We've had those words." He started to say something else but I cut him off.

"Yes, that's right. And, probably the most important thing is you are going to need to call a lawyer. No way around it. Probably should talk to a lawyer right away before the maelstrom gets worse."

Grady motioned for me to hang up.

Elyk was still sputtering when I talked over him, "Thanks for checking in," I said and pushed the button to hang up. I'd had my chance. I hoped it worked.

Grady grabbed the phone from my hands and shifted the gun back my way. He flipped the cell open and started clicking through the levels to find the photo.

Casey sucked his thumb and clung to his mom with tears running down his face.

"There's no photo there," I said. I had to lure Grady out of this house. "The phone is in my car. The one you're holding is the loaner I needed after you took my *first* borrowed phone."

"That explains so much." Grady grabbed my arm and jerked me toward the back door. I touched Casey's leg as I was passing, just long enough to get a few seconds of eye contact. I mouthed the words, "Lock the doors." He could read lips; he'd been doing it his whole short life. I prayed he did it one more time.

Grady dragged me down the four steps into the lawn.

We'd only gone a few yards when the huge wolf I'd seen before charged from the trees. I screamed and backed away.

Maybe my luck was changing. When Grady stopped to fend it off, I'd have the distraction I needed to break free and run.

The animal was enormous. Its teeth were bared as it loped closer and closer. That I would die a painful death seemed inevitable. I'd finally be with the rest of my family, I thought only half in jest... But I wanted Grady to go down with me, and for Honey and Casey to make it out alive.

Grady raised his free hand and said, "Sit, Puma."

My heart sunk as the animal skidded to a stop and sat.

Grady laughed, "I think you've met my dog, right?"

I nodded. Another piece of the puzzle. "Yeah, the day I let Beryl's dog loose."

"You know, I wasn't going to keep the old man's dog. I didn't need another beast to haul around, especially a deaf one. But then you took my picture and he was the only bait I had to try to get near you."

I thought of the day the wolf had charged across the road in front of my car. "I almost hit him once. How did you plan that?"

"You kept the same schedule each week so I had him sitting on one side of the road and I called him across when I saw you coming. You were supposed to stop." He yanked my arm. "Let's go."

We continued around the house. Puma remained where he had been told to sit.

I needed to slow this whole process down in case Elyk had understood my message. And if he called Lawyer and if Lawyer remembered the last name of Lester. It was a lot of 'ifs.' The closest police department had to be 20 minutes away while the trip to my car was going to take about 20 seconds. Once Grady had the phone, he wouldn't need me anymore and that's when things would turn ugly.

I stopped walking and planted my feet, refusing to move.

"I can drag you," he said roughly.

I knew he could. "I need to know Beryl is fine."

He pulled me off the ground and moved me a few feet before he set me down again. "When I get the phone and if it's the right one, I'll let everyone go."

I tried again, "No one has seen you. Even now, I couldn't pick you out of a line up. And there aren't any other copies of your picture either."

He snorted, "At least not now. The photo shop had an early morning fire after I found out where you developed it. And the copy the old man had didn't really show my face behind the binoculars, but it's gone too."

Add arson to his record.

We walked past his truck. No sound came from inside and I felt sick. Beryl needed to be alive, and The Dog, too. They'd been hurt because of me and that was painful to grasp.

"The phone's in the glove box," I said as we approached my car. That's when I remembered the mace. It was also in there and I felt like I had another chance.

I unlocked the passenger door with my key fob and he immediately snatched the keys from my hand. "I'll hang on to these," he said.

I wouldn't be driving out of here.

I dropped one knee onto the seat and leaned in, blocking the view of what I was doing as best as I could. I opened the glove box and fumbled around, although the phone was right there. I saw something else that might come in handy. I grabbed the rattlesnake tail and dropped it down my blouse into my bra. Then I got the mace and popped the cap off with my left hand making sure the canister pointed in the right direction. I tucked it in the front pocket of my jeans.

During the same time, I'd pulled the cell phone out of the glove box and held it backwards out the door for Grady.

He accepted it.

I stood up, telling myself that this was it.

In one smooth move, I turned and lunged, jammed him in the neck with the fingers of my right hand and sprayed him in the face with the mace I'd grabbed from my pants with my left.

Although I didn't get a full squirt off before he knocked the canister out of my hand, he dropped to the ground holding his throat and choking; the gun bounced into the grass.

I grabbed the gun, thought about using it, but knew he'd just get it away from me. First and foremost, I needed to lure him away from this home. I turned and sprinted down the dirt lane toward the main road. I ran as if the hounds of hell were on my heels.

For all I knew, Puma might soon be.

I ran the quarter mile fast, probably in two minutes, which was amazing with the loose footwear I had to work with. I was nearly to the end of the dirt lane when I dropped the gun into a thicket of berry bushes with thorns the size of grizzly claws. I tried to part the branches, but when I didn't immediately see it, I knew I was wasting time. I tried to convince myself Grady would just take the cell phone and leave. Why chase me down now? He had what he came for and we all were still oblivious to his identity. The sensible thing would be to pack up his wolf and leave the state. Find another backwoods place to land and continue stealing chickens and building campfires.

I almost believed it. I felt the stress start to leave, my breathing slowed just a bit. Then I heard the roar of his truck coming on fast.

Glancing over my shoulder, I didn't see him yet, but I knew within seconds he'd be cresting the rise behind me. Even if I made the main road before he reached me, it was two miles into Vixonville and I had no hope of getting far. Flagging anyone down on the main road was impossible since traffic was so sparse.

I had no choice; I'd have to go into the woods for cover and to find my way to town.

Sprinting off the road to my right, I chose an area where the trees looked less dense and I could move faster. Slipping down the slight embankment, I got my feet under me and high-stepped it through the weeds and painful thistle, swatting aside the growth, trying to find the best way into the forest.

The noise behind me grew louder.

I dashed into the green cover, pushing away the branches of the lower bushes, plunging into an area filled with fallen, moss-covered trees, lacy ferns and rocks. I kept moving, heading for a stand of tall pines where the ground seemed less cluttered. Weaving around the pitfalls on the ground, I continued deeper into the woods until I couldn't see the road, which I hoped meant, from the road, I couldn't be seen either. Grady would expect me to stay on the pavement or near it.

Wearing pink and tan was not to my advantage, but when I dressed that morning, the idea I'd be running for my life, looking like a lone salmon flopping around in bear country, had not even remotely occurred to me.

I held my breath trying to hear if the vehicle had passed by while my blood banged in my ears. Sounds of scampering broke from the trees above. I whirled, then flinched as a pine cone fell to the ground.

Squirrels. I had freaked out over squirrels. I tried to picture Elyk beside me as I headed deeper still into the trees, remembering his reassurances that the forest was safe.

It wasn't working.

The sound of something big thrashing around in the underbrush behind me stopped me short. The growl of the engine had stopped.

Grady was in the woods! I listened, and it sounded like he might be getting nearer. It was too hard to locate the direction the movement came from because the forest muffled some sounds, but echoed and amplified others. I moved backward, staying in the pines in case I needed to move fast. The ground was soft and spongy under foot, a decade of pine needles padding it.

I pulled the rattlesnake tail out of my bra and clutched it in my hand. This dead-end part of a snake was my only hope for scaring Grady away.

The crashing noises sounded much closer now. There was no doubt. Something was headed my way.

Then, Grady called out, "You're in my playground now, Pinky." He laughed and my blood froze.

I whirled around. He might be able to see me but I couldn't see him anywhere. He was right: he was in his element and I couldn't be more out of mine.

Remembering what Elyk had taught me about where rattlesnakes lived, I ran as hard as I could toward the darker recesses of the forest, heading uphill, batting branches away with my arms. The undergrowth snapped back or broke off under my feet and stuck into my shins and calves, but I couldn't feel anything at the moment as adrenaline masked everything but the will to live.

Branches broke behind me, and I knew I had to outrun Grady.

The terrain became more rugged as I headed into the underbrush and any sense of a trail diminished. My left ankle turned as my foot landed on a log and I nearly fell. Pain ripped up my leg. I stopped at the crest of the hill to survey the area below, my lungs rapidly sucking air.

Become one with the forest, Elyk had said, although it now seemed a lifetime ago. I needed to lose my scent because there was no way I was out-foxing a wolf. And I had to lose the pink shirt since it was a beacon. I pulled it off and dragged it over the bushes around me, just like I'd seen on a tv show. Then I bundled it around a rock and whipped it as hard as I could in the opposite direction I was heading. The rock sent it sailing 20 feet away.

Hopefully, Grady and the wolf, if they made it this far, would be thrown off my trail. Otherwise, stripping down to a tan bra had been a very bad idea.

The swampy area at the bottom of the hill was a flat spot in the ravine catching the drainage from the hills around it. Trees had rotted and died where they stood, leaving disintegrating trunks, stumps of all different heights, sticking up through a patch of watery ground a half-mile wide.

I splashed into the greasy water and yellow-ish muck until I was knee deep, with shoes mired in the bottom. I stifled a thousand screams, from the cold and sliminess to the putrid gases breaking free from the mud, the bubbles racing up my legs fighting for the surface, feeling like creatures crawling up my goose-bumpy skin.

I heard nothing more from behind me. What I thought was a tiny wail of sirens in the distance a minute earlier, probably was the scream in my head when something shifted and my left ankle turned again.

The sun was mostly lost in here. I was halfway across the swamp, trying not to make sounds. My plan was to reach an outcropping of rocks and logs on the hillside to my left, a place that looked rattlesnake friendly. Grady would know these hills; he'd know a rattler wouldn't be here in the bottom of the valley, in the open. I'd hide, and if he managed to somehow track me through the swamp, I'd scare him away with my rattle, which would give me a chance to get out before dark.

I stepped out of the swamp, my arms and chest coated in mud, my chinos stuck to my legs, and bare-foot. I wished for the boots Elyk had let me wear, even if they'd been too large. And as long as I was wishing for things, I wanted to be back at the Bed & Breakfast getting taken for $10 bucks by Milt.

Milt! 'Wolf and man,' he'd said. How had he known Grady had the wolf?

Something big crashed through the underbrush just beyond the swamp, from the direction I had just come. The shirt toss had not slowed them down by much.

I ran for the hillside, trying to ignore the pain in my ankle. When the sounds behind me stopped, I knew Grady had reached the swamp.

I scrambled up the last of the hillside, weaving from tree to tree, before I slipped behind a large outcropping of rocks. I checked below.

Grady had removed his mask; he didn't think I'd be leaving the woods. He studied the ground along the edge of the swamp. The wolf circled the watery area and was nearing the place I'd exited the muck.

I started shaking. How do I fight a wolf? I searched the area around me. There were fallen logs, jumbles of rocks, and about 20 feet away... an old rusty car. What a ride that must have been, getting to this remote hillside. Devoid of windows, the abandoned vehicle's doors were splayed open like the torso of a murdered animal.

I knew I had only moments before the wolf arrived.

I hurried around the front of the car to where vines from a nearby tree grew over the roof, creating a tent covering the back half of the vehicle. I crawled inside the green tent and waited. In a closet sort of way, it gave me an ounce of comfort: soft, quiet, dark.

Through a tiny opening I could see the front of the car. I heard the animal's panting even before he rounded the hood. He had stopped running and lowered his head, slowly stepping toward me.

His stance was not a good sign.

It was only five feet to the edge of my enclosure.

I had no idea if the animal was afraid of snakes but the only way to find out was to try. I held the rattle up in front of me and shook it for all it was worth.

Only a soggy thud came from the rattle, my pulse sounding louder than the bead inside. The tail had been damaged.

I was going to die.

Grady appeared and stopped beside his animal. His police uniform was disheveled and his shirt was out and ripped. "What do you have, Puma?"

They both breathed hard and I nearly passed out trying to control my own ragged breath.

They moved closer to a position only a yard from my hiding place when I tried the rattle again, as if something could have changed with its functioning. Then the beautifully horrible sound of dry beads scratching around inside of the segments came to life.

Grady stopped and halted his dog. The wolf's ears jerked to the side and he sniffed the air. As Grady tried to hold him, the wolf turned and charged off in another direction.

"Puma!" he scolded. "Come!"

When I stopped shaking the tail, the rattling sound, multiplied now, continued right next to me.

I turned my head slowly, remembering that snakes sensed movement. In the dim light, in what was left of the back seat, I saw a nest with three entwined reptiles, one stretched forward with a flicking tongue.

I screamed. Loud and long. I couldn't help it. A primal scream programmed into my head that had its own exit strategy.

Grady made his move. He charged toward me and parted the vines, a sneer on his face.

In that split second, I acted out of instinct - I grabbed his shirt and pulled him toward the nest and then things happened pretty fast.

He fought to balance, his arms tangling in the vines and he fell toward the car's interior. Snakes slid out of the car like overcooked linguini.

I heard Grady yell, and I watched him slap away two snakes as he tried to push himself out of the backseat.

Something nicked my arm as I parted the vines and ran for the road, vowing not to look behind me. Either I was being followed or I wasn't. I'd make it or I wouldn't. I didn't think. I ran.

A few minutes later, as the trees thinned, I saw sunlight through breaks in the branches above. I was almost to the road, which was good because something was wrong with my legs and I wasn't feeling well. I assumed I'd reached my capacity for terror and my body was quitting on me. I was a speech therapist. I'd never trained for survival or warfare.

My vision flickered in and out but it could have been the sun through the leaves above. I pushed on. Only 30 feet to go but it seemed like miles. I wobbled and almost fell, and wondered what the hell was happening to me. My mind turned to Casey and Honey and Beryl and I grew furious, and through fury found a reserve of strength to push me forward. I would *not* drop in the woods and give up.

I stumbled from the tree line and clawed my way up an embankment. The fresh air hit my lungs but it didn't clear my vision. It felt like I was looking through oil. I gathered the last of my strength and stepped into the road, barely avoiding the grille of a big, white truck skidding to a halt a foot away.

I swayed on the pavement and in a dream-like trance, saw Lawyer appear. I couldn't decide if he was real or my final thought. He reached for me just as I started to fall and caught me. I watched him shrink as the world closed down into a gray circle and then everything went black.

Bitten

This time when I awoke in an ambulance, I knew immediately where I was. You couldn't fool me with that blindingly white ceiling more than once. We were moving fast and the siren wailed, clearing a path on the highway. Lawyer knelt on my right side and a paramedic with a thick, blond mustache was doing something with my left arm.

Lawyer shook his head but smiled. He looked tired. He brushed the damp hair off of my forehead. "You're a hero," he said. "Jonathon Marshall, or Grady as we all called him, will finally be in police custody thanks to you."

I thought about what had happened. Surely Grady had been bitten by at least one snake. "Will be?" I asked. The oxygen mask at my nose made me sound nasal.

"He's got a coupla snake bites to get bandaged first. The paramedics were reluctant to give him the anti-venom but after ten minutes, they decided to be professional." He smiled.

The blond paramedic laughed. "Not like you. You got the first shot." He finished bandaging my forearm and laid it across my stomach. "Course you only had one bite."

I'd been bitten? I blacked out again.

FAMILY

This time I awoke in a hospital room. Rose and Richard stood to one side while Elyk leaned against the wall in the narrow space on the other. The Pfoltzes told me all they knew about what had happened and answered all of my questions.

Beryl was fine. He'd been cared for at the hospital and already released. He was drugged a good portion of the time he was with Grady, and hadn't been hurt. The Dog was examined by a veterinarian and although he lost some weight, he was also fine. Apparently the wolf and Beryl's dog had become instant friends, which made it easier for Grady to keep The Dog with him. The wolf was awaiting shipment to a preserve in Montana despite Grady having raised it as a pet. It never actually attacked anyone, so it wasn't killed.

I turned to Elyk. "You figured out my clues."

"I thought you'd lost your mind, then what you were saying clicked. You're pretty creative under pressure."

"Thanks for teaching me to hunt rattlesnakes."

He blushed, "By the way you aren't supposed to do it half-naked and then get yourself bitten."

It was my turn to go red.

"You stumbled onto a pretty big nest. There was a seven-footer in there when I checked it out. I'm drying the tail for you."

I nodded, worn out. Then I remembered something else. "Berimbau," I said.

They all stared at me.

Rose squeezed my hand. "You're tired and not making sense, Sweety. We'll let you sleep."

"No." I grabbed Elyk's sleeve. "It's the answer to the puzzle. Berimbau."

He scowled and then I saw the gears moving in his head. "Oh my God, you're right!" He looked at his watch, as if calculating how much time he had left, then ran from the room without a good-bye.

I smiled. He'd saved my butt and I'd just saved his.

Richard said, "Milt has been a mess since we told him you'd been hurt. He's moving everything all over the place and muttering how he hates you for leaving and saying wolf and man. Did you teach him those words?"

I shook my head. "No, but he said it this morning to me and I thought he'd seen the picture of The Dog and Troy."

"Which we all know now wasn't Troy," Richard said.

Rose had been quiet. "Do you know what? Last week I took Milt with me to Blackout and he'd been staring out the window and all of a sudden, he went completely berserk. He must have seen the wolf and Grady."

It wasn't lost on any of us that if he could speak, we might have avoided all of this trouble.

I nodded. "I will get him talking more. I promise." Then I asked, "Did Lawyer leave? I need to thank him."

Richard answered, "He said he had an errand to run and he would be back."

I was fading. The Pfoltzes said good-bye and for a moment the room was quiet. I hadn't heard much about Honey and Casey, although Elyk said they were found safely locked inside the house.

Casey had read my lips and followed my directions.

I closed my eyes and thought of Casey and Honey. The terror on their tear-stained faces. Their love for each other. Honey might not have the best child disciplinary techniques, but she loved her son very much. Even as I thought of him I heard his little voice clearly in my head.

Then came the sound of feet running into the room. My eyes flew open. Casey launched himself onto my bed and nuzzled into my armpit. "Ah is oo."

I stifled a scream as all of my muscles flared with pain. I rubbed his head, "I missed you, too."

Honey walked in with Lawyer.

She smiled. "How do you feel?"

I said, "I'll take that drink now."

Laughing, she said, "Right, just when I decide to get on the wagon. But really. How are you?"

She was actually concerned. "Lots of sore spots, but all things considered, I'm good."

Tears brimmed in her eyes. "You saved our lives by leading that crazy loon away. I can't repay you, and just saying 'thank-you' doesn't seem to cut it."

I brightened. "There's one way you can thank me."

Her eyebrows shot up. "Okay?"

Casey sat up and started investigating the pulse meter on my finger.

"Get his hearing checked tomorrow. You'll find he has a major hearing loss. The audiologist will fit him with hearing aids and then I'll be back to work with him. His speech will absolutely take off once he can hear."

I watched Honey's face register what I said. Then she burst into tears.

The water built in my eyes and ran down the sides of my cheeks and into the pillow.

Casey hopped off the bed and raced from the room. "Get back here!" she yelled as she went after him. She'd catch on that he couldn't hear soon enough.

Lawyer moved to the side of my bed and carefully sat on the mattress. "I knew you would want to see them."

"I did. Thanks for bringing them by," I said, too tired and in pain to wipe the tears away.

I felt Lawyer's hand touch my face.

"And that was some fast thinking you did when you had Elyk on the phone."

Weepy, I said, "I guess my fast-talking profession pays off sometimes."

He took my hand and studied me. He finally said, "Could I ask you a question?"

"Was that it or is there another?"

"Funny." He took my arm with his other hand. "You aren't thinking of quitting, are you?"

"I'm not going anywhere," I said. "I'm going to finish the contract. And you are going to help me figure out who my birth parents were."

"I am. I know they got mixed up with the mafia and they came here with the Witness Protection Program. They gave you up when it looked like they had been found again."

"I was two."

"They had no choice really."

"They were protecting me? My California parents must have known the situation and that's why they never told me in case I went looking. They might have actually wanted me."

He nodded, "My guess is you meant more than the world to them."

He tilted his head to the side. "I have another question."

"Yes."

"Do you think it's possible you will still be alive this Friday?"

I laughed, and although it hurt, it felt good. "I have plans to stay alive until at least Saturday at noon. Why?"

He leaned forward and pressed his soft lips to mine. They fit perfectly. We stayed that way for several seconds then he dropped his face into my neck. "You see, I like being with you, talking, holding you and kissing you. I'd hoped to have a proper date with you this Friday, a non-emergency kind, where we could let ambulances take care of someone else for a change."

I wrapped my arms around him and said into his ear, "I'd like that very much."

Acknowledgments

A writer never makes it to publication alone. Thank you to those who read and gave me feedback on the first rough draft, and the subsequent revisions. I hope I have you all listed here. To my critique group: Bill Dennis, Sherri Curtis, Rick Christensen, Linda Orvis, and Ericka Prechtel, thank you for your monthly feedback. To my early readers: Karen Nickell, Judy Hardy, Janet Kirsh, Marjorie Welker, Lane Cohen, Brittani Jay, Alex Garcia, Val Walsh, Angela Bradbury, Jenna Lillywhite, Michelle Hard, Marvin and Shirley Jay, thanks for saying the book was funny enough to keep revising. To Julia Hardy, Scott Brendel and Kristy Pappas, thank you for your amazing attention to detail and wonderful editing advice. To Sarah Warner, thank you for falling in love with this story and for making it a much better book. Thanks to Haley Sisco for all of your help in getting the book ready. And finally, to my husband John Hardy, thank you for believing all along this story would make it to a store bookshelf, so much so you built a writing room so I had the space to work on my dream.

INTERVIEW WITH THE AUTHOR

Interviewer: They say write what you know. Since you are a speech therapist, is that how *Speaking in Tungs* came about?

Karla Jay: Probably. I've been a therapist for 30 years and lots of quirky, strange things have happened while I was working with patients, especially during the 10 years I worked in home-health. I started out writing this as non-fiction, a let-me-tell-you-some funny-things kind of book, but soon realized that by fictionalizing a story, it made it more fun.

Interviewer: With that in mind, are you Marleigh?

Karla: People who know me will see flashes of me in Marleigh although her situation of working in a very remote area was nothing I have ever experienced. All of my work was in Salt Lake City or its suburbs. I love being a speech therapist so her dedication to trying to "fix" everyone most certainly is "essence of Karla."

Interviewer: What do you want readers to take away from this book?

Karla Jay: Well, I hope they laugh! I also hope they think about the characters after the book is finished. I like when that happens to me. Above all, I want them to say, "I had no idea speech therapists do so many things!" I do think my profession is a mystery to people.

Interviewer: Is this the first book you've written?

Karla Jay: No. I spent 10 years working on a book called *Grasshopper Soup*. It followed two brothers after Pearl Harbor was bombed, and their horrible experiences while trying to survive in POW camps in the Philippines. Definitely not humorous women's fiction!

Interviewer: What made you want to write that kind of book when humor seems to be a strong voice for you?

Karla Jay: I love books about people overcoming great odds. Spending 10 years writing and rewriting taught me HOW to write so I don't feel like I wasted any time. And, believe it or not, the book was full of humor, between the prisoners, which was how they survived.

CPSIA information can be obtained at www.ICGtesting.com
Printed in the USA
BVOW08s0409100915

416770BV00015BA/56/P